Masters of the Shadowlands:
IF ONLY

Cherise Sinclair

LooseId.

ISBN 13: 978-1-62300-674-7
MASTERS OF THE SHADOWLANDS: IF ONLY
Copyright © November 2013 by Cherise Sinclair
Originally released in e-book format in November 2013

Cover Art by Anne Cain
Cover Layout and Design by April Martinez

Printed in the U.S.A. by
Lightning Source, Inc.
1246 Heil Quaker Blvd
La Vergne TN 37086
www.lightningsource.com

AUTHOR'S NOTE

To my readers,

The books I write are fiction, not reality, and as in most romantic fiction, the romance is compressed into a very, very short time period.

You, my darlings, live in the real world, and I want you to take a little more time in your relationships. Good Doms don't grow on trees, and there are some strange people out there. So while you're looking for that special Dom, please, be careful.

When you find him, realize he can't read your mind. Yes, frightening as it might be, you're going to have to open up and talk to him. And you listen to him, in return. Share your hopes and fears, what you want from him, what scares you spitless. Okay, he may try to push your boundaries a little—he's a Dom, after all— but you will have your safe word. You will have a safe word, am I clear? Use protection. Have a back-up person. Communicate.

Remember: safe, sane, and consensual.

Know that I'm hoping you find that special, loving person who will understand your needs and hold you close.

And while you're looking or even if you're already found your dearheart, come and hang out with the Masters in Club Shadowlands.

Love,

Cherise

ACKNOWLEDGMENT

With eternal gratitude to my brilliant critique partners, Monette Michaels, Fiona Archer, and Bianca Sommerland, who walloped me over the head until I got the story right.

Much love to my Shadowkittens for their amazing pouncing and playing. Life would be so dull without you. And a special bow to Leagh and Lisa who (quite sadistically) laced my corset for RomCon.

A thousand thanks to my new editor, Maryam Salim, who cheerfully hammered this manuscript into submission.

Hugs to the incredible Liz who blessed a group of stressed-out authors with a laughter-filled weekend. (I'll never look at a dinosaur in the same way again).

Kisses to my dearheart who manned the kitchen during my last deadline.

And to you, my readers: if this book gives you a few happy moments of escape, then I am well rewarded. You are the reason I write.

CHAPTER ONE

I f only trying to be a hero wasn't so disgusting.

The center of the Tampa police station stank of sweat and fear and blood. And death. Holding her breath, Sally Hart trotted across the noisy hub to the investigations department.

In the quiet hallway, she slowed, giving her stomach time to crawl back out of her throat. When she'd started school to be a computer forensics specialist in the law-enforcement arena—as close to a hero as a nerd could get—no one had mentioned these minor details.

Really, blood and bodily wastes should remain in a body, not out. She gave herself a shake. *Onward.*

Dan Sawyer's office door stood open. Seated at his desk, the detective waved her in.

"Hey, Dan." Sally walked in. "The lieutenant said you needed my help."

Before Dan could speak, Sally spotted the owner of Tampa's exclusive BDSM club standing inside the door. "Mas—"*Duh, don't call him Master Z.* "Uh, it's a surprise to see you here, Sir."

Black-haired, gray-eyed, in his midforties, Master Z was one of the most gorgeous men she'd ever met. In the Shadowlands, he wore only black, and she was a bit scandalized to find him in a pure white shirt and dark tie. But not even standard business attire could diminish the sense of power he exuded.

She had a feeling her jeans and tucked-in polo shirt didn't convey anything except, maybe, clean.

"Sally." Master Z held out his hand. When she put her fingers in his, he tugged her a step closer to study her with a frown. "How are you doing?"

I'm lonely, and I want to come home to the Shadowlands. "I'm fine." *God, she was such a liar.*

And he knew. One brow inched up.

"Actually," she said in a rush, "I wanted to talk to you. I broke up with Frank and..." And she just couldn't tell him her request. She hadn't been able to call the Shadowlands and ask, and now, here she was in front of him and still choked on the words.

"I'm sorry it didn't work out, little one," he said.

"Oh, well." She looked down, absurdly relieved that enough time had passed for her bruised face to heal. Why did choosing a creep for a boyfriend make the *girl* feel like a loser? How could she possibly ask Master Z to—

"Would you like to return to the trainees?" he asked gently.

She clamped her jaw shut, fighting tears, and nodded.

"It will be nice to have you back, Sally. I'll put you on the schedule starting Saturday."

Joy welled inside her. She could return to her friends. Could try again to find someone...special. A Dom of her own. "Thank you, Sir." And just like that, she found a smile.

"You're very welcome."

God, she loved Master Z. Not as a potential master—no way—and she'd been thrilled when he married Jessica. But he always made her feel...special. As if he found her delightful.

After kicking Frank out, she'd felt as enchanting as a hair ball hacked up by a cat.

"It'll be good to see you in the club again." Dan tossed his pen on his paperwork and leaned back in his chair with a smile.

"Thanks, Dan." On his desk was a photo of his wife and son. "Awww." Could the beaming black-haired baby really be over seven months now? "Zane looks adorable—and Kari looks tired. How's she doing?"

Although he answered, "Fine," his mouth had flattened. He was obviously not a happy camper, which was strange, since he adored Kari and his baby.

Sally frowned. As soon as school was out, she'd try to catch up with her friends. Kari and Dan lived only a few blocks away. Easy enough to make a little impromptu visit.

Meantime... "Lieutenant Hoffman said you had a laptop you needed me to get into?"

Dan nodded. "I do. One of the men forgot his password, and we need the files he has on the hard drive. You got some time right now?"

"You bet." Breaking into computers was one of her favorite things.

Her phone rang, and she gave the display a quick check. *Ugh.* Frank. He'd taken to calling her every couple of days since they'd split up, which was ridiculous. She swiped the REJECT CALL icon.

"So, where's the laptop?" Dan's desk held only a regular computer flat screen. Beside the monitor lay an open folder labeled *Harvest Association.* Oh, she knew that name. They were the organization who'd been kidnapping women for slaves. Leaning forward slightly, she casually did an upside-down read, and... *Wait just one little minute here.* "Why's my name in there?"

Dan frowned and moved the paper out of reading distance.

Spoilsport.

Behind her, Master Z chuckled. "You might as well save yourself some nagging, Daniel, and indulge her curiosity."

"Guess it's not confidential information any longer." Dan glanced up at her. "Last fall, they had you targeted to be kidnapped." A corner of his mouth pulled up. "Seems they thought you'd be perfect for the rebellious slave auction."

"Me?" A chill ran through her as she realized she'd have been a slave if Master Z hadn't sent her away. Linda and Kim had suffered horrors at the hands of the slavers. "Haven't those stupid Federal agents closed the Harvest Association down yet?"

"All but the northeast section." Turning his chair around, Dan motioned toward a table against the wall. "There's the laptop. After I escort Z out, I'll be back to give you some ideas of what Brendan thought his password might be."

Oh please, as if I need help? "Sure." As the two men left, Sally started toward the laptop...and paused to stare at the report containing her name. She could swear it was calling to her.

Saaaaally. What had the asshole kidnappers said about her?

Curiosity itched at her worse than any mosquito bite. And, look, her cell—complete with camera—was conveniently right there in her hand. Ignoring her second—and third—thoughts, she snapped shots of the papers scattered over Dan's desk.

God, I am a bad, bad person.

After shoving her phone into her pocket, she virtuously sat down in front of the laptop.

Such was the power of a guilty conscience, she'd finished the job before Dan returned. Not that hacking in was difficult. *Seriously, what kind of fool uses a pet name for his password?*

———✦———

In the Shadowlands that weekend, Sally set dirty glasses from a table onto her tray. The pounding bass of Nine Inch Nails from the dance floor drowned out her heavy sigh. *I'm tired. My bare feet hurt. I want to go home.*

As she stretched the ache out of her back, she looked around. On the left, a new Dom had completed setting up a suspension scene.

On the right, Mistress Anne was flogging a lanky male submissive.

At one time, Sally would have stopped to admire the slender brunette's technique.

Then again, at one time, Sally had loved being in the Shadowlands.

But somehow, the magic had faded—*damn you, Frank*—and she wanted it back. Maybe she could carry a Tinker Bell wand. Instant magic, right? Or maybe a stick like Harry Potter used. No, Tinker Bell's wand was prettier and required less effort.

"Here you go." A sour-looking Dom walking past handed her a dirty glass.

"Why, thank you, Sir," Sally said in a saccharine voice. Someone was in dire need of a little happiness charm. What would he do if she bopped him with a magic wand? Nah, the sparkling dust might catch in his overabundant chest hair and look like stars in bondage.

Shaking her head, she swiped a wet cloth over the table. Jeez, she was in the Shadowlands. Why did she feel so miserable?

The BDSM club hadn't changed. The sounds were familiar— the music, the slapping of whips, floggers, and hands against tender flesh, the crying and moaning punctuated by occasional sharp cries. The perimeter of the mansion's bottom floor held St. Andrew's crosses, spanking benches, cages, rope spiderwebs, stocks, and chain stations. In the center, at an oblong, gleaming wooden bar, members chatted with the gregarious bartender.

So if the Shadowlands hadn't changed, the problem must be with her. What a purely upsetting thought.

She swung by the bar to unload the empties and nudged past some single Doms scoping out a group of unattached submissives.

Sally knew the Doms. Had played with most of them. Had usually annoyed them. None had clicked for her. And wasn't that a stupid phrase? *Had clicked.* Did that mean when meeting the right person, something inside would make a noise like hitting a button on a mouse—*select* this man.

Didn't that sound a little ridiculous to anyone else?

And yet, what she wouldn't give to have some clicking going on. But face it, her God-I-want-you mouse selector was busted. None of her scenes had been that great, and she was tired of playing with bungling Doms.

She nodded a greeting at the men and headed out to clean more tables and take orders. *Be fair.* Most of the guys weren't incompetent. She was too fussy. And...and withdrawn. Even with skilled Doms, she somehow tucked her emotions away to a place where nothing could reach them...probably in the same location as her broken clicker.

With a snort of exasperation at her idiotic thoughts, she stopped to watch Master Marcus restrain Gabi in the stocks, then tease her with his hands until her face flushed pink.

Gabi and Marcus had clicked right away.

Why could everyone else find a good Dom, when she couldn't?

For a little while, she'd thought she had found someone. She'd even quit the club's trainee program to be his slave. Yes, Frank had been intelligent. Had been masterful. Had been perfect.

Frank had been Frankenstein.

"Hey, it's good to see you, Sally. Where've you been?" A burly, older Dom smiled at her.

"I-I just took some time off for a bit." *Thinking I'd found the Dom of my dreams.*

Her smile was so unsuccessful that his eyes narrowed in his bulldog face. "Right. I heard that you hooked up with—"

Before he finished, she pretended to recognize someone and hurried past. She felt the heat in her cheeks. Poor submissive couldn't find herself a Dom, even after being a trainee for so long. Master Z felt sorry for her that she'd fallen for a loser. Maybe all the other Doms did too.

Excuse me, but did I issue invitations to a pity party? She was the only person allowed to feel sorry for her.

"Oh, sister, what's wrong?" Rainie walked over, a tray in one hand. The trainee's belly dancer's costume made the most of such lush curves that Sally felt underendowed. "You look like you just stepped on your pet turtle."

Sally shuddered. "Ew. Major disgusting." She could almost hear the crunch of the tiny shell.

"True, but that's how you look." Rainie bumped a hip against Sally's. "You're supposed to be overjoyed to be back, not all quiet."

Bouncy Sally, that's me. Scene with anyone, fuck them as well. The more the merrier. Why had she thought screwing around with everyone would find her a Dom? "Guess I need to work my way back into it."

"I know what you need—some fun. It's time to raise some hackles, upset some Masters. How do you feel about pissing off the unpissoffable Mistress Anne?"

"Well." Picking on the average Doms wasn't a challenge, but going after the experienced, powerful Shadowlands Masters and Mistresses? That took skill. Courage. Daring.

Intrigued, Sally leaned a hip against an unoccupied leather couch. Pulling a joke on Mistress Anne would be about as safe as playing catch with nitroglycerin. Perilous pranks—a surefire way to raise her spirits. "We'll die in pain, but it will be worth it. Got some ideas?"

"You know her submissive, Joey?"

"Sure."

"He says she's squicked out by big bugs. Any big bugs."

"Reeeaaally." The idea was awfully tempting. "Being supportive trainees, we should help her overcome such an unreasonable fear."

"My thought exactly."

"Uzuri will want in." Who else? Sally saw Maxie near the back of the room and shook her head. "Not Maxie or Tanner. Way too nice."

No one ever called Sally nice. She'd never aspired to such a designation...until Frank. Then she'd tried, bent over backward to be his sweet slave. And failed miserably.

Rainie tapped her fingers against her tray. "We could get spiders. Cockroaches. Beetles..."

Sally yanked herself back into the plan. "The bugs have to be fake, or Master Z will make us catch them, then clean the entire room with toothbrushes."

Rainie winced. "Not a good chore for me—my tits would drag on the floor. Imitation insects it is."

"I'll gather what I can. You and Uzuri do the same. Then we'll figure out the perfect date for the Night of the Monster Zombie bugs."

"There's my Sally girl. Been really boring here without your clever, twisty brain." Rainie glanced over at the front wall clock. "We're off duty in a couple of minutes. The new Dom, Saxon, is going to commandeer the poly room for furry play. Want to be a kitten or puppy?"

She didn't feel at all bouncy and cute...more like a badger. A very bad-tempered badger liable to bite off dangling boy bits. Imagine the mess. "Not this time."

"Then I'll see you later." After a quick squeeze, Rainie cheerfully sashayed toward the rear of the room. Even the tattoos covering her back looked happy.

Sally felt the prickle of tears in her eyes. Face it, she'd only returned to the Shadowlands because she'd missed her buddies.

Not to find a Dom. As she filled her tray again, her shoulders slumped. Pretty sad to realize a dream had died. Years ago, her mama had blown bubbles, sending the iridescent balls floating over the green lawn. Sally had caught them. Time after time, the bubble would pop, leaving only a wet spot on her little hands.

There was a dirty analogy in the story, she knew, wet spots and things blown up and deflating too soon. But she wasn't in a naughty mood. More of an all-my-bubbles-escaped mood.

Whining again. Sheesh. She set her tray down on the bar top with an annoyed thump and realized she stood next to Master Dan.

"You look tired, sweetheart." Although he wore the gold-edged black leather vest indicating he was serving as a dungeon monitor, he still came across as a detective.

Scary thought since she had a guilty conscience the size of Master Cullen. "My graduation's coming up. Is Kari here tonight?"

"No. She's home with Zane."

"Home? But..." *Kari loves the Shadowlands.* Sally bit back the words. She'd been immersed in grad school and hadn't kept current. Her friend had a baby now; maybe her idea of what was fun had changed.

Instead of moving away as she'd hoped, Dan leaned an elbow on the bar. "Is Hoffman overworking you?"

"Nah." Digging information out of computers was even more entertaining than playing online war games. "And the lieutenant is a good guy. Did I remember to say thank you?" Dan had pulled the strings to get her the computer forensics internship at his station.

She owed him...and instead, she'd snooped. Guilt tightened her shoulders.

"Not a problem. He says you're more skilled than any software person there." A smile lightened the angular lines of his face. "You going to stay on after you graduate?"

"Thinking about it." As her remorse built, she couldn't help shifting her weight and retreating a step.

His eyes narrowed. "Sally, what have—"

"Sir." A young male submissive skidded to a halt beside them. "We need a DM in the back."

"Coming." Master Dan nodded to Sally and followed the sub toward the theme rooms.

Oh boy, saved by the subbie. I'm a bad Sally. If he knew she'd snapped pictures of those Harvest Association documents—or worse, what she'd done with the information—he'd put her in handcuffs and not the fun kind. But really, that list of e-mail addresses on paper was a God-given sign she must lend a hand.

Those stupid Feds needed a good geek in their corner.

"How's it going, pet?"

Sally blinked and pulled herself out of software-land to find Master Cullen watching her with his thick brown brows drawn together. "Uh. Fine." She forced a smile. "All finished cleaning up my section." She gave the tray a push forward.

He glanced at his submissive, Andrea. "Can you get that, love?"

Andrea smiled. "*Sí, Señor.*" Before picking up the tray, the tawny-haired woman patted Sally's hand. "You okay?"

Christ on a crutch, did she appear that wrung out? "I'm good. Just tired." And frustrated and lonely and starting to grasp a sad truth. Even after she finished her Master's degree and left school, her love life might not improve.

"The first shift of trainees is free to play now. Has Nolan set you up with someone yet?" Cullen asked.

She shrugged. The idea of doing a scene was...blah. She didn't feel playful. Or sexy. Or anything. "No."

She leaned her forearms on the bar top, her shoulders sagging. Might as well go home. She glanced around for Master Nolan. He was in charge of the trainees tonight and would get pissed off if she left without permission. Annoying Master Nolan wasn't something any submissive wanted to do...although his sub, Beth, said she poked at him occasionally just to watch his face go all hard.

Wish I had someone to poke at. She'd thought Frank would be that Dom, but his response to being teased had been horrible. The yelling hadn't bothered her much, but when he'd backhanded her?

That was not only the final straw but the entire pile of hay.

How humiliating to realize she'd chosen a man like her father.

"Sally."

She turned toward the sound of Nolan's gravelly voice.

Oh hell. At the sight of Galen Kouros beside the Dom, Sally almost cringed. Surely the FBI agent hadn't discovered what she was up to with Dan's records. She took a hasty step back, bumped into a bar stool, and a person. "Sorry," she said, glancing over her shoulder. Her stomach dropped.

The big man behind her was Vance Buchanan, Galen's partner. He gripped her arm with a powerful hand to steady her. "Easy there, sweetie." As he smiled down at her, his sharp blue eyes held both humor and something unrelated to crime—the potent regard of a man.

When she looked away from Vance, Galen had moved closer. Meeting his intense dark eyes was like being sucked into a black river whirlpool...and drowning.

"Breathe, little girl," Vance said in her ear, making her jump.

God, these two. He still had his hand wrapped around her upper arm. She glanced over her shoulder. "Let go."

Vance's lips twitched, drawing her attention to his face. Square jaw, flat, hard cheekbones like a Celtic warrior. Brown hair just long enough to tie back with a leather band. Yeah, she could envision him running over the Highlands beside Liam Neeson, wielding a broadsword.

And bedding everything in sight. After all, he and Galen were players. They didn't do serious, wanted only fun and fucking. Normally how she preferred her guys, but these two were...scary. "Please, let go."

He lifted his chin in acknowledgment and released her. The loss of his warm hand created an unsettling ache deep inside. But she could breathe again. She turned to Master Nolan, ignoring the FBI agents. "Master Nolan, I want to leave."

"I agreed you'd have a scene with Master Galen and Master Vance," Nolan said, his voice laying out her doom.

Her mouth went dry. How'd she forget the Feds were now *Masters?* In the Shadowlands, the title was given only to very experienced, very powerful, and very conscientious Doms. In return for teaching and monitoring activities, the Masters received extra privileges, especially with the trainees.

In other words, she was screwed.

The infinitesimal deepening of the lines at the edge of Galen's eyes meant he'd followed her thoughts. "Show us your cuffs." His voice was deeper than Vance's, with a strong Maine accent, and his dropped *r*'s turned *your* into *yo-uh*.

Wordlessly, she held her arms out.

"Yellow, blue, green ribbons means you enjoy mild pain, bondage, and sex. Is that correct?"

The pushy jerk. He'd have already pulled her records and checked her limits list. Any Master would. So his question was pure intimidation to build anticipation—or apprehension—of what they might do. And it would be *they*, since the two topped together. The tingle creeping up her spine said his technique worked, whether she recognized it or not. She nodded.

A tug on her hair drew her attention over…and up…to Vance. "You've never had a problem verbalizing anything before, sweetie. Don't start now."

Why did she let these two get away with shaking her up? She straightened her shoulders. "Yes, Sir. That's very clever of you, Sir," she said to Galen in a snotty tone before looking at the trainee Master. "Master Nolan, I don't intend to stay. I'm not feeling good. At all. I need—"

"Are you ill, Sally?" Master Z's rich voice made her close her eyes with a combination of hope and despair. No telling what the owner of the Shadowlands would decide. He could overrule Nolan. But he undoubtedly knew she didn't feel ill. No one successfully lied to Master Z.

Fuckity fuck fuck fuck.

The skeptical tilt of Galen's black eyebrows indicated he hadn't bought into her I'm-so-sick story either. Not even close.

"I'm quite tired, Master Z," she said truthfully.

Master Z smiled slightly and squeezed her shoulder. "You are, indeed. But I'd call it mostly mental and emotional exhaustion." His brows drew together. "I don't know what's happening in your life, little one, but if you don't shed some stress, you're going to get flattened."

"I just need to sleep," she protested.

"Do you actually sleep when you go to bed?"

Step by step, he was backing her into a corner. She shook her head.

"I thought not. After your graduation, we are going to have a long talk. For now..." His attention shifted to the FBI agents. "She's not up to her usual speed, so be careful," he said quietly. "However, I think getting out of her head will be good for her."

She actually glared at Z. "Don't I have anything to say about this?"

His face turned...not cold, but unyielding. "In the Shadowlands, submissives always have a safe word. As a trainee, you have little else. That's why you wanted to be a trainee...to surrender control." He touched her cheek lightly. "That's what will happen tonight."

He nodded to Galen and Vance and walked away, Nolan beside him.

Sally's gaze went from Galen to Vance, and she felt surrounded, even though they were only two men. "Well, you won. Now what?"

Galen studied her for a minute, his expression unreadable, and her flippant words bounced off him as if he wore armor. He stepped forward, invading her personal space, so close she could feel his body heat.

Her retreat bumped her into the concrete wall called Vance. He gripped her shoulders, firmly enough to stymie any chance of moving. He had her restrained without rope or chains.

A tremor ran through her at the exciting sensation. *Dammit.* "Is all this crowding necessary?"

Galen cupped her chin in his palm, and his gaze effortlessly trapped hers. "I know we scare you, pretty little pet." His lips twitched. "In your case, that's a good thing. But don't let fear lead you into being disrespectful, eh?"

He held her gaze...held it and held it, and with each fleeting second, she sank, dropping into acceptance, into calmness.

After an ocean of time had passed, he murmured, "Good."

When he took his hand away from her face, she'd have staggered if Vance hadn't had his body pressed to hers.

"Bondage table?" Vance asked.

Galen nodded and led the way across the room. Dressed in black slacks, button-down shirt, and shoes, he presented a smoother appearance than Vance—also in black but wearing jeans, tight T-shirt, leather belt, and boots. Forceful versus laid-back, sleekly muscular versus football-player size, darkly Greek versus Scottish warrior, smooth versus rugged. They shouldn't be able to work together, let alone co-top, but they managed without missing a single step.

Vance tucked her against his side, his arm behind her giving her no choice except to follow.

Her heart was already hammering so violently she felt as if she were choking.

How could they affect her like this? She didn't have this problem with the rest of the Masters. Sure, each of the Masters could and had made her submit, but they didn't worry her. Maybe these two were more frightening because they ganged up on her? Every time she tried to take a stand, one would push and the other would trip her.

But she didn't like being...intimidated. Not by them. "Listen, I don't..."

Galen turned to regard her, and the words dried right up in her mouth. Was he always so...intense?

"Stand here, Sally." His dark clothing made his eyes even blacker and more ominous. He ran one finger over the edge of her halter top, down the curve of one breast. "Remove this, Vance."

Vance undid the ties and tossed her top onto a chair.

For the first time in forever, she wanted to shield herself. Her hands came up and, at a glance from Galen, went down. Galen studied her, his gaze lingering on her boy briefs.

Her breath stuttered as warmth pooled low in her belly. Damn him, she didn't want to have sex with either one of them...and yet, she really, really did. When his lips quirked, a flush heated her cheeks.

"Not this time, pet," he said. His smile transformed his face from terrifying to gorgeous. Compelling. "We'll enjoy your body eventually, but tonight is for you."

She stared at him. Seriously? But they liked sex. She'd heard the submissives marveling over how *much* they liked sex. Was something wrong with her that they didn't desire her?

Galen patted the top of the bondage table and turned away without seeing if she obeyed.

Then she realized why he hadn't worried. Vance gripped her waist and set her on the table like a doll to play with. Under his tight black shirt, his shoulders were huge and his biceps curved like boulders. He made her feel tiny.

"Down you go." He pushed her onto her back.

To her embarrassment, her bare breasts showed just how bunched and tight her nipples had become. She tried to look away.

"Relax, Sally." Tilting her chin up, he bent and kissed her. His lips were firm, his movements slow as he coaxed a response. When his mouth left hers, she tried to follow, and he chuckled. Then his hand was on her cheek, his mouth over hers, and he turned the kiss deep. Carnal. Making her tingle in a long surge downward.

And before she'd even caught her breath, he was using the straps on the table to restrain her arms to her sides. He put another over her waist.

"Did you know I like tying up naughty submissives?" The hunger in Vance's gaze confirmed his words. His hands were firm as he roped her thighs together and then her ankles. A strap went across her knees.

Finished, he crossed his arms and surveyed his work.

She lifted her head and saw the ropes and straps covering her body. Jeez.

"Missed one." Vance pushed her down and pulled another strap across the top of her forehead so she couldn't lift her head. Couldn't move at all. Feeling more immobilized than she'd ever experienced, she couldn't keep from squirming. From attempting to get free.

Her body understood she was caught—trapped—and the table beneath her seemed to shake.

Vance's mouth tipped up. "Now that's just pretty," he said before giving her an easy kiss. "She's ready, pard."

Both Doms walked around the table, tugging and checking the straps.

"Numbness, tingling? Cold?" Galen asked, his New England accent broadening his deep baritone.

Her attempt to shake her head got nowhere and set up an instinctive flutter in the pit of her stomach.

Vance's smile increased at whatever he saw in her face. Although he seemed more easygoing than Galen, the depths in his dark blue eyes were disturbing.

"Well?" Galen prompted, pulling her attention to him.

"No, Sir," she whispered, then scowled. *Where oh where, has my backbone gone?* "I'm really quite fine, thank you, Master Galen. And how are you today?"

"You going to chatter the way you do for other Doms?" Galen asked.

"Of course."

He pulled a leather strip from their toy bag and tossed it to Vance. "Gag her."

"Hey, I don't like gags." She started to struggle. What if she *needed* to talk?

Galen took out two small rubber balls and squeezed them to make them squeak. "These are if you need to safeword." He tucked one into her left hand, then the right. "Show me you can use them."

Her heart slammed against her ribs. She made the balls squeak and continued until they sounded as if someone was murdering a flock of baby birds.

"Sally." Just one word in Galen's bottomless voice and Sally couldn't force her fingers to continue. Even though the squeaky toys went silent, her pulse made waves of sound in her head.

"Open, sweetheart." Vance lifted the leather strip, snorted when her mouth clamped shut, then pressed a spot on the hinges of her jaw to open it. As he pushed the gag in and strapped it on, her hand closed convulsively on a rubber ball, getting a high squeak.

Vance leaned a forearm beside her and smiled down, his light brown hair falling over his forehead. "Too tight?"

"Umh."

"You are so cute." His grin was devastatingly handsome and totally scary because he didn't appear concerned about her answer at all. "One blink is yes. No blink means no. Is the gag too tight?"

Everything in her yelled for her to blink, but the straps weren't uncomfortable. What scared her was their lack of concern for what she wanted or what she thought. They'd just shut her right up. She glowered.

His smile widened. "We pissed off a submissive, Galen," he said.

"Oh, damn." The amusement in Galen's response made Sally want to hit him. He rested his hand against the side of her face. "We're not going to hurt you, pet. Not even going to touch your pussy. We'll play with you some and release you."

Her muscles untensed...slightly. But why hadn't he explained earlier? Her eyes narrowed.

"Why didn't I tell you before?" Galen drew a finger over her cheek and around her ear. She saw no mercy in his face. "I didn't want to."

His voice wasn't cruel...just matter-of-fact. They'd do what they wanted. She knew they weren't careless like some Doms, but they were dominant, no ifs, ands, or buts. Why was the knowledge so very exciting?

With a faint smile, Galen moved down to the end of the table and grasped her left foot. Rubbing, massaging with firm hands.

Oh God, it felt good. Her feet always hurt after a couple of hours of going barefoot. She couldn't keep back the sigh of pleasure.

As Galen continued, something brushed her stomach and moved slowly toward her breasts. Her eyes popped open.

Leaning on one arm, Vance trailed a finger across her belly, just above the waist strap. Making circles. Crosses. Each movement brought his touch higher on her body. His face wasn't—wasn't excited or filled with lust. He was simply amusing himself.

His light touch on her belly was so different from Galen's strong hands on her foot that she felt...confused.

Galen switched to her other leg, and oh God, she might die from the pleasure. Why were they being sweet to her?

Before she could settle into enjoying Galen's ministrations, Vance ran a finger along the extremely sensitive underside of her breast. Her back tried to arch—the straps kept her flat. *Jeez.*

She looked up to see him studying her face, reading her every little twitch. Undoubtedly mentally marking that area as one "of interest." His finger circled her left breast, then her right.

She stared back. He was just plain gorgeous, his size and big nose keeping him from being too pretty, but otherwise, he'd take the lead in the hottie category. The laughter lines fanning out from his eyes contrasted with the square jaw and firm lips that warned he could be a very, very dangerous man.

She felt her nipples contract as he spiraled in toward the aching peaks.

Then Galen massaged her calf, hard enough to hurt. Taking his time. When he finally moved to her left calf, the right was gloriously limp and happy.

Vance's fingers closed on her left nipple, teasing and sweet, and her clit began to tingle. Galen said he wouldn't play with her pussy, but her body wanted sex. Now.

Vance moved down to her legs.

Galen took his place. He cupped her breasts and pinched one nipple. Controlled but hard. Her back tried again to arch. Electricity sizzled straight to her core.

With her legs roped together, Vance's confident hands stroking up and down the front of her thighs were tantalizing her aroused clit.

Wetness seeped into her briefs. Like a drug, lust pulsed in her bloodstream. What were they doing to her?

Galen switched to her right breast, and the cruel pinch was a shocking contrast to Vance's easy massage. He rolled her nipples, one and then the other, relentlessly enough to make her squirm and test her straps. Nothing gave.

She made a garbled sound through her gag.

Galen's smile flashed white, transforming his stern face into sheer sexiness and increasing her nervousness. She couldn't fall back on sarcasm. Had been completely silenced. A shiver shook her as the last lingering hope of manipulating them disappeared.

"That's the girl," Galen murmured. "Give it up." He closed his hands on her breasts, massaging powerfully enough to approach pain, and she felt her tissues swelling, tightening the skin, increasing the sensitivity.

Vance had reached the tops of her thighs and skimmed his palms upward past her pussy on each side to stroke over her briefs on her mound.

Her clit begged to be touched—and the instinctive effort to open her legs failed. The ropes kept them pressed firmly together. A crease flickered in Vance's cheek as he ran his finger next to the strap crossing her belly, then glided back to her pelvis.

Her body tensed—*oh please, touch lower*—and then Galen's hand curved around her throat. Not pressing, just there...yet a very palpable threat. Her gaze shot to his unreadable face. His eyes were fixed on her.

Vance scraped his fingernails along the top of her low-cut briefs, on her tender belly. The skin tingled in his wake.

"Pretty Sally," Galen murmured, "can't move, can't yell." His lips curved slightly. "Can't come." His hand still rested ever so gently on her throat in an unstated threat.

He kissed her cheek, his lips grazing her jaw, along her neck. His scent was spicy with a subtle richness, and she breathed him in.

Vance licked over her left nipple.

Her brain spun and threw her thoughts into disarray. Gentle and painful, sweet and cruel.

Her breasts ached; her pussy throbbed. Burning. Needing. Vance nibbled lightly on her bare shoulder and down her inner arm. His lips were warm, firm, and velvety contrasting with the slight scrape of his five-o'clock shadow.

Galen lightly bit her right nipple, sending a wildfire of sensation to her clit.

Oh God. She couldn't think.

As Vance pressed a kiss into her palm, Galen licked each peak, leaving them wet.

Vance's lips closed around her thumb. He sucked lightly…and it felt as if he were sucking on her clit. Her thigh muscles tensed as if she could draw him to the ball of nerves.

He moved to her index finger. And sucked.

Galen blew air on her nipples, turning them impossibly tight, then nibbled each one. Rougher, his bites harder, until she was at the whimpering edge of pain—making her want, want, want.

When he straightened, her breasts were almost painfully swollen. "Look at me, pet."

Her eyelids drooped as she obeyed. Her body felt cocooned in sensation.

His eyes were black without a glimmer of light as he stared at her, absently caressing her breasts. His doll to play with.

Vance rested his palm, then his weight on her mound, creating a growing sense of needy pressure.

Her body thrummed with arousal, begging for more. Begging that they make her come. She managed to drag her gaze from Galen's, only to be caught by Vance's burning blue eyes. The table seemed to drop a foot.

Nothing existed except Vance's eyes and his hand on her mound, the heat swirling around her body, Galen's demanding touch on her breasts. Her breathing slowed…the entire world seemed to halt in its spinning.

GALEN SMILED AS Sally's eyes glazed and the tension drained out of her sweet little body. Now, wasn't she just a responsive little thing? She'd been as much fun to play with as he'd always imagined.

Definitely a mouthy submissive—enough to annoy some Doms. Not him though. A bit of sass, if it was intelligent sass, could liven up any scene.

But this one had more to her. She hid her caring nature, but he'd seen her looking after the newer submissives as often as she'd created havoc at other times.

He glanced at Vance, enjoying the way his partner kept the girl locked tight in his gaze.

Letting the moment unwind, Galen idly caressed her nicely swollen and beautifully taut nipples. Be a pleasure to have her in his lap in the evenings, having these to play with while he watched television. With her hair down, her breasts would be covered in a waterfall of rich brown silk.

After a bit, Vance broke off, leaving Sally blinking and obviously trying to find her way back to reality. He gave Galen a quick grin as the sub pulled in a shuddering breath.

Galen sighed and moved his hands. For months, they'd watched the little sprite. Never silent, never modest. She didn't submit gracefully. Both he and Vance had wanted to take her on. Nothing serious—they didn't do serious—but just for the challenge.

Now they had her, and he was tempted to drag those briefs off her and take her in every way two men could enjoy a woman. But that wasn't what she needed right now. Might not be what she needed for a while. She'd been gone for well over a month, and the girl wasn't the same. Her bubbling enthusiasm had disappeared, and he felt the absence like an ache inside him. What had happened to flatten her—and put a wounded expression in her eyes?

But this wasn't the time to explore such things. She'd never done a scene with them before. Didn't really know them. So they'd keep this to merely a short, sensuous session.

He took a baby wipe from the toy bag, removed her gag, and cleaned her face off.

Her liquid brown eyes focused on him, a slight wrinkle between her brows. Confused, was she? Excellent.

Her upper lip was slightly shorter than average, curving into a bowed shape. *Kissable.* He leaned down to check if appearances could be believed. Under his, her mouth was reluctant. He nipped her lower lip in reprimand and felt her soften.

And then she gave so generously to his demand, to his tongue, that his cock stiffened to actual pain. A woman's kiss revealed much about her, and Sally's was teasing. A bit impertinent. And fucking *sweet.*

Hell, he wanted her. Badly.

Not the time, Kouros. Raising his head, he pulled in a breath.

She stared up at him, and her wide eyes held a hint of worry. As if she'd given him more than she wanted. Her lack of sass was amazing.

"Tell me how you feel," he said, not revealing what he knew— that she was very, very aroused.

She swallowed. "I feel good." Her voice came out husky, as if she'd already climaxed. The sound definitely didn't decrease his discomfort. She shook her head, and he watched reality snap back in.

Time to stop. One by one, he and Vance removed her restraints, then helped her sit up.

He closed his fingers over her shoulder and steadied her. Under his hand, her skin was warm and slightly damp. And incredibly soft. Contrasting with her golden tan, her creamy white breasts seemed to beg for his touch again.

But no.

She looked around, glanced up at Vance and him, and frowned. As if Little Miss Know-It-All didn't know what to do. So she attempted to push off the table.

Vance grabbed her arm. "Stay put, sweetie."

Apparently, if she was at a loss, she'd retreat. Galen curved his hand around the back of her head, needing to use some pressure to force her to face him. Damn, he loved the way she tried to resist. "Want to tell us what's been bothering you?"

She stiffened, then shrugged. "Nothing. I'm just tired."

Bullshit. He heard Vance's annoyed growl. Holding her gaze, Galen said, "You're a shitty liar, pet."

She tried to pull back, got nowhere. Her rounded jaw set. "Okay, I'll just say it's none of your business."

Well. Galen glanced at Vance, caught his resigned expression. The girl had the right to play that card. This had been a light session, they hadn't scened before, and she didn't know them. She might be a trainee, but they didn't have the prerogative to plumb her depths.

But he had a craving to do just that.

— ✦ —

Hearing footsteps in the quiet house, Vance turned to see his partner detour around a stack of paint cans and rollers in the unfinished dining room and limp into the kitchen. The work on remodeling their place had turned the floor into an obstacle course. But they'd almost finished the kitchen, at least, and done a hell of a job.

Seeing the weariness on Galen's face, Vance shoved the package of cream-filled cookies across the marble-topped island. "Have something to eat."

"Good plan." With obvious stiffness, Galen eased onto a black leather-covered bar chair at the island.

Vance frowned. Their case was getting tougher to put down, and after they'd returned home from the Shadowlands, the idiot had worked for another hour in the office. "Leg hurting?"

"Some."

That much of an admission meant it hurt like hell. Vance retrieved the ibuprofen from a cupboard, shook out a couple of tablets, and handed them to Galen with some water.

"Thank you, Mom," Galen said sourly but drank the pills down before taking a cookie.

Vance rewarded him with a Johnny Walker Black and soda, and then poured himself a shot of vodka. "Bad day."

With his leg resting on one of the backless stools, Galen leaned an elbow onto the island, glass in his hand. "Till this evening." His lips curved. "Pretty little bit, wasn't she?"

Vance grinned back. "She made it difficult to stop." He took a sip, letting the Russian Standard slide down his throat. "Didn't have her usual perkiness though." Odd how much that had bothered him, but a subdued Sally was like a bird with a damaged wing.

"Her month plus off from the club didn't have a good effect."

The Shadowlands rumor mill said Sally had hooked up with a Dom who wasn't a member of the club. And for over a month, he'd missed seeing her bouncy body and hearing her infectious laugh. He and Galen had been delighted she'd returned. "At least we got her out of her head for a bit. I'd like to know why she's so unhappy."

"Yeah." Galen rubbed his hands over his face. "Be a change to have something we could actually fix."

"Wouldn't it though." Darkness edged into Vance's good mood. In New York, Lieutenant Tillman's home had been burned. The arsonist hadn't tried to hide what he'd done, and it had been ugly. The Harvest Association had not only eliminated a cop who'd made headway into their affairs, but the savagery of the murder—burning Tillman's home with him and his family chained to their beds—served as a warning to potential informers. If a cop wasn't safe, a mere civilian sure wouldn't be.

"Nothing we could do," he said, knowing Galen would follow his thoughts.

"Won't help his children feel better. They're adults, but still..."

Vance frowned at the edge in his partner's voice. Tillman's death would raise cruel memories for his partner. Galen's wife had died at the hands of criminals Galen had been after, and the wound of losing her to such an ugly death hadn't healed as much as his partner wanted everyone to believe.

"Think Sally will show up tomorrow?" Vance asked.

Galen looked over, his bad mood derailed. "If she does, we'll take her further."

"If she agrees." Vance dipped his cookie into his drink before taking a bite. Vodka-laden chocolate with a cream filling. Not bad. "You suppose she's still rocky from breaking up with that guy?"

"Doubtful. She didn't seem the type to want to settle down."

"There is that." He heard she'd played with most of the Shadowlands Doms. No different from what he and Galen were doing—checking out the submissives. "Maybe he got serious and she dumped him. Would have given a few bucks to watch that fight."

Galen actually grinned and answered in Maine slang. "Ayuh."

Definitely *yes*. God knew they preferred subs who didn't get attached. The time to settle down hadn't yet arrived...although sometimes he envied his married friends. Not that much though.

Vance took a drink of his vodka, remembering a pretty blonde from a month ago. Beautiful. Totally into serving his every need. But after two scenes, she'd been ready to get married. Sally wasn't that type. "Good thought, gagging her. Seems like she uses that mouth on her like a sword and shield."

"And we rendered her defenseless. She might see it that way too. Might not like how much she surrendered." Galen rubbed his jaw. "Interesting little submissive. I bet she shores up those defenses now. She might not even want to play with us."

Vance shook his head. There was chemistry between them and...something else he couldn't put his finger on. "After the way we left her? Needing to come so bad she was shaking? Fifty bucks says she jumps at the chance to play." And fuck but he wanted her in his ropes again. Wanted those sweet, vulnerable eyes looking up at him.

"I'll take that bet."

CHAPTER TWO

I'm the man! Sally did a seated victory boogie that netted her startled glances from the others in the coffee shop. Ignoring them, she grinned at her laptop display. E-mail after e-mail had filled the folder she'd set up for the Harvest Association.

The folder bore the name *Scum Suckers* in honor of Kim, who'd been an unwilling guest in their establishment. *Fucking slave traffickers. You are going to be sorry you targeted me.* And Dan would be sorry for keeping such a messy desk. The photos she'd taken included a list of e-mail addresses from suspected members of the Harvest Association. The temptation to screw with them had been too much. So, last week, fueled by a bit too much alcohol, she'd sent e-mails with her special custom-designed computer worm to each address.

As Sally sipped her turtle mocha coffee, the sociable noise of the coffee shop surrounded her. Having others around was comforting, considering she was kind of snooping around the den of a very big bear. She'd be much safer if the bear—aka the Harvest Association—never discovered her tracks, right?

Harvest Association. Sheesh. The Midwesterner in her was offended by the name. Harvest meant crops like corn and beans. Good things. Harvesting shouldn't refer to humans, let alone enslaving women.

They needed to be put away, but Galen and Vance's team hadn't managed to identify the top dipwads. *But I can.*

And ta-da! E-mails now filled the *Scum Sucker* folder, showing her sneaky computer virus had gained access to some mail systems. *I'm the man!* Now every e-mail those men received or sent was blind copied to Sally.

With anticipation making her bounce in her chair, she opened the folder. But the first e-mail held nothing interesting. Or the second. Or the third. *Well, spit on a snowball.* Just as well that she'd been too busy to check the folder until today. The fourth revealed a man was cheating on his wife. Sally blinked at the suggestive language he'd sent to his girlfriend. *Could two bodies truly get into that position?*

However, the next e-mail had been sent to one of the Association people they titled an overseer. One step up. *Perfect.* Slowly Sally worked her way through the *Scum Sucker* folder, adding new people to gift with her worm. Since the sender was familiar to the receiver, her e-mails would be opened.

Almost at the end, another overseer's e-mail mentioned several New York "shipments" being ordered. A chill slid down her spine and lodged in her stomach. The shipments were women scheduled to be kidnapped. All too soon, the Harvest Assholeyation would auction them off to rich, sadistic buyers.

Now what? Last week, she'd sent off the worm for oh, so many reasons. Like getting revenge for what the bastards had done to Linda and Kim, and yeah, because she still felt guilty for almost getting Linda killed. And definitely because finding out they'd targeted her for kidnapping had sorely pissed her off. And—*okay, admit it*—she'd always wanted to be a hero.

She totally hadn't expected to discover they were planning another auction. How should she deal with this information?

She took a sip of her coffee in an attempt to warm her frozen insides. Knowing how Kim and Linda had suffered, she needed to warn the targets, somehow.

And then maybe the Feds could plant another decoy. Galen and Vance were clever that way. Last year, they'd had Gabi pose as a bratty trainee in hopes of getting kidnapped. Lord, Gabi had been so good she'd fooled everyone.

When Linda joined the Shadowlands, Sally had learned about the horrors of human trafficking. Linda was older than Sally's usual girlfriends, but too young to be a mother figure...although she was the most motherly person Sally had ever met. Last

January in the Shadowlands, Linda had heard the voice of a slaver—one she'd never actually *seen*.

Sally sipped her coffee, forcing the liquid past her tight throat as she remembered her own stupidity. She'd blithely suggested Linda should join the trainees to help search for the slaver.

Great suggestion. The psychopathic slaver had caught Linda. Sally's teeth ground together. One minute Linda had been in the Shadowlands, gone the next. Just like with her mother, Sally couldn't fix it. If Linda had been murdered, her death would've been Sally's fault. Although Linda acted as if Sally had nothing for which to apologize, Sally wouldn't ever forgive herself.

Galen and Vance hadn't been there that night. They'd had to deal with some problem in the northeast. But Linda had mentioned that the two men felt responsible as well. What a horrible, horrible feeling. How could they stand making those kinds of decisions?

She stared at her drink, recalling the harsh lines in Galen's face. He seemed so driven sometimes. At least Vance watched out for him. Funny that they were so close. She smiled slightly. She'd asked the other subs if the guys were gay. They weren't—they just liked to share a woman.

As Sally remembered the previous weekend, a slow slide of desire vanquished the last of the cold. They sure did a good job of sharing—and dominating—together. She'd never, never felt so totally at a loss, knowing she couldn't...*manipulate* was a bit extreme...couldn't *influence* the Dom's decisions. But they hadn't given an inch.

And the way they'd watched her and touched her. Gentle and edging on cruel.

As her core throbbed at the memories, she squirmed in her seat. Wasn't it odd how she was just dying for them to play with her again and yet...uncomfortable...at the thought.

But even beyond that, how awkward that the Feebies were in the Shadowlands at all. If they ever found out she'd hacked into the bad guys' e-mail systems, they wouldn't be happy.

Unhappy Doms weren't good for a submissive's health, especially since Galen looked as if he had a bit of sadist in him. She sighed. Really, it would be smart to keep her distance from them.

The decision was a relief, and then a letdown. *Hart, you're schizoid.*

Well, she didn't have a choice in who joined the Shadowlands, after all, so she'd better be careful.

She shrugged and drank her coffee. On her laptop, the display flickered to the screen saver and the flash of light sabers as Obi-Wan fought Darth. She grinned. Guess she'd never be a Luke Skywalker-type hero; she was more like R2-D2.

But she was an amazing droid. She'd been hacking into computers since she was a teenager, and no one had caught her yet. Darned if she let any more women be kidnapped if she could prevent it. Besides, this was good practice for her forensic computer specialist career...kind of. Aside from being really, really illegal.

Of course, that just meant she was playing a digital Robin Hood. Stealing info from the rich slave traffickers and giving it to the poor cops. *Didn't that sound nice?*

Remotivated, Sally clicked the keyboard and continued reading through the e-mails. Mostly junk until she ran into warning e-mails sent from an overseer to someone the next level up. A *manager*. The e-mails said a cop, Lieutenant Tillman who was working with the FBI, had ordered surveillance on a Harvest Association private investigator.

And...Sally caught her breath. The manager had replied. *Awesomesauce!* She had her first hit on someone in the upper ranks.

She slowly read the rest of the e-mail and frowned. Quite the sarcastic douche bag, wasn't he? The e-mail concluded with Sarcastic Douche Bag telling the overseer to watch the news that night. Why would the douche bag expect something to be on the news? Sally lifted her hands from the keyboard, dread setting up residence in the pit of her belly. She couldn't do anything about whatever had happened though; the e-mails were from last week.

Biting her lip, she did a search for the name Lieutenant Tillman. Articles filled the screen. Her hands trembled. After a sip of suddenly tasteless coffee, she carefully set the drink back on the table. The news reports led to images and videos: the cop's house, gutted by fire, black and smoking, covered stretchers carried out to the ambulances, and neighbors weeping as they watched.

Tillman, his wife, and her mother had been chained and left to burn. *Oh God.*

"Are you okay, miss?" A man's voice broke through Sally's fugue.

She looked up.

Rich brown hair, green eyes. Jake from the Shadowlands. Staying as discreet as the club rules required, he didn't let on he recognized her. He simply acted like any guy checking on an upset woman.

From the buzzing in her ears and nausea, she probably looked about ready to puke. "I'm okay. Just some bad news." She pulled in a slow, calming breath and then gave him a nonchalant nod. *You can leave now.*

He didn't move. *Doms.* They displayed that overprotectiveness 24-7. He studied her for a second longer. "Maybe I should take you home. Do you live around here?"

"Uh, no. I'm on my way somewhere and stopped to get coffee." Kind of. She'd decided to never send Harvest Association e-mails from her home, so on her way back from Orlando, she'd pulled off I-4 near Plant City to do her checking. Sure, she could bounce her IP address around, but using the free Wi-Fi in a store added a bit of extra safety. "No need to worry."

His eyes narrowed. He was a newly titled Shadowlands "Master" and slightly younger than the rest, but he sure had the same instincts. To her relief, he didn't push. "I'm across the room with friends. You call me if you feel worse, and I'll take you home."

"I will. Honestly, I really am fine." She would be. Maybe. "But thank you."

As Jake walked away, she sighed. Galen and Vance had been like that—all concerned about her. Not all Doms were. With Frank, she'd thought his dominant behavior meant he'd be as protective and caring as the Shadowlands Masters. Boy had she been wrong.

Just as well she'd sworn off wanting a Dom of her own. Much safer to stick to lightweight scenes at the club.

Safer. The word sent her gaze to the laptop, to someone whose world would never be safe. With a keystroke, she brought up the reports about the fire. Even as a quiver of fear ran through her, she straightened her shoulders. *You just look out—I'm on your trail, you bastards.*

CHAPTER THREE

"Hey, Ben." Along with Vance, Galen walked into the entry of the Shadowlands. "How's it going?"

The oversize security guard lifted his chin in greeting. "Going good. You two are running late."

"You suppose there are any interesting submissives left in there?" Vance asked.

"For you two? You bet." Ben grinned. "Hey, you ever hear Nolan grumble about how much work is it to say 'Shadowlands submissives'?"

"Christ, Nolan bitches about any sentence over two words long," Galen said.

"Yeah, well, Cullen started calling the submissives 'Shadowkittens.' Says even Nolan can spit that out."

"Shadowkittens?" Galen exchanged an amused glance with Vance. The term certainly fit one little sassy sub.

"I like it," Vance said.

"Let's see if we can catch one, eh?" Galen lifted a hand to Ben and opened the door. His ears were assaulted by dungeon music and the enticing sound of impact toys hitting flesh. The room held the distinctive sex and pain scents of a BDSM club with the added fragrance of leather. Z had a preference for expensive equipment. The ambiance of the Shadowlands washed over Galen, pushing him into a different zone. No longer an FBI agent, but a Dom.

Near the front of the room, he spotted Nolan. His submissive—and wife—stood quietly in front of him as he tied her in an intricate rope bondage. The dark blue rope was a marked contrast to her fair skin. Her eyes were closed, an expression of peace on her face. Galen shook his head. Although many submissives said rope restraints could be as comforting as being wrapped in a toasty snug blanket, he didn't have the patience for long, involved bondage sessions.

Z was sitting on a bar stool. Galen and Vance joined him.

Z's wife, Jessica, was perched on the bar top. The submissive's wrist cuffs were clipped to a leather waist belt, keeping her arms at her sides. The low neckline of her knit dress had been pulled down far enough to expose her full breasts. Brows together. Eyes filled with fire. Spitting mad.

Galen felt grateful she was gagged.

Out of kicking range, Z sipped his drink. "I expected you two earlier. Problems?"

"The good kind of problem, but time-consuming," Galen said. He rested his hip on a bar stool and lowered his voice. "A New York police station got an anonymous e-mail tip with the name of a young woman targeted to be kidnapped."

"Interesting. Why not the FBI offices?" Z asked.

Vance scowled. "The cop who'd been working the case died in an arson fire earlier this week. The e-mail was addressed to 'Tillman's Captain.' And the sender went to considerable trouble to ensure he wouldn't be traced."

"Do you believe the informant is someone on the inside?" Z set his glass on the bar.

"Probably. The information seems accurate—the named woman fits their target parameters." Galen rubbed his chin. "A New York special agent will see if she wants to help. Even if not, we might be able to discover if anyone has done a background check on her." Every cog in the wheel called the Harvest Association would yield up more information. Galen was determined to get all the way to the top of the organization. And bring the bastards down.

"Good." Z eyed the agents. "But while you're here, let go of the police work. Whatever submissive you play with deserves your complete attention. And you both need the break."

Vance snorted. "I bet they call you Mama around here, don't they?"

"Not within my hearing." Z rose and pulled his wife off the bar. "Perhaps you can speak in a polite tone now, kitten?"

When she glared at him, he chuckled and fondled her breasts. The color in her cheeks heightened in a charming mixture of embarrassment, fury, and arousal.

A loud laugh drew Galen's attention.

"'Tis our favorite Feds." Behind the bar, Cullen grinned. "What'll it be, gents? You playing or drinking?"

"Play first," Galen said. "Hopefully with a little brunette."

"Sally anywhere around?" Vance asked.

"She was negotiating a scene with Casey," Cullen said. "You might check the dungeon room."

Well, hell. He'd looked forward to taking her another step further this evening. "She's obviously not jumping at the chance to play with us. You owe me fifty bucks," he said to Vance.

"Fuck. You've got the soul of a loan shark." Vance rubbed his face. "Might as well go watch."

"Ayuh." When Galen turned, he saw Jessica on her knees, delivering a sincere-looking apology to Z. *Very nice.*

Vance grinned. "Aren't spitfires cute?"

As Galen led the way to the back and down the theme room hallway, he saw a Dom and short Uzuri cleaning the medical room. On the other side, violet-wand play cast intriguing lights and shadows in the darkened office theme room. The dungeon was the last room on the right.

Vance stepped in beside him and leaned against the wall. After a few minutes, he murmured, "Well, damn."

Exactly so. Sally had her arms restrained above her head from the rafter chains, legs open. In between flogging sets, the Dom was finger fucking her. His face held the dark red of arousal, and a hard-on bulged the front of his jeans.

Sally didn't look excited. At all. Even worse, the flogging appeared to be hurting her. Over the last few months, Galen had observed that the girl wasn't a masochist. She needed an erotic component to enjoy pain. And right now, the arousal wasn't there.

He saw her open her mouth, undoubtedly for one of her unsublike orders, but she said nothing. Weariness tugged at her features, then disappeared.

The Dom was jamming his fingers into her cunt and rubbing frantically at her clit. Her movements—that he undoubtedly took to be of arousal—looked more like discomfort to Galen.

"As Masters are we allowed to intervene in that debacle?" Vance asked in a low voice.

"I prefer you leave that to me unless there's some urgency." The owner of the Shadowlands stood in the door, his face tight. "But it does need to be—"

The moaning scream cut off his words as Sally had a noisy, obviously quite satisfying orgasm.

A very, very fake orgasm. From the way the Dom puffed up, he'd been taken in completely.

Z growled under his breath. "That I didn't need to see."

"You plan to let her get away with that bullshit?" Vance's lips pressed together. Galen knew dishonesty in any form eradicated his partner's laid-back nature. Good thing Sally hadn't faked an orgasm during their scene, or she wouldn't have been able to sit down for a week.

"No." Z sighed. "But I prefer the newer Dominants not discover their shortcomings in such a public fashion...especially from a trainee."

Yes, that would hurt.

The grinning Dom finished freeing Sally and ran his hands over her body. She had a sweet smile on her face. Wasn't mouthing off. What was wrong with the girl?

Z walked forward. "Casey, I'm afraid we have a problem."

Galen leaned a shoulder against the wall.

As Casey turned, Sally saw Z, and her face turned white.

"Sally, explain what you did and apologize to the Dom." When she seemed paralyzed, Z added coldly, "From your knees, trainee."

She dropped to her knees and stared at the floor. Her voice shook as she said, "I didn't get off. I faked it. I'm very sorry."

Casey's mouth fell open, and the flush of arousal faded from his face and left him looking as if he'd been punched.

Galen felt a fair amount of sympathy for him. They'd all been inexperienced at one time, and it took a while before a man's cock didn't lead him around. Casey had been a sloppy Dom for not paying attention, but Sally had been a worse submissive for not simply telling him she wasn't getting anywhere.

Odd she hadn't. He'd seen her ream out Doms if they botched restraints, flogging, or other BDSM techniques. Yet he couldn't recall her complaining about sexual techniques or saying she wasn't aroused. Galen frowned. Had she ever shared how she actually felt?

She was so mouthy he might have missed those times. He rubbed his chin.

Casey started to speak and then bit the words back, taking the time to think first. Two points to the lad. "I'm disappointed in you, Sally, both for faking and for not telling me your head wasn't in the scene." He said to Z, "I screwed up, obviously, in not paying closer attention."

"Let's go talk about that now." Z's voice chilled. "Sally, remain there without speaking until someone returns for you."

Her shoulders hunched slightly, but she didn't move otherwise.

As the Dom cleaned the equipment, Z rejoined Galen and Vance. "Masters, I think it's time to put you to use. Do you feel up to giving a class on how to detect if a female is faking an orgasm?"

Vance shrugged. "Sure. Just let us know when and the location."

A slight smile appeared on Z's face. "The when is now. The medical room has the best lighting."

A theme room? Galen stiffened. "I take it this isn't a whiteboard and lecture venue?"

"No. A demonstration." Z glanced at Sally. "Use her."

Vance smiled slowly. "We can do that."

—✦—

"Sally."

Sally looked up to see Uzuri in front of her. She didn't know how long she'd been kneeling in the dungeon room. After a few minutes, misery had simply swarmed up and buried her. Faking an orgasm was one of Master Z's crash-and-burn offenses. The time Andrea had pretended to get off, she'd been forced to ride the fucking machine.

Unfortunately, Master Z would know that getting off with a machine wouldn't be much of a punishment for Sally. "Hey. What did Master Z choose to do to me? A whipping?"

Uzuri's gentle brown eyes filled with sympathy. "You might like that better." The trainee held her hand out.

Sally winced as Uzuri pulled her up. Her knees hurt like hell. She stretched and worked the kinks out, wishing she could just go home. At one time, she'd have been excited and scared about what might happen. Now…now her punishment was just something to suffer through.

She had a feeling she was nearing the end of her time as a trainee. The Shadowlands Masters had been almost the only ones who could give her what she needed—who were dominating enough to compel her surrender. Now they all had their own submissives, and any hope Sally had was gone.

Of course, the Feds weren't attached. Doubtful they'd ever be, considering what the other submissives had said. Players. She huffed a miserable laugh. At least they were new enough that Master Z wouldn't use them to punish her.

She pulled on her short, stretchy minidress—she hadn't had the enthusiasm to come up with flashier attire—and followed Uzuri into the hallway.

Uzuri stopped at the medical room.

Surprised, Sally bumped into her. "Here?"

The beads in Uzuri's braids clattered softly as she nodded. "Good luck."

This really didn't look good. There was already a crowd in front of the oversize window into the room. And the window had been opened so everyone could hear. Sally pushed her way through and stopped two feet inside the room. She felt the

Masters' eyes even before she saw them. *No. No no no.* It wasn't fair.

Vance and Galen were waiting for her.

She took a step back.

Galen shook his head and held out his hand. "Come here, trainee." His gaze was...direct. Firm. But she saw sympathy in his expression.

However, Vance's eyes held the warmth of a frozen lake. He'd never looked at her like that, and the loss hurt her inside. "I'd thought better of you," he said.

She pulled in a miserable breath, wanting to run. Knowing she wouldn't. A trainee knew the rules. She'd lied to a Dom; no matter what nasty punishment the Feds'd planned, she deserved it.

Her feet took her forward, and she set her wrist in Galen's grasp.

Palm under her chin, he studied her face with a frown. "I don't know what's bothering you, but you should've discussed it with your Dom. Or refused the scene. Lying—verbally or physically—isn't permitted."

Her shoulders slumped. "I know. I'm sorry."

"Me too." Somehow his words—no matter how soft—were like a slap in the face. He pulled her dress over her head, then patted the table. "Put your bare ass here."

I don't want to. With a lowered gaze, she climbed onto the table. Dammit, she did scenes in public all the time. She liked the thrill of being observed, of taking what a Dom had to give. And at the Shadowlands, she didn't worry about her safety. So why was facing this so difficult tonight?

"Head in the game," Vance said, his rumbling baritone as authoritative as Galen's resonant voice. "Lie on your back."

She complied, and he positioned her with her butt at the edge of the table, then set her feet into the stirrups and strapped her legs to the supports.

Vance spread the leg rests widely apart, exposing her pussy, then lifted the stirrups until her pelvis tilted upward. Undoubtedly wanting her asshole available.

She glanced nervously at the tray tables. No needles. Not even the urethral dilators. Thank God for that. She'd far rather be whipped than punctured or dilated. But no floggers or whips or canes were visible. What did they plan?

Vance tightened a strap over her waist, lifted the head of the table slightly, and clipped her wrist cuffs to the top. He tied an elastic satin blindfold behind her head and then shoved it up onto her forehead. Not using it yet, but...obviously he planned to.

Galen addressed the viewers through the window. "As you undoubtedly know, Master Z asked us to give a short talk on how to tell if a female fakes her orgasm. I see no need for any submissives to be present, so please have them wait for you elsewhere or chain them in the subbie section."

Several submissives, including Rainie and Jessica, left. A couple of Doms led their collared slaves away. Most of the remaining observers were male with a sprinkling of Dommes.

Sally felt a sinking in her stomach. There was only one reason they'd have strapped her to this table.

"Sally, you are going to show them how a submissive fakes an orgasm."

What kind of a punishment is that? A flare of anger bit into her. "My pleasure. It's not as if fooling a Dom is difficult." *You asshole.*

Galen actually grinned. "So you fooled everyone?"

"Well, yeah. Sure, Master Z could tell, but others...?" Her shrug lost its effectiveness with her arms over her head.

"Actually, pet, Master Galen and Master Vance noticed your dishonesty even before I did," Master Z said from the doorway. His arms were crossed over his chest, his gaze less disapproving than disappointed, and she felt tears sting her eyes. "Thank you, gentlemen, for giving up your time to teach this class," he said.

Murmured thanks came from the other Doms.

Vance's easy nod of acknowledgment was annoying. Damn Feds. Like they were all knowing and all powerful? What would they do if she made their scene into a farce? A *When Harry Met Sally* hammed-up orgasm. *Oh yeah.* Her lips curved.

Galen moved into Sally's line of vision. "Trainee. If your

performance isn't convincing, you'll get another chance. But before then, we'll use the toys in the drawers to motivate you. Is my meaning clear?"

The *meaning* made her impulse shrivel into a tiny screaming ball. The equipment in the medical room drawers was ghastly—needles and urethral sounds and enema kits. The bastard must have noticed her anxious look at the instrument trays. Then again, he was good at screwing with a submissive's mind. "Yes," *you fucking*, "Sir."

"Good." Galen ran one finger over her cheek, gently enough to surprise her. "Oddly, we don't enjoy humiliating submissives, even for punishment. I'm sorry you earned this, pet. We'd hoped for a different kind of play this evening."

Her lips trembled. The sympathy in his low voice was far more difficult to take than his uncompromising tone.

He took a step back, his features turning unreadable again. "For realism, we'll play with you briefly. Your job is to pretend excitement—whether you are or not. When you see me say, 'Now,' show everyone how wonderfully you can fake arousal and an orgasm."

See him say? That didn't make—

Vance put noise-canceling earphones over her head. The white noise they emitted drowned out everything.

Galen turned away from her and spoke to the audience.

She couldn't hear a word he said. And she began to feel like...an object. A nothing.

This was so different from the last time she'd been with the Doms. Before, they'd been sweet to her. Not like this. Ice formed inside her.

Even more tears welled up. Closing her eyes, she rested her head against the leather padding.

Hands ran over her body, cupped her breasts, and pinched her nipples lightly. A finger carefully pushed inside her. She was fairly dry, and under the weight of their disapproval, not even their hands could get her to moisten.

Her mouth tightened, and she set herself to suffer. This felt all too much like her time with Casey earlier.

The fingers pushed in and out. Then the Dom—Vance?—grabbed one buttock and pulled on it, more fully exposing her asshole.

A tap on her cheek made her open her eyes. She stared into Galen's face.

His lips formed the word, *Now.*

She'd rather hit him than perform for him, but had no choice. She mouthed, *I hate you.*

His gaze softened. Then he pulled the blindfold down from her forehead and over her eyes.

Couldn't see. Couldn't hear. A shiver ran through her. But she had a chore to perform. She took a second to gather her thoughts, then let out a low, aroused moan.

VANCE'S LIPS TIGHTENED as he watched the pretty submissive go into her act. Fuck, he hated liars. His ex-wife had been a master at it. And he'd been too young and gullible to realize what she was doing. Even divorcing her hadn't stopped the damage. By the time she finished, his best friend had been convinced he was an abuser. His buddy had eventually figured it out, but their friendship hadn't survived.

Do the job, Buchanan.

"Aroused women are usually flushed. Their lips are redder and often more swollen than normal," Galen said from his position near the top of the table. "See how her nipples are flaccid rather than peaked as they should be."

"She's barely wet," Vance said, "although a woman's vagina can moisten somewhat in sheer self-defense." He separated her labia to show her clit. "Still hooded."

And then Sally went into her orgasm.

Vance tightened his jaw. All fake. But, he had to admit, the sound would have made him erect if he hadn't been so pissed off.

"Her moan is good theater," Galen said. "The way she arches her neck and back is typical of orgasm—although, if you check her face, it appears oddly slack." He grinned. "Think of when you get off. Facial muscles will tighten—in fact, most of us look like we're dying."

Laughter ran through the crowd.

Vance caught Galen's glance and took over. "The pumping of her hips was usual for a woman coming. Her cunt and asshole would also pulse and clench. Being a very smart—as well as sneaky—submissive, Sally deliberately tightened her vaginal muscles—rather like those Kegel exercises they recommend for women." He pulled his slightly damp fingers out and held them up. "However, at this point, she should be thoroughly soaked inside."

"Her nipples never spiked," Galen pointed out as Sally lay, panting slightly. "She does the after-orgasm limpness well. But...do you see any flushing anywhere?"

Another murmur came from the crowd.

Vance said, "Usually you'll find redness over the sternum, cheeks, upper thighs, lower stomach, and ass. Her labia and clit would be more swollen and pink as well."

"Hellfire," one daddy Dom muttered. "I think my baby and I are going to have a chat."

"Now," Galen said. "The second half of this demonstration is to show you what she looks like when she really does get off." He turned and started stroking Sally, running his hands over her breasts.

Vance smiled as she stiffened. *Not ready to be aroused, were you, pet?*

"Bear in mind," Vance said to the crowd. "Women are all different. Every sign may not be present, but you should get some of them."

He bent and licked over her pussy, not trying for finesse or teasing. One part of the punishment was to teach her that her body could be used against her...despite her anger. Some women might be able to resist, but this little one was accustomed to submitting in public.

And she was fucking responsive, whether she wanted to be or not.

Under his lips, her clit swelled and pushed out from its hood. He took a step back to show the Doms. "That's an aroused clit. See how her inner labia have puffed up and darkened with blood."

Galen motioned to her face. "Her lips have reddened, cheeks are pinker. And, even without direct stimulation, her nipples are tight. She's aroused"—he chuckled—"although she doesn't want to be."

Normally, Vance enjoyed such a challenge, but, like his partner, he'd started to feel sorry for her. Although Z's choice of punishment was appropriate, Sally was a sweet little sub. It would be best to find out why she had a need to fake her orgasms.

He and Galen had decided not to drag the lesson out. Vance said to the Doms, "We don't want to keep you here, so we'll finish this up." He pulled a condom-covered bullet vibrator from his pocket and applied it to Sally's clit.

As he teased her for a bit longer, just for his own pleasure, he heard Galen point out the changes in her breathing and the increasing rigidity of her thigh and stomach muscles.

A second later, she climaxed.

"Her eyes would be dilated, but you can't see that from where you are," Galen lectured.

Pretty arch she had. Attending to the job at hand, Vance pointed out the visible contractions of her entrance and asshole and how a light red flush covered her thighs and belly. As Vance slid his fingers into her cunt, she jerked and spasmed around him. He held up his hand to show the ample amount of glistening fluid.

"Questions?" Galen asked.

The applause was quiet to avoid disturbing other scenes, and then their audience moved on.

Vance rubbed his hand up and down Sally's soft inner thigh. "That went well enough." He glanced at her face and saw the anger and unhappiness, despite the lingering glow of her orgasm. He sighed.

Galen gave him a wry glance. "Don't think we won her over by punishing her."

"The lecture we'll give her won't improve matters." Sally could fill an entire room with her bright spirit; darkening her light felt wrong. "Fuck, I hate making submissives cry."

"For punishment, yeah." Galen tilted his head. "Have we ever seen her cry?"

Vance paused, trying to remember a time. "Maybe not. I can say for sure, though, that she now hates our guts."

"Ayuh," Galen said. "So let's end this on a better note."

SALLY LAY QUIET, waiting for them to set her free. What was taking them so long? Damn them.

She'd given demonstrations before but never as part of being punished. It galled her that she'd deserved the punishment.

But they were complete douche bags to make such an example of her. To show everyone what she'd been doing. Some of the Doms she'd played with had been observing, and they'd looked... disillusioned.

One side of the earphones was pulled off, and she heard Galen's flat New England voice. "The audience is gone, and the curtains are closed, pet. This orgasm is just for you, because you took your punishment like a good girl."

What? Her whole body went stiff. "No. No, I don't want anything else." She growled and tried to bring her hands down. They'd left her arms chained. Left her legs strapped, her pussy open. "Let me..."

A demanding mouth closed over her left nipple; another over her right. Their tongues circled her nipples as the men targeted one of her most erogenous zones. When they sucked rhythmically, her back arched up as if to offer them more.

Their hands were stroking her stomach, her waist, and her upper thighs. So different from when they'd picked on her before, teasing her out of her head. This time, they headed in a straight line—arousal to climax. Do not stop at go. Their determination and single-mindedness was terrifyingly erotic.

Her body seemed to sink into the table as one Dom moved down. The other played with her breasts. Pinching mercilessly, licking softly, rolling one nipple, and sucking on the other. *God.*

Cloth—probably someone's pants—brushed against her inner legs, and then powerful hands fondled her butt cheeks and squeezed her thighs. She couldn't control anything they did. Couldn't move. Couldn't even hear. Heat rolled over her skin as if she were sinking into her bath.

Determined fingers pulled her labia open. His lips closed around her clit, hot and wet, and his skillful tongue was ruthless.

There. No there. Even better. Pressure grew inside her, driving her toward an orgasm, and she hated that they could manipulate her so easily. A few minutes ago, they'd forced her to climax; somehow this wasn't the same. Their hands were gentle, more teasing. Their coldness had disappeared. She felt almost as if they were truly treating her.

The coil in her belly grew as need climbed within. Tighter, tighter.

Someone pulled her headphones off. Lifted her blindfold. Galen stood above her.

She tried to close her eyes, but he gripped her chin. "Look at me, pet."

Vance's tongue skittered across the top of her clit, and he slid two fingers inside her. Three fingers. Stretching and pressing, thrusting in and out. Pushing her toward the top. His tongue never stopped.

Her breath caught as Galen's burning eyes kept her pinned to his gaze, and she felt the surge as her moorings broke loose, as her climax threw her into the riptide.

Somehow Galen was in there with her, pushing past her defenses to see who she was.

She shuddered and, as she came down, tried to turn her head.

"Not yet, pet," Galen murmured, his thumb stroking over her cheek. "I like that you can't hide from us. Not when you come."

She couldn't look away, was held by his gaze, his voice, his hand as her being dissolved.

"Shhh." The lines at the corners of his eyes deepened with his smile. "Relax for a minute." He kissed her lightly. Lingeringly. His spicy, masculine scent wrapped around her.

When he moved away, she felt the invisible restraint of his determination snap.

As Galen released the straps, Vance took his place, laying his big hand along her face. His eyes were dark, deeper than sky blue. His light brown hair angled past his broad cheekbones to end slightly below his collar. "Pretty Sally," he murmured and kissed her, slowly, surely, coaxing a response she didn't want to give.

Smoothly, Vance pulled her to a sitting position. The straps were gone. His arm braced her, and he fondled one breast, almost absentmindedly. "Blanket?" he said to Galen.

Blanket. Like for aftercare? She shook her head. "No. I don't need— My dress is there. I need to get back to work." Surely they wouldn't know she'd finished her trainee's shift.

Galen pulled a blanket from the white cupboard over the sink. His displeased stare shut her up. "You've already worked your stint, and I find your attempts at prevarication annoying."

Oh poop and shit and crap. Her chin lifted. Too bad for him that she annoyed him. "I don't need any aftercare. Not for this kind of scene. And I don't want you to touch me." She gripped Vance's wrist and tried to push him away.

"I like touching you, and since I'm the Dom and you're the trainee, guess who gets what they want?" Vance didn't move. "You're with us because you fucked up, Sally. Maybe the club members got a treat, but this demonstration happened because Z thought *you* needed a lesson."

She waited until her voice would emerge without quavering. "I understand. Lesson learned. I'm sorry, Sir, and I won't do that again."

"Good to know." Vance had seemed the more even-tempered of the two, but boy, he changed when he was pissed off. His square chin looked like a chunk of granite. He still didn't move.

Instead Galen came to stand in front of her. Although the sympathy he'd shown her before was gone, he wasn't furious like Vance. He looked as if nothing would upset his confidence. His black hair in a conservative business cut wasn't mussed. No wrinkles showed in his black shirt or slacks. Totally in charge.

The assholes. She never had any trouble with scenes until the Feds showed up. They made her feel stupid. As if she didn't have any say over what was going on. Which seemed strange, because she wanted to give up control, but not to them. The other Masters, yes, but not to these two.

Two. Maybe she could deal with one—although she'd begun to wonder about that—but both of them? She closed her eyes and tried to clear her mind.

Gregorian chants drifted in from the main club room. Sweat was cooling on her body, and a trickle ran down the hollow of her back. Vance stood close enough she caught whiffs of his aftershave. Old Spice maybe. The one that smelled like the outdoors with sex added. He shouldn't smell so good; one more strike against him.

Against them both. Galen wore something rich. Amber and sandalwood. Damn them.

Okay. She pulled in a breath. "I apologized to Casey and you. I did as you asked for my punishment." Her voice came out level and reasonable. She couldn't help the way her teeth clenched before and after.

"You aren't a new trainee, pet," Galen said. "Surely you've learned honesty is integral to a BDSM scene."

"Yes. I know. And I messed up."

He pinned her with those dark eyes again. "I'd like to hear why you weren't honest."

The two of them kept backing her into a corner, and she scrambled for a way to escape. One came to mind: fight back. "You're not my Dom. Neither of you. I didn't negotiate with you for a scene, and I wouldn't have volunteered to do this."

Vance narrowed his eyes. "You feel you didn't earn it?"

"I did, but the punishment is over now. And I don't know you. Or trust you enough to want to talk to you." That was a hit. As new Masters, they probably wouldn't push a trainee—and they were digging deeper than the others ever had. "I have some say in who I want to work with." *Kind of.* Unless Master Z stepped in.

"Sally—"

She jumped off the table. "Thanks for the lesson. *Sirs.*"

—✦—

In his New York condo office, Drew Somerfeld frowned at the e-mail from one of his managers. What the hell? Two of the women chosen for his Harvest Association summer auction had disappeared before they could be abducted.

Suddenly. Without any advance notice to their family or employers.

Could they have been warned?

He uncurled his fingers and forced them flat on the black desktop as he considered possible reasons. Complications. What his next step should be...

Perhaps one of the contract agents had talked or been compromised. The overseers occasionally hired less than ideal individuals, after all. Kidnappers weren't exactly at the top of the character charts.

He'd have to play a wait-and-see game for now. Meantime, he'd put in an order with a different manager. He not only needed more women for the auction, but Ellis had used up his slave when he'd slaughtered that cop. His twin needed to be rewarded for his excellent work—and his favorite bonus was a new slut to play with.

A shame Ellis went through them so fast.

CHAPTER FOUR

S ally parked at the side gate of the Shadowlands, turned off the car, and wearily leaned her head back against the seat. Maybe she shouldn't have agreed to meet Jessica and a couple others for the afternoon. She was seriously short on sleep.

Why the punishment demonstration would give her nightmares all week, she didn't know. Or perhaps the cause was the poor police officer that the Harvest Association had killed? She'd been unable to keep from watching the funerals for him, his wife, and her mother. At least he hadn't left little children behind—but his boy and girl were about Sally's age.

Damn the Association. According to their e-mails, they were still planning an auction. She'd sent a warning to the New York police about another woman targeted for kidnapping. Hopefully the cops weren't blowing off her information.

This Robin Hood business wasn't for the faint of heart.

Since she'd be working as a trainee tonight, she picked up her diet soda and finished off the last few sips. *Come on, caffeine.*

Her cell phone rang, startling her. After a glance at the display, she accepted the call. "Hi, Father."

So stiff a word. Father. Back before she was ten, she'd called him Dad. But then her mom died and the world changed. Darkened.

She shook her head at the maudlin thought. *Gonna get all self-pitying now?* But...it was true. That year, the sky over the cornfields had seemed to turn from an Iowa royal blue to a cold gray.

"Sally." Her father's voice was as frozen as usual. "I received the message about your graduation. I will attend the ceremony."

Very dutiful. God, but it hurt to know he only came because his absence would look bad to the people in their small Iowa town. They'd undoubtedly told him: *Take lots of pictures at her graduation.*

Everyone else in the town liked her. Just not her father. Because she wasn't supposed to have been born. Because it was her fault Mom died. Sally closed her eyes and pulled in a slow breath. "Would you like directions to—"

"No need. I can find my way to the ceremony."

They weren't alike at all; she could lose herself walking around the block. Thank God for GPS and smartphones.

"Then I'll see you there." She ended the call. With a gentle hand, she opened her car door and slid out. The Confederate jasmine covering the fence was in bloom, the white flowers scenting the air with sweetness, dispelling the bitterness of the conversation.

Inside the gate, in Master Z's private backyard, she hesitated. No one was on the veranda behind the mansion. Would the others be on the third story where Z and Jessica lived or...

Laughter came from the other direction. Back somewhere in the extensive gardens. Sally turned and followed the sound.

Under a huge umbrella, three women—all Shadowlands submissives—sat around a patio table. Jessica, blonde, short, and curvy. Kim, black-haired and slender with a day collar around her neck. Linda, probably in her forties, fair-skinned, with red hair. A slight silvering showed at her temples.

"There she is!" Jessica held up a glass. "Finally!"

"Sorry about being late."

"Girl, you look overheated and tired." Jessica pointed to the pool. "Jump in before you join us."

Jessica knew her too well. Veering toward the pool, Sally shed shirt and shorts, leaving on her bra and thong. She dived in. Clear and cool—not the bathtub temperature it would reach later in the summer. Just right. The whoop she gave as she surfaced shattered the unhappiness that lingered every time she talked to her father. *Put him out of your mind, girl.* She swam a couple of laps to wash away all the nightmares and sadness and anger.

Maybe after she graduated and got a good job, she could afford a place with a pool. A small one would be okay. After climbing out, she squeezed the water from her hair and left it to hang in tangles down her back.

A glass pitcher, beaded with moisture, sat on the table. She eyed the contents warily. Jessica often got pretty creative with beverages. "What are we drinking?"

Jessica poured and handed the drink over. "This, my child, is a screaming orgasm. And Z says to be sure to sober up before the Shadowlands opens. I heard him leave a message for Ben to not let us in if—how did he put it?—'if he doubts our sobriety.'"

"Only Master Z could say that with a straight face." Too thirsty to sip, Sally drank about half before slowing and savoring the flavors. *Yum.* "I'm tasting Kahlúa and amaretto and...?"

"Baileys and vodka. Be warned—the drink packs a kick," Linda said.

"A kick is good." Sally dropped into a chair and considered the older woman.

Linda's creamy sundress was the perfect backdrop for her thick, shoulder-length hair. Her toenails were painted a sparkling raspberry color that seemed to match the glow of happiness about her.

"I think living with Sam agrees with you, although I'm not sure how. Sadists are just plain scary." Sally shook her head.

"I like his brand of scary." Linda gave the others a slow smile. "Besides, I always wanted a cowboy, even if my rancher considers himself a farmer."

"Ugh. I grew up on a farm." Sally leaned forward and refilled her drink. "Cornfields and beans and pigs."

Kim toasted her. "And now you're a city girl getting a master's."

"In what?" Linda asked.

The alcohol buzz had hit already—maybe because she hadn't had any lunch. Stupid, but she'd relish the feeling for a few minutes before digging into one of the deli sandwiches piled on a platter. "Computers. Digital forensics, actually. Does that sound sexy or what?"

"What—like crime stuff?" Linda tilted her head.

"Kinda. Like if someone's dead, I do an autopsy on his hard drive instead of his body. So much more sanitary, right?" But she could still do good. Be a hero, even if a nerdy one.

Jessica snickered. "God, yes. I'd rather deal with a pile of papers any day than a stinky corpse. But computers... Is that like legal hacking?"

"It really is." Sally tipped her head back, enjoying the balmy early evening. Enjoying the alcohol. She felt relaxed for the first time in ages. "I used to be a hacker, you know? Snoopy Sally, the nerd."

"Seriously?" Linda narrowed her eyes. "I never thought of you that way."

Woo-hoo, I'm good. "My sorority sisters taught me how not to look—or act—like a dork. Bless them."

"Huh. I figured you as smart, but a teenage hacker is a whole different level." Kim swirled her drink and eyed Sally. "I'm trying to visualize that. Did you make viruses or something?"

"Well..." Sally set her empty glass on the table. Maybe she should eat. *Nah.* She poured herself a refill. *Screaming Orgasm. Awesome name.* "Not exactly. Um, stuff like—a college jock figured he could assault a girl because she was black." Sally scowled, remembering how angry she'd been. "She wouldn't press charges. So I copied and sent his racist, sexist—and porn-ridden—e-mails to the college faculty and dean. He was gone a week later." *The asshole.* "I've improved the program a lot."

And it's working just fine on some true douche bags. A bit of caution made it through the blurring in Sally's head, and she kept the revelation from spilling out. "Don't tell anybody, okay?"

The other women nodded, and she gave them a happy smile.

Linda patted her hand. "You, my dear, are already blitzed. Eat something or Z won't let you into the Shadowlands tonight."

"But it feels good," Sally grumbled. How long had it been since she'd felt so...open. Free. With a sigh, she obediently accepted the sandwich Jessica handed her. "Hey, as anyone talked to Kari recently?"

Jessica shook her head. "Some teacher went out on maternity leave, and Kari is filling in more. Between extra work and the baby, she hasn't had any free time."

"Oh. No wonder she isn't at the club these days." Perhaps a visit should wait until the Hillsborough elementary schools started their summer break in June.

"Probably," Jessica said. "But I miss seeing her and how content Dan looks when he plays with her."

Sally smiled. "Yeah, he really does." Working in the police station, she saw an awful lot of cynical cops. Master Dan had been headed in that direction until he'd met Kari. But no one could stay bitter around the sweet-hearted schoolteacher.

"Speaking of the club, what happened with the Feds last week?" Kim asked. "Jessica said you were punished."

"Christ on a crutch, it was awful." Sally giggled, pleased the pain of the memory seemed so distant. "I'd faked coming and got caught."

— ✦ —

Galen walked down the outside steps from the third story to the veranda and leaned on the railing to pacify his aching leg. *Damn knee.* The gunshot wound from years past had healed, but the underlying damage had slowly surfaced. Getting older didn't help. Soon, he needed to man up and get surgery. Maybe he'd have the time once the case was wrapped up, if that ever happened.

"Nice of Z to help out," Vance said as they reached the bottom.

"Ayuh." They'd asked the psychologist to counsel a recovered slave—a girl so young Galen couldn't think of her kidnapping without getting enraged. She'd been so traumatized she'd stopped speaking, and Z specialized in nonverbal communication. God knew the Dom understood the psychology of slaves, voluntary or involuntary.

Galen and Vance had swung by to drop off the girl's information, as well as a thank-you bottle of Aberfeldy 21 single malt, which Galen had picked up during a Scotland trip.

Near the gate, Vance halted. "Listen."

Women were laughing somewhere in the gardens. One giggling voice was like water over a stony creek bed. "Is that Sally?"

"I've never heard her sound like that." Vance headed toward the gaiety.

Galen noiselessly followed him down a path into the gardens, remembering his hunting days. Stalking the prey.

Words became distinct, and Vance stopped.

Galen leaned against a convenient tree and listened. *Not very gentlemanlike behavior, Kouros.* But how could a Dom resist? After a minute, he laughed silently and mimicked tipping up a bottle. The ladies were drinking and had been at it for a while.

Vance nodded. He crossed his arms over his chest and settled in.

"I was so mad," Sally told the women. "I mean, yeah, I shouldn't have, but sweet Jesus on a pogo stick, they announced to everyone I'd been faking getting off."

Yes, he could see how that would bother her. But why had she needed to pretend? And it hadn't been her first time. He and Vance had spoken with Z about that very matter.

"You and the Feds?" Galen recognized Kim's voice. "What do you think of them?"

Interesting question. He leaned forward as the pause continued.

"Well, one minute I think they're nice, and the next I think they're total dipwads. Manipulative bastards."

Galen bit back a laugh.

Jessica snorted. "Sounds like the definition of a Dom?"

"Well, maybe. And their two-to-one stuff is…"

Galen sighed and jerked his head at his partner. Not fair to be listening to private conversation, no matter how interesting. But the draw of Sally's open laughter had been irresistible.

Vance gave him an annoyed, then rueful expression, and they retreated quietly.

"You ethical bastard. She'd just gotten to the good stuff," Vance said, holding open the gate to the parking lot.

"True." Galen smiled. "But I like to think we're honorable—even if we are dipwads."

"Pretty sure she only meant you." Vance frowned. "She sounded different."

"Yeah, she did." Galen limped across the concrete, as always, annoyed to see his partner shorten his stride and slow. "Notice she talked about how she felt?"

"Because she was intoxicated."

"Exactly. She certainly doesn't share if not under the influence." Galen frowned. "Why would a lovely woman close herself down?" And why did the vulnerable expression he'd seen on her face last week pull at him?

"Good question." Vance slid into the driver's seat. "Let's find out."

———✦———

Oh boy, she should've stopped drinking a lot earlier. After a quick shower and change in Jessica and Z's guest room, she took their private stairway into the Shadowlands. Carefully. Screaming orgasm—the drink that kept on giving, cuz she sure wasn't sober. Ben would probably turn her away if she went in the front door.

A long gauze skirt and a makeshift scarf tied around her breasts served as her outfit. Thank God Z preferred the trainees barefoot; she'd have busted an ankle in heels.

She'd missed the trainee lineup and inspection. Master Cullen would be displeased. But since she didn't barmaid until the second shift, her lateness wouldn't upset service.

Members packed the room. To her fuzzy brain, the music and conversations sounded awfully loud, and people moved too fast.

At the bar, she waited for Cullen to see her. On her left, a Domme in a motorcycle jacket, black latex pants, and boots was chatting with a couple of newer submissive women. On her right, a group of older Doms discussed service protocols.

"'Bout time you arrived." Master Cullen in his brown leathers gave her a long look. "You've still got an hour to play before your shift starts. Do you have a Dom lined up or someone in mind?"

Sally winced. How many of the Doms would think—or know—that she'd faked getting off? "I—"

"She's been drinking and can't even walk in a straight line, Cullen." The word *drinking* somehow had changed to *drinkin'*; *can't* had been transformed into *cahn't*.

At the sound of Galen's down-east accent, Sally stiffened and turned.

As usual, he wore black slacks and shirt—similar to Master Z—but Galen's dress shirt was broadcloth rather than silk. Kouros wasn't a silk kind of guy.

He continued, "Perhaps she can wait tables now and have the second shift off."

Vance's big hand came down on her shoulder. "Galen and I would like to play with her. But not until she's sober."

"I'm not—" Sally knocked Vance's arm away and turned back to Cullen. "I'm perfectly fine."

"Fuck, I hate when she lies," Vance growled. He gripped her hair, tilting her face up. His eyes were cold. "Are you seriously telling Cullen you're sober?"

"I…" She couldn't lie. "No. I'm not completely sober."

"No one does a scene if under the influence." Frowning, Cullen rested his thickly muscled forearm on the bar. He said to Galen, "Thanks for the heads-up. Sally, you're assigned to cleaning tables. Check back with me in an hour."

Stupid, interfering, know-it-all Feds. When she glared at Galen, a line in his right cheek deepened, showing his amusement. She realized he had more than a five-o'clock shadow, as if he hadn't shaved earlier.

Andrea, Cullen's submissive, who'd been listening, set a big mug of coffee in front of Sally and winked.

"As for later," Master Cullen said, "Sally, I've heard what the members think of a trainee playing them for fools. There won't be more punishment, pet, but I can't do anything about your reputation with the Doms."

Master Cullen usually had a smile, but not now. He was serious and…unhappy with her. Everyone was unhappy with her. Like in the beginning of the Wizard of Oz, when Dorothy realized she couldn't do anything right.

Sally stared at the bar. *Why didn't I just stay home?* "I understand."

"Tonight, you're assigned to Master Galen and Master Vance. They can work with you on honesty." Master Cullen's expression was troubled. "I know you didn't fake an orgasm with any of the Masters, love, but we also never pushed you for more than light submission. We don't usually. Emotional vulnerability is given to a long-term Dom, but we should've caught on to how much you were hiding from us."

The sting of tears had her dropping her gaze again. She'd disappointed everyone.

Cullen set a tray on the bar next to her mug. "Finish the coffee; then get to work."

Vance ran his knuckles over her cheek. "It's not that bad, sweetheart. This will pass." Sympathy warmed his eyes. "We'll find you in a couple of hours. Here at the bar."

Even as a thrill ran through her at his touch, she couldn't suppress her glance at the door.

His hand curved under her chin, and he tilted her face up. "Sally, don't try to leave early."

Bossy Dom. "No, Sir. Wouldn't think of it, Sir."

When Galen raised an eyebrow, she flushed. Dammit, he'd probably gag her again.

—✳—

Seated near the middle of the club room, Galen smiled as the little black trainee handed him a bottle of water. "Thank you, Uzuri."

"You're welcome, Sir." Watching her trot away, he shook his head. Her smile had been one of the sweetest he'd ever seen, but her dark eyes said *watch out for pranks.*

He looked forward to the upcoming scene with her fellow mischief maker, the imp named Sally. Propping his feet on the coffee table, he watched Vance work with a newer Dom, showing the knots best for rope bondage. For the past couple of hours, they'd wandered through the main room, helping out, answering questions, even demonstrating. Part of Z's purpose in establishing the Shadowlands had been to provide education to the BDSM community, and the Masters were expected to put in their time. He and Vance would start as dungeon monitors next month.

He checked the clock. Sally should be getting off duty about now. Galen caught Vance's attention and tilted his head toward the bar.

Smoothly, his partner finished his instruction and walked over. "Time to pick on a sassy brunette?"

"That's the idea. If you run down the girl, I'll get my toy bag from the locker room and meet you in the back." Anticipation was a swift stream in Galen's veins.

"Good enough." Vance grinned.

A few minutes later, Galen walked across the main room to the far side. Murmurs of low conversations, sounds of sex, the slap of a hand on flesh were louder than the music coming from the front. Tall containers of plants divided the sitting areas into secluded niches for aftercare and quiet talks.

It was like wandering through a maze.

At the sound of Vance's rough voice, Galen headed in that direction.

His partner had found an unoccupied area with a leather couch and two comfortable chairs. On her knees, Sally waited, her hands on her thighs, her back straight, gaze down. Vance sat on one of the chairs.

"Very nice," Galen said.

After her initial start of surprise, she relaxed. Her lips softened in a submissive's deep-rooted pleasure at receiving approval.

By God, she was pretty. He bent, tilted her chin up, and took her lips—not demanding, but wanting a taste of the sweetness that was Sally.

And she gave it to him.

Moving away, Galen set the bag down. They didn't expect to use any toys, but the bag held water and chocolate and a blanket.

"Time to start," Vance said. "Remove your clothes, Sally."

"Um." She glanced around as if expecting to see bondage equipment magically appear. "This isn't a scene area."

"No. It's not," Galen said agreeably. He took a seat on the couch.

She rose, taking a step back so she could face them both. Confrontational—or defensive?

"I prefer to play in the regular areas," she said.

Galen exchanged a glance with Vance. Wasn't it a pleasure to keep this one off balance, little Miss Sassy who'd ruled over less experienced Doms.

"This spot is better for what we have in mind," Vance told her.

Her eyes narrowed. She was obviously considering how far she could push them. Damned if he'd figured her out. Despite her impertinent behavior, she was submissive. Given no choice, she'd relax into giving up control.

"Clothes off now, Sally. Not next week." Galen leaned back and extended his legs.

After a long hesitation, she stripped off her almost see-through skirt and the scarf she'd wound around her pretty breasts. She wasn't a big woman but was solidly built. Amply padded with a curvy ass, heavy thighs showing she had some muscle underneath. He smiled as she bent to pick up her clothes. Jiggly, lush ass—Vance's favorite kind.

As for Galen, he simply liked women's bodies. Skinny or lush, muscular or soft. Full breasts or thimble-sized.

Naked—beautifully naked—Sally set her hands on her hips and frowned at Galen.

"Is that posture one Master Z teaches the trainees?" Galen asked levelly.

Her face flushed, and her arms dropped. "No, Sir."

"There's a relief," Vance said.

Galen had to suppress a laugh at the flashing anger in her expression. "Come and sit on my lap."

Her mouth flattened. She really didn't like them, did she? Then again, he doubted her feelings were personal. She wouldn't like anyone who'd punished her as they had—and she wasn't going to enjoy what they'd planned for tonight, either.

With obvious reluctance, she seated herself on his thighs. He let her sit there, rigid as a pissed-off cat. Probably as dangerous.

"Now what?" she asked.

"We're going to talk a bit, Sally." Vance pulled his chair closer. "Nothing painful."

"Lean against me, please," Galen said. He enjoyed the hell out of making her comply with his voice alone.

Without relaxing a mite, she shifted until her shoulder met his chest.

"You smell good, pet. Like springtime." He put his arm around her back, holding her still so he could rub his jaw along her neck and inhale the clean fragrance. Almost like green apples. "What's the name of your perfume?"

"Be Delicious," she muttered.

He chuckled. "Sounds like an invitation to me." When he nibbled the top of her shoulder, she jumped.

Vance lifted her legs onto the couch and slid his chair close enough to rest his hand on her thigh. They wouldn't tie her down. But she was a small woman, and their large sizes and positions would give her the feeling of imprisonment.

Now, the true point of this not-scene would begin. "I heard you're going to get your Master's degree. In what?"

Her disbelieving stare made him smile. She acted like a mouse cornered by a cat that didn't immediately pounce.

Galen waited.

"Um. Computers."

"A master's in computers?" Vance prodded. "That's vague."

Her cheeks darkened slightly. "Master's of Digital Forensics."

Galen blinked at the unexpected answer. The girl was not only smart, but she might be pointing her sights at criminology. "Why that?"

"It's interesting."

"What exactly interests you?" Vance asked.

"Oh please, I'm not going to talk computers with someone your age. You probably think a mouse pad is where a rodent lives." She scowled at them. "Is this an interview or what?"

"No, it's a conversation between two Doms and a rude submissive," Galen said, barely managing to keep from laughing.

She froze as if shocked to be called on her behavior. After a second, her head bent. "I'm sorry."

SALLY FELT GALEN'S warm hand stroke her shoulder. She'd annoyed him, but he still handled her gently.

And under his slow touch, her body responded in a way these Doms achieved far too easily. To her unease, Vance moved her legs apart before running his palm up and down her outside thigh.

Two men at once. She'd enjoyed threesomes in the past, but...not with these two. They were—

"So, trainee, what kind of a Dom are you looking for?" Galen asked as if not too interested in her answer. He seemed more engrossed in the way his fingers ran over her collarbone. Her nipples tightened as if begging to be touched as well.

Vance moved his hand higher on her thigh so his fingers dipped into the—*dammit*—wetness of her pussy. A brush against her clit made her jump.

She tried to move away.

"Stay still, pet," Vance warned as he pressed a finger up inside her. His thumb rested beside her clit.

Biting her lip, she didn't move, although her center quaked like force screens were disintegrating. *Shields up, Scotty.*

"That's a good girl," Galen said. Approval turned his voice to velvet.

When he cupped her breast, she realized they'd restrained her in an incredibly intimate fashion.

"Look at me, sweetheart." Vance's sapphire eyes met hers. Held hers as he slowly pulled his fingers from her pussy and then thrust deeper.

Despite Sally's anger at them, heat blossomed in her core.

"Galen asked a question. Answer him."

Question? Oh, right. Vance's thumb pressed into the flesh

above her clit, so close to where it would really feel good. *Question.* "Um, I don't want a Master-type Dom." *I don't want a Dom at all. Not anymore.* "Not if he needs a real slave. I like to play."

"A Dom just for some fun times in the bedroom? To tie you up and fuck you but not dominate in any other way?" Galen plucked her nipple, then recupped her breast as he waited for her answer.

Her body shimmered with heat. Damn them, they were doing this to her again. She tried to remember what she'd once desired. Before Frank. It didn't really matter though. She could say anything. "Just for the bedroom."

Vance slid his fingers in and out. "Odd. Her pussy lie detector says she's lying."

Sally stared at him. "You can't—can't tell anything like that."

"The technique isn't one we're allowed to research." Vance smiled. "But it works fine."

He couldn't possibly tell if she lied. "Let me go."

"No, I don't think so." Galen played with her breasts. The center of his palm was more calloused than Vance's. Because of the cane?

She realized her not inconsiderable weight rested on his legs. "Let me up." When he lifted his eyebrows, she lowered her voice. "I'll hurt your leg."

His hand stopped moving for a moment, and then he shook his head. "No, you won't. The damage is already done—you're not going to make it worse." He smiled and touched her cheek. "I'm glad to know you care."

"I don't." Angry she'd been so stupid, she tried to push his hand away. Shoving an eight-foot Wookiee would be easier.

"Haven't you ever wanted a Dom at home to worry about you?" Vance asked. "To spank you for not carrying your cell phone? To push you to try harder? To force you to share what's bothering you?"

Yes. At one time. Back when she was naive. Now, she really didn't. "No."

"Z did a piss-poor job of training you. I had a wife who lied constantly, and I have a low tolerance for it," Vance said with disgust. "What part of honesty don't you understand?"

Her chin came up. "I honestly don't want to answer your questions."

"*No* isn't the answer we're looking for." Galen pinched her nipple, a short, painful reprimand.

She winced.

"You're obviously comfortable with physical intimacy." Galen ran his hand over her, proving his point. "Why are you so guarded with your thoughts?"

"I feel left out and worried if you don't tell me what you feel," Vance said, apparently trying to demonstrate how to share.

"I like you, Sally," Galen said softly. "We've been watching you. Have wanted to play with you for quite a while. But we worry you. Why?"

"Don't give yourself airs," Sally snapped. "I'm not worried."

"Lie," Vance said softly. When his thumb brushed over her clit, she couldn't help squirming.

"I talked to the other Masters about scenes they've done with you," Galen said. "They've realized that, although you submitted physically, they'd never pushed past your emotional defenses. Never reached your feelings. Normally, that's not a concern since deeper emotions are best explored by a long-term Dom."

"Exactly. You're not that, are you?" she muttered. How dare they talk to Cullen and Nolan and Dan and Raoul? The thought of them discussing her was...humiliating. Terrifying.

"No, we're not." Galen pushed her hair off her forehead, then laid his hand along her cheek to stop her from averting her face. "However, you have a problem other subs don't. You're not honest or even revealing a hint of your emotions. That's disturbing, pet."

"I think you're overreacting," she said. "Yeah, maybe I don't meltdown after a scene like a PMSing teen without a prom date, but that doesn't mean there's anything wrong with me. I enjoy playing. What more—"

"Enjoy playing?" Galen pinned her with those dark eyes again. "Then last week, why didn't you tell Casey you weren't getting anywhere?"

The question was an unexpected bull's-eye. She stiffened.

"We're not going to judge you, sweetheart," Vance said. He

sounded so…concerned. "Just tell us why."

"I don't know." She blinked away the dampness in her eyes, her stomach twisting uneasily. What was wrong with her? "I just *couldn't*."

"All right, pet," Galen said, his deep voice soothing. "Maybe you can make some guesses?"

Neither of them was going to back off.

Why *had* she let Casey continue? Usually, if a scene wasn't working out, she'd annoy the Dom enough to end it early. But that evening… "I was just too tired to fight, I guess."

Galen's eyes narrowed. "To fight? Why would telling a Dom you weren't into a scene have to be a battle?"

Her mouth opened. Closed.

"You never do tell them if a session isn't working, do you?" Vance asked. "Instead you prod until the Dom gets annoyed and lets you go."

Her cheeks felt too hot.

"Why, Sally?" Galen hadn't moved, and yet she felt as if he was in her face. "We're here to listen to what you have to say."

His statement flattened her with its weight, compressing her chest and lungs. She couldn't do anything right. Couldn't even be a good submissive after so long. She began to fight Galen's hold, and when he didn't release her, she glared at him. "Red. Red, red, red. Let me go *now*."

Galen lifted his hands. Vance moved back.

Sally jumped to her feet and snatched up her clothing.

Before she could run, Galen gripped her arm. "You safeworded, so I'm letting you go, but pet, the problem you have won't disappear. Talk with someone about this. Master Z, if no one else."

Never. "Just stay away from me. I don't like you." She glared at Vance. "Or you. Is that honest enough for you?" Wrenching her arm from Galen's grasp, she fled.

CHAPTER FIVE

S ally used her thumbs to tap in the phone number to the Shadowlands, winced, and frowned at her hand. Every nail was bitten down to the quick...and now a bit past. Ugh.

Sitting in the shade near the University of Central Florida's reflecting pond, she tried to let the noise of the fountain calm her. Didn't work. Even the stupid stubby St. Augustine grass annoyed her. In kindergarten, she and her best friend would roll down the tiny playground hill. But silky-soft northern grasses didn't like Florida. No one would roll on this crap.

She used her index finger on the small cell-phone screen. Got to admit, short nails made it easier to type. But she really should stop chewing on herself. She'd thought she'd gotten past the nervous habit in college. Did they still sell that nasty stuff you could put on your nails?

"Sally, I've been worried about you." The voice on the other end was deep, rich, and powerful.

Damn caller ID and double damn the call hadn't gone to voice mail. Sally rolled her eyes. And didn't that make this a typical Monday? In a totally crappy month. In fact, the entire season had sucked the big one. "Master Z, I appreciate you letting me return to the trainees, but it's not working out with my schedule. I'm sorry to do this to you, but I'm quitting. Again." *Forever.*

The pause seemed far too long. "Would you trust me enough to meet me so we can discuss this? I'd consider it a favor."

Oh, sneaky, guilt-inducing question. If she said *no*, the implication was that she didn't trust him. "No need." She forced a light tone past her clogged-up throat. "I'm finishing up my semester and am overloaded right now. Afterward, I'll probably move out of state to wherever I find a job. This is as good a time as any to quit."

"Little one, did Galen and Vance—"

"No. My decision has nothing to do with them." God, how many people could she lie to? She blinked back tears, already missing everyone. "Thank you for everything you've done for me over the years, Sir. Give Jessica a hug for me." It took all her determination to push the red Disconnect button.

After staring at the blank screen for a minute, she turned the phone completely off. Just in case.

He knew she was quitting because of the Feds. Would he give the men a rough time? Master Z was very protective of the submissives—especially the trainees.

A breeze ruffled her hair. Wind was wonderfully soothing in a muggy climate...until it was disturbed, turned into a hurricane, and flattened everything in its path. Much like Master Z.

She shook her head. She'd bet Galen had a ferocious temper as well. And he and Vance hadn't done anything terribly wrong. They'd only asked her some questions.

Hard questions.

Chin on her knee, she wrapped her arms around her legs. She not only didn't know the answers, but the idea of sharing her emotions creeped her out.

She'd never talked to Frank about her feelings. Like her father, he didn't want to know.

She scowled. So they wanted her to blurt out every thought? How boring. Wouldn't that take all the fun out of a scene?

Her brows drew together. Would it, though? Other submissives talked to their Doms about their impressions—even if not during the scene, at least afterward. But—Sally wrinkled her brow—why hadn't she told a Dom something like, *I prefer finger fucking to be gentle at first*. In aftercare, she'd snuggle, not talk, even if the Doms wanted to discuss the scene. And most of them had.

She frowned. Frank never asked. He'd never done much

aftercare for that matter. He might've talked the talk, but he sure hadn't walked the walk.

The Feds had him beat there. They'd been affectionate. Caring. Acting as if they liked who she was...aside from her reluctance to spill her guts. What was their problem anyway? Guys weren't supposed to like that emotional baring stuff...which was probably why no other Doms had gotten upset. But the Feds had been all over her evasions like white on rice.

Sheesh.

Well, she couldn't deal with this now. She had a couple of final papers to hand in, graduation practice, and résumés to send out.

Job hunting to do. She hadn't lied to Master Z about relocating away from Tampa.

She'd planned on trying to find a job in the area. Leaving might be smarter. The BDSM community was small enough that the local Doms would learn she'd faked orgasms. Or she'd run into Frank. How awkward would that be?

She straightened her shoulders. *Three easy steps. Graduate. Find a job. Move.*

But I like Florida. She shook her head. *No whining.* Miami might be fun. Or better yet, New Orleans.

But she'd leave behind all her Shadowlands friends. When tears burned her eyes, she had to bite her lip to keep control.

I can do this. She could do anything. She'd survived losing her mother. Survived her father's anger. Put herself through college and grad school. Being lonely... Well, she'd make new friends.

She was "fun." No one had ever wanted more from her than silence and service or entertainment.

Not until the stupid Feds.

CHAPTER SIX

On Tuesday night, Kari was sitting on the living room floor facing her son, Zane. His little face scrunched up in a grin. And his eyes looked so much like Dan's that she felt as if her body couldn't possibly contain all the love.

Her husband sprawled in his favorite chair behind her. On the sofa to the right, Dan's FBI friend was idly petting her German shepherd. In total doggy heaven, Prince leaned against the man's long legs to show his approval.

As the men talked quietly, Kari dropped a napkin over a small black-and-white plastic animal. "Where is the cow, Zane? Where did it go?"

Zane looked around, then with an almost audible click, he got it. With a squeal of glee, he pulled the napkin off the toy.

"Oh, aren't you smart? Aren't you the smartest, most gorgeous boy in the whole world?" She lifted her black-haired baby and blew raspberries on his tummy. The cascade of baby laughter made her heart feel as if it had been tenderized.

Vance grinned down at them.

She didn't smile back. The agent was definitely a handsome man. And charming, as well. But after hearing from Jessica that Sally had safeworded out of a scene and then quit the Shadowlands entirely, Kari wasn't feeling very friendly toward him. Sally was an experienced submissive and as sweet as could be, even if she was—how had Master Marcus put it?—as full of mischief as a basket of kittens. So the two Federal agents must have done something awful.

Holding a beer on his stomach, Vance stretched his legs out. "Now, loyalty forces me to say that my three nephews, naturally, take top prizes for smartest and most adorable, but Zane is right up there in fourth place."

Dan laughed, and as always, the sound of his voice stroked over Kari's skin like a fuzzy blanket. He could always make her yearn for him. If only she had the same effect on him.

She set Zane in her lap and kissed his baby-soft cheek, feeling clumsy and overweight and...ugly. She looked down at her clothes. Dumpy and boring. But after having Zane, she'd been so exhausted, emotional, and—face it—depressed, that it had been an effort to keep moving, to care for the baby. Being attractive had been low on the list. Having sex, even lower.

Although her depression had finally wafted away like dark clouds after a storm, she still felt ugly. The weight she'd gained during her pregnancy hadn't disappeared, her stomach was on the flabby side and had acquired a fine set of stretch marks.

Dan spent his days in a life-altering, dangerous world with beautiful, intelligent women. She spent her days babbling at a baby.

She knew he was tied up with work; she shouldn't feel as if he was neglecting her. But...if she was more attractive or sexier, would he be home more?

"He looks like a miniature of you, Dan," Vance said. "Nice job."

"Kari did all the work," Dan said. "I was just along for the ride."

She managed to summon a sweet smile for him before stacking blocks so Zane could push them over. "I'm going to take Zane upstairs once your game starts. I don't want him corrupted by all the swearing if some poor player misses a pitch."

Dan snorted, then asked Vance, "Is Kouros joining us?"

"In a bit. He was tiling the kitchen backsplash and wanted to finish."

"You two have your work cut out for you with that old house."

Kari agreed silently. After the two agents had bought the place last February, she and Dan had visited. Dan had come right out and said it: *"What a dump."* But maybe that was what they deserved.

"True enough," Vance said. "But some days, I like having something to pound on."

"Yeah," Dan said under his breath. He'd understand, she knew. He wasn't assigned to the FBI agents' slave-trafficking project, but he kept informed and helped where he could.

Watching Kari restack the blocks, Dan frowned. "You look tired, sweetheart."

"I'm fine." To shift Dan's attention away—and because she couldn't be openly rude to her husband's guest—she said to Vance, "I don't know if you'd be interested, but did you know Sally quit the trainees? And the Shadowlands as well?" *And you're one of the jerks who drove her away.*

"She quit?" Vance stared at her before turning to Dan. "Is she fucking kidding?"

"Nope. Z called last night. Today, I caught up to Sally at work and—"

"What work?"

"She's interning in the station's computer department—concentrating on fraud. Good at it too."

Vance nodded. "She mentioned digital forensics. So what'd she say about quitting?"

"Some bullshit about being too busy with graduation. That she wasn't planning to stay in the area."

"Hell. We pushed her too far. Too fast." Vance's concerned expression softened Kari's heart. Slightly. "We told Z afterward. Z should've been the one to work with her. Or someone who knew her better."

"Maybe. But you two were the ones who saw her clearly enough to notice all those defenses. Seemed logical you should continue." Dan took a long, slow drink of his beer. "Your questions shouldn't have provoked such an extreme reaction."

Kari frowned down at the blocks and guided Zane's hand to stack a block of his own. She'd just sit here and see what explanations the Dom came up with.

VANCE SILENTLY WATCHED Dan's wife play with her son. Maybe what Dan said was true. The guilt didn't decrease any. All they'd wanted to do was help; instead, they'd made her problem worse.

He felt his jaw muscles grind his teeth together. The thought that they'd damaged that bright, spirited submissive so much that she'd fled the Shadowlands made him want to put his fist through the wall. True, he wanted only short-term relationships, but for the time during a scene, the submissive was his. And he—and Galen—had screwed up.

"I talked to Z after I spoke to her," Dan said. "He's feeling fucking guilty himself. Says he'll hold off until after her commencement, but then they'll have a long chat whether she likes it or not."

Vance wasn't sure he had that amount of patience. He and Galen had been the ones to screw up; he needed to make it right.

Or would seeing him just make everything worse for her?

Fuck.

—✦—

Sally took a long, very hot shower, scrubbing and shampooing to erase the stench of violent death. What an absolutely crummy day.

First, Dan had shown up in her department and asked why she'd dropped her Shadowlands membership. Despite what she'd thought was a perfectly fine answer, his expression said he knew she was bullshitting. He'd never looked at her that way before, as if he didn't trust her to tell the truth. Like he really was a cop and she was a criminal.

But too bad. He didn't have any right to question her; she wasn't a trainee anymore.

Next week after graduation, she'd still go see Kari. Their place was just a nice walk away, in the residential section. But she'd make really sure Dan wasn't home.

Right after he'd left, the crime scene guys had asked for her help on scene at a homicide. The victim had an intricate computer setup that needed to be dismantled and taken back to the station.

Honestly, when she'd first thought about getting into the field of digital forensics, she'd assumed the computers or drives or memory sticks would be delivered to her at the police station. Her plans hadn't included working in a room where there were dead bodies. And blood. Everywhere.

Just the memory had her stomach doing an I'm-going-to-puke dance. After a few deep breaths, she dried off and pulled on her favorite dark red silky pajamas, then her fluffy blue robe. The ankle-length, shabby garment was her comfort garment, and she needed it this evening. Her tiny apartment seemed far too empty.

Then again, empty was better than sharing with a jerk. Kicking Frank out had been a most excellent decision.

I wish I had someone, though. Even a pet.

With an effort, she pushed away the memory of Vance's arms around her, of Galen stroking her hair. Such assholes. They'd ruined the scene with stupid questions...and now they were ruining her evening by making her crave them. She scowled and tried to forget how they'd paid attention to...everything.

To her.

She shook herself. *Get over it.*

In the main room of her apartment, she hesitated. Normally, she'd jump into World of Warcraft and do some fighting. Vanquish evil. Assuming she didn't get slaughtered, she'd return to real-time victorious. Having saved the town or whatever, she'd be a heroine, which was the best feeling in the world.

But not today. No blood. No death today.

Instead, she brewed a pot of chamomile tea and settled into a corner of the couch with her Kindle. On the screen saver was a boring picture of some author. Maybe she'd put a cute kitten there instead. And hack into the software and set up a routine so the kitten would meow at the device's startup. A virtual pet would be better than no pet.

Slowly, the sounds of her apartment settled around her. The hum of the old refrigerator in the opposite corner, the drip of the faucet in the bathroom. From the apartment above drifted classical music. Beethoven. Rather sedate, but easier on the ears than the acid metal the previous tenant had enjoyed. The thin walls meant she could hear Joanna's cranky baby on one side and the chugging of Harvey's dishwasher on the other. Wasn't it strange how the sounds could be annoying one day and so very reassuring the next?

She sighed. The last time she'd walked over to Dan's house, she'd played with baby Zane while Kari cleaned up the kitchen. The rattle of dishes had reminded her so much of Mama that the surge of homesickness had almost laid her flat. After her mother had died, that feeling of...safety?...love?...had disappeared forever.

Sipping her tea, she pulled up a nice historical romance to read. Tomorrow, she could worry about the two job offers she'd received and go through another set of the ugly Harvest Association e-mails. Tonight, she'd keep herself firmly in a fictional past. With a happy yawn, she settled in to read.

"Sally."

The voice percolated through her dreams, and she blinked. Geez, she'd totally fallen asleep. Lifting her head, she saw her e-reader had fallen to the floor. Above the television, the wall clock read just before eleven at night. She pushed her hair out of her face as she sat up and froze.

Frank stood at the other end of the couch, staring down at her.

"What are you doing here?" Annoyance burned away her grogginess. She rose to her feet. "How did you get in?"

"Made a spare." He tauntingly waggled a key before shoving it in his jeans pocket. "I need to talk to you."

My life sucks. "It's late, Frank. Give my key back and go home." She stopped in front of him and held her hand out.

He shoved her away and stomped toward the tiny kitchenette in the far corner. "You got anything to drink?"

"Hey!" Had she really thought his pushy attitude was sexy? "There's nothing we have to talk about. We're over. And I'm tired." She opened the apartment door and made a shooing motion.

His face turned a dusky red. "Get your ass over here, bitch."

God, being infatuated had sure blinded her. How could she ever have let him talk to her like that? Let him treat her like dirt? Master Z would be so disappointed she couldn't tell the difference between a caring Dom and a nasty control freak. Well, better late than never. "No. Just leave, dammit."

Moving faster than she expected, he grabbed her hair, yanked her out of the doorway, and kicked the door shut behind him.

She scratched his face with her nails, pulled in a breath to scream, and he backhanded her across the face.

As pain burst in her cheek, tears flooded her eyes, blurring the room. Shock held her immobile.

"Now that I have your attention..." The sloppy smirk on his face gave him away. He'd been drinking. He shoved her toward the couch.

Her insides tightened. Frank was a mean drunk. During their negotiations before he moved in, she'd made him agree that if he drank, he'd stay somewhere else for the night. She hadn't thought alcohol would become a problem...but then he'd lost his job.

She touched her burning cheek and felt liquid. Blood. The skin had been torn by his ring.

Her heart started to hammer. *Okay, smarty, how do you get out of this?* Gritting her teeth, she shoved her emotions down, a talent she'd mastered as a child and never lost. Men didn't want an emotional woman, no matter what those stupid Feebs said. "What did you want to say to me?" she asked politely.

And why the hell didn't she have something useful like a baseball bat or stun gun in her living room. Definitely shortsighted.

"There. That's my sunny girl." He smiled at her, proud he'd made her do what he wanted.

And he had. Could she hit him with the lamp? No, the cord would slow her down. Her cell phone was in her purse.

"Stay there." As he headed for the kitchenette, he bumped into the armchair—and that set him off again.

Sally winced as he kicked the chair across the room. "Stop it!"

He didn't even seem to hear her. The coffee table followed and hit the wall with a crunch. One leg broke. Beside the couch, her cup lay on the carpet next to her Kindle. Frank glared at the e-reader. "That thing. Always more important than me." He lifted his foot to stomp on it.

Not my books! "No!" She shoved him away.

Losing his balance, he staggered sideways and tripped over the overturned coffee table. His landing shook the floor.

Oh shit.

With her foot, she slid her Kindle under the couch. "Frank, you need to leave before you get in all sorts of trouble. Remember where I work?"

He sat up. "You hit your Master."

Her father had turned that purple color when enraged, but he'd never hurt her. *Much.* Frank, however... Fear slid cold ice into her belly, but living with her father and brother had also taught her—never show fear. Her voice came out level. "I'm sorry, but you're not my Master any more. Remember?"

Ominously silent, he pushed to his feet. He stood between her and the door, blocking her escape. "You need to learn. Need to learn..."

She retreated. Not much choice. He was a foot taller and outweighed her by a hundred pounds. Why the hell hadn't she picked self-defense for one of her electives?

A grizzly bear in a black T-shirt, he lumbered toward her, leaving destruction in his wake. The pictures on the television stand, candlesticks...each item that she'd saved up to buy, carefully chosen.

He'd break her next.

Not enough space to get past him to the door. No chance to get to her phone. Her heart pounded wildly, trying to escape the cage of her ribs. She'd misjudged—he wouldn't stop until he hurt her. She had neighbors. Maybe...

She yelled with all her might, "Get away from me! Help!" And then she screamed, high and long.

He lunged for her, and she dodged. Then dodged again. *Stall.*

"Frank. Listen, we need to talk about this." She sounded hoarse. Terrified.

Stopping, he panted and glared. "Don't think so."

Maybe she could circle around toward the door. The blood seemed to be pounding in her head as she backpedaled toward the back where her bed was.

He lunged, sweeping his arms before him. The crash of her television made her pause. A second too long.

She ducked a punch aimed at her face. Stepping forward, she punched, trying to hit his throat. Arms too short. He grabbed her hand and nailed her right in the stomach. The shock hit first—she couldn't inhale—and then the pain exploded.

As she staggered back, he grabbed her. *No.* Blinded by tears, she punched. Got his shoulder. Tried to knee him.

Rather than hitting his balls, her knee thumped his thigh. With a roar, he threw her across the room. She tried to catch herself. Her ankle twisted with a horrible stab of pain. As she fell, her back smacked into the side of her desk.

Half sitting, she shook her head. No birds tweeted like in the cartoons; she heard only a roaring in her ears.

He stalked toward her, his hands opening and closing into fists. "Cops won't get here in time for—"

The pounding on her door halted his advance.

"Sally? Sally! You okay?" Harvey's voice came from the hall.

"Get the manager. He's got a key." Joanna's voice was high and terrified.

The old lady across the way quavered, "I called the police. They said—"

"Fuck!" Frank kicked.

She twisted so his boot smashed into her left hip rather than her ribs. Sobbing with pain, she rolled blindly. *Escape. Get away.*

Voices spilled into the room. Grabbing the lamp from the end table as a weapon, Frank shouted at her neighbors, keeping them from entering the apartment. No one was big enough to take on the brute.

Yelling and yelling. A standoff. Frank sounded more and more out of control.

She needed to do something before her friends were hurt. "Don't—" She tried to push to her feet. A knife seemed to stab into her ankle, and her leg gave out. She landed on her right side so hard that her head went all blurry.

"Let me pass." The unfamiliar voice had an effect.

The shouting died away into silence.

Sally lifted her head.

A uniformed police officer stood in the doorway, confronting Frank. Her neighbors had retreated. "Sir, you need to—"

"Get the hell out of here," Frank roared, brandishing a heavy iron lamp. "My girlfriend and I are just talking."

He's lying. Don't go. Don't leave me here. "No." Her voice came out only a whisper.

The police officer held up his hand. "I'm sorry, sir, but you—"

"Fuck diplomacy." Dan pushed past the cop and walked into the room. Frank swung the lamp like a baseball bat.

Dan blocked, grabbed the lamp, and used it to swing Frank at the two men who'd just walked in.

The darker one sidestepped.

The other—*Vance*—caught Frank, twisted gracefully, and slammed him face-first into the wall so violently that the pictures rattled. The lamp dropped to the floor with a nasty thud.

"Nice catch, Buchanan," Dan said, pulling out a set of handcuffs.

Sally's breathing faltered as she took in the miracle of a rescue.

Despite his position, his face pressed against the wall, Frank yelled. "Fuck you. She's mine. Fucking cops."

Chills swept across her body as she listened. As she tried to find some strength to move.

Galen stalked across the room toward her, his eyes black with fury.

Angry with her? She tried to roll over so she could sit up and gasped as daggers of pain stabbed through her hip, her shoulder...everywhere. She moaned.

"Hold on, Sally." He went down on his knee. "Stay put while I see how bad you're hurt."

Too close. On her back, she couldn't defend, couldn't...do anything. "*No.*" She struggled wildly, trying to sit up.

"Ah." His eyes softened. "Easy, pet. Let me help you." Putting an arm behind her back, he raised her to a sitting position.

The moan that escaped her gritted teeth was humiliating. Gradually the sparkles blurring her vision cleared so she could make out Galen's face.

"Why are you—" She tried to pull away. She hadn't called him, had she? No, she didn't have his number. Dan must have. But now Galen must think she was selfish. And he was so *mad*. "I'm sorry. I didn't ask—"

"Shhh. I'm not upset with you, Sally." He didn't let go but closed his eyes and drew in a slow breath. The anger faded from his face.

She relaxed slightly, leaning back against the leg of the desk.

"Just sit still for a minute, so I can check how badly you're hurt." He used a corner of her pajamas to apply pressure to her cheek, holding her firmly when she tried to pull away. "Anything broken?"

Surely not. "No."

"How about I take a look, sweetheart?" Vance knelt beside her. His intensely blue eyes were calm and so, so reassuring. He quickly ran his hands over her skull, then her neck and back. His gaze never left her face. He checked her shoulders and arms, not stopping at her flinches. "Right shoulder a little sore, but so far, so good."

But his fingers on her stomach made her suck in a pained inhalation.

"Caught one in the gut, did you?"

"It's getting better," she said. And it was. She could draw in a real breath.

And had started to relax. Frank had stopped screaming. That helped. Having Galen and Vance beside her helped even more. Even if they were angry with her, they'd never let anyone hurt her. She knew that.

Vance pressed over her right hip, then her left—and she flinched, then had to endure more probing.

"Bruised—didn't bust it, as far as I can tell." Vance moved his hands down her legs.

At the blast of agony when he squeezed her left ankle, she barely smothered a scream.

"There too." Vance traced around the area. "Starting to swell."

"Did a number on her face," Galen muttered. He lifted the corner of her pajama top to show Vance her cheek.

"Looks like the bleeding has stopped," Vance said.

"Ayuh."

"Ready to get off the floor, sweetie?" Without waiting for her answer, Vance simply picked her up.

The movement made her dizzy, and the pain overwhelmed her. Rather than protesting, she buried her face against his shoulder. His white T-shirt was well-worn and soft. Each breath brought her the clean scent of laundry detergent and a hint of his aftershave.

He carried her so easily, and his strength was even more reassuring than the presence of the police officer. After a few moments, she lifted her head.

Hands cuffed behind his back, Frank was talking—loudly—to Dan and the cop. "Yes, my name is Frank Borup. It's right there on my driver's license. No, I haven't been arrested before." He gave Dan a smile. "I'm sorry about overreacting. This is all a big misunderstanding."

Could he charm his way out of this? She shuddered. Frank could be awfully convincing. Look how well he'd taken her in. She pulled herself together.

"No. There's no misunderstanding," she said in a loud voice. "He let himself into my apartment with a key he'd made without my knowledge."

Dan's eyes narrowed. He muttered to the other cop, "Make sure we get that from him."

"He hit me and kicked me and broke..." Hearing her voice shake, she stopped. Vance's arms around her tightened, lending her strength. She said firmly, "Arrest him. I'll file charges."

"Sally. You're being foolish," Frank said. "You—"

Dan jerked his head at the uniformed officer. "You know the drill. Get him out of sight and hearing."

"Yes, sir."

Yelling protests, Frank was escorted into the hallway.

"We need an ambulance for her?" Dan asked.

Sally's voice came out a whine. "No. I'm fine."

"I'll have her checked out in the ER," Vance said.

Dan nodded. "Make sure they know to document everything. I'll send someone to get her statement."

"Right."

"But, I don't want to go to the hospital."

Vance looked down at her. "You can skip the ambulance, but not the emergency room. I want your ankle checked out, if nothing else."

"What about afterward?" Dan asked.

After the ER, she'd come back here. Sally turned her head to look at the destruction of her cozy apartment, and tears blurred the sight of broken furniture, glass glittering in the carpet. No longer a refuge.

Not even safe. She'd have to pay the manager to change the locks—who knew how many copies Frank had made. She shuddered. What if they let him out and he came back here?

She could stay somewhere else. But her friends had duties, work, families, and taking her in would be a horrible imposition. And what if he followed her to their house?

No, she couldn't take the risk that someone else would be hurt.

If only she had family she could call...but she didn't. Misery slid into her heart like a knife of ice.

But she'd manage. She always had. After blinking the blur from her eyes, she lifted her chin. "I can manage. Don't worry about it."

THE LITTLE SUB was like a cornered feral kitten, Galen thought. Despite her trembling, she was still hissing and spitting defiance. Yet, her big eyes had such a lost look that he wanted to simply hold her and promise she'd never be hurt again.

"Shhh." Galen couldn't keep from touching her. As he brushed her hair from her face, the purpling bruise on her cheekbone was exposed. His gaze met Vance's to find a similar fury. "You're going to need someone to take care of you for day or two, pet."

"I don't—"

"You have two choices," Vance told her. "After the ER, I'll either drop you off at one of your friends, or you'll stay at our house for the night." He smiled down at her. "To sleep and recover only."

"Pick one, pet," Galen prompted. If she chose a friend, he'd call and give them a quick rundown.

Vance's expression was as gentle as Galen had ever seen it. "Sally, you can trust us, you know."

She looked at each of them. "You won't...push...me?"

Galen wanted to hit something. They'd fucked up during that session. "No, baby girl. No pushing."

She glanced at the doorway through which the perp had disappeared, and the shudder that shook her small body made Galen want to kill the bastard. But her nod of acceptance was one of the finest rewards Galen had ever received. Even if she'd fled from them before, there was still trust there.

Vance kissed the top of her head. "Thank you, sweetie." He glanced at Galen. "You'll wind up matters here?"

"Ayuh." He'd kept an ear on the bullshit that the perp—Frank Borup—was spouting. Some damage control might be needed.

"You can put me down now," Sally said to Vance.

So independent. She was trembling and holding Vance's shirt with a death grip, and still demanding to stand on her own feet. By God, she was something.

Vance merely smiled—patient bastard that he was. "I'll put you down in the car. Galen will lock up for you after everyone leaves."

Her whispered *thank you* was heartbreaking.

Vance brushed his lips over her hair and carried her out.

As the uniform brought the Borup bastard back into the apartment, the neighbors crowded around the open door.

Considering the crew had been willing to take on the bulky asshole for Sally, Galen didn't give a fuck if they got a thrill by listening in. With a sigh, he leaned against the wall. His knee ached like a son of a bitch. But he wanted to see this through.

In the midst of the destruction, the uniform was checking for prior arrests.

Seated at the small kitchenette table, Dan was taking the Borup bastard's statement. The detective's expression turned to granite.

Galen's attention sharpened.

"Yeah, I know it looks bad. But hey, we were just playing a little rough." Borup's expression was so sincere that Galen thought he might puke. "My girlfriend likes that. Asks for it."

Time to shut him up before he damaged the little sub's reputation with her neighbors. This was Dan's town and he had rules to follow, but Bastard Borup wasn't connected to any of Galen's cases. He strolled over to stand beside Dan.

Hands still cuffed, Borup was seated sideways on a kitchen chair. Good-looking enough, muscular, and a complete asshole. What had Sally been thinking?

"She's my slave," Borup protested. "She wants me to treat her like—"

Galen's snort of disgust turned the man's attention to him. "I've had a fair amount of women who like calling themselves a 'slave'—especially since that *Fifty Shades* crap. Women are funny that way, and judges know that. There's no law against wanting to serve someone." Galen crossed his arms over his chest. "Unfortunately for you, there are laws against slavery. And even more laws against beating the crap out of someone if you're drunk. Especially a girl half your size. Especially since she broke up with you"— *what had Z said?*—"over a month ago."

"She didn't—"

"You shithead, everyone in the building heard her kick you out," a man called from the doorway.

"Yeah, because you were 'too rough,'" a young woman added, using her fingers to put quote signs around the phrase.

Excellent. Galen grinned. "Good witnesses there."

"Agreed." Dan caught the uniformed policeman's attention and jerked his head at the doorway. "Get their statements. Including if they know why Miss Hart dumped him."

"Yes, sir," the uniform said, obviously pleased.

"Who the fuck are you?" Borup rose to glower at Galen.

"FBI." Galen showed his ID. "Working on human trafficking in the area. I'd like to hear more about how Ms. Hart was your slave."

The man's face turned a pasty white. "I didn't—" He took a step back. "We were just playing, never like for real."

"So you got drunk, came over, and beat her up." Galen prompted. "Nothing to do with any Master/slave business?"

"No. I mean, that's right."

Dan turned his head and winked at Galen.

—✦—

After parking beside Galen's black sports sedan, Vance jumped out of his truck and walked around to the passenger side. Good thing they'd driven separately to Dan's house to watch the game. Even better that Dan had his dispatchers bribed to tell him if any problems occurred at the homes of the Shadowlands trainees. That altercation could have been an ugly mess otherwise.

He opened the door and scooped Sally into his arms. He'd held her before at the Shadowlands—tonight she seemed so much lighter. So fragile. She was wearing a fuzzy robe, and it felt as if he held a kitten.

She slapped his arm and wiggled. "Hey, I can walk. I'm not broken, remember?"

He snorted and then smiled. In many ways, spitfire submissives were even tougher than the Doms. "No, you're certainly not broken."

But, despite her protests, he carried the stubborn little sub into the house. Maybe she could walk, but he had a need to hold her. With reluctance, he settled her into Galen's favorite spot—the recliner section of the sectional.

Carrying a pillow, Galen walked into the great room and over to Sally. "Feel better?"

Ignoring his question, she sat forward, holding her stomach. "What about Frank? The guy who talked to me in the ER said they'd arrest him. Will they? Or do I need to go there and—"

"Easy, pet. He's all tucked away in jail." He handed her a key. "This is the one he had, but I talked with the apartment manager. He'll change the locks tomorrow."

"Oh God, thank you."

At Sally's smile, Vance felt his chest tighten. It was the first time he'd seen her brighten all evening.

"No problem." Galen frowned slightly. "Are you going to relax now?"

"Okay." She leaned back on the recliner.

Good enough. She was in their home. It was a step in the right direction. He glanced at Galen. "The docs said no bones are broken. Ankle is sprained but not badly. Bruises will heal."

Galen nodded.

"If you do cleanup, I'll get her crutches, then make tea," Vance said to Galen.

"That works." Galen was already rolling up the sleeves of his shirt.

By the time Vance returned with a tray of tea, Galen had cleaned the remnants of blood off her face, propped her left leg on a pillow, and put a bag of frozen peas on her ankle.

Sitting on the sectional beside Sally, Galen glanced at the tray and cleared a space on the flat armrest. "Vance makes tea for anyone who's upset."

"Happened to be my mother's remedy for anything that ailed us," Vance said.

A shadow crossed Galen's face. Mrs. Kouros was as cold a woman as walked the earth. Very doubtful that she'd made her son any home remedies. Or shown him much love.

Vance had been luckier. He set the tray down.

"You don't need to wait on me," Sally protested and struggled to get up.

"Stay put." Galen gave her a level look with the order.

She stared at him, then sank back onto the couch.

"Take it easy for now, sweetheart." Vance took her hand and rubbed his thumb over the back. Such little hands. He handed her the cup, then sat on the coffee table.

After blowing on the steaming liquid, she sipped, then huffed a little laugh. "I like chamomile tea too, but how many teaspoons of sugar did you dump in this?"

"Lots." Nothing like getting the blood sugar up.

As if to verify his statement, after a few more sips, some pink returned to her face.

"All right, now. Let's have a report on where you're hurting." Galen leaned a hip on the arm of the couch.

"I'm fine."

Galen grunted his annoyance. "Try again."

"I—okay, *fine*. My head feels like someone is hitting it with a club, my stomach and hip hurt, and every time I move, a knife jabs into my ankle. All on the left side." Her defiant glare faded into an adorably rueful smile. "Guess I didn't do a very good job of defending myself."

"You're alive and moving—that's good enough." Galen frowned. "We don't have much for painkillers."

"I don't want any—and that's what I told the ER doc too." She shook her head. "Being fuzzy-headed right now would bother me more than hurting."

Because she'd be liable to start reliving the attack. Vance knew far too well how that felt. "I don't like them either, especially after...situations."

Without speaking, Galen disappeared into the kitchen. When he returned, he handed her a couple of ibuprofens. "They'll help keep the swelling down without sedating you."

As she choked them down, her eyes filled with tears.

Before Vance could move, Galen bent forward and tilted her chin up. "What's wrong, pet? What can I do to help?"

She blinked hard, as if that would prevent them from seeing her distress. *Fat chance.*

"Sally?" Galen's brows drew together.

"I'm fine. It's nothing."

"No," Galen gritted out. "You are not fine." He let her go and stalked across the room.

Christ, Galen.

But his friend didn't react well to not being able to fix...everything. Especially if he cared. She'd learn that if she stuck around long enough.

"Sally." Vance waited until her damp brown eyes lifted. "Only an idiot would lay out her emotions for just anyone to stomp on, but there are times you need to share how you feel. To be able to say, for example, 'I'm unhappy because my boss yelled at me. I need a hug.'"

"I—"

"No, we won't talk about this now. You've had a hell of a time." He tucked her hair behind her ear. He'd damn well like to give her that hug. She needed one, but probably not from a man. Not right now.

He continued, "You think about it, sweetie. If you can't share, you'll deprive yourself of a lot of support as well as hurting your lovers' feelings. Especially if they're Doms. I like being able to help, you know."

Her mouth opened; then she shut it and shook her head. But she hadn't immediately rejected his statement. With a big swallow, she finished her tea.

He pulled her carefully to her feet, helping her balance on one foot. "Let's get you ready for bed."

When she stiffened, he knew he'd read her right. Here she was, pretty fucking vulnerable and alone with males after being attacked.

Her little hands fisted. "I...I'm not sleepy. I'm not ready to—"

"Sally." Galen turned, his face unreadable. "You'll sleep alone in the guest room. We'll be home, so if you need anything, just call out." He paused and added, "If you want me to call you a friend or take you to a friend, I will."

Surprise and then relief filled her face. "Thank you." After a second, she said, "I'll be okay."

Vance nodded satisfaction as he lifted her into his arms. Despite all that had happened to her tonight, she'd heard Galen—and believed him. Odd how hopeful a little progress could be.

—⁜—

In the guest bedroom, snuggled under the covers, Sally eventually started to relax. Maneuvering with the crutches was exhausting, but she'd managed to clean herself up. After bundling up her bloodstained pajamas and robe, she had donned the huge T-shirt Vance had given her and crawled into the king-size bed.

The sound of the men's low voices from downstairs was more soothing than any white noise device.

The pillow was wonderfully soft...

In the quiet, she heard the door rattle. Her Kindle fell from her hand and broke on the floor, shattering into a million pieces. Her heart pounded as she sat up. Frank stood, staring at her. His eyes were a weird color. Wrong. His face was too long, twisting into cruel patterns like rubber melting in a fire. But his hands didn't melt as he hit her. Blow after blow. She couldn't move, couldn't scream—couldn't scream. No one would save her this time.

"Wake up, baby girl."

Frank grabbed her shoulder, and she hit out as forcefully as she could. "No!"

Unyielding fingers closed around her wrist.

She gasped. And opened her eyes.

The light in the bedroom was on. No shadows anywhere. No monster. Galen sat on the bed, still holding her arm. Vance leaned against the door frame.

Lying down seemed far too vulnerable, and she tried to sit, gasping when pain stabbed into her stomach, then her hip.

Galen put his free arm behind her, helping her up. "Just a nightmare, pet," he said in his smooth baritone, then pushed her hair away from her sweating face. "Not surprising, considering the evening you've had."

"I almost hit you."

His lips quirked. "Be a sad thing for my rep, to be downed by a bit of a submissive."

She glared at him.

"There she is." He dropped a kiss on her lips, surprising her so much she lost her frown.

Vance disappeared into the bathroom, returning with a damp washcloth. After sitting on the other side of the bed, he gently wiped her face. "That better?"

The coolness cut through the last of the dream. When she nodded, he brushed her damp cheek with his knuckles. "Hell of a time you've had."

"Want to talk about it?" Galen asked.

"No." Her voice came out raw, as if she'd actually managed to scream.

"I see." Galen slid his hand down from her wrist and curled his fingers around her hand. If she'd been drowning, his grip would have pulled her to safety. "Can you go back to sleep?"

"I guess." Exhaustion dragged at her body, but the thought of being alone in the dark was terrifying. *Don't leave me. Please.* She stared down at the bedcovers. A second later, she realized she was gripping Galen's hand so tightly her fingers ached.

"Baby girl, you're a piece of work." Galen shook his head. "Since you won't ask, let me offer. Do you want one or both of us to sleep in here tonight? Just sleep."

They'd stay with her. She'd never wanted anything so much in her life. "Yes," she whispered. A double dose of safety. "Both."

Galen touched her nose with a gentle finger. "That's a start."

She had a feeling he didn't mean that they'd managed to get into her bed.

Vance grinned. "Want the bathroom before you're pinned in the center?"

The surprised laugh she gave hurt her bruised face. "Yes." She painfully crawled out of the bed.

To her relief, Galen merely handed her the crutches.

By the time she returned, both men had stripped, leaving only their jeans on. She stopped, realizing she'd never seen them shirtless. Vance's chest was a solid wall of muscle under a light dusting of golden-brown hair. In contrast, Galen was all streamlined muscle under taut olive skin. His black chest hair made a triangle pointing downward toward his jeans.

After a second, she kicked herself back into moving, regretting that she was too tired to properly appreciate the view.

On the far side of the bed, Vance got in, then held up the covers for her. "You prefer on your stomach, back, or side?"

She froze, and the fear swept back in, more shocking from being unexpected.

Vance slid out of the bed and walked over to her, his eyes gentle. "Cold feet are best dealt with by letting someone warm them up for you. Come on, sweetheart." He took her crutches, leaning them against the foot of the bed, then waited for her nod.

This was so wrong. This cowardice wasn't her. At all. But as he simply waited, as she met his steady, so very controlled regard, she knew he was nothing like Frank. She pulled in her lips...and nodded.

He ran his knuckles down her cheek. "Thank you for your trust, Sally." And with the easy strength she'd started to expect, he lifted her and set her down in the bed.

Oddly enough, she hadn't "slept" with that many men. Most of her sexual play had been at the club. And, aside from Frank, she'd always kept some control. Galen and Vance had taken that away, only permitting her the courtesy of making a few decisions because she'd been hurt. The realization set up a quiver of worry—and need—inside her.

He followed her in and lay quietly.

Oh, right, wanting to know how she slept. "On my side."

"Got it." He rolled onto his back and, to her surprise, adjusted her so her head was on his shoulder, her stomach pressed against his side. Watching her closely, he gently lifted her left leg over his thighs. Her sore hip and ankle jolted with pain, then subsided. "Comfortable?" he asked.

"Yes." Too comfortable. She flattened her hand on his wide chest. So big and muscular. His skin held the scent of soap.

And then Galen slid into the bed and moved behind her to spoon against her back. She tensed when his hand brushed her sore hip, but he moved his hand up to her side.

Warmth surrounded her along with his rich, masculine scent. She gave a soft sigh. "Thank you."

"You're welcome, pet."

"Get some sleep." Vance stroked her hair.

Although her body was comfortable, her mind wouldn't turn off. Vance's statement kept swirling through her brain. "...*there are times that you need to be able to share how you feel.*"

She actually agreed. So why, when she wanted the guys to stay with her, hadn't she been able to say that? Other submissives—other women even—had no trouble asking for hugs, for help, for a shoulder to cry on. She'd never realized she didn't.

Under her hand, Vance's chest slowly rose and fell, the curly hair tickling her fingers. He had just the right amount—somehow making him seem even more masculine.

He'd give her that hug if she asked. But at the thought of actually doing so, her brain just...stopped. Her insides tightened, her mind retreating at the thought of opening herself to ask for anything.

Galen curled his arm around her waist and pulled her against him firmly, despite the way she startled. His voice was a rich growl in her ear; his breath ruffled her hair. "Sleep, Sally. You'll have time in the morning to stew about everything."

Snuggled in compassion, embraced in safety, she let herself slide away.

CHAPTER SEVEN

After showering and dressing, Galen checked the guest room. Still buried in covers, Sally's body was a rigid stillness, indicating she was awake. He wanted to talk to her, to know she was all right, but he'd promised her the time to stew. He'd give her a few more minutes.

In the kitchen, Vance sat at the long granite-topped island with a cup of coffee and the morning paper. "Morning. You taking the day off too?"

"Seems like a good plan." Galen had put in so much overtime he felt no guilt at taking a few hours back. "Think she'd let us send a cleaning service to her place?" He poured a cup of coffee, added cream and sugar, then snagged the discarded front page before settling onto one of the wider counter-height chairs.

"Doubt it. She'd probably consider it either an invasion of her privacy or her rights or something."

"Stubborn little thing, isn't she?" And the way she'd lingered in his mind since she'd safeworded and stormed out of the Shadowlands was worrisome. He'd never had a problem dismissing a submissive before, never had one keep him awake. Not since his wife had died.

"Too stubborn. After what she went through, she should have been bawling her heart out."

Galen glanced toward the stairs at the sound of the shower coming on. "She'll have another chance to weep—it's your turn to cook."

Vance didn't grant the insult a reply, but returned to reading the paper.

As Galen took the last sip of coffee, Sally limped into the kitchen. She'd donned the jeans and soft pink T-shirt he'd brought from her apartment and left for her on the bathroom counter. The shirt had been folded, and he hadn't seen the front. A robot-like Dalek from Dr. Who was saying: *Exterminate All Males.*

Christ. He grinned. She really was one of the most interesting women he'd met in a long, long time.

But seeing the scabbed purple bruise on her left cheek wiped out his smile. Be a pleasure to rip the bastard's balls off and stuff them down his filthy mouth and... With an effort, Galen tamped his fury down. The imp needed cuddling today more than anger. "Crutches?"

"The doc said I can abandon them if I keep the ankle brace on."

Her wet hair lay in tangles halfway down her back. No makeup. Barefoot. She looked far too young for either him or Vance, but her Shadowlands records gave her age as twenty-six. That meant she'd probably worked for a couple of years before entering the Master's program.

Part of the impression of youth was how awkwardly she was holding her body and the absence of her cocky self-confidence. His every instinct shouted for him to fix her—her hurts, her problems—and he didn't even know where to start.

"Hungry?" Vance's eyes narrowed as he undoubtedly picked up on her defensive posture.

"No." She bit her lip. "I mean, yes, but first...I'd like to talk."

"Of course," Vance said easily. He pushed a chair out from the island with his foot. "What's up?"

Rather than sitting, she stood behind the chair, her hands gripping the leather-covered back as if it might attack her. "I was thinking."

Ayuh, she'd been stewing. "Go on," Galen said. Now they'd hear about Borup and the attack.

"You said I don't share. Or ask for what I need." Her gaze dropped to her hands.

She wasn't talking about the bastard, after all. And she

normally looked a Dom straight in the eyes. What was bothering her? "Were we wrong, pet?"

"No." She swallowed, and her fingers turned white-knuckled. "I hadn't realized that. It's a problem I didn't..."

"You didn't realize you avoid talking about your feelings?" Vance summarized.

She nodded. "But I'm trying"—she gave them an unhappy look—"and it's so hard."

She was breaking his heart. Galen patted his thighs, wanting to feel her as well as hear her. And face it, he needed to give some comfort if that was the only fucking thing he could offer. "Come here."

When she walked to him, he pulled her stiff little body onto his lap and wrapped his arms around her. Slowly she relaxed against his chest, and that much trust from her after yesterday was the sweetest of compliments.

His glance at Vance got a nod that left the direction of the conversation to Galen. So he kissed her temple. "Now tell us what you need."

"I don't know how to fix this problem. To ask. Or share what I'm feeling." Her head was down, her voice barely above a whisper.

Vance leaned forward and rested his elbows on the island. "You want us to help?"

She gave an infinitesimal nod.

"Look at me." Vance waited until Sally lifted her head. "Now, ask."

Her body stiffened again.

Warm, fresh from the shower, soft in all the right places, and so fucking scared. "Go on," he prompted.

GOD, WHY WAS this so difficult? Sally felt as if her body had turned to granite. Her hands were cold in spite of the comfort of Galen's arms around her. *But I can do this.*

"Help me?" she whispered.

Galen's arms tightened. "Good girl," he murmured against her hair.

"Of course we will." Vance's devastating smile made her heart skip a beat. "Brave girl for taking the first step."

She closed her eyes for a moment; their approval soaked into her like the sun's warmth on a bitter cold day.

Galen chuckled. "And now you feel as if you just ran a mile?"

"More like ten," she muttered. Christ on a crutch, that had been just one tiny request.

Vance rose and cupped her chin, tipping up her face. His shrewd eyes were a knife blade penetrating straight to her soul. "I need to know why you have such a problem, Sally, but that can wait a bit."

Oh, thank you, God.

"For now, your job is to try to tell us what you need when you need it."

And that was supposed to be easier?

Vance waited until she nodded against his hand, and then released her.

"In addition, you'll honestly share what you feel if asked," Galen added. "Be warned, pet. I'll question you often."

Did she really want to do this? But she did. In all these years, she hadn't found her own Dom. What if it wasn't the Doms who were lacking? What if it was her? "I'll try."

"That's all we ask, sweetheart."

With Vance's smile, her trembling slowed.

Thinking they were done, she tried to stand.

"Not yet." Galen tightened his arm around her waist, holding her on his lap as he massaged the stiffness from her shoulders. His firm hand ran down her arm. Tugged on her damp hair. Curved around her nape.

As she leaned her head against his shoulder, she realized he was *petting* her in the same way she'd comforted frightened barn kittens. When he nestled her closer, she softened into him and fell into a contented haze, letting him do whatever he wanted to do.

Next life, she wanted to be a cat.

"That's better," he said eventually. After giving her a light kiss, he set her on her feet. "Although I'd enjoy holding you longer, you need some food."

"Pancakes or eggs?" Vance asked. He rose and pulled a skillet from the cupboard.

Sally stood in place, confused. Frank had always made her cook. "Um. I can cook."

"You will, sooner or later. Everyone helps in this house. So...?" Vance raised his eyebrows.

A sugar rush would be wonderful. She'd worry about the calories later. "Pancakes."

"Done."

Something brushed against her leg, and she squeaked and jumped a foot, almost losing her balance. Trying to ignore the throbbing of her ankle, she looked down.

An annoyed steel-gray cat stared at her with yellow-green eyes.

Galen laughed, and the deep, resonant sound had her mouth curving up. Had she ever heard him really laugh before? "Glock rules the house. Are you bothered by cats?"

"No." Sally bent and held a finger out. The cat craned his neck in a long sniff, then curved to bump his head against Sally's hand. His fur was short and thick, completely gray except for a slightly paler stripe from the top of his head to his nose. "Oh, you're so soft," Sally crooned. "So sweet."

"He was here when we arrived. Half-starved," Vance said. "Using a broken window in the cabana for his personal entry."

"He's sure not half-starved now." Hurting in too many places to remain standing, Sally eased herself onto the tile floor with only one tiny grunt of pain. Then, she happily gathered the solid, purring body into her arms. Oh yes.

When Sally looked up, she realized she'd leaned her shoulder against Galen's legs.

Elbow on the island top, he'd rested his chin on his palm, a finger stroking his lips as he studied her. His black eyes had softened. "Like cats, do you?"

As Glock rubbed his head against her cheek, Sally pulled in a shaky breath. "I miss having pets." They loved her, never let her down, never turned their—

"What are you thinking?" His question jerked her out of her memories.

"I—nothing."

"Try again, pet." Galen's voice was even, firm. The command of a Dom.

She'd already screwed up—the very first time she'd been asked a question. She stiffened, waiting for the sarcasm, the coldness.

Vance continued cooking.

Galen hadn't moved. He didn't appear angry or even upset. He was just...waiting for her to get her act together.

The purring cat in her arms was like a security blanket. *Take my back, Glock. I'm going in.* "In Iowa, I'd sneak out to the barn, take treats to the cats and dogs, and just...hang out...with them." Blackie, the lab, would try to crawl in her lap. The barn cats would weave circles around her feet.

Galen frowned. "Why did you have to sneak out?"

"My father didn't believe in house pets. Said it would ruin them for hunting so they had to stay in the barn."

Vance turned to look at her; then the men exchanged glances. The pity in their eyes was unbearable.

Sally stiffened her spine and lifted her chin. "It was no big deal. I just like animals."

"Me too." Vance pulled eggs, milk, and bacon from the fridge. "We always had a couple of dogs and a cat or two. My sisters would dress them in doll clothes. Poor beasties found it a relief when the girls got too old to play with dolls."

"Good thing you were older. But, on second thought, you'd look quite endearing in a baby bonnet." Galen ignored Vance's scowl and grinned at Sally. "His sisters are like a pack of poodles."

Vance snorted. "All yap and no bite." And his love for them came through clearly. He put the pancake ingredients on the island and handed Galen a bowl and spoon. "You mix, pard. You got brothers or sisters, Sally?"

She pulled the cat closer. "A brother. Half brother." She added the qualification as Tate always had. He hadn't hated her. *Much.* He was the one who'd told her that her mother wasn't supposed to have her. That Father hadn't wanted more children—especially not a *girl.* "We're not close. He's not coming to my graduation ceremony." But her father was.

"There's a good frown." Galen leaned forward and traced his finger over her downturned lips.

She looked up into intent eyes that seared like molten lava. Her worry about her father's presence at the graduation ceremony burned away under the heat. Galen might be very controlled, but now she knew he wanted her. God, she wanted him too, wanted his dark voice whispering to her as he took her.

His lips curved slightly; then he sat back. "You're not looking forward to the ceremony—or is it your family?"

Darn perceptive Dom. She shrugged. "No big deal."

"Sally." This time the reprimand came from Vance.

"I-I don't l-like this," she exploded. "I feel naked."

Vance's grin was like sunlight breaking through storm clouds. "That's exactly how you should feel. Get used to it, little girl."

Despite his grin, the merciless resolve in his voice made her shiver.

"Now, explain." He turned back to putting bacon into the skillet.

Pushy jerks. Naked, huh? Guess she'd better start emotionally stripping.

With a sigh, she set the cat on the floor. When she struggled to rise, Galen stood, lifted her to her feet, and released her. "Thanks," she muttered as he took his seat again.

"Not a problem, pet."

At the sink, she washed her hands, taking her time and keeping her gaze away from them. Like how at the club, she'd turn her back to strip. Less disconcerting. Less intimate. She raised her voice slightly over the running water. "The ceremony is nothing unusual. But a classmate's parents are throwing a reception afterward for us and our friends and families. I don't know if my father will go."

Everyone else would have hoards of family and friends.

"And you feel…" Galen prompted softly.

She glared at her soapy hands to keep from smarting off. She'd wanted them to push her, so why did she resent it so much? *You're being illogical, girl. Man up.* The words still came slowly as if drawn up from a deep well. "I feel like the scrawny, mange-ridden dog left at the pound that never gets adopted."

"Poor puppy." Vance wrapped his arms around her and pulled her back against his solid chest. "We'll be at your graduation and your party too."

"Really?"

"Ayuh." Galen agreed.

All her unspoken emotions dammed her throat. Finally she managed to speak. Her words came out husky. "Thank you."

—✥—

Vance watched as Sally came to a sudden halt just inside her studio apartment. *Poor girl.*

"Christ in a cave," she whispered.

He put his arm around her and surveyed the mess. She'd undoubtedly been too upset last night to comprehend all the damage done to her apartment. Broken glass glittered from everywhere, including on the bed and embedded in the carpet. Spilled liquids and bloodstained walls and carpet. Broken furniture. "It's a mess, sweetheart."

"Yeah." She leaned against him, pleasing him.

What was there about a woman's need that made a man stand straighter? "We can pick up the worst of it, but the wall stains and carpets need professional help."

"But—"

He gave her a level look. "Galen and I will handle that part. And if it bothers us, we'll visit Borup and make him foot the bill." Galen said the guy had no priors so he wouldn't do much time. More like probation, alcohol and anger classes.

Yeah, a quick visit after the asshole was released would be fun.

"Vance. I can handle this."

"I know you can." He ran his fingers through her silky mink-colored hair. Fuck, he loved long hair. Instant hard-on. Reluctantly he released her and watched her limp into the apartment. "I'm going to help anyway."

"Right." Awkwardly, she turned in a circle to study the room, her forehead endearingly wrinkled.

He waited, figuring she needed more time to adjust to the trauma. Considering how the senseless destruction outraged him, he could only imagine what she must feel. Despite the small size of the studio and the extent of the damage, he could see she'd made herself a cozy, colorful place. The apartment had the typical off-white walls and beige carpet, but her couch was dark red, the chairs black. Floral pillows blended the colors together, as did the scattered rugs on top of the carpet and the black-framed pictures.

Bold yet warm, much like Sally.

"Okay," she said finally. "I saw a good-sized box at the end of the hall. I can use that to toss the broken stuff and glass into, if you'll put the furniture back into place. If I can just get the worst of it up, I can vacuum, and then as long as I remember not to jump out of bed without putting on shoes, I can manage."

While he'd thought she was mourning, she'd been formulating a plan of action. How did he keep underestimating her?

But did she seriously think they'd let her try to live here? "Sally, you do realize that after we've cleaned up, you're going to pack some clothes and come home with me."

Her jaw dropped. "I'm what? No way."

Good God, she'd thought he brought her back to drop her off like that fucking puppy at the pound? "Sweetheart, if we're going to work with you, we need you available, don't you think?" Leaning a shoulder against the wall, he watched her face.

It clouded over like a Tampa thunderstorm. "I can't live with you."

She'd make a lousy poker player, but once they finally got her in bed, those unrestrained expressions would be a delight. "Why not? Do we make you that nervous?"

Her back straightened. "Of course not."

Liar. "Try again."

"I..." She bit her lip. "Kind of. Besides, putting me up would be an imposition."

She really was cute. And more fucking vulnerable than they'd realized. He and Galen would have to walk carefully around her. Oddly enough, the thought didn't bother him at all. He pulled her back into his arms and rested his chin on top of her head. "Do either Galen or I look like the type of Doms who'd do something we didn't enjoy?"

"Actually, yes." She rubbed her forehead on his chest. "I think you really do take on a lot of stuff you don't like."

Mmm. Very perceptive. "But not with women."

In fact, they'd been careful to pick ones who wanted a fun night or scene and nothing more. He molded her against him, enjoying the soft curves. "You're going to be a bit of work, sweetness, but we'll demand things from you to compensate."

"Sex."

He chuckled at her matter-of-fact tone, then without warning, fisted her long hair and tugged her head back so he could watch her face. When he cupped her breast, her nipple peaked immediately. Pink surged into her face, and her pupils dilated. As he slowly caressed her breast, feeling the heat against his palm, he said quietly, "If we didn't think sex would be a treat for all of us, we wouldn't have played with you to begin with. Were we wrong?"

He held her in place although she looked down and tried to pull away. No, she wasn't going to hide her face. "Eyes on me." He waited until her gaze met his. "Answer my question."

"No... I mean, you're not wrong."

"Do you like my hands on you?"

The pink increased to an alluring red. "Yes," she muttered.

Damn, he liked throwing her off balance. "Good answer. As to compensation for room and board, I think Galen wanted you to recover a hard drive that a virus trashed."

She blinked, looking so startled he laughed. "Oh. Well, sure. I can do that," she said.

"Good. Let's get your place cleaned up, and you can fill a suitcase." He waited until she made it to the middle of the room before adding, "I will—of course—help you decide what clothes you should pack."

Definitely not a poker player.

—✦—

That evening, Sally followed Galen into a room she hadn't seen before. She stopped and stared. *Wow.* The entire house was a rehab patchwork. Some rooms were a broken-down mess; some were spectacular. This office was fantastic—very masculine with hardwood floors and light wood wainscoting. Leather chairs. A dark wood filing cabinet and bookcase shared one wall. At least, the oriental carpet and arched windows softened the testosterone. A bit.

Two antique desks held computers—and as far as she was concerned, that juxtaposition of old and new never looked quite right.

A massive round table filled the center of the room; the polished wood surface looked big enough to hold a person, which was a very...interesting thought. When Galen stopped at the table and tapped the surface, her cheeks flushed.

One of his eyebrows quirked up. He didn't comment on her undoubtedly red face—*thank you, God*—but simply said, "You can set up your laptop here. The center compartment holds electrical plugs."

Plugs. She'd heard the guys liked everything anal. Oh God, her mind was totally in the gutter, because the thought of his lean, ruthless fingers pushing a plug into her ass totally fizzed her hormones. She could feel her color heightening, so she shrugged and turned away. "Nice techie setup. And quite amazing. Considering your age, I figured you'd think a hard drive was a long trip on the road."

His fingers gripped her chin and turned her to face him. He gave her a level look. "Yes, I probably have a decade on you. I definitely have enough years to know a little subbie is tossing out insults because she's nervous."

Oh shit. She could actually feel her color moving past red into fluorescent levels.

And she couldn't think of any response to his dead-on conclusion. None. She retreated to get out of reach and tried on an I'm-just-adorable nose wrinkle. "You guys actually remodeled the office before the dining room?"

"Hell yes." His rare grin made her insides quiver like jelly. "Of course, Vance insisted the great room come first so we could hook up the television. Can't miss seeing the Buckeyes play."

She laughed, half with relief and half with amusement. Once they'd returned from her apartment, Vance had checked the time and disappeared into the great room to watch his basketball game. "Good to know. I'll remember to speak of them with respect."

"Excellent plan. Insulting Ohio State would earn you a bare-ass spanking." He tilted his head, watching her. "Of course, he'd probably hand you off to me for the punishment. He has a soft heart."

His dark look sent a current running between them, heating her insides at the same time. She swallowed. "And you don't? Have a soft heart?"

"No, pet." He moved closer and ran his thumb over her lips. In the sunlight streaming through the windows, his eyes weren't completely black, but a dark, dark brown around the outer iris, and lightening near the pupil. Mesmerizing... His lips curved. "I look forward to turning your pretty ass red. To seeing tears in your eyes. And making you come so hard our neighbors will hear you scream our names."

Their neighbors weren't that close.

It was very hot in the room; the air-conditioning needed to be turned up. "Ah, right." She took a careful step back and set her laptop on the table.

Time to get to work. She had a zillion texts and voice mails to answer. Apparently the Shadowkittens had heard about Frank's attack.

And there were even more e-mails. Unfortunately, she also needed to catch up on the Harvest Association e-mails. Wading through their filth made her sick each and every time, but she wasn't going to quit. Not as long as she could help. Heroes didn't quit.

Amusement gleamed in his eyes. "Want some help setting up?"

She tensed. Her e-mail program came up first. Galen might recognize some of the bad guys' names. "Nah, I can handle it."

His eyes had narrowed. Frigging Feds, keen to notice the tiniest hint of guilt.

"Can I have your wireless security code?" she asked hastily.

After an intimidating pause, he walked over to desk on the left wall and scrawled the password on a sticky note.

"Thank you." *Leave. Leave now. Go on.* And the first thing she'd do would be to check those e-mails and bury the program.

"We'll be in the great room." As he walked away, actually obeying her mental commands, she started to relax...until he turned in the doorway and gave her a long look. "If we decide to fuck you on the table, you'll have to move your stuff—so don't leave it too messy, eh?"

Oh. My. God. He really had known what she was thinking.

She couldn't help looking at the table...imagining. Spread out like a feast, open to their hands, their mouths. After a long, shuddering breath, she turned to glare at the empty doorway. Now she had to sit at that table with an overheated imagination and a damp thong.

An hour later, Sally appeared. Galen frowned. The girl looked as white as she had last night; it made the bruising on her face stand out even more. "Problems?"

Her attempt at a smile failed badly. "Nah. I'm just tired."

"Bullshit," Vance said from where he was sprawled on the sectional. He picked up the remote and turned the TV off.

On the other end of the couch, in his recliner, Galen noted the game had only been in the third quarter. The little sub had better watch out.

After a nervous glance at the blank television screen, she amended, "Some...acquaintances...are upset because they lost some...money. And I hate reading profanity. But it's not anything you can fix—or that I can share." Her chin lifted, and she gave them a spirited glare. "Okay, *Sirs?*"

Galen's lips twitched, and he worked to suppress his smile. He sat his recliner up, tossed a heavy couch cushion on the floor at his feet, and pointed to it.

Her hands formed little fists—and he had an appealing vision of how her hands would feel on his shoulders...or dick—then she obeyed.

He watched closely as she went to her knees. Moving better. No tightness around her mouth indicating pain. She was clever and used a hand on the coffee table to balance as she kept her weight off her braced ankle. And the cushion was high enough that her ankle didn't have to bend. Good.

Galen tipped his chin at Vance. They needed to set some ground rules, and Vance would start out more gently.

Vance accepted the handoff. "We haven't spoken about your place in the household, have we?"

She blinked, as if he'd sidestepped her anticipated argument. "Um. Right. I'd like a bit of clarity on what's expected. Maybe even some negotiation." A trace of sarcasm had crept into her tone.

Appreciation flashed in his partner's eyes. The last submissive they'd brought home had been sweet but not too bright, and she'd missed a lot of subtext. He and Vance preferred the smart ones, even if they were more trouble.

From comments at the Shadowlands and her documented history and his own observations, he was beginning to realize the imp was very, *very* intelligent.

"We can do discussion," Vance said agreeably. "Normally, we don't get into full-time D/s relationships. We have no interest in picking a sub's clothing—except for scenes. For example, I'm rather partial to French maid costumes, especially ones with short skirts. And no underwear."

Sally's color heightened.

Be interesting to arouse her verbally and keep her on edge all evening. But not now. Galen sighed. "Focus, Buchanan."

Vance tossed him a grin before returning his attention to his instruction. "So. We don't need a maid or cook. If you pull your own weight in the house, that's enough." Vance pushed the coffee table farther away, angled himself to face Sally, and rested his forearms on his thighs. "However, you requested our assistance for a task that can't be limited to an occasional scene. Am I right?"

Her huff of breath was audible. "Yes, Sir."

"This is how it will work. If we ask you a question in casual conversation, we expect an honest, forthright response. If you can't provide one, we'll drop into a D/s dynamic until we get the answer."

She actually paled.

"However, that D/s dynamic isn't limited to the times we catch you being evasive, pet," Galen qualified. "That's up to us."

"You're such a fucking lawyer," Vance muttered, then returned to her. "What he said. Any problems with the plan so far?"

She shook her head.

"Answer aloud, please," Galen said softly. His partner didn't particularly care, but Galen enjoyed hearing changes in a submissive's tone and word choices.

Such as now, as Sally murmured, "No problems, Sir." The sarcasm had disappeared; her sharp edges had disappeared. From her expression and posture, he could see her sliding into a submissive mind-set, but by God, he really enjoyed hearing it as well.

"Good. Next, we do like sexually oriented play," Vance said.

As she stiffened slightly, Galen added, "Sally, if you're uncomfortable with that, you can still live here. We'll work with you without sex involved...but we need to know."

Vance nodded. "You seemed to enjoy sexual scenes at the club. But things change. We won't be upset with either choice, but you have to be the one to choose, sweetheart. Sex or no sex."

Her gaze dropped to her hands, and Galen's respect for her grew when she looked at them directly and said, "Sex." She didn't pretend to be pushed into the answer, didn't deny the sexual tension among the three of them.

"Well, I can't say that I'm not pleased," Vance said lightly. "Are you on the pill?"

"Yes."

A shame to have to deal with ugly topics, but better that it was done.

"While you're here, you'll be our only partner, and we expect the same from you. And we prefer no barriers during sex," Vance said. "Galen and I have no diseases, and as members of the Shadowlands, we're all tested often, but let's swing by the doc tomorrow and get us all checked again."

She nodded. "Frank had...loose ideas about monogamy, so we never had unprotected sex." Her lifted chin showed that insisting upon that had, perhaps, been an adversarial position. Good for her. "I'm clean, but I think the extra testing is wise. Thank you."

"Next, your limits list was filled out for a club venue. But we won't be playing in a public venue most of the time. Would you like to restrict—or add—anything to that list?"

She thought for a second and shook her head. Then with a glance at Galen, she spoke her answer. "No, Sir."

There it was. Her resistance was disappearing. *Sir* could be said in many ways, but when it slipped out easily, without thought, the title was one of the most beautiful words in the English language. Coming from this little imp made it all the more special.

"Thank you, Sally," he said, showing he recognized her surrender. And prized it.

She tried to shrug it off, but the sweet pinkness of her cheeks said she valued his approval.

And they all knew she'd fight them now and then—especially since they would push her into uncomfortable mental places to break down her barriers. Speaking of which... "We don't know why you have a problem, and we're going to work on helping you overcome it, but you might try counseling instead or in association with this. If finances are a problem, we can help."

She gave him a surprised look. "Um." Her expression changed as she considered his suggestion. Her thinking mode was interesting to watch—as if she heard music that played only for her.

After a minute, she shook her head. "I'd like to work with just you guys for now, but I'll tell you if I think it's too stressful or if I change my mind."

"Good enough," Vance said. "For sleeping arrangements, the guest room—your room—has the biggest bed. Simply close the door if you don't want company at night."

Vance's nod at Galen handed back the reins.

"Take your shirt off, pet," Galen said.

Her eyes rounded. But she obeyed. After pulling her pink T-shirt over her head, she hesitated with her hands on her lacy bra.

Galen nodded.

The bra followed. She really did have pretty breasts. Ample and high with pink-brown nipples. Her stomach was rounded and just the right softness for enjoyable nipping.

She laid her clothes neatly on the coffee table. "Sirs," she said quietly. "Do you prefer any type of address?"

"As long as you're polite, we're not fussy," Vance said.

"Stand up and remove the rest, please," Galen said softly. He leaned forward and offered his hands to help steady her.

Her hands were cool, her grip strong as she let him help her to her feet. He tossed the cushion back on the couch.

As she started to unbuckle her silver belt, a flush started at her breasts and flowed upward.

"Stop." Vance smiled as she paused. "You're blushing, sweetheart. Why?"

Her mouth fell open as if to say *you're questioning me...now?* "Um. This is embarrassing. That's why."

"Really?" With his elbow on the recliner arm, Galen rested his chin on his palm. "I've seen you strip in the Shadowlands without blushing."

Her color deepened.

SERIOUSLY? SALLY FELT almost...outraged. She was ready to have sex. They liked her body. Wanted her. She knew it. But to stop and question her about her feelings. Again? When Vance's gaze lingered on her clenched hands, she forced them open.

Okay, they were just doing what she'd wanted. Why did she have to keep reminding herself of that? And why in heaven's name was she embarrassed anyway? "I'm just—"

Her voice trailed off at the serious expression on Vance's face. He hated her evasions. She bit her lip and tried to think. He was right; she didn't mind being naked at the Shadowlands. Then again, the Masters didn't try to make her feel—vulnerable—and the younger Doms couldn't.

"You make me feel...exposed. More than naked."

"Keep stripping." Galen studied her as she pushed her jeans off. "We *want* you to feel exposed. Inside and out."

As her nipples contracted into tight peaks, Vance's gaze dropped there. "You have pretty breasts, Sally, and I like breasts."

A bit of the nervous fluttering in her stomach eased. At least until Galen said, "Present yourself, please. Standing. Wrists crossed behind your lower back. And let me know if you find anything uncomfortable or if your ankle starts to hurt."

Her legs started shaking as she widened her stance, straightened her posture, and put her arms behind her back.

"If you arch your back more, you'll please Vance," Galen suggested.

Even as her back arched, she recognized the manipulative technique. He was pushing her into pleasing them.

"It seems you like making him happy," Galen observed.

She stopped her automatic nod and said, "I guess."

Galen smiled at her, his midnight eyes softening. "A verbal answer. You like pleasing me as well?"

She hesitated.

Vance rose and wrapped his big hand around her wrists tightly enough she couldn't move her arms. He cupped her right breast. "Answer Galen."

She felt his calloused fingers scrape over the tender underside of her breast. "I do." When she managed to look away from Galen's dark gaze, she added under her breath, "I don't know why."

"Aside from the fact that you're submissive and like to please?" Vance asked.

She nodded.

He tugged at her nipple. "Probably more than one reason. You trust us or you'd never have come here, let alone asked for help." Still holding her hands behind her back, he nudged her chin up and took her lips.

He kissed like—like himself. Firm but direct. Gentle, yet holding her so she'd take whatever he wanted to give her. "And there's something between us, sweetheart. You've attracted us from the beginning, and from the way you've retreated, you feel it as well."

His perceptive eyes caught hers, sending her sliding downward into quicksand.

He kissed her again. Deeper. Wetter.

Then Galen stepped in front of her, and a quaking built inside her. Vance was straightforward. Galen was...unpredictable. His unreadable eyes watched her as Vance released her wrists.

"Vance likes to make sure you don't move. I want you to do that yourself." Galen smiled slightly. "It will please me if you maintain that position until I say otherwise."

Oh God. She swallowed against a dry throat. "Yes, Sir."

"Now let's see where your threshold lies. Tell me when something actually hurts. Not fun pain but hurts, eh?"

She trembled, the fluttering working its way outward. Her skin felt hot, her insides cold.

Galen walked around her in a Dom's inspection of his naked submissive. She stayed silent, feeling herself sink further into the happy state of no control.

He ran a finger down her arm, stroked over her shoulders, fondled her buttocks. Firm fingers, hard hand. "Very nice."

Once in front of her, he cupped her breasts and rubbed his thumbs over her nipples. A smile played along his lips as he pinched one nipple and the other. The tugging sensation was wonderful. Her toes curled.

Then he increased the pressure to where it hurt.

A squeak escaped her.

He didn't ease up. "Does that hurt, Sally?"

She nodded. Her eyes filled.

"Why don't you say so?"

She stared at him. Admit that something hurt? She just didn't. *And how stupid is that?* "It hurts," she whispered.

"There you go." He rubbed her nipples to reduce the sting. "Do you think the world will come to an end if you tell someone you hurt?"

"No." But she felt odd. Tense. As if he'd...be crueler now that he knew.

"Physical and emotional?" His eyes narrowed, growing darker. Sterner. "Who used to hurt you, pet? Who made it so you didn't want to admit to hurting?"

She couldn't answer. Her brain ceased to function, as if someone had pulled her power plug and shut down the processor.

"Hell," Galen said under his breath. He took her wrists, put them around her waist, and pulled her into his arms.

Shuddering, she sagged against him. Cold currents swirled through her like an insane whirlpool. But in his firm embrace, she knew she wouldn't spiral out of control. He had her. As his body warmth poured into her, she gave a tiny sigh and laid her cheek against the solid wall of his chest.

"Vance?" Galen murmured. "Ideas?"

"You didn't have siblings, pard," Vance answered. "Sally, think back. Do you remember saying, 'You can't make me hurt.'" His voice was high. Young. Defiant.

Familiar.

"I-I said that to my brother." Her voice came out high and hesitant. She'd never said it to her father—just thought it so many times.

"Go on." Galen flattened his hands on her back, confining her against him.

She was silent.

A touch on her cheek broke her paralysis. She opened her eyes and found Vance beside her. "You didn't want your brother to think he could hurt you?" His gaze was understanding. "Or make you cry, right?"

She nodded. "He made fun of me if I cried." His taunts were somehow worse than the occasional pain, somehow making it clearer that her mother's death had destroyed her family as well.

"What did he do to make you cry, sweetheart?" Vance's hand was gentle on her face.

"He would push me sometimes. If I got in his way," she whispered. Cold Iowa winter. Ice on the sidewalk. A narrow, shoveled path between the house and barn. Two could squeeze by—or one could be shoved out of the way.

"Did he hit you?" Galen's voice was almost a growl.

"Not...really." Not Tate. A slap on the back at the school as he pretended he'd been congratulating her for her test scores, but the spot had burned. "But...Tate just didn't like me."

"And your father?" Vance asked quietly.

She closed her eyes, unable to tolerate his keen gaze. Because... On the rare occasions that she talked too much or asked for something or complained, her father *would* slap her. Because he hated her. *Hated* her. She realized she was shaking and pushed at Galen. "Let me go!"

"Shhh," Galen said. "We're stopping now, baby girl." He took a step back and sat on the couch, pulling her with him.

Even as he adjusted her position on his lap, she realized how careful he was being with her injuries. And she didn't care. "Let me go," she said again. "I don't want to—"

"Settle, pet." Even as he rubbed his chin on the top of her head, his steel-hard arm remained around her waist. "No more questions. You've worked hard enough for now."

Settle. She wasn't going to settle. Couldn't. Didn't want to remember things.

He was talking to Vance in a low voice, finishing with, "I set her off. I'll hold her for a bit. Make us both feel better."

A hand ruffled her hair, and somehow she recognized Vance's touch. "I'll be back in a while."

His footsteps faded. Galen didn't move, and his concern filtered through her cold shell, into the ice that filled her insides.

Muscle by muscle, she slowly relaxed against him.

"That's better," he murmured. He snuggled her to him even more closely. "I'm sorry, Sally. It isn't easy to face what has happened in the past. But whatever happens, I'll be here to hold you afterward." He kissed her temple gently. "Whether you want me to or not."

Doms. Demon Doms. How could he be stern one minute and so comforting the next? She gave a little sigh and put her arm around his waist. Under her cheek, his heartbeat was as slow and measured as the Gregorian chants played in the Shadowlands, and each thud dissipated more of her memories.

He rubbed his chin over the top of her head, teasing her with the scent of his rich aftershave, and she remembered another occasion she'd been close enough to smell that hint of lavender— when she'd been tied to a table in the Shadowlands. He'd been touching her. His gaze intent on hers...as she came.

God, she'd never orgasmed like that before. Never felt so exposed as she did.

A shiver ran through her at the memory...and with a small jolt, she realized she was still naked. On his lap.

She traced her fingers over his crisp shirt...and the contoured muscles of his chest. God, he reminded her of an all-black leopard she'd seen—sleek and powerful. Every time Galen moved, she could feel his muscles ripple under the skin. She stroked up his chest, almost mesmerized by the valley between his pectorals, the dip at the hollow of his throat, how his deltoids transformed into rock-hard biceps. She pressed closer.

His arm around her tightened, and she felt the power of his eyes on her. The silence from him seemed to grow, taking on an almost palpable weight. "Give me a kiss, Sally."

A kiss—a kiss with Galen? With his directive, she was suddenly aware of how her breasts were flattened on his chest and how his hand cupped her bottom. His hands were calloused...and she wanted those hands elsewhere. Covering her pussy. Pushing inside her. *A kiss.* When she curled one hand around his nape, his thick hair teased her fingers. She tipped her head up to press her mouth against his.

He took control immediately. Good God, the man could kiss.

Deep and hot and panty wetting. Only she didn't have on panties.

His tongue tangled with hers, pushed deep, retreated, lured hers into the play. When he sucked on her bottom lip, she felt the pull low in her core. He did nothing but enjoy her, choosing different angles, taking his time, going nowhere.

And where ice had reigned, a fire started to build. An urgency. She was naked; he should be too.

With one hand, she tried to unbutton his shirt. She'd reached the second one before he noticed.

He glanced down, a snort escaped him, and he muttered, "You're definitely an imp." After setting her on her feet—holding her until she found her balance—he rose. His voice louder than normal, he called, "Vance."

Before she could move, he captured her wrists, putting her arms behind her back. The position arched her back—and pushed her breasts out. Holding her firmly, he kissed her again, even as he rubbed his chest against her breasts. The stiff material abraded her jutting nipples, making her pussy dampen.

Finished, he glanced over her shoulder. And smiled.

Vance's big hand replaced Galen's as he pressed against her from behind, warming her skin with his body. Reaching around, he flattened his free hand over her breast, sending need clawing through her in jagged patterns.

Galen took her face between his palms, tipping his hand to avoid her bruise, and took himself another kiss, a totally demanding one, while Vance held her for him, not letting her move.

God, God, God. The unyielding hands on her wrists, the plunder of her mouth—her insides liquefied like butter on a summer sidewalk.

Vance reached around to tease her nipples into rigid peaks.

Her knees simply buckled.

Laughing, Galen grabbed her waist and held her up until she could stand again. "You kiss like a wet dream," he said. "Enjoy for a bit, Vance."

Vance didn't release her wrists; instead he fisted his free hand in her hair, pulling her head back and back until he had her arched far enough he could capture her lips.

Different was all she could think. Galen...took, demanded, plundered, but Vance was simply overwhelming, swamping her in sensation.

She was standing on one leg; the toes of her injured leg were barely touching the floor to help her balance.

Now Galen's hard hand grasped her calf as he carefully moved her injured leg outward and held it there. Opening her. At her wobble, Vance simply tightened his grip and continued. Her head spun under the assault.

Then she felt Galen stroke up her leg, heading directly to her pussy. Heat sizzled through her when he touched her folds. One finger ruthlessly circled her clit until burgeoning need made her moan. She was very, very wet—she could tell from the slick feeling of his hand.

"How sore are you, baby?" Galen asked, lightly touching her bruised hip. "Want more, or should we stop?"

After nipping her bottom lip, Vance let her answer.

Stop? Now? "I'm fine." The silence reminded her they didn't always believe her. "Really. I'm fine." She wanted to ask them to continue. Needed to ask. Couldn't. "I... More would be good."

Vance huffed a breath, laughing, and yet she realized he was watching her carefully, making sure. "All right, sweetie. More, it is."

AND HE'D GET a kick out of giving her as much as she could take, Vance thought.

The half smile on Galen's face said he was on board with that idea. But she wasn't ready for the usual way they made love...and in all reality, he wanted a more "hands-on" approach first too. The first scene they'd done with her had given him a good idea of many of her erogenous zones. But by the time he finished today, he intended to have a whole lot more mapped out.

He glanced at Galen. The tightness around his eyes said his knee was hurting. And Sally had been roughed up—they'd need to be very careful. "How about a quilt on the bar? I'm in the mood for a feast."

Galen's eyes narrowed—he hated any accommodation made for his injury—but his fingers touched the bruise on Sally's hip again. "Good plan."

"A feast?" Sally asked.

"Yep. Galen and I are hungry—for you." With a smile, Vance lifted her into his arms. And wasn't it lucky that he'd stocked the island drawers for *fun* after the kitchen was finished.

Galen swept a fluffy quilt off the back of the couch and led the way into the kitchen. After he'd spread the quilt on the marble-topped center island, Vance lay Sally on her back with her feet toward the backless bar stools.

As her wavy brown hair spilled across the blue-green fabric, Vance picked up one silky lock. "She's color coordinated with the cabinets."

Galen glanced at the brown walnut cabinets and snorted. As he took his seat on a bar stool, he said, "Might as well continue the color scheme. You put those blue thigh bands in the drawer?"

Restraints? Vance's cock thickened so fast it almost brought him to his knees. "Damn straight." He smiled into Sally's worried—excited—eyes. "Say your safe word."

"Red."

"Good. Use if it you need to, sweetheart." Playing in a private home had to be more frightening than in a club where dungeon monitors could intervene. He had to respect the courage of submissives who'd let someone tie them down. He bent down to take the straps from the island's bottom drawer and, as long as he was there, a couple of condoms as well. And after a moment of thought, a packet of lube.

Galen saw the packet and grinned.

Oh yeah. Vance wrapped one strap just above her left knee and almost got distracted. Women had such soft skin on their inner thighs. "Move her down, Galen."

Galen gripped her thighs and slid her, quilt and all, until her ass was at the edge of the island counter and positioned perfectly for Galen to play.

The strap had a short lead ending in a D ring. Vance clipped it to one of the eyebolts spaced at intervals along the underside of the island. He grinned at her. "You get to be the first to break in the island."

"Lucky me." Her breathless voice had a slight tremble in it. Nice.

After walking around to her left side, Vance ran his hand over her bare pussy lips, enjoying the way her breathing hitched. Yes, she was ready for more. Carefully, he strapped her other thigh, clipping it at an angle that ensured her knees would stay splayed apart. "Is this going to hurt your hip?"

She moved, tested, and shook her head. "No, Sir."

"Good enough." Just for fun, he ran another strap across her lower stomach and made it snug. Running a finger around the purple bruise well above the strap, he wished he could have a few minutes with the bastard who'd hurt her.

Galen waited patiently, one palm stroking the inside of her right calf. "Wrist restraints?" he asked, bringing Vance back to the present.

Wrists... *Hmmm. Should he?*

"No, I like letting her experience a token amount of freedom even while knowing she can't move her cunt away from anything you do to it."

When her legs jumped as if to test his statement, Galen laughed.

"And I want to feel her hands in my hair." With a grin back, Vance kissed the center of Sally's little palms before putting her arms around his neck. Being a smart subbie, she ran her fingers into his hair as he bent down and licked over her right breast. Her fingers gave a reflexive yank as her body jumped.

Sensitive breasts. Fuck, he might kill himself playing with her. And, unlike the sensuous scene they'd done in the Shadowlands, this time he could indulge himself as much as he wanted.

He gave her a long introductory kiss, like the ceremonial toss of the ball into the game. And then he started working his way down, nuzzling her neck, licking the hollow of her collarbone. Her breasts were full, the nipples the color of her lips, already peaked. The tiny bumps around the nubs teased his tongue. Using his lips, his teeth, his tongue, he teased first one nipple and the other before using his hands on her breasts. As he kneaded them, he enjoyed the way the skin tightened as they swelled. He pushed them together so he could alternately lap at the nipples.

From the way her back arched, pushing her nipples into his mouth, she was dying for him to suck.

Not yet.

He looked into her pleading eyes.

Her last trace of anxiety had disappeared.

"We're just starting, sweetie." And the kitchen was damn hot. He stripped off his T-shirt and savored the desire in her gaze before he bent over again, this time to tease the soft roundness of her belly. A light nip made her squeak. Running his tongue downward toward her pussy had her muscles tensing. He could feel her trying to lift her hips toward his mouth—unsuccessfully.

Not going to happen, sweetheart. She'd shown them how easily she could come—and Vance wanted to see how high they could take her before that.

A glance toward the end of the table revealed amusement in his friend's face as well as lust. But Galen wouldn't let Sally get off too quickly. He was talented at gauging the moment to back off—better than Vance—and maybe because of that healthy streak of sadism.

Galen leaned forward and kissed the inside of her thigh, just above the strap. The sharp sound of her inhalation was tantalizing. And Vance decided to hang back for a few minutes and watch his partner drive her crazy.

SALLY'S BREASTS WERE so swollen she could feel the beat of her pulse. Her nipples ached and burned for more attention. Her pussy was worse. Without even having been touched, the labia were swollen, hurting.

With her knees pulled up and outward, she was wide open to whatever Galen wanted to do—but he wasn't doing anything, the annoying asshat.

Still sitting on the bar stool, he'd leaned forward. His forearms on the edge of the island pressed against the outside of her buttocks, giving her disconcerting pressure, but not where she wanted it. *Touch me; touch me; touch me.*

Instead of hearing her silent plea, he brushed his lips over her inner thigh. One, then the other. After a minute of torture, she realized he was drifting slowly, but surely, toward the *place*. She rocked her hips, trying to angle him, to move him—

Slap.

The startling pain on her inner thigh blasted through her. "Ow!" Yet the smarting eased into an erotic burning to match her pussy.

Galen didn't even lift his head, so she transferred her glare to Vance.

He chuckled. "He's never liked moving targets. He gets cranky."

Cranky? The most intense, controlled, dominating Dom she'd ever met got cranky? A giggle escaped her.

Then she choked as Galen's merciless fingers pulled her folds open.

The brush of cool air on her entrance and her engorged clit made her moan. *There, there, there.*

Nothing happened.

She raised her head slightly. Galen was simply looking at her pussy with that indefinable manner of a Dom inspecting what he considered to be his.

Her flush of embarrassment disappeared in the inferno that rolled right up her body until she could feel her cheeks glowing. Hopefully he wouldn't notice...

He lifted his head; his keen eyes studied her face for a long moment before meeting her gaze. She saw his amusement, his hunger, and something...more. As if he cared how she felt.

She felt Vance's hands on her breasts...but Galen's gaze kept hers trapped.

As Galen held her open, he ran a finger from his other hand around her entrance, and slowly, slowly slid it up toward her clit.

Her eyes started to close as the pressure inside her grew, as—

"Eyes on me, Sally."

At Galen's soft command, she forced her eyes open. He never looked away as his finger slicked up one side of her clit. Her muscles tried to tighten, and his fingers implacably held her open. When he wiggled the hood, the sensation of his calloused finger was too intense, and she flinched.

His touch lightened, and he slid his finger down the other side of her clit. Electricity seemed to sizzle there, right under the skin.

But as he moved his finger down farther, she wanted to groan with frustration. The finger slid into her, awakening new nerves. It withdrew, and she felt him insert two fingers, moving them inside her pussy as if exploring—yet his gaze never moved away from her face. In and out. Back in.

Oh God, it felt so good. A quiver coursed through her, and she felt a coiling of arousal growing deep within her.

With insistent fingertips, he rubbed an area inside her, over and over. He gave a tiny shake of his head and changed to a new place.

She started to wiggle to tell him to move on but... *No, Sally. No moving targets for this Dom.* Somehow, she managed to force herself to hold still.

He had sun lines at the corners of his eyes, and without even a smile, they deepened as he watched her. Then he rubbed a place that made her vaginal muscles jerk tight, squeezing around the hardness of his fingers.

"Well, that's easy enough to reach," he murmured and slid his fingers out.

No! A moan escaped her.

He chuckled and looked up at Vance. As Galen's gaze moved away, she felt as if she'd been drawn over a rack and suddenly released.

After nodding at Vance, Galen smiled at her. A...worrisome smile.

"Hang on, sweetheart." Vance pressed her breasts together, his hands rougher than before. No more gentle, teasing touches from him.

Galen bent his head, and his tongue skimmed over her bare outer labia and up to her clit, circling slowly inward with fluttering licks. His other arm wrapped outside her thigh so his hand could cover her mound. His fingers curled, pulling up on the skin so the hood exposed her clit and made the nub stand out.

He slid two fingers back inside her to rub ruthlessly over that sensitive spot, and her muscles tensed around him, making him smile. Over and over, he stroked...right on that spot.

As her insides clamped down, he thrust in and out occasionally, as if to keep the entrance wakened.

She felt as if she was swelling inside, and there was a feeling of needing to pee that made her squirm. The pressure grew as his mouth paused directly above her clit. She could feel his sultry breath against the unprotected button.

"Say please, Sally." Galen's voice broke into her need.

Her mouth closed. *Couldn't.*

"You can, sweetie," Vance murmured. He took one of her nipples into his mouth, licking around it.

At the same time, Galen licked a circle around her clit, round and round, even as his fingers tormented that...spot...inside. The need to come was like the inevitable surge of the ocean, breakers rising up out of the sea, rolling toward—

Everything stopped. Vance, Galen, tongues, fingers.

A protesting groan broke from her.

Vance's lips closed around her other nipple, lightly. Not moving.

"Say please, Sally," Galen whispered. "Nothing else. Just one word, pet."

Her mouth moved, *couldn't.*

He blew a stream of air onto her appallingly sensitive clit.

Cold contracted the overheated tissues; her hips strained upward toward release. "*Please.*"

"Good girl." His voice was a purr of approval that wrapped her heart in warmth.

Vance pulled her nipple into his mouth...and sucked strongly.

Galen's mouth closed over her clit—the sudden engulfing wetness shocking—and cartwheeled her right toward an orgasm. And, oh God, he sucked on her clit in fast pulls as his tongue rubbed one side and the other.

Up, up, up.

Her body tightened. Her breathing stopped. Her hands fisted in Vance's hair as she clutched him against her breast. Everything poised for that moment of...

With a rushing sound she felt rather than heard, everything drew together into one glowing, glorious cosmic ball before exploding outward. The splendor of it took her air, her mind, her body as she rode the waves of the orgasm. The blackness of space filled her world, meteors streaked through her vision, and sensation after sensation sparkled through her like newly born galaxies.

Finally the roaring in her ears diminished, and she heard Vance's low chuckle and Galen's hum of satisfaction.

As she lay, limp and gasping, Vance unstrapped her legs. Before she could move, he picked her up. Galen folded the huge quilt into a rectangle. After nudging together two backless counter-high stools, he arranged the inches-deep, puffy "pillow" over the tops.

Vance laid her belly-down across the stools. "Does that hurt your stomach?"

There was more than a feather mattress. "No, Sir."

When her toes tapped on the floor, Vance bent her left leg and wrapped a rope around her thigh and lower calf, ensuring her knee stayed bent. "No pressure on this one, remember?"

Right. Only that left her even more helpless, she realized with an anticipatory shiver.

"Sally." Galen's voice.

Getting her hands under her, she pushed her head and shoulders up slightly. "Yes, Sir?"

"I want your mouth around me, pet," In front of her, Galen unzipped his jeans, and his cock bobbed out. Like the rest of his body, it was perfectly shaped and beautiful even to the plum-shaped head.

Oh, she wanted that—everything in her wanted to satisfy him. To hear the way his voice deepened and hummed if she'd done something to please him.

She breathed in his musky scent, licked her lips, and opened to allow him to guide himself into her mouth. Velvety skin was stretched tight over inner steel. "Mmmmh."

He huffed a laugh. "Go to work, Sally." He pulled her hair out of her face, tangling his hand in the strands to direct her movements. The sense of being controlled, being helpless curled inside her, growing in urgency.

She worked him, licking and sucking, loving the chance to give, loving the appreciative under-the-breath sounds he made.

"You're as good at this as I'd heard," he said once, making her lips curve around his hardness.

She felt her legs pushed apart and muscular thighs moved between them. Vance's big hand tested her wetness, and something pressed against her entrance...an extremely thick cock. Almost too big. But she was so soft and slick that, despite Vance's size, he could push in.

Not easily. A quiver ran through her as his shaft stretched her, sparking off orgasmic aftershocks. He didn't slow, pressing in with the ruthlessness of a bulldozer, until he was deep inside her and his groin rubbed against her buttocks.

God, she felt filled, top and bottom. Used. Taken. Controlled.

She wanted it all. Wanted *them*.

As Vance pulled back, the slick slide of his hefty cock kindled every nerve back to life and, like a struck match, ignited her clit all over again. As he bent over her, his wide hand slid under her lower abdomen to tilt her ass up higher. His grip on her right hip tightened as he slid slowly back into her. And, as if satisfied she could take him, he increased the pace, each powerful thrust pushing her forward onto Galen's cock.

GALEN GRINNED EVEN as his body started to tighten. He wouldn't push her limits today, not until he knew how well she handled oral sex, but by God, she felt good. When he pulled back, the air struck his wet dick with a wash of coolness. He pushed forward into her hot, wet mouth. Her tongue swirled over him. With each thrust, he was immersed in heat and softness.

Vance's gaze met his in mutual enjoyment of sharing a little subbie—and, he had to admit, this one was something special. *Christ.* He'd need to think carefully about where they were going with her. Later.

Slowly, he sped up, careful not to get too deep or forceful—yet, directing her to ensure she knew she wasn't in control of any part of this. He could see her hands tightening on the stool legs. Looked like the little sub was going to get off again. Excellent.

Hopefully after he did, since Cullen had mentioned that the imp was known to nip with orgasms. Why was he not surprised?

As she sucked on the tip of his cock and lashed him with her tongue, he'd swear the room temperature was increasing to sauna-like levels. She gave generously of herself, didn't she?

Pleased, he stroked her hair. "You make me very happy, Sally. And now, I'm going to get off before you do. You okay with swallowing?"

Her head came up slightly, eyes surprised. Surprised that he'd ask? But she nodded, her lips curving around his cock in the prettiest sight he'd seen in a long time.

Well then. With an indulgent groan, he pumped in and out, harder, faster, deeper, and felt the unmistakable boiling sensation begin. The climax ran down his lower back, tightened his balls into rocks, and blew out of his cock in scalding jerks of pleasure. He fisted her hair, holding her tightly as he checked that she could get air.

Her throat squeezed the tip of his increasingly sensitive cock as she swallowed and swallowed again.

Fuck that felt good.

And he breathed out, not moving so he could savor her warmth around him. Her tongue made lazy circles as his shaft decreased in size.

Finally, he pulled back and bent to kiss the top of her head. "Thank you, Sally. You were wonderful."

The flush that stained her cheeks showed her happiness at having perfectly served her Dom. And she had.

Little witch. With every flash of sweetness she showed, she was pulling him further under her spell.

Stroking her hair gently, he nodded at Vance, who had slowed to let Sally focus on the blowjob.

"My turn?" Vance picked up the packet of lube he'd placed on an unused stool. After ripping it open, he spread Sally's cheeks apart and drizzled the contents over her asshole.

COOL LIQUID DRIPPED onto her overheated flesh. Onto her asshole. *What the heck?* Sally's head came up so fast her neck almost got whiplash. "What are you doing?"

Galen laughed, his hand still rested on her hair in the most comforting way. "He's just playing this time. You're not ready for more."

More. Hell, she knew they'd want *that*. The other submissives had said as much. The Feds' penchant for anal sex was just one of the reasons she hadn't particularly wanted to be with them. Anal wasn't high on her list of favorites. At least not for anything the size of a cock. Every time she'd allowed the act, she'd regretted giving in to a Dom's pressure.

But, oh God, what would it be like with these two? They were so…different, always so careful. They treated her like something—someone—special.

And yet, even as they cared for her, they took what they desired. And she *wanted* that sense of being overpowered, mentally and physically. *Needed* it.

A tremor ran through her as Vance's cock slid in and out of her pussy, slow and inexorable.

His strong hand clasped her right buttock, pulling it apart so…

She squirmed as his thick finger circled her anus, penetrating slightly before withdrawing. Every time his cock pulled back, Vance pushed in his finger, slowly but surely working his way deeper.

Nerve after nerve flared awake, like birthday-cake candles being lit until the entire region was flaming brightly.

"There we go, sweetheart. No more today," he said, caressing her bottom, his cock deep inside her. Filling her. "I hope you enjoy anal plugs, because you'll be wearing one every day until you can take me."

A shudder shook her—and she wasn't sure if it was from fear or anticipation.

He laughed, and his hand moved to take her right hip in a tight, ruthless grip. "Ready?"

No!

A moan escaped her as he set up a mind-blowing rhythm by alternately impaling her anus with his finger and her pussy with his cock. The effect confused her senses as her body responded, pressure inside growing in an undeniable way. Her breathing turned to fast panting as she knew—knew—she was going to come again. His thrusts grew more powerful, sweeping her before them, pushing her up a mountain. Pinning her on the edge of a precipice over an abyss.

Her ass tilted up, begging for more, for *one more, one more.*

"All right, sweetie," he murmured. As he slammed into her with his cock, her insides clenched around him, and this time, he didn't withdraw. Instead, he pushed his finger deep, deep into her back hole, filling her completely. Throwing her off the cliff.

"Oh, oh, oh." The sparkling nerves erupted with the fury of a wildfire, taking over her body, making her buck and cry out. The sensations ripped through her, the pleasure almost unbearable. She gripped the legs of the stool as she mewed and shook, unable to escape from his grip, his impaling finger, his cock.

She heard him laugh, echoed by Galen, and then he powered into her as he sought his own satisfaction. He felt even bigger. Huge. As she still shook from the strength of her orgasm, he pressed deep and groaned as he came.

And oh God, she loved that feeling, the knowledge that she, Sally, had given him that pleasure.

CHAPTER EIGHT

The nice thing about dirt roads in the Catskills was he could easily tell if someone was following him. Drew Somerfeld stopped on a rise, got out of his vehicle, and checked his back trail. The dirt hanging in the air was from the tires. The soughing wind ruffled the spruce and fir forest; a creek gurgled over rocks. All quiet—aside from the whimpering of the woman in the trunk. She must have been wakened by the bumpy road.

He slapped the metal to shut her up and climbed back into his car.

A half hour later, he pulled to a stop in front of the isolated cabin he'd bought for his twin. Best decision he'd ever made. His brother couldn't cope with civilization, but he functioned fine if interactions were kept to only one or two people. No noise, no distractions.

In the turmoil of a city—or mental institution—Ellis couldn't cope. Here, he did very well, with an occasional outing to satisfy his obsession.

Drew's lips curled. He'd been quite clever to turn Ellis into the Association's private executioner.

On the rough excuse for a porch, his brother rose from the ugly chair he insisted on carting around wherever he went. Burn marks covered the chair's wooden arms.

Hell, his brother was no prettier. White burn scars marred Ellis's left cheek and jaw, and his eyelid was puckered, pulled askew, giving him a monster-like appearance. Mesmerized at watching their father die in the fire, Ellis had stayed too long.

Almost died under the collapsing roof.

Before the fire, he'd been as handsome as Drew. He'd never been as stable though.

Drew had been born first. Their mother always said Drew was greedier, blaming him as if an unborn child could have decided something like that. But the fact was Ellis had been deprived of oxygen, and he just wasn't as…bright. Or balanced. Something in his brain was off.

But Drew saw to it that he never lacked for anything. Who knows, maybe he owed his twin that.

AS HIS BROTHER got out of his car, Ellis grinned, expectation rising inside him. Had Drew brought a replacement slave?

The job on Tillman had been fun. Ellis had done exactly what his twin wanted, and enjoyed every minute. Especially killing his former slut in front of Tillman, seeing the cop's helpless fury. Afterward, he'd burned the house to ashes around the lawman and his wife—and hey, he'd even added Tillman's mother-in-law to the mix. *Fun times.*

But hauling the slave's body back out to the car had been an effort. Might have strained his back. Drew's fucking hired gun hadn't helped at all, said his job was to guard, not to carry.

But Ellis had followed the rules since his twin was fussy about the body count being right. And once he'd gotten the body into the car, it hadn't been that difficult to dispose of her in a deep body of water. The fish had to eat too.

Heh. Clever Drew. He'd been the one to realize they could use a bloody, terrified slave to gain entrance to a target's house.

And Ellis did enjoy making sure each woman was bleeding like a stuck pig. Even gave each one a broken bone or two to ensure they were really crying. Begging to get in.

The door to the house always opened right up. The woman would go through, and Ellis would follow right after. *Definitely fun times.*

But Drew had decreed no witnesses, so each fire meant he'd lose that slave.

Drew always brought him a replacement. Had he this time?

"Do you have something for me?" He couldn't help hurrying forward. New slaves were always fun.

Drew grinned and opened the trunk, yanking out a young blonde woman. Blindfolded, handcuffed, wearing leg shackles. "One pretty treat for you, Ell."

Oh yeah, indeedy yeah. "I like the blonde ones."

"But you gotta make her last this time. The Feds are getting too close, so I'm shutting down a lot of the *services.*"

"Right." Ellis scowled. That meant he wouldn't be burning anyone for a while either. "I only killed one by accident."

"True. You've done well." Drew patted his arm. "And you did a fine job with the Tillman fire."

—✦—

In a spacious Orlando hotel ballroom, Galen moved through the crowd of celebrating graduates and their friends and families. The music from the orchestra was soft, allowing people the option of dancing or being able to hold a conversation. At one end of the room was a buffet table. A well-stocked bar had been set up in another section, and Vance had headed there to procure drinks.

Galen turned slowly in a circle. His task was to spot a curvy, long-haired brunette in the midst of all these people. A short woman. No longer limping—unlike him—since her ankle had mended nicely in the four days since the asshole's attack. But since she knew her ankle was weakened, she'd chosen to wear flats rather than heels. Smart woman.

He liked that about her. Liked *her.*

She was still in their home, and he had gotten far too accustomed to her sprawling over him in the night. When she curled next to Vance, her round ass snuggled against Galen's groin. She had the prettiest heart-shaped ass he'd ever seen.

And the most tempting. Each day he had increased the girth of the anal plug she wore. She was ready for them now, and he looked forward to seeing her come undone. The sweet little imp gave of herself more generously than any woman he'd ever known.

Finally, he saw her, speaking to a man near the linen-covered tables of food. Although she looked gorgeous in a flame-red gown, the glowing pleasure she'd shown during the ceremony was gone, leaving her face pinched and unhappy. Who the hell was she talking to? Someone from her family?

Galen detoured so he could approach from behind Sally. Study the situation before butting in. Although masculinized, the man's pointed chin, thin nose, and wide forehead were very similar to Sally's. Family, all right. This must be the pet-hating father. Galen already disliked him.

"So you've finally graduated," the man was saying to Sally. "You going to get a real job now?"

Galen stopped. That sure wasn't a loving tone of voice. Or a proud one.

"I've always held down a job, Father, starting at twelve," Sally said, her voice stiff.

"And spent your money on clothes. You'd think you would have learned what was important after you got your mother killed," the older man said, bitterness in every word.

Christ, what kind of fucked-up shit is this? When Sally flinched at the cruel words, Galen's hand curled into a fist.

Sally pulled in a shaky breath before straightening her shoulders. How many times had Galen seen her do that? She was so fucking brave.

"Well, thank you for coming, Father," she said politely. "It was nice to have family present."

Protectiveness welled in Galen's heart. He was used to physically shielding his women; looked like this one he'd need to protect emotionally, as well. "There you are," he said, raising his voice. He stepped up behind her and curved his arm around her waist, feeling the tension in her small body, seeing the guardedness in her eyes. In meth houses, he'd seen children with such eyes.

But he had years of dealing with assholes, so he smiled and prompted her. "And who is this?"

"Um. Right. Father, this is Galen Kouros with the FBI. Galen, this is my father, Hugh Hart."

Had to say, Hart seemed to be sorely lacking any heart. "Good to meet you." *Sally has nothing but bad things to say about you.* He stuck his hand out, ignoring the reluctance the father displayed. The man had the same velvet-brown eyes as Sally, but the lines around his downturned mouth showed a sour personality. His skin was leathery, his build muscular, his hands thick with calluses. She'd spoken of cats in a barn...and she was from Iowa. Probably a farmer.

"FBI?" Hart's gaze was assessing. "Are you her boyfriend or did you come to arrest her?"

"Boyfriend," Galen said. *Lover. Dom.* He was tempted to go on the attack. There were certain people a man wanted to step on as simply a gift to humanity. Something like squashing a cockroach. But this wasn't the time. *Her father. Graduation. Be polite, Kouros.* "You must be quite proud of your daughter. She's done very well." *God knows, I'm proud of her.*

"Ah-huh."

The enthusiasm was underwhelming. Why the hell was this bastard here? "Long way to travel."

"It was." The father pulled a camera from his suit-coat pocket. "I need pictures. People in town want to see them."

Sally posed, her smile so fake that Galen's gut twisted. Hart started snapping pictures, and after a couple, Galen stepped between them. "That's enough." *Enough of this bullshit. Enough of messing with your daughter's emotions.*

The man glared and pocketed the camera. "Guess that's good enough."

"Tell everyone hi for me." She glanced up at Galen. "You'd like the people there. Iowans are just plain nice."

Knowing Sally, he might agree with that...if he hadn't met her father.

The old guy frowned at Sally. "Now you're finished with school, come by and get the rest of your junk."

"Uh. Sure. Is there any hurry?"

"Not particularly."

Which meant the father just wanted Sally's stuff gone. Galen could feel the girl absorb that blow.

"All right. As soon as I get a permanent address, I'll do that." She gave her father an obviously forced smile.

"See that you do."

Couldn't punch an old man for being an asshole...could he? Couldn't slaughter him verbally—Sally might not like that.

"Excuse me." Vance took Sally's other side. "I brought you a drink, sweetheart."

AS SALLY TOOK the glass, she realized the men were doing their guard-dog maneuver again, taking up positions on each side of her. Her overprotective warriors.

From the look on Galen's face, he was seriously pissed off at her father.

With good reason. Why had she ever sent her father an invitation? When would she learn that nothing she did would please him? But no matter how much she tried to tell herself that, it never stuck. She kept trying.

Galen's arm was rigid around her back. "Excuse us, Hart, but we have places to go, people to see. And you can just—"

Before he could finish, a group of her classmates descended on her. In the flurry of congratulations and introductions—and admiring stares at the Feds—she regained her composure. And wasn't it fun to show them off, because jeez, they looked gorgeous in their tailored suits. Galen in the darkest of grays, Vance in a steel gray with a hint of blue. She could see the women wondering which man Sally was with.

Hands off—they're both mine. Then she shook her head. *Delusional much, Sally?*

As the crowd thinned again, she turned back to her father. "Well, I know you have to go," she said. "Thank you for coming."

Her father opened his mouth to say something, undoubtedly cruel, and halted at the sound of a happy scream.

Jessica?

A second later, the blonde tugged her away from Galen, and Sally was engulfed in people, congratulations and handshakes and hugs. Master Cullen's enthusiastic squeeze actually lifted her off her feet. As he set her down, she stared around her in wonder. It looked as if all the Masters and Mistresses—and their submissives—had come all the way to Orlando.

At the edge of the group, her father glared at her before walking away. Her chest hurt, her heart echoing with the emptiness there.

"Not worth being miserable over," Galen whispered in her ear. "You have people who care about you. Love you."

So it seemed. The flood of calls and texts and visits after Frank's attack had astonished her. Made her cry. And now…not just her subbie friends were here, but the Dominants as well. She smiled at them all, then frowned. "I thought I quit the club."

"You were mistaken." When Master Z turned to her, Galen surrendered his place. The owner of the Shadowlands cupped her chin and studied her face. His gaze fastened on the bruise she'd thought she covered so well, and his mouth went hard.

"Mistaken?" she asked quickly.

"You are no longer a trainee," he said quietly. "Not while you're with Galen and Vance. But you will always be a member of the Shadowlands, Sally."

Oh God, she was going to cry after all.

His thumb stroked her cheek; then with a faint smile, he gave her to Vance.

She looked at the Fed with blurry eyes, and he gently pressed her head against his shoulder, holding her firmly against him. "Go ahead, sweetie; let it out."

A couple of choked sobs escaped her before she pulled it together. Party. Friends. She didn't have time to have a wussy breakdown. As she pulled back, Vance accepted a tissue from Gabi to blot her tears and undoubtedly the running mascara.

"Nice job, stud." Mistress Olivia grinned at him. "You learn that from making your subbies cry?"

"I practiced on my little sisters." He winked at Sally and finished, "I *perfected* the technique from making subbies cry."

Galen handed her drink back, his dark eyes studying her. She stiffened, expecting him to grill her about her father, but he shook his head. "Relax, pet. Enjoy your party."

Oh boy. She'd be in for an interrogation later. Bloody, fucking hell. But for now, she'd take Master Fed's advice and enjoy herself. She'd finally graduated and had friends with whom to celebrate. Her mood brightened as if she'd emerged from a cave into crisp morning sunlight.

She held up her glass to them. "Thank you all for coming." Her first sip was great. The second...familiar. "This is a Screaming Orgasm!"

Vance's lips quirked. "We heard you have a fondness for them. But since we might want to play with you later, two is your limit."

"Pffft." Sally turned to the other Shadowkittens. "What kind of a limp-dick loser tells his girl, *only two orgasms?*"

Her girlfriends busted out laughing.

And under the joking, she heard Galen's amused mutter, "The brat is back." Before she could comment, he told her in a low voice, "We're serious, pet. Only two drinks."

Good luck with that, boys.

To Sally's delight, the Shadowlands crew stayed, mingling with the grads and their families. Lawyer Marcus, fire inspector Cullen, bounty hunter Anne, and the Feds hooked up with the professors with law-enforcement backgrounds. Their voices stayed low as opposed to the more raucous group containing Linda, who owned a beach shop, Jessica an accounting business, Beth landscaping, Andrea cleaning and some of the grads' mothers who also ran their own businesses. Apparently taxes could bring out the worst in a woman.

Z, Gabi, and one of the forensics professors were discussing serial killers, causing a quick retreat. Surely there were less disgusting conversations somewhere.

Having heard Sally's feelings about blood and death, Gabi gave her a wink.

Moving from group to group, Sally finished her first drink and got another. The second tasted fully as nice as the first. She spotted Kari coming across the room.

"Don't you look wonderful?" Kari beamed at her. "Sorry for bringing up the rear, but I got stuck talking to my mom on the phone. Zane's giving her trouble. Oh, and Rainie and Uzuri called to say that they were stuck working late today, but to give you hugs from them," Kari said, putting action to words. "I'm so happy you've graduated."

"Me too." Sally rolled her eyes. "Even though I didn't have classes at UCF every day, the commute from Tampa was killing me."

"Do you have any idea what you want to do now?"

"I'm looking for a job in a police station."

Kari grimaced. "That should be interesting."

"The work really is. But ugly sometimes. I saw a murdered guy; my stomach was doing rollercoaster flips for a couple of days." And longer.

Kim turned from where she stood beside Raoul and gave Sally a worried look. "Those images don't really go away, you know." As a former slave, she'd probably seen more than her share.

"So I'm finding." And yeah, she should never have hacked into the New York police station database. The pictures of that murdered New York police officer... *God.* Rather than counting sheep at night, she was counting bodies. "But I don't leave the station very often, so it's probably not a problem." She wouldn't *let* that be a problem.

"That's good." Kari glanced over at the huddle of law types, which her husband had joined. "Dan says you're living with the two Fed hunks. How's it going?"

"They're nicer than I thought," Sally admitted. "It's not serious. I mean, hey, they're players and there are two of them, so I'm totally not wanting long-term. But for right now, it's like indulging in Halloween candy. I'll enjoy it until the sweets run out."

"That sounds smart." After a sip, Kim frowned at her glass. "Wine might be healthy, but it's so boring at a party. Maybe I should try that Orgasm drink of yours. What about you, Kari?"

She hesitated, then shook her head. "Probably not a good idea. But I could use some water."

"In that case, ladies, follow me." Sally led the way to the bar.

The lanky bartender grinned at the three. "What can I get you?"

Kim set down her wineglass and glanced over her shoulder at her Master, where he was illustrating something on a napkin while Nolan and Sam looked on.

"He's too busy to worry about what you drink," Sally said. "Besides, orgasms are healthy, aren't they?" Perhaps not up to Master Raoul's standards.

Sally looked around and grinned. *Oh gee, my Feebies are awfully occupied too.* Wasn't that too bad? She emptied her glass in two gulps and set it with a thump in front of the bartender. "I need another one as well."

"You're going to get in trouble with those big doofuses, you know. But I'm in." Kim told the tall bartender, "Two Screaming Orgasms, please."

"Coming right up."

Sally grinned at Kari. "And you?"

Kari shook her head. "No. I haven't had anything stronger than a glass of wine since Jessica's bachelorette party."

Guess ordering one for her wasn't a good idea. "Hard to drink much with a baby at home."

"Actually, my mom took Zane home with her for the night." Kari wistfully watched the bartender making the drinks.

"So are you and Dan gonna party at home tonight?" Kim put her arm around her friend.

"Doubtful," Kari said under her breath.

Sally frowned. New baby. Dan was working too many long hours. Unhappy look in Kari's eyes. Sounded like problems in the Sawyer household. "Make a drink for my friend here too," she told the bartender.

"Hey!" Kari said. "No."

"If we're going to get in trouble, so are you." Sally smirked. "I bet Dan hasn't had a good reason to spank you in ages."

The bartender stared, mouth open.

Kari turned red. "I'm going back to the others." She got two steps before turning to scowl at Sally. "And bring me that drink." After a glance at the bartender, she added, "If he ever makes it."

"Huh?" The bartender looked down. "Shit!" Most of the glass

was filled with Kahlua.

Oh God. Sally put her hand over her mouth to try to smother her snickers.

Kim, the bitch, had no control and was laughing her fool head off.

The guy pushed the bad drink aside and started making a new one, carefully not looking at them.

As the bartender's face kept getting redder, Sally couldn't stop. Giggles broke out so hard she had to hold her stomach. And when she noticed Galen watching, her attempt to stop laughing almost blew her brains out. A horrible snort escaped instead.

"God, stop. I'm going to wet my pants." Shaking, Kim leaned against her.

"Shit," the bartender muttered and set them both off again.

Composure finally regained, Sally straightened and wiped her eyes.

Lips still quivering, Kim picked up her drink from the table, sipped, and told the bartender solemnly, "Thank you. It's very good."

"Good to hear." He offered Sally her drink.

When Sally reached for it, he held on to the glass. "So, you like spanking?" he tried to say casually.

"Ah—"

"She does." Galen's dark voice sounded a second before his arm wrapped around her waist and pulled her back against his rock-hard body. "But my hand is the only one that gets applied to her pretty ass."

The bartender released her glass so quickly she almost dropped it.

Galen turned her and guided her back to the group. "Enjoy your third drink, pet. Because I'm going to enjoy punishing you for it." He rubbed her bottom, and she could feel the hardness of his palm through her silky dress before he left her beside Kim and Kari.

—✳—

Leaving Galen to check the mailbox at the end of the drive, Vance held open the front door for Sally.

In the entry, Glock was sprawled out like roadkill on the tile floor. He opened his eyes and obviously decided his humans didn't require more effort than an ear swivel.

Sally detoured around him; Vance stepped over.

The reception had lasted past midnight, and Sally had sobered up somewhat, but she was still in a chatty, cheerful mood. As she whirled around in the center of the room, her hair fanned out around her. "I had so much fun."

Fuck, she was a cutie.

Glock scooted out of her way, retreating with an indignant tail flick into the game room.

"Thank you so much for coming to my party." Sally spun again. This time, her ankle gave out, sending her staggering back.

Grinning, Vance caught her before she landed on her ass. He bent and took himself a long, slow kiss, gathering her against him. Full breasts, lush butt, all that hair like silk over his arm. *Oh yeah.*

And she melted into him, returning his kiss with enthusiasm.

"You're living with us. Why wouldn't we come to your party?" He stepped back, telling his cock to ease down.

"Well." When she shrugged, he could almost see her reason: that her own father hadn't wanted to attend, so why would her casual lovers?

"We enjoyed ourselves." He'd have done a whole lot more to see her so happy. Smiling, he patted her ass. "Why don't you get comfortable? Go take a nice shower. We'll be in the kitchen."

"Okay." She danced through the foyer and up the winding stairs, one steadying hand on the wrought-iron railing.

"Nice to see her in such high spirits, isn't it?" Galen stood in the doorway, his gaze on the stairs.

"Yep. Bet her mood would lighten even more if we could get her to open up. That father of hers made me want to flatten him."

"Same here." Galen came into the room, leaning heavily on his cane. The obstinate fool hadn't used it at the reception. "Before you joined us, her father said something about Sally killing her mother."

"Are you fucking kidding me?" Vance stared at him.

"Made her cringe like a kicked puppy."

The spitfire wouldn't react like that if she didn't buy into the dickhead's logic. Not good. "She's taking a shower now. How about we grab us a clean little subbie and get some answers."

Galen winced. "Hell of a way to end a party."

"We have to do it, sooner or later."

He got a slow nod from his partner. "Ayuh. But where? Not a bedroom. Don't want an interrogation where we sleep."

"The moon's up. Let's use the cabana." Vance estimated how much time Sally had been scrubbing. "I should have enough time for a shower."

"Best if you take the good cop role tonight."

"Works for me." He made a lousy emotional surgeon; he didn't have the heart to dig deep enough to open up past traumas. But he was excellent at the recovery stage—one reason he and Galen worked so well together. "I don't want to be the villain for this."

Not with Sally. She already pulled at his heart. Truly hurting her would turn him inside out.

Galen's mouth tightened. "This might not be pretty. Not from what I saw tonight."

"Yeah."

Galen smiled slightly. "How 'bout you start the evening by showering with our pet? Work her up a bit. Get her ready to be grilled. Then we'll take her higher."

Vance's spirits lifted. He certainly couldn't add to that excellent plan.

On second thought, he could. "She disobeyed us. I think she'd do better if we enforce the rules, even if they were in fun."

"Maybe." Galen rubbed his chin where his heavy beard growth was showing. "Yes. It would leave her more open for questioning— and it won't be any hardship to beat on that sweet ass."

"Didn't think so."

———✦———

After pinning her hair on top of her head, Sally stood in the shower, letting the hot water roll down her body. Enjoying the feeling, letting herself relax. She loved showers—and this one was almost as wonderful as the one in Master Z and Jessica's place.

She stroked her hand over the marbled tile walls and smiled at the space around her, more than enough for three people. Larger than the men's own showers...

And, speaking of men, she should probably get out and tell the guys good night. What a wonderful evening she'd had. Finally graduating was satisfying, but even more splendid was to share that step with everyone. A small, sour feeling ran through her at the memory of her father but was erased by remembering Galen and Vance beside her. And how the whole Shadowlands gang had come to her party. She sighed with happiness.

The shower door opened.

Sally gasped and recognized her intruder a second before she screamed the house down. "Vance! This is my shower."

"And this is my house." His lazy smile creased his cheek as he pushed her back far enough that he could step in. "I need someone to wash my back."

God, faced with that utterly confident gaze, she'd do anything. But he certainly didn't need to know that. "Oh please, as if you haven't been—"

"Sally." He was so easygoing she forgot how he could jerk her power away with a mere word.

Her insides turned liquid. Even more disconcerting was the way her heart turned to soft goo. *No. No no no. Keep it together, girl.*

"Well, okay then." She clapped her hands and gave him a simpering smile. "Want me to wash your back, Master Buchanan, Sir?"

"Why yes, Sally. That would be very nice." His cordial tone somehow didn't negate the steady, assessing look in his eyes.

Oh man, she was in so much trouble—because that look made her want to go to her knees. She squirted his spicy-scented liquid soap on a washcloth and set to scrubbing his back. A very wide back, broad shoulders, muscles that bunched every time he moved.

"That feels good." He turned, grasped her wrists, and set her hands on his chest. Christ on a slippery slope, but she'd never, ever get tired of touching him.

Of serving him. Of lo— She deleted that thought before it could even run.

Reboot.

Back to the subroutine programmed for sex, please.

He put a finger under her chin, eyes narrowing when she gave an involuntary shake of her head.

No. Stay out of my brain.

Her hands were flattened on his chest. She could feel his heart beating against her fingertips as his face gentled and the look in his eyes...changed.

His deep blue gaze held her, pulled her in, filled her world.

And he kissed her, slow and deep and more wonderful than any kiss she'd ever had before. He rubbed his nose along hers in a gentle caress and smiled.

"You planning to wash me, little subbie?" he murmured.

"Anything you want," she whispered, then blinked. *What?*

He laughed and put her hands back on his chest.

Right. Don't look at his eyes. Or his face.

So she soaped up his chest, getting mesmerized by how he had just the perfect amount of hair sprinkled across his solid pecs. The inverted triangle changed to a narrow line down to where...he had a gorgeous hard-on.

Well, that could keep her busy and her mind off...other thoughts.

He chuckled and wrapped her fingers around his erection. Thick. Long. Veins curving around the silken skin. She had the time now to look. To enjoy. She slid her hand up and down, teasing with squeezes, adding her other hand. She leaned forward so her breasts would rub on his lower chest. Oh, she definitely wanted him. *But just his body. Not anything more.*

And she'd start by driving him crazy. That would be an excellent end to the evening.

But before she could go down on him, he stopped her, picked up the soap, and started to suds her breasts. *Oh holy God.* An insistent pinch brought her up on tiptoes. "Pay attention to what you're doing, sweetheart," he said. "Keep those hands moving."

—∗—

Having taken a quick shower, Galen carried his toy bag down the tiny path that angled off from the back of the house. The foliage grew thicker as he approached the lake where the cabana rested on stilts near the water's edge. The place was perfect for housing guests who desired privacy—or it would be once they got it remodeled. Since the building had a tiny kitchenette and bathroom, he and Vance had slept here when they'd first moved into the house. But the only restoration done so far was to yank out the small window overlooking the water and put in a wall-sized one.

He stepped inside and looked around. One corner held a small fridge and stovetop with cupboards over them and a nearby tall cabinet. Twin beds were pushed against two walls. A sturdy square table and two wooden-backed chairs were close to the front door. On the wall to the left, the window showed the moon over the lake sending fingers of light across the black water.

Yes, this would do nicely. He took ropes from his bag. The table would be a fine height for play.

As Galen finished setting various implements around the room, he heard Sally's voice outside. Not good the way it made his heart lift.

Followed by Vance, Sally walked in, attired in a long fleece robe.

Her flushed cheeks and swollen lips looked as if she'd been nicely aroused. Galen gave his partner a nod of approval and tried not to grin. Bet his jeans had been difficult to zip up over that hard-on.

"This is a great place." Sally spun in a circle and came to a sudden halt. She'd spotted the paddle on the table, the crop on the bed. "You're going to punish me? But...I just graduated."

"I heard a rumor to that effect." Galen stepped closer and undid the ties of the robe. As the sides opened, he caught the fragrance of aroused woman, soap, lotion. "You smell good, pet."

"I'm not wearing any perfume."

"You don't need any." He pushed the robe farther back so he could caress her soft breasts. When he scraped his thumbnail over one pointing nipple, her sharp inhalation was his reward. And, as he'd expected, she automatically tried to step back. Already standing behind her, Vance blocked that retreat.

"Do you run away because of instincts, or do you really not like my hands on you?" Galen asked. He curved his fingers under her breast, feeling the heavy roundness. Her spiked nipple, her response to his touch had already told him the answer, but she needed to acknowledge it to herself.

"I-I guess instincts."

She'd even dodge verbally. "Do you like my hands on you?" he asked her directly.

Her gaze dropped. "Yes."

And even though he knew her answer already, hearing her admit it made him feel like he'd reached a mountain peak. He cleared his throat. "All right. Do you like Vance to touch you?"

"Yes." Her voice had lowered, as if she were confessing a crime.

"That's good, pet. We plan to do a great deal of touching tonight." Time to rev up those nerves a bit. "Some you'll like. Some you won't."

His fingers on her breast registered the increase in her pulse.

Very nice. "Now, before we do anything else, let's get your punishment out of the way." And start her off on her journey to another plane.

She jolted slightly. "I get punished because I graduated?"

"Sally. You get punished because you had an extra drink after I told you not to," Vance said.

"B-but it was a party. My party."

"We wanted to play with you afterward," Galen replied.

Vance said, "And we didn't want you breaking your neck if your ankle gave out." At her flush, he added, "Alcohol and gimp legs don't mix well."

Wasn't that the fucking truth, Galen thought sourly. But his mood lightened as he looked at the imp. Even subdued, she still seemed filled with joy. By God, she was something. He smiled and touched her cheek. "Ready, imp?"

When she raised her big brown eyes, Vance grinned at Galen over her head and tugged her robe completely off.

Galen doubted he'd ever get tired of seeing her without clothing. The faint moonlight slid across her bare skin like a lover's stroke, highlighting areas he planned to touch, shadowing those where the scent of woman would be strongest.

Vance curled his hand around her upper arm. After taking his seat in the chair next to the table, he firmly pulled her down over his knees.

The moonlight turned her full round ass to a marble white.

That skin was just begging to be pinkened.

SALLY SPLAYED HER hands on the floor, trying to stay balanced on Vance's very muscular thighs. Her pulse had sped up; her skin felt overly sensitive, as if even the air was scraping across it.

When she shifted uncomfortably, he ruthlessly arranged her position so her bottom rose higher in the air. "You know why you're being punished. Do you have any questions?"

Had she ever seen the guys doing a punishment scene? How bad was this going to get? She turned her head so she could see Galen's face. "What are you planning to do?"

His expression hardened with disapproval. "I'm not impressed with Z's lessons for the trainees."

God, no trainee would ask a question like that. Why did she keep forgetting her self-discipline with these guys? "Sorry, Sir."

Galen leaned his hip on a corner of the table and regarded her with a grave expression. "Is obedience too much to ask of you?"

The question took her breath away. "No, Sir." Knowing she'd disappointed them created an ugly feeling in her chest. They'd been kind to her, she'd asked them to be her Doms, and then she kept smarting off. And deliberately disobeyed a direct order.

Did they even like her anymore? She swallowed past a tight throat.

After a minute, Vance laid his hand on her bottom. The warmth sank into her cold skin. "Pretty little ass, don't you think, Galen?"

"Ayuh." Galen pulled the empty chair out from the table and moved it so he could rest his injured leg on the bed. Obviously settling in for the show.

She gritted her teeth and prepared for the worst. At one time, she'd thought Vance was the easygoing one. That assumption might have been incorrect.

He stroked and massaged before slapping lightly all over her bottom. She closed her eyes as a kernel of worry sprouted. The care he was taking meant he planned a longer session.

Slap, slap, slap. He worked his way up and down her bottom in sets of three, pausing briefly before hitting harder. As he established his rhythm, the mild sting turned to a burn. To the beginning of pain. But he stopped and returned to rubbing her bottom.

She started to smile. That wasn't bad at all. Almost erotic. She'd been right after all; Vance wasn't into dispensing pain. She relaxed, enjoying the slight scrape of his calloused palm over her tenderized flesh.

He leaned forward, reaching toward the table. But the surface had been empty except for…that narrow wooden paddle.

No!

The paddle smacked her right in the sweet spot, the rise of her cheek from the crease of her thigh. The sound was startling, the bite meaner.

She gasped, and her fingers curled, finding only cold wood to hold.

Smack, smack, smack. "You disobeyed us, Sally." *Smack. Smack. Smack.* "Didn't you ask us to take you on?" He paused.

Oh God, he really did plan to punish her. Her breath shuddered into her lungs as his words registered. She'd been the one to ask them. "Y-yes, Sir. I did."

Smack, smack, smack. "Where we come from, submissives obey their Doms. Is it different in Florida?"

The pain crept in; the blows blurred together, leaving the burn and pain behind. He'd paused so she could answer. What could she say? She hadn't even tried to obey them. She closed her eyes, feeling like a failure. *I'm sorry. Don't be mad...please. I didn't mean to make you mad.* "No, Sir. I should have obeyed you."

Smack, smack, smack. "Since we're just getting to know each other, I'm not all that upset. Or disappointed."

Her relief actually overcame the pain for a second. *Don't hate me. Please don't hate me.*

"We try not to give many orders. But you'll learn that we take obedience seriously."

Smack, smack, smack.

Tears prickled at the back of her eyes. He'd been so good to her. Caring for her after she'd been hurt. *"Ready to get off the floor, sweetie?"* Holding her so gently after the nightmares. So patient. And look how she'd rewarded him.

Smack, smack, smack.

"If you disobey, you get punished. And not in a sexy, fun way. Is that clear?"

Fire bit into her skin. She tried to blink the tears away; the pain was coming from her heart as well as her skin. "Yes, Sir."

After setting the paddle on the table, he rubbed her bottom. His hand felt cool against her burning skin.

With a long sigh, she let herself relax. That was it. Not so bad—except for the shame simmering deep inside her. The worry that he'd find her too much trouble.

He could easily find someone who'd work hard to please him. A *good* submissive.

She let out a breath. She should be relieved that this hadn't been so bad. Not a deterrent at all. Was that good? Some submissives worried about upsetting their Doms, knowing they'd get an ass walloping nasty enough to make them think twice about—

"Up you go, sweetheart." Vance helped her stand. Rather than pulling her into his arms for some after comforting, he rose. With a cop's grip around her upper arm, he led her across the room to Galen.

"Warm-up finished. All yours." Vance's words didn't register for a moment, not until Galen stood up.

Warm-up? That was a warm-up? And Galen would... She shrank back against Vance.

The corner of Galen's mouth tipped up. "This is the difference between playing at the club and actually having a Dom. Your own Doms will take disobedience a bit more seriously. Because they care enough to make you obey."

Your own Doms. The phrase ran like liquid sunshine over Sally's soul before her mind scrambled back behind her defenses. "Are you saying you'll beat on me because you care?"

Galen's black gaze softened. "Actually, yes." He stroked her cheek with his fingertips, holding her gaze with his.

Her breathing stopped. He cared. *For me?*

And then he took a step back. "Bend over the bed. Rest your weight on your forearms."

Oh fuck fuck fuck. As she complied, her arms sank down into the puffy blue quilt. The bed was low, positioning her bottom higher.

"Move your feet out."

She inched her bare feet outward. The position lowered her butt slightly but put more weight on her arms and made it more difficult to stand. More helpless.

He picked up a thin rattan cane. "All right, pet. I'm not going to count. I will continue until I think you're properly repentant."

"But I am. I—"

His sigh was loud. "Don't bother to talk to me. I'm not sure you even know what true remorse means."

The first slash of the cane struck her bottom and it *hurt*, blasting across her skin like fire.

No! She tried to stand and realized Vance sat at the foot of the bed. His hand curled over her nape, holding her in place.

Blow after blow smacked into her flesh with a nasty stinging pain. And suddenly, shockingly, she was crying. Hard horrible choking sobs that hurt her throat. "I'm sorry. I'm sorry. I didn't—didn't mean to disappoint you. I'm sorry."

"There we go." Galen's voice was rougher than normal, raw as the pain of her skin. "That was repentant."

Vance released her.

Hard hands mercilessly pulled her onto a lap. Her bottom scraped on the harsh material of jeans, and she tried to jump up—and was pulled back down, secured with muscular, adamant arms. His hand—Galen's—tucked her head against his shoulder, holding her as she cried.

Her face pressed against his chest, wetting it with her tears. "I'm sorry," she whispered again.

"I believe you, pet." She felt his lips against the top of her head, and the jagged glass fence around her heart began to thaw.

His scent, masculine and rich, wrapped around her, confirming his presence with each breath she took. As the burning subsided, she could feel, even more than his strength, the controlled gentleness with which he held her. How his hand cupped the back of her head. His slow breathing. His patience.

Gradually her crying changed to hiccupping sobs.

Vance sat on the bed and took her hand. "All done, Sally." He stroked her head and tried to release her hand, but her fingers closed around his.

Stay. Somehow she needed him there—both of them. Their presence was as comforting as having a man in the house if opening the door after dark. Knowing, despite the monsters in the night, that they'd keep her safe.

GALEN FELT THE tightness in his chest ease as Sally clung to him. A true submissive, she wasn't fuming at her punishment but had let the tears wash away her shame and free her from guilt.

When he checked Vance, his partner made a small rotation of his shoulder. No trouble interpreting that unhappy movement.

Galen too, had been surprised at how long it had taken to break through her defenses. This one didn't cry easily. And he hadn't liked administering the last few strokes needed to push her there. He liked erotic pain—and maybe a touch beyond—but this had gone past his comfort level.

But apparently she'd forgiven them both, and damn, she was wonderful to hold.

As Sally's breathing evened out, Vance rummaged through the fridge to get bottled waters. He drank one and set Galen's on the table. After handing Sally one, he plucked her out of Galen's arms and sat down with her on his lap.

Galen nodded approval and rose. She'd need Vance's arms around her during the next phase. Meantime, he circled the room, drinking his water, stretching out his leg...and formulating his strategy.

She'd finished drinking by the time Galen took the bottle from her. She gave him a wary look. Smart little submissive.

Galen moved the chair to the bed, straddled it, and leaned his arms on the back. "Interesting man, your father."

She flushed.

"You know, my parents are almost as uncaring as he is," Galen said lightly. Even as a teen, he'd compared his parents to frozen fish. Vance's family had shown him how much he'd missed.

Sally frowned at him. Her color had returned to normal, although her eyes were still reddened. "My father isn't—"

Vance squeezed her in warning.

She closed her eyes for a second. "Yes, my father is cold." She reached out to touch Galen's hand. "I'm sorry if your parents are too."

There was that compassionate heart he'd seen before. The little brat had a generous spirit. "How did your father punish you when you messed up?" The bastard hadn't let her have pets. This evening, he'd edged into what Galen would consider verbal abuse. How far had he gone with a child?

As she stiffened, Vance combed her hair with his fingers, saying, "Now my dad was a firm believer in spankings, but my mom preferred time-outs. Personally, I'd rather be spanked than be stuck inside all afternoon."

Good guy; bad guy. If Galen couldn't scare a perp into talking,

Vance's sincerity often lured the answers out.

"He usually sent me to my room." Her expression darkened, like ink spilled into clear water.

Galen felt his instincts twang.

"Without supper?" Vance asked lightly. Over her head, his worried gaze met Galen's.

"Huh. At least." She turned her head into Vance's chest.

At least? Galen controlled his voice, keeping it even. "How long did he usually leave you there, Sally?"

"Oh, just till the next day." Despite her efforts to make the words flippant, the strain—and hurt—came through. "I'd get to come down to breakfast."

And if she'd screwed up at breakfast? "And the longest?"

"Uh. Not much—"

"Be honest, sweetheart," Vance said, and she stiffened, catching the warning note.

"Three days," she whispered into Vance's chest. Her laugh was thin, filled with pain. "If the school hadn't called to ask why I was absent, I wonder if I'd still be there."

Why hadn't someone sent the bastard to hell and gone? Galen's jaw muscles clenched, hindering his ability to talk.

"How old were you?" Vance was doing better than Galen at keeping the questions coming.

"I think I was twelve. My mother had..." Her mouth pressed into a thin line of pain.

There it is. Like in his favorite childhood game, clues would eventually line up to reveal the crime. Colonel Mustard in the library with the candlestick. He hadn't planned to ask this so soon, but the opening was there. "Sally, why did your father say you killed your mother?"

Every bit of color drained from her face.

"YOU..." *MOM. OH, Mom.* Sally couldn't—couldn't believe he'd asked such an unspeakable question. Her thoughts fled, disappeared, hollowing her mind into dark emptiness. Like a dog's choke chain, tightness circled her throat until only strangled wheezing escaped. Unable to even look at the cruel beast who would ask such a thing, she pushed her face against Vance's chest.

"Answer the question, Sally." With a determined grip, Vance turned her to face his partner.

No. I won't.

Galen's gaze met hers, ensnared hers. The patient expectation in his expression was impossible to ignore. After a moment, he threw her something easier to answer. "How old were you when she died?"

"Eleven." Saturday afternoon. Her straw-filled hair had been in tangles from playing in the barn with half-grown cats. Her homework had been finished the night before, because she was a geek. Called into the house to answer the phone. Lauren was having a semisurprise birthday party that night and invited Sally. A *popular* girl had asked *her*, the chubby nerd, to a party. Her excitement had made her feel like a balloon ready to pop. Then it all went wrong. "And I got a new dress."

She shut her stupid mouth, knowing it was too late.

Galen's expression had sharpened. "Why was a new dress a problem?"

"Please, Mom. Please. I'll do my chores and I'll clean the barn and..." She'd begged and promised, because she just knew that looking *right* would let her be one of—maybe not the *in* crowd— but maybe the normal girls. She wouldn't still be stuck in with the losers, the really overweight ones, or those on welfare. The ones who had pimples. Or never washed. God, how shallow they'd all been. *She'd* been. "Father had said no. No more money for clothes."

"So how did you end up with a new dress?" Vance asked gently.

"Mom drove me into town. It was snowing. Blowing." *Leaving the store, she'd been blinded by her hair whipping around her face. The car shook with the gusts of wind. The snow hitting the windshield sounded like sizzling bacon. A storm turning to a blizzard.*

Galen's intent eyes lit with comprehension. The ancient Greeks loved tragic plays; did his heritage mean he'd understand?

"An accident?" he asked softly.

"The bridge was old. There was ice under new snow." Skidding. She swallowed, her mouth tasting like metal. "The car... The railing broke." *Screaming and falling and screaming.* The smash, breaking, shattering sounds, the horrendous impact that could still knock her out of her nightmares. "We went over the side." *So much pain, blood everywhere, like a kicked-over can of red paint. Mom. Mom! Not answering. Shaking her. Screaming and crying and—*

"Shhhh." Vance stroked her hair.

As Sally had finally stroked her mother's. Soft hair. Pretty. *Had Mom felt her attempt at comfort, even in heaven?*

"And your father blames you because she died?" Vance asked.

Her voice came out harsh. "Yeah."

"Because you'd..." Galen's voice trailed off, an invitation for the rest.

She tried to look away. He caught her chin gently. Firmly. Turned her back. *Damn him.* "Because I begged. She didn't want to buy anything, didn't want to spend the money, and I thought only of myself and made her go to town"—her voice rose—"because I'm selfish and stupid and always wanting stuff."

Her shouting should have made him back away. Should have made Vance release her instead of holding her tighter.

Galen's lips turned up, his gaze filled with approval that...that she could actually recognize. "That's a good baby girl," he murmured. His mouth touched hers for a second, his lips soft. "Thank you for sharing with me."

The taste of salt made her realize tears were running down her cheeks.

Vance wiped them away gently. "You're not selfish. Or stupid. Your father is the stupid one."

"Exactly." Galen squeezed her shoulder before rising to walk around the room, his cane forgotten in the corner.

Exhausted, she lay in Vance's arms and just watched his slow, limping circuits.

Eventually, he came to a stop in front of her. "Homework for you. We'll expect it tomorrow night."

Homework? Had she slipped into an alternate universe, one where a crying outburst was followed by school? "Excuse me?"

His lips quirked. "Homework. Use one of your school notebooks. I want an essay about what a parent can reasonably expect from a preteen. Specifics, please. Include quotes from people about whining and begging and adolescent temper. Use the Internet—and document your sources."

"What?" Her brain wasn't keeping up, no way, no how.

"There are quite a few parenting sites out there," Vance said helpfully, obviously on board with the insane scheme. "You might try those first."

"But I got my mother killed."

"Baby girl," Galen said. "You didn't. You were a typical irritating teenager, wanting something and whining to get it. If we put every teen who displayed that kind of obnoxious behavior in jail, we'd depopulate the world."

"You'd have to start with my nieces and nephews." Vance chuckled. "'I want. I want. I want,' alternates only with 'I need. I need. I need.' Sweetheart, you were a normal young girl. Not someone evil."

As she looked at Vance and Galen, her eyes filled with tears again, blurring the room's walls to an underwater montage. Vance made a soft sound and tucked her back under his chin, rocking her slightly.

"I think you've had enough, pet," Galen said. His eyes crinkled. "But do your homework before bedtime tomorrow night, or you'll be bending over the bed again."

And suddenly she could again feel how sore her bottom was. *Ouchers.*

No wonder Kim thought twice before disobeying Master Raoul.

CHAPTER NINE

After a stop in the kitchen, Vance stepped out the back door, feeling more battered than after a college football practice. The moon was high, illuminating his way across the patio, down the walk to the lake. The muggy night air wrapped around him, making him shake his head. Back in Ohio, he'd still be wearing a sweatshirt.

The lakeshore frog chorus was silenced by the thump of his feet on the wooden dock.

Galen sat in one of the two chairs near the end of the dock, his sore leg propped up on his ancient upside-down canoe. Vance handed his partner his whiskey and dropped into the other weathered chair.

Glock, curled in Galen's lap, looked up long enough to evaluate a possibly better resting area, but resettled where he was. Galen stroked the furry head before asking, "She asleep?"

As water lapped quietly against the pilings, one courageous frog chanced a croak, soon joined by the rest.

"Out like a light—after another crying fit." Broke his heart too.

"She had it stored up." Galen tipped his head back. "Bet her father threw her mother's death in her face for every request she made. And whenever she displayed an emotion."

"Not surprising she doesn't ask for anything now." Vance tamped down his anger, remembering the hurt in her big eyes. The incomprehension. A person might mature, but the vulnerable child inside would never entirely leave. "She told me her dad hadn't wanted her. That her mother wanted a child, but he didn't. Especially not a girl."

"Hell."

Not wanted. Actively put down. "Be a pleasure to beat the fuck out of her father."

"We'll take turns." The softness of Galen's voice didn't conceal his red-hot anger.

A corner of Vance's mouth lifted. He happened to like justice. Right and wrong. Protecting and serving. Law enforcement filled a need in him. But in Galen, the need to protect was...more. Deeper. It was that burning drive that had first attracted Vance's attention. Had made them friends. Sucked that it was now starting to scar his friend's soul.

However, the desire to beat the hell out of Hart? Sounded healthy enough to Vance.

And watching Sally sass his partner while she was stealing his heart was a true pleasure.

Vance stretched his legs out and drank his vodka. The moon's glow was a blanket over the lake until a breeze broke it into choppy fragments. Like life—smooth sailing, then rough water. Excitement and disaster, then calm seas. "She's more vulnerable than we figured."

"Ayuh." Silence.

Vance felt the burn of the alcohol as he swallowed. They'd always been careful to scene only with women who held the same expectations, those who agreed that play was for fun, sometimes for sex, never permanent. Who required nothing beyond the demands of the scene. "We agreed to help her, but..."

But they hadn't realized the barrier to openness was because damage had been done. Helping a wounded soul wasn't a short-term obligation.

"She trusts us." Galen stroked the cat, his gaze on the darkness of the far shore. "I don't like having someone here long-term, especially not while we're on the Harvest Association case, but she might not survive what she'd see as another rejection."

"Pretty much what I figured." The scent of the gardenias growing on the bank drifted past, mingling with the green fragrance of the burgeoning growth around the lake. Sweet, clean, and alive. Like the young woman who had trusted him with her tears.

In the cabana, Sally had fit into his arms as if she'd been designed for him. She had a generous and spirited personality, brown eyes that could soften the hardest heart, and a brilliant mind. More than just her body fit him.

But it was fucking bad timing. Why did they have to find her *now?* He wanted a woman—a submissive—to keep and share with Galen. Eventually a family, if they could figure out how to make that work. But not for years. Not until he changed to a more settled career. Certainly not while he was hunting a vindictive bunch of bastards.

Galen tapped his finger on the arm of his chair. "We can't let her get attached, Vance. Permanence isn't in the plans."

And there was where they differed. Galen didn't want a real relationship again. Ever.

Vance had planned on beating that obstinacy out of him when needed. But the time was not now...wasn't supposed to be now. But he was experienced enough to know how rare Sally was. Character, intelligence, strength...she was perfect for them.

And how many women could accept two men, could learn to care for them?

Maybe Sally wasn't the one, but damned if he'd go along with Galen this time. They'd see how this played out for a while— maybe Sally wouldn't be happy with men in risky careers; maybe she wouldn't be able to take how often they were away. But if she started to get "attached," he was going to have a come-to-Jesus talk with his partner.

"Odd." Galen swirled his drink and took a slow sip. "After being in the FBI so long, I forgot a woman can be destroyed by more than the fists and bullets."

Vance pulled his mind back, setting his thoughts aside for a future time. "It's amazing that she's survived—and is who she is." He grinned, remembering her blithe spirits earlier. "She's definitely a treat when she feels safe."

"Ayuh. Got some work cut out for us."

"Think she'll do her homework?"

A smile lightened the shadows in Galen's face. "If she doesn't, she'll have to recite aloud for us."

"Naked. Naked recitations would be good." Maybe he should hide her notebook.

—✦—

In the darkness, Sally roused, wakened by the men's voices coming from somewhere outside.

Amazing. She'd actually fallen asleep.

She still lay curled in a tight ball from when Vance had tucked her into the king-size bed. She huffed a laugh. Over the course of the evening, she'd bawled her head off on both Galen's and Vance's shoulders.

Poor guys. They'd had no idea of the consequences of letting her stay here. Then again, they were apparently like the other Shadowlands Masters. Tears didn't bother them.

At her attempt to apologize, Galen had snorted and said she had a few years stored up. *"Get it out, pet."*

Funny how comfortable she'd felt crying all over them. Sure, a little embarrassed that she couldn't stop, but they hadn't made her feel worthless or stupid. They'd acted as if they expected her to cry, and so it was okay when she did.

Scary guys.

Annoying too. She'd been expecting sex in that cabana, and instead she'd had her butt walloped red and been interrogated into a meltdown.

And she was sleeping alone.

Not fair. This was her graduation night and should be a celebration. She should demand her rights.

Shivers seized her as she considered how the men might react. With an ordinary Dom, she'd have no worries. But not only were Galen and Vance *Masters*, but there were two of them.

Nonetheless, she had rights. *Right?*

She slid out of bed, trying to ignore the nervous fluttering of her stomach. *This might be a horrible mistake, but hell, what was one more?*

Her silky gown floated around her, and her toes wiggled in the carpet as she took condoms from the well-stocked bedside table. The other submissives had extolled the Feds' preferences in playing—one cock in a vagina, one cock in the anus.

God. It sure hadn't worked that well the one and only time she'd tried double penetration. Talk about awkward. The two Doms hadn't been used to playing together—not in that way, at least. She grinned. The one with the shorter cock had kept falling out. Not sexy at all.

Do I want to let Galen and Vance do that?

Heat started in her center and washed all the way to her fingertips. Hell, she'd already answered that question every time she'd let Galen bend her over and push in an anal plug. *Okay then.* She picked up the lube and whispered, "Happy graduation to me. I hope."

She wandered through the downstairs rooms. All empty.

They were outside. She stood in the back door and felt her nerves increase. Could she lure them back in? What if they didn't want to...or laughed at her...or— She closed her eyes and forced her feet across the patio to the dock.

Outside in a midthigh-length nightgown. How decadent was that?

At the first creak of warped boards, they turned. The moon was starting to set, and in the waning light, she saw Vance smile. Why did he have to have such a mind-blowing smile?

"What's up, sweetheart?" Vance reached out and took her hand, pulling her onto his lap.

Ouch. Sore butt! She exhaled past the burn. "I woke up and—*"And I wanted to have sex.* "And..." Her voice died.

Galen leaned forward, elbows on his knees in his study-the-foolish-submissive posture. "And what?"

Like a frog sucking down a bug, she felt her throat close over the plea. Nothing escaped. With a shaking hand, she held out the condoms and lube.

Comprehension flashed in his face as he took them, and his

expression gentled. "I won't make you ask, pet. Just say *please* like a polite little subbie."

Demon Dom. Still determined to shove her out of her comfort zone. Maybe he didn't give her the impossible—just the unbearably difficult. She swallowed the sharp edges of fear, pursed her lips, and forcibly pushed the word out. *Please.*

No sound. Dammit. Her second *please* didn't take longer than a few years to gather. "P-please?" A whispered question rather than the assertive demand she'd hoped for.

Galen kissed her lightly. "Good girl."

Vance hugged her, echoing his partner's compliment, piercing her heart. And then he pulled her gown off over her head. Right out there on the dock.

"Hey." She pushed his hands away from her breasts. "No. Not out here."

The pinch on one nipple made her jump, and Vance growled in her ear. "Did you just tell me no?"

She swallowed. Why did she want their dominance over her, crave it, and yet find that it scared her? It was like walking up to the super roller-coaster ride with terror shaking her insides...and still paying for a ticket. Wanting the ride. Fearing it. "Sorry, Sir. But we're outside." *And I'm naked.*

"We don't have near neighbors, Sally," Galen said. "Not even Tarzan could get through the jungle on either side of this place." He moved his chair close enough to run his warm hands over her outer thighs.

Vance shifted her so she faced away with her back against his broad chest, then pushed her bottom forward, almost off his lap. The determined way he cupped her breasts, in both a restraining yet erotic move, made her toes curl.

"Open up, pet." Galen lifted her left leg up and over Vance's thigh, letting her foot dangle outside it. He did the same with her right leg, ensuring she was spread widely apart. Giving himself unimpeded access to her most intimate places.

The sultry air caressed her pussy, and oh boy, she was already growing damp. Preparing for them.

She set her palms on Vance's hard thighs, wanting to push up.

To close her legs somehow…or to stay put and see what happened.

He gripped her wrists and lifted her arms up so her fingers curved over his nape. "Keep them there, sweetheart. I don't like obstacles in my path."

Under her palms, even his neck was muscular, and his almost shoulder-length hair brushed teasingly over the backs of her hands.

Nerves zinged as Galen slid his palms up her inner thighs. Her clit ached as if it hoped he'd keep moving all the way up.

Rather than touching her there, Galen cupped her buttocks with both hands. And squeezed.

Pain blasted across her tender spanked and caned skin. "Christ in a cave!"

Vance's low chuckle made her realize she was yanking on his hair. *God.*

As the shocking pain subsided to a thick, sweet burning, she felt as if she was dissolving into Vance's immobilizing hold.

"I like the way you respond." Galen's perceptive gaze was focused on her face as he rubbed her sore bottom, keeping the sensation alive, feeding her nerves like wine, making her drunk with arousal.

When Galen slid his fingers through her increasingly wet folds, Vance adjusted his hands to play with her breasts. Two sets of hands forged a four-lane highway of arousal between her breasts and her pussy.

Watching her closely, Galen slipped one finger inside her. Two. The knobby sensation of his knuckles made her whimper as he pushed in deep.

Vance rolled her nipples between his fingers, sending lightning sizzling right to her clit.

"That made her clench," Galen commented.

"Well then." Vance pinched harder, tugging her nipples into long, tight peaks. Her breasts swelled under his attentions, growing more and more sensitive as he played her body like a person would make a squeaky toy perform for a baby. Like he knew exactly how to make her writhe.

Galen's grin showed his appreciation. And the feeling of his fingers deep inside her and Vance's determined exploration above was so erotic that she moaned.

Galen pushed another finger in, stretching her pussy—making her hips try to rise. The intensity of his gaze and the slow turn of his fingers as he stroked different areas inside her pulled her from the slow river of desire into a stronger, faster current. His lips curved. "I might have to try fisting with you, pet."

She shook her head and shivered. Let him put his whole hand inside her? God, no.

Vance wrapped his arms around her, holding her completely immobile, and yet his strength was comforting. Safe. "Not tonight, sweetie," he whispered in her ear. "Tonight we're going to do other things to your body."

Her shudder shook her whole body.

Even as Galen's fingers moved slowly in and out, Vance nipped the edge of her ear. "You'll have us both inside you, pushing you past thinking, past reason. You won't have any control, sweetheart. We're going to take it all away."

Oh God.

ENJOYING THE DAZED look on the little submissive's face, Galen slid his chair forward and set a slickened forefinger on her clit.

Nice satisfying gasp. With his other hand, he curved his finger up and pressed it right onto her G-spot. The ridges were pronounced; the area wasn't puffy enough to drive her mad. But it would be soon.

Circling her clit, he felt her cunt tighten around his other finger. By God, he loved how she responded. Glancing up, he caught Vance's eyes and nodded. Time to take it up a notch.

Vance grinned and changed his position. His hands covered breasts that were more swollen than a few minutes ago. Her pink-brown nipples had turned a dusky red from his play.

Even in the moonlight, Galen could see Vance's face darken with arousal as he played. Total breast man.

And Sally's were not only beautiful but very, very sensitive. He smiled, enjoying the quivers of her body and cunt as Vance teased her. His partner could have some serious fun with her while she stayed with them.

Galen kept up a light stimulation of her G-spot as Vance played, and her wetness soon covered his palm. Her breathing turned shallower until she was panting. There was something special about the way she gave herself to them. Openly. Holding nothing back. She might have defenses around her emotions, but her body was honest.

Her labia were swollen, and her cunt was sucking at his finger. When he lifted his other hand, he could see the way her clit protruded. With the hood pulled back, the glistening pearl was fully exposed. He stroked around it once and heard her breathing hitch. Delightful.

Her eyes were closed, her body starting to stiffen as all her attention moved to her pussy. Almost anything would set her off now.

So he pulled his finger out, moved his hand away, and exchanged grins with Vance at her protesting whine. Lovely sound.

After picking up a condom, Galen reclined his chair and undid his jeans. His cock sprang up as if released from prison. Jeans could be an uncomfortable jail for a hard-on. He rolled on protection.

Vance rose, hands around Sally's waist, and set her down on hands and knees over Galen.

Galen moved her legs to each side of his hips, curving his hands around her thighs, securing her. Her pussy rubbed over his cock, making her moan. The slick, hot feel of her was amazing.

"Hands up here, sweetheart." Vance curled her fingers around the wooden chair frame behind Galen's head. With Velcro straps, which were attached to the top bar, he restrained her wrists.

She stiffened.

Galen laid his palm on her cheek. "Sally. Your safe word still works, no matter where we are. Am I clear?"

Her big eyes, even wider than normal, stared into his, and she pulled in a breath. Some of the tension flowed out of her. She started to nod, then whispered, "Yes, Sir."

Afraid, restrained, and still remembering his preferences. This one was something special.

She straddled him, her breasts dangling down over his chest. He fully intended to play with them a bit. But first, he grasped her hip with one hand and, with the other, guided his cock to her pussy. He pulled her down until he was in an inch. *Hell.* All that heat tugged at his control, begging him to yank her down hard and fast. But he stopped, his teeth grinding from the strain.

When she made a soft, inarticulate sound and tried to lower herself, he nodded at Vance before moving his hands to her breasts.

Vance gripped her hips, ruthlessly holding her in place. She might be positioned on top of one man, but she still had absolutely no control.

HER BODY WAS shivering, not with fear, but from the waves of desire. Galen caressed her throbbing breasts, which had swollen until the skin stretched taut.

Vance's fingers curled around her hips, immobilizing her. She couldn't move. Couldn't escape. Her hands gave an involuntary tug, and despite the restraints being Velcro, she couldn't pull free.

"Eyes on me, pet." Galen's command was low but resolute enough that her gaze flew to his. His eyes seemed darker than the night sky.

And Vance slowly, mercilessly pushed her down. Galen's cock filled her, stretched her. Vance didn't stop, ignoring her squirms, until she was fully impaled and her buttocks brushed the coarse hair on Galen's upper thighs.

With the back of his chair reclined, she was bent forward, her bottom readily available. Her insides pulsed with sensation; her clit burned. She...needed. Her attempt to rub against Galen's pelvis caused Vance's viselike grip to tighten.

"Not allowed, baby girl." Galen gave her nipples a reprimanding pinch that made everything inside her clench. He chuckled.

Galen's gaze was steady on her face as Vance took her over, working her hips up and down onto Galen's cock. It felt so good, revving the hum of desire even higher.

A shudder ran through her at the realization that she'd get only and exactly what they gave her. Her leg muscles went limp as she surrendered, giving all control to Vance.

"That a girl," Vance murmured.

Galen nodded at him before his hands replaced Vance's on her hips.

She heard the crinkle of a condom wrapper.

Even as she started to comprehend, she felt her buttocks pulled open. Cool liquid lube drizzled between her cheeks. Vance ran a finger around the rim of her asshole.

Galen cut short her involuntary attempt to wrench away.

So many different nerves. Her core was filled with Galen, yet all her attention shifted to Vance's finger—how it circled and probed. He pressed past the rim of anal muscles, inserting one finger. Two fingers. The small burn from the widening made her pussy clench.

She swallowed and closed her eyes.

"Eyes on me," Galen repeated.

Her eyes met his even as Vance's cock replaced his fingers and pushed in slowly. Despite the lubed-up slickness of his shaft, as her asshole stretched, the burning sensation took over her world.

He pressed in, always farther. "You can take me, sweetheart. Push out and breathe."

The sound of Vance's voice, his rumbling, calming voice, made her want to try. To please him. Her hands seized the chair back as he surged in. Too much. Her vagina was already filled by Galen's cock. There was no room for more. She started to shake, feeling as if she'd split.

Galen's hands tightened on her hips, keeping her immobile.

"Almost in, sweetheart. You feel so good," Vance said, squeezing her still-tender buttocks, adding a different kind of pain to the brew.

God, God, God. Her eyelids lowered, then rose again at a sound from Galen. He stared into her eyes, reading further than anyone ever had. Even as her body was penetrated, taken over, his unrelenting gaze pierced through to her soul.

When she whimpered, he moved his hand up to cup her cheek. "Shhh. Let us in, baby girl. Take a breath now."

As she managed to pull air in, suddenly she felt Vance's groin hit her abused bottom. Everywhere back there seemed to be in flames, and she stiffened, unable to move.

Vance braced himself with his right hand on the chair back next to hers.

Galen locked both hands on her hips. "Look at me," he reminded her. As she lifted her head, he moved her, working her up and down on his cock in an implacable slide that felt...stunning and terrifying.

So full; everything in her lower half was stretched and throbbing. Even her clit was pulled tight, brushing over his pelvic bone as he moved her. She whimpered, and her toes lifted upward. *My God.*

He broke his gaze long enough to look past her shoulder at his partner. "She's ready. Let's do it."

"Breathe, sweetheart," Vance reminded, and she realized she'd been holding her breath. At the sound of her gasping inhalation, the men laughed, low and deep.

Vance wrapped an arm around her and pinched her so-sensitive nipples. She clenched involuntarily, and he groaned. Then he straightened slightly, gripped her waist, and slid his thick cock from her asshole.

The devastating, wonderful, impossible sensation made her shudder. "Oh God!"

Galen pushed in, withdrawing when Vance surged back in. The sliding, the stretching, even the slight burn from both her asshole and abused butt was like a lightning storm of nerves that crashed over her. She had no control. She was too full.

She was taken. Taken. Taken.

Their pace increased, and yet, like a dance, they never missed a step. Shudders shook her as her body overwhelmed her mind, as the sheer sensation centered everything in that region as if a sizzling lightning strike had hit and stayed on, flaring the world to utter brightness.

Every little movement pushed her higher, closer to coming, and she fought it off. It would be…too much. Take the last bit of her senses from her. She shook her head. *No.*

"Stubborn little sub." Vance sounded almost sympathetic. But he shifted his hand from her breast, down her stomach, lower, until his fingers slid through her wetness and slickly across her clit.

"Aaah!" Everything in her seized, throwing her into a whirlwind, a hurricane. The sensations spiraled up and up, setting every single nerve to firing in the most supreme burst of pleasure she'd ever felt. She writhed on them, unable to breathe.

A long wail escaped her as another wave hit. Her back arched, and each clenching spasm sent another engulfing sensation through her.

Vance gripped her waist, holding himself deep inside her.

Galen hammered into her, powerful and fast, until he made a guttural sound and she felt his cock jerking, shooting inside her.

And then Vance pulled out. He yanked her back onto his shaft, setting off new pounding waves of pleasure inside her. In and out in long, merciless thrusts of his thick cock. One hand still gripped her waist, but as he came with a growling roar in her ear, he pinched her clit. Hard.

Sally screamed as her body clenched around the impossible impalement. She exploded into another orgasm, crying as she shook from the force, unable to escape the restraints, the hands, the cocks.

Some distant time in the future, she blinked as the roaring in her head receded. Her head drooped; her arms trembled. Someone—her—was gasping for the humid air, dragging it in as if the moist air was a nectar.

After another minute, she realized Galen was stroking her hair, murmuring, his voice more gentle than she'd ever heard before. "Pretty pet, sweet Sally. Thank you for sharing."

Her body was wonderfully satiated, but his words filled a well far deeper inside her, as if she'd been thirsty and hadn't known.

Vance was running one hand up and down her back, his other arm around her waist, holding her up. "Good, good girl," he was murmuring. "Brave girl."

Both caressing her. Both focused on her.

Vance pulled out slowly, laughing under his breath as her body shuddered around him. After undoing her hands, he tucked her down on Galen, letting her lie limply on his partner's chest. He ruffled her hair and walked away.

Using an immense strength of will, she managed to raise her head and look at Galen. "He—he's leaving? Is he mad?"

"Not even close, Sally." Galen cupped the back of her head, tucking her against his shoulder. His shirt was open, and her breasts flattened on his steely chest. Slowly, he was softening inside her, but they were still connected in the most intimate, wonderful way. He resumed stroking her hair, petting her absentmindedly. "Since we both enjoy holding you, we take turns. He was with you upstairs."

"Oh."

"Since you're awake enough to ask questions, you may kiss me now."

She tipped her face up to look. His black eyes were amused...and tender. No longer blazing like a bonfire, but warm enough to fill all the lingering cold spaces inside her.

And he lured her into a kiss like no other she'd ever received.

Oh, she was in trouble.

CHAPTER TEN

When Vance returned from work on Monday, he walked through the quiet house. Galen was still in a meeting, he knew, but Sally's car was in the drive. No one in the kitchen or great room—except for Glock, who greeted him with an indifferent tail flick. Obviously not hungry. Gone were the I've-been-starving-for-days pitiful meows and ankle bumping. Looked like a little submissive was a soft touch.

Vance picked up the gray tom. "I think you've already put on a couple of pounds, cat."

A slit-eyed smirk was his only answer.

He carried the cat with him and found Sally in the office working on her computer. With a smile, he wondered what mood she'd be in today.

Last Saturday, she'd been sweet. Accepting them, loving them. Afterward, she'd slept in their arms, snuggling against them both. She didn't play favorites. As far as he could tell, she liked them both. No matter how often she and Galen butted heads, they also were a lot alike. And her tender affection was good for his partner.

Felt fucking good to Vance, as well.

And he liked that sassy mouth of hers, the attitude she could put on like a uniform. Her conversations with Glock had him wondering if the cat really could communicate.

She'd fished with him early Sunday for a long, contemplative hour and seemed as contented as he'd ever seen her.

Last night, he'd heard her shriek and had run into the office. The room had been empty except for her, a wide-eyed, furious young woman ranting about health potions and being surrounded by demons, abandoned by her comrades and left to die.

She had quite a mouth on her sometimes.

And now she'd assumed another personality—the focused intellectual typing so fast she hadn't even heard him walk in.

"Sending out job applications?" he asked.

She jumped as if he'd goosed her with a cattle prod. "Vance!" Her hands flicked over the keyboard. The screen changed from an e-mail program to a document. "I didn't expect you back so early."

She spun in the chair to face him. Dressed in faded jeans and a Darth Vader T-shirt with the logo: *The Dark Side made me do it!!!* Her hair was pulled back with a band. Makeupless. Not out to impress anyone, was she?

"It's actually rather late, sweetheart." If he'd ever seen a guilty expression, she was wearing one. But they hadn't told her not to communicate with her friends. "You have the code for the wireless, right?"

Her expression eased. "Yes. Thank you for letting me use it."

So that wasn't it. Well, unless she was running an e-mail banking scam and asking recipients to send her a few thousand to save her baby from starving, he didn't need to be involved. Neither he nor Galen restricted a submissive's communications—and he wanted her to keep in touch with her friends. "How good are you with construction?"

"Well, not too bad with basic skills, but I can't read a diagram and make it come out right."

He smiled and tugged her hair. "Top of your class and you don't do diagrams?"

"Hey, flow charts are one thing, spatial skills another. I can get lost in a cornfield." She wrinkled her pert nose. "Bet they don't let you into Fed school if that happens."

"Nope. Takes all the fun out of a car chase if you get turned around." He held his hand out, pleased she didn't hesitate before putting her hand in his.

As he pulled her to her feet, her eyes held curiosity with just a touch of trepidation. Good. She was the type of submissive who would do better if kept on her toes. But he needed to be sure she knew she was valued.

"What's up?" she asked.

"We'd planned to use the cabana for guests, but we're going to convert it into a dungeon instead."

"It will make an awesome dungeon. And be a lot nicer than those typical fake stone wall ones. What can I do to help?"

He gave her a slow smile. "I thought I'd take you on as a carpenter's apprentice...so to speak."

She gave him a puzzled look.

"Every schoolgirl should learn a trade to fall back on." Teacher-schoolgirl had been listed as one of her favorite role-plays, and he had a fondness for that kind of power exchange. He looked her up and down. "I left a pair of overalls for you on my bed. Schoolgirl socks and tennis shoes. Braids."

Her eyes lit up. When she was happy, she almost sparkled.

He added, "Meet me in ten minutes in the cabana."

"Yes, Sir!"

SHE'D WORRIED THAT he'd make her wear ugly farmer's overalls. She grinned at what he'd left on his bed. Yes, the material was denim with a bib front and shoulder straps. But without a T-shirt, the bib barely covered her nipples. Lacing on each side of the waist made it formfitting. And rather than long pants legs, the bottom was a skirt. The hem ended just short of her butt. She put on knee-high socks and denim sneakers. Her hair hung in two long braids. No makeup. Just to be contrary, she pulled on a pair of bright pink panties.

Whoever thought one of the stern Feds could be into role-playing? A check in the mirror showed her grin. Poor guy. He'd never seen her playing schoolgirl, or he'd know better.

She paused on the stairs as she remembered Vance's really big, really strong hand slapping her bottom. That had hurt.

She huffed in exasperation at her worries. He wouldn't do a true punishment for a role-play. The only reason to play schoolgirl was to be able to be sassy. Maybe that's why she enjoyed it so much.

She frowned. If she enjoyed it so much, why hadn't she been like that at home? Or had she been? In kindergarten, she'd lectured her mother about throwing away recyclable glass. And hanging out of the hayloft, she'd teased her brother, knowing he was afraid of climbing the ladder to enact retribution. And informing her father at supper that companies headed by women made more money. Sally grinned, remembering the appalled look on her father's face. How old had she been that time? Nine?

Her smile faded. That was before he'd started to hate her. After her mother's death, his disapproval—and occasional backhand—eventually silenced her complaints, her requests...her voice.

Being mouthy was something she'd lost when her mother died, and only regained once away and in college.

The humid lake air wrapped around her as she walked out the back door and down the narrow dirt path to the cabana. Out on the lake, two bright orange kayaks left trails of miniwaves behind them. In the rough vegetation on the lakeshore, an alligator lifted its head to check her out before returning to drowsing. She shuddered. No one thought twice about jumping into a lake in Iowa, but here? Not a chance.

In the cabana, Vance stood in the center of the room, tapping a yardstick on his palm and surveying the potential construction site. The ancient white T-shirt that stretched across his broad shoulders was so thin she could see his shoulder muscles bunch as he turned.

"There you are," he said.

She held still while he prowled a circle around her.

"Very nice."

When he ran his hand under her skirt, she shoved him away. "Sir! What are you doing?"

"Apprentices in our company don't wear underwear. It's a danger in a work environment." His voice was stern, his eyes dancing. "Gets caught on things." He hooked a finger in the waistband and yanked her panties down. "Remove them."

She huffed and slithered out of the panties without exposing anything. "Fine." And added in a mutter, "I don't think I'm going to like this job."

"Truly a shame that your uncle indentured you to us for the next five years."

Christ in gator-land, but that was a terrifying thought.

"Of course, he might not have done that if you'd been a good girl." Vance swatted her butt with the yardstick he held. Thank God the skirt cushioned the blow—not enough. She was still tender.

"I am a good girl," she told him, hands on her hips, scowling. "You'll see." *Or if you hit my ass again, maybe I'll kick a paint can over.* "What should I call you?"

"Boss will do just fine." He handed her a paintbrush. "You can paint the trim."

He'd chosen a nice beige for the baseboards, and the walls would be a dark but rich cocoa. Much like the Feds' personalities. She concentrated on painting quietly. He'd put country-western on the player, and oddly enough, the work was more soothing than she'd thought. It was rewarding to take something ugly and make it beautiful.

After a bit, she realized he was standing over her, checking her work. The light-filled room brightened his beautiful eyes, showing the paler blue rays in the iris. She'd always loved blue eyes.

His hand stroked down her hair. "Very nice work, Miss Hart. You can take a break now. Lid on the paint. Brush in a Baggie."

After setting things to rights, she walked over to where he sat on one of the twin beds, looking at a catalog.

He patted beside him. "Sit here."

She dropped down and checked out what he was looking at. A BDSM equipment catalog. "Whoa. That's very cool. I've never seen one."

"Z lent it to us. Says this company is known for building both solid and comfortable." He turned the page and tapped a picture of a St. Andrew's cross. It was padded with leather. Gleaming eyebolts studded the ends of the arms. "You like crosses?"

She shrugged. "What's not to like?"

"How about this?" He opened the page to a vacuum bed with a

pump to pull the air out of a latex bag, letting the submissive breath through a tube.

A shudder ran through her. "Never. Not for me. Ever." Just the thought of being enclosed—almost mummified—like that could give her nightmares.

He nodded and opened the page to a bunch of bondage tables. "We'll probably get one of these."

One had the prettiest strapping system that— She realized he was studying her. "Uh. Right. Every dungeon should have one."

His lips quirked before he turned the page again. "Or at least a spanking horse."

God, those had to be her favorite. Like a hybridization between a picnic table and a sawhorse on steroids. Somehow being strapped into that doggy position was just too darned exciting.

He ran a finger down her cheek. "Definitely one of those." He set the magazine to one side. "I was looking through your history in the Masters' files. You got your bachelor's, worked a bit in a software company, before going to grad school for your Master's degrees. No marriage or engagements in all that time?"

She shook her head. And maybe now she knew why. She hadn't trusted anyone enough to lower her defenses. "What about you, Sir? Engaged? Married?" She gave him a slow smile. "The trainees don't have files on the Masters to check."

"There's a mercy." His mouth tightened. "I was married—and divorced—in college."

"Is that the wife who lied all the time?" Sally hated that he'd once compared her to some scumbag of a wife. He'd been so angry at the thought of being lied to.

"I did tell you that, didn't I?" Leaning back against the wooden headboard, he studied her. "And you? Are you a liar, Sally?"

Her chin came up. "*No.*"

He lifted an eyebrow.

Frigging A. "Okay, so faking orgasms was kind of a lie. And I guess if I say, 'I'm fine,' even though I'm not, it's kind of a lie too. But..." She bit her lip.

His eyes were starting to chill, and he crossed his arms over his chest. How could he look so relaxed and so threatening at the same time? "But?"

"But I do it because...because I don't—can't—share." *Don't hate me. I don't want you to hate me.*

"I know that." His voice was so neutral as to be unreadable.

"But I don't *cheat*. Cheating is different. I don't steal or betray my friends or poach boyfriends. And if you ask me if your hips look fat in a dress, I'll tell you the truth. And—"

When he grinned, she realized what she'd said. A flush crept into her face.

"Next time I go out looking for a nice gown to wear, I'll know who to take with me," he said.

Jeez. She looked down and muttered, "You know what I mean."

He tucked a finger under her chin and lifted. "I know what you mean." His eyes were the blue of a sunlit Iowa lake. "I want to get you to the point where you can share—honestly. That time will come."

The relief of his understanding made her eyes swim with tears.

He made a tsk sound, kissed her cheek, rose, and pulled her off the bed. "Time to put you back to work, little apprentice. You've lazed about long enough." Beside the kitchen area was a tall cabinet. Vance opened the three-foot box in front of it. Inside were straps, ropes, gags, spreader bars, blindfolds, and hoods. What every well-equipped dungeon should have. "I want you to put these away neatly in the cabinet."

Still feeling unsettled, she frowned at him. Boy, this wasn't much of a schoolgirl role-play, was it? He actually acted as if she was his apprentice. And he was being awfully polite. *Bad Dom.*

After putting a few items on the shelf, she found the nipple clamps—tons of them. He'd already gone back to painting the wall. So she put some clamps on a shelf. Tossed one at him. No reaction. Put a few more clamps away. Tossed another—aiming for his ass. Fine, fine ass. Hit. No reaction. Put a few more and turned to—

"Eeek!" Heart pounding, she looked up at the man looming

over her. Vance's face was grim, and jeez, how had he gotten so tall? He made her feel like a mouse. "Christ on a pogo stick, give a girl a heart attack, will you?"

He opened his hand, showing her the nipple clamps.

"Uh. Guess I just dropped them. Boss man, sir." She gave him a simpering smile. "Ooops."

"I see. Well, seems a waste to not put them to use." He undid the straps to her overalls, letting the bib flop down, exposing her breasts. He cupped his hand under one, weighing it, his thumb teasing her nipple into a point. "Odd that you're not wearing a bra—I thought breasts needed some kind of support."

She stared at him. What kind of a comment was that? "Um. Guess I just forgot. Boss."

"Well, I don't have time to let you run home and put one on, so we'll just have to make do. I wouldn't want anyone to think we're not taking good care of our little apprentice." He picked up two lengths of chain from the box and clipped a nipple clamp on each end of the chains. Four nipple clamps?

"I don't think I have four breasts, sir," she said politely. *Just trying to be helpful, boss.*

"Good to know." He put a clamp on her left nipple and tightened it right up to where she was starting to sweat. After placing the chain around the back of her neck, he pulled the flopped-over bib back up and clipped the other end of the chain onto the left edge of the material, using the second nipple clamp.

When he let go, the weight of the heavy denim pulled on the chain...and upward on her breast. "Ow!"

A smile flickered over his lips. And he did the other chain the same way on her right side, running the chain around to the material on the right. Her nipples were now holding the bib of the overalls up. *Ow, ow, ow.*

And the chains were pulling her nipples in an upward direction.

He grinned. "There, see? Support for your breasts. Maybe I should patent the system." He turned her around, the movement pulling on her breasts and making her squeak. "Keep working, little apprentice. I'll give you a break in a couple of hours."

What? Fuming, her nipples burning as she bent over the box, she considered throwing something really, really heavy at him.

Even worse, she had to pee something awful. She stood up and shifted from foot to foot, hoping he'd notice.

He turned his back on her.

Fine then. She started for the door.

"Sally, you don't have permission to leave." He hadn't even bothered to look at her.

Oh God, if she didn't get out of here, her bladder was going to explode. "Um." She couldn't ask. Dammit. Teeth gritted, she headed for the door.

"Sally, did you need something?"

Saying no...wasn't an option. "Yes, Sir." Maybe he'd just tell her to leave?

"Good answer. So, ask." His gaze met hers. Patient. Understanding. Resolved.

Demon fucking Dom. He was going to pay for pushing her. Her hands were cold, her heart beating too fast as she tried to get the words to come out. Why was it more difficult today? She pulled in a breath. "May I go to the bathroom, Sir?" came out in a rush.

He smiled at her, eyes lightening, and despite her anger, she felt warmed through and through. "Now that's a good request, sweetheart. Use one in the house and bring us both back some iced tea."

"Yes, Sir."

———✦———

After stopping to pet Glock in the front yard, Galen found Sally in the kitchen, holding two iced teas. And didn't she just look cute? In the Shadowlands, he'd thought schoolgirl clothing was particularly suited to her bubbly nature. The overalls Vance had found were even better. "Interesting way to hold up your clothes, imp." He gave a gentle tug on one chain and she winced...and her eyes dilated slightly.

She must have done something naughty to get in this fix. Good. He and Vance had hoped some role-playing might help her get her sass back. "What have you and Vance accomplished in the cabana so far?"

She gave him a slightly disgruntled look. "Painting."

So was she missing more domination or more sex...or something else? He might start with both and see if her reactions would give him a clue. "Nothing strenuous, eh? I daresay you'll have enough energy for this." He unbuttoned his jeans. He'd learned the benefits of going commando when there was a submissive in the house.

He saw the spark of delight in her eyes as well as something he remembered and hadn't seen enough of. If she was planning mischief, the corners of her eyes tilted up slightly, as if by holding her smile back, her eyes had to do it for her. It had to be the most adorable look he'd ever seen. But...what was the imp up to?

She turned her back to him, putting the glasses of iced tea on the counter. Facing him again, she dropped to her knees. After she pushed her braids out of her face, she enveloped him in sultry heat. Licking and sucking energetically, bobbing her head so energetically that his eyes almost crossed. She was damned good at sucking cock.

When she lifted her mouth away, she kept one hand caressing his balls as she looked up at him. She gave him a little smirk, then rubbed her mouth with her free hand before lowering her head again. She caressed his balls for a bit, building his anticipation, before closing her mouth over his cock.

His heart almost stopped with the shock. His cock felt as if he'd stuck it in the polar ice cap. "Christ!" Grabbing her hair, he pulled her off. As his blood pressure lowered and the roaring in his ears receded, he could hear her giggling. Lovely sound, but not for the right reasons.

Holding ice in her mouth to give her Dom a heart attack during a blowjob wasn't what he called a well-behaved submissive. *Don't laugh, Kouros.* He pressed his lips together. "Okay, Sally. You've had your fun." Holding her in place by her braids, he zipped his jeans with the other hand. Carefully. If he caught himself in the zipper, he was liable to scream like a girl.

She peeked up at him, starting to look a tad bit worried. Smart subbie.

"Eyes down." He glanced at the two drinks, chock-full of ice. "Didn't know you liked ice play, pet. But since you do—" He tossed her belly-down over the counter, so her legs dangled. Before she could move, he yanked up her short skirt and secured both it and her with his forearm, putting more weight onto her when she started to squirm.

The tall ceramic jar held a variety of wooden spoons. He picked one up and whapped her ass half-a-dozen times. Quick and hard. His dick perked right up at the satisfying sound of the impact on bare flesh.

Her short scream was almost as fun.

"I'm guessing you felt neglected," he said, waiting long enough for the burn to decrease before adding another six to her count. "You wanted attention?"

"No." She gripped the other side of the counter, holding on for dear life. A nice pink began to bloom on her ass. He avoided the places that still held marks from her previous punishment and made a mental note to go lighter with the cane next time. And considering her penchant for brattiness, there would undoubtedly be a next time.

"Your Doms are pleased to give you attention, Sally, but this might be the wrong way to ask for it." He smiled and dipped his hand in one iced tea glass. "I'll let you decide." Pulling out two ice cubes, well rounded and the size of a fingertip, he pushed one in her cunt and took a second to enjoy the shrill scream before he slid the other one into her asshole.

Her shriek of outrage made the windows rattle. He and Sam had enjoyed a conversation once about heartwarming screams. This one ranked near the top, he had to say. He leaned more weight on her ass to keep her from kicking herself off the counter.

To top off the lesson, he reddened her cheeks with a few more whaps of the wooden spoon, concentrating on the sweet crease between upper thigh and curve of the ass, judging carefully the effect. He wanted it to sting—didn't really want her crying. But every time she kicked, he added an extra-vigorous smack. She figured that out within three strikes. Clever girl.

After he stopped, he ran his fingers between her legs. Nice and slick. She liked being spanked. Liked being under control.

Some of her pushing was undoubtedly her way of getting more of that. He had a feeling some of it was sheer testing, her way of questioning if they'd still like her if she acted out. And perhaps if they'd manage the art of keeping control without making her feel insecure or unworthy. He stroked over her round ass, feeling her quiver under his touch.

There was nothing unworthy about this imp, but she wouldn't believe the words. Just time and consistency.

So, to be consistent, should he have her finish the blowjob? No. He grinned. He didn't want his pride and joys anywhere near a vengeful little mouth. It would be challenging to piss with a one-inch stub of a dick.

Instead he lifted her off the counter, set her on her feet, and pointed to the floor.

She dropped to her knees, expression fairly subdued. "I'm sorry, Master Galen," she whispered. "I won't do that again."

"Probably a wise decision," he said gravely. "We have the mold for making ice dildos, and from your response to a tiny cube, I think you wouldn't enjoy a larger one."

She actually cringed, and he had to cover his laugh with a faked cough.

"I'll be good, Sir," she promised.

Oh, he really doubted that. He pulled her to her feet and gave her a hug and a long, lingering kiss. Her stiff little body soon melted, undoubtedly like the ice in her hot cunt, and she softened against him. "I like you, Sally," he murmured into her hair. "You're a natural imp, and I like that part of you. We don't want to change you—just keep you within a few bounds."

Her head moved up and down on his shoulder.

He kissed the top of her head. "However, I was raised in Maine. Cold is not my friend."

When she giggled into his shoulder, he grinned. Yeah, this one was special.

—*—

Drew slammed the door of the rental jeep as he stalked to his brother's cabin. Fucking Feds. Fucking cops.

He probably should shut everything down, but letting the assholes win made him want to kill something. Someone. More someones. And he didn't want to lose a *business* that pulled in millions of dollars.

Nonetheless, he wasn't stupid. Right after the first woman he'd sold, he'd set up backup plans in case things started going sour. Today, he'd sent off the e-mails to his handful of managers to put the entire business on hold. Hopefully that would be enough to throw the Feds off the scent.

His thin lips tightened. He'd taken precautions while setting up the network. Compartmentalization was the key. The lower levels were contracted hirelings; each knew the one overseer who hired him. The managers knew only the overseers in their area. In turn, Somerfeld contacted only the handful of managers and only through e-mails.

But he hoped to keep the nucleus of the organization intact and ready to rebound once the FBI turned their attention elsewhere. He'd also given the managers a big bonus as an incentive to remain quiet. That was the carrot. The stick was the knowledge of how the Harvest Association dealt with informants.

He grinned. Who would have thought his pyromaniac brother would prove so useful?

HEARING THE CAR door slam, Ellis snapped the chain on the slave. Drew must be here. Maybe he'd have some work in mind. Ellis grinned and rubbed his thickening cock. He really enjoyed meting out vengeance for his brother. So much that he would leave behind a battery-operated wireless video camera in the room so he could record their pleading, the crying, and the screams as their skin started to crisp. A shame the cameras usually died about the same time.

But he'd accumulated a good set of recordings. In fact, he'd viewed one last night. *Oh yeah, indeedy yeah.*

He stepped into the doorway, breathing in the tang of the forest, the silence. His twin's face was tight, brows pulled together. "Is something wrong?"

"The Feds haven't stopped. I shut down the network." Drew

shoved past him to enter the cabin.

Ellis scowled. That meant no nice fires in his future. "That sucks." He leaned against the door, watching Drew unbuckle his pants. "What are you doing?"

"Got rid of my slave. Just in case."

"And you didn't call me to kill her?" Anger welled up in him.

"You only want to burn them, and I didn't have time for that. She's at the bottom of the ocean instead. And I'm without a fuck toy." Drew nodded to where Slut knelt with her forehead pressed to the ground, ass in the air. "I came to use yours."

"Whatever."

"Thanks. And don't break this one for a while. You'll get no new ones until I start the network back up."

All bad news. He wanted a fire, to sweat at its nearness, hear the roar as it caught and grew, watch the victim's eyes widen. The struggle. The itch was under his skin, pulling at him.

CHAPTER ELEVEN

"Hey guys." Sally walked into their home office, her clothing soaked from the rain, her backpack dripping, her feet dragging. Sometimes the world just sucked. And this had been one of those days.

"You're running late," Vance said without looking up from the paper on which he was making notes. The classic heavy metal of Deep Purple played in the background, showing he'd lost the toss for music selection to Galen.

"It's almost seven." Galen turned from his computer, saw her, and narrowed his eyes. "What's wrong, imp?"

Vance spun his chair around.

She looked at them, one on each side of the room. Unsmiling, lines cut into their faces. They looked as grim as she felt. "Just a bad day." She dropped her backpack on the floor and wrapped her arms around herself. Could she really smell death on her clothes, or was it her imagination? "I don't think I like reality."

"C'mere." Vance opened his arms, and she walked into them. He tucked her down on his lap, cradling her to his big chest. Over the past few weeks, she'd come to realize he gave excellent hugs, engulfing her in the wonderful feeling of being cared for. She pressed closer and rubbed her cheek on his soft T-shirt. His clean scent erased the horrible stench from her mind...at least for a moment.

"What happened?" Galen leaned forward with his forearms on his knees, his attention completely on her. The way he so readily put aside his work to focus on her was a little disconcerting. He made her feel...special. "Sally?"

"Nothing that bad." She sighed. "I just don't like dead bodies. Or violence."

Galen's smile held sympathy. "I've heard police stations tend to have a bit of those."

"So it seems." But she had her heart set on law-enforcement support. "Maybe Illinois will be quieter. I got an interview request from a sheriff outside Chicago."

Galen's mouth tightened at her reply.

"So how's your case against the Harvest Association going?" she asked, hoping to take his frown away.

Vance tilted her so he could see her face. "How do you know about that?" He glanced at the papers on his desk. "You can't look through—"

"Oh please. I have never, ever touched your desks." Or even hacked into their computers, which she thought entitled her to a halo, for sure. "You do realize the Shadowlands submissives always learn what's going on. Which means the trainees eventually know."

Vance's smile turned rueful. "Should have known. Sorry, sweetheart, I wasn't thinking. You're not the kind of person to sneak."

Oh, that hurt. Under the guise of being insulted, she pushed to her feet. God help her if they found out she'd snapped pictures of documents on Dan's desk. But that had been different, after all. Her *name* had been on those papers. "So, can you tell me anything?"

"Although this isn't classified, you may not discuss it with anyone." Galen gave her a stern look.

"No problem."

"We're in a foul mood because the activity in the Northeast territory has halted. Accounts we were monitoring have been closed."

"They stopped?" she asked. "Isn't that what you wanted?"

Vance took her hands. "We wanted to arrest the ringleaders, not have them go to ground like hunted foxes. The chances of finding them went down; the search will take longer."

"Oh." The bastard who killed that nice cop wouldn't pay for it? And he'd start running auctions again. Anger flared inside her. "That would make anyone mad." She twisted and squeezed Vance around the waist, wanting to give some comfort back. The way his arms tightened around her said he'd needed a hug.

When he released her, she glanced at Galen and saw, beneath the impassive look, a hint of longing. He didn't offer affection as readily, but she was slowly learning he needed her touch...as much as she needed his. With a small smile, she walked across the room, pulled him to his feet, and wrapped her arms around him.

His hug was long and grateful. Yes, he'd needed her care. Both Feds were driven, but Galen didn't put the job aside as well as Vance did. She could almost feel the cuts in Galen's soul.

His arms loosened, but before he let her go, he murmured against her hair, "Thank you, pet."

As she stepped back, he glanced down. His shirtsleeves were wet where they'd contacted her wet clothing. "You're soaked. Go shower and get into dry clothing."

"I'm fi—"

He jerked his head, back in his nonhuggable Dom mode. "Go."

Sheesh. A few nasty words nearly escaped her...until she met his darker-than-night gaze, and the words turned to smoke and dissipated as she walked away, managing—barely—not to stomp her feet. Bossy. Why sometimes she adored a bossy Dom and sometimes she hated one wasn't exactly clear. Why Galen could give her a rush of lust and still make her feel like kicking him wasn't clear either.

She picked up her backpack and glanced at Vance. He was laughing.

Bastards, the both of them.

She trotted up the curving stairs and detoured to the end of the hall. To Galen's bedroom. He liked antiques and dark wood. The cream-colored walls held paintings of lighthouses on the New England coastline.

His bed was covered with a burgundy-colored satin quilt and

felt like clouds, she knew. The time she'd brought him up a gooey chocolate-chip cookie just out of the oven, he'd eaten the treat, tossed her on the bed, and thanked her in a very...carnal...fashion.

She pulled in a breath. What that man could do with his mouth...

Focus, girl.

Galen kept his toy bag in a carved chest at the foot of his bed. The anal plugs were there, she knew, since they still occasionally "prepped" her beforehand.

Soooo... Her own backpack held colored markers. On the slimmest purple anal plug, she used her silver marker to draw a smiling face. Yeah, just like Happy from Snow White and the Seven Dwarfs.

For the ridged black anal plug, Sleepy seemed like a good pick. Her silver marker drew a slack face with half-closed eyes. The clear blue plug got Doc's big nose and tiny glasses. The oversize flesh-tone and cock-shaped one soon boasted a scowly face for the dwarf named Grumpy.

"Wonder how long it'll take him to notice?"

Would he recognize the dwarfs? She grinned. Considering how he'd teased her about her collection of Disney films, he very well might.

Mood lightened, she took a hot shower, scrubbing energetically and washing her hair to try to erase the prickling feeling that seeing violence left on her skin.

Once out, she donned old jeans and a soft pale blue top—*no red colors today, thank you*—and skipped the bra as well. *Want comfort.* The Doms wouldn't mind. They liked seeing her comfortable...and they'd never had a problem making her change.

She smiled. She liked knowing they wouldn't hold back when they wanted something. Somehow it reduced all sorts of anxiety. But they didn't play the Dom card all the time—not like Frank. They made sure she knew she had boundaries, but not so much that she felt as if she were on a choke chain.

Actually, despite the stress from the Assholyation case, they'd been very careful with her. Sweet and thoughtful. She stood in her pretty pale blue and ivory bedroom, which they'd filled with her belongings brought from her apartment. Her colorful pillows brightened the room...and drove the men crazy because they had to toss them off the bed.

They kept buying her things. Like the rich blue fuzzy robe Vance had bought her after finding her old bloodstained one in the trash. On the bedside tables were stained-glass lamps from Galen because she'd mentioned she liked to read in bed.

Thinking of the anal plugs, Sally bit her lip. She really was an ungrateful bitch, wasn't she?

Needing a way to show her gratitude, she pulled her laptop out. After booting it up, she checked her e-mail, going through the *Scum Sucker* folder slowly.

She sat back and pursed her lips. *Well.* G and V were right. Over the past few weeks, she'd managed to infect only three managers. All three had been contacted by someone even higher. The High Muckety-muck had ordered them to shut down and wipe their files. The Harvest Association was going on hiatus.

She glared at the screen. Well, didn't that suck?

Now what? The infected managers had replied to the High Muckety-muck, and, unless the boss's fire wall and antivirus program was brilliant, his e-mail system was the proud possessor of her virus. She'd reached the top and hadn't a clue what to do about it. Tracing him back to who he really was might be more than she'd planned. But her Feds were unhappy.

And an ex-student like her who was no longer inundated with homework had an awful lot of spare time, right?

She grinned. And, just for the hell of it, sent the three managers' e-mail addresses to the New York police station.

—✦—

Their little subbie was in a better mood, Vance saw, as she entered the kitchen. Dressed in one of the soft tops he and Galen had picked up, she looked incredibly cuddly. The slight tilt of her nose made her seem younger than her real age, and her wavy hair rippled across her shoulders. Glock lay in her arms, furry chin resting in the curve of her elbow.

"You look as if you're about five with a teddy bear," he said. Except for the way other parts of her bounced as well. Fuck, he loved her breasts.

Dimple flashing, she sniffed in a derogatory way. He was pleased to see her eyes clear and free of shadows. "Whatcha making? It smells good."

Vance glanced at the long windows running over the sink and dishwasher. The solar lights around the covered porch, down the sidewalk to the dock, were dimmed by the heavy rain. Lightning flashes illuminated the whitecaps on the small black lake. "Seemed like a good night for tomato soup and grilled cheese." He started to set the fixings out on the island.

After putting Glock down and washing her hands, Sally perched on a leather-topped stool. "What can I do?"

Vance smiled, enjoying her. There wasn't a lazy bone in her curvy body, and he was experienced enough to appreciate that. Aside from some defensive responses ingrained in childhood, the little sub didn't back away from anything—not work, not arguments, not sex, not laughter. "If you put together the sandwiches, I'll grill them."

"Got it." She started cutting cheese. "What will you and Galen do if you can't find the Association jerks?"

He put a shred of cheese between Glock's paws. After a sniff displaying his opinion of the inadequate offering, the cat took a delicate bite. *Fussy feline.* "We'll try awhile longer, but soon we'll have to put it on the back burner and start working a caseload here in Tampa."

"Is that good?"

Now that was a tough question. He took the sandwich from her and put it in the skillet. The butter sizzled, sending up a savory fragrance to join that of the soup. "Probably. Galen might take time off and have knee surgery." Before too long, they both might need to look at where their careers should go.

"Definitely surgery." Galen limped through the kitchen door and sat down beside Sally with a huffed groan. "I'm ready."

Vance shook his head, turning back to the stove. Odd to come to love the idiot like the brother he never had. It drove him nuts not to be able to fix his pain, to take the tightness from Galen's voice.

As if she'd followed his thoughts, Sally glanced between them. Her dimples showed again. "You know, I thought you guys were gay at first."

"We get that a lot." Galen gave her a sour look, then grinned at Vance.

Yeah, the rumor had come as a surprise. Years past, on one drunken night, they'd even discussed the gossip. They'd both been in the lifestyle for years and had friends in polyamorous relationships. But their boundaries turned out to be same. Male-male action didn't appeal. Fucking a woman with a brother was more than fun. Actually fucking the brother? Nope.

"How did you two come to be...whatever you call yourselves? Co-Doms?"

Vance smiled. Sally's curiosity was one of her most annoying—and appealing—traits. "We met in Quantico during training. Galen for the FBI; me for the DEA. Didn't see him again for years until coming face-to-face at a drug buy. Hell of a shock since we were both undercover—and on opposite sides."

Galen snorted. "I was part of the gang doing the buy."

"And I was with the seller as one of his enforcers." Vance shook his head. "The local cops got wind of the meet, and the whole thing turned into a clusterfuck."

Her eyes widened, and Vance realized his tone had turned grim.

Galen gave him a wry half smile.

The inside of the deserted warehouse had turned into a nightmare. Indiscriminate shooting, blood everywhere, bodies, men yelling...screaming. Vance had tackled a cop to keep him from getting shot and caught the bullet instead. The impact of the slug hadn't hurt...at the time...but the sound and the crack of his humerus breaking had twisted his guts. The perp's next shot had killed the cop he thought he'd saved. Blown his head to—

"Vance." Galen's even voice snapped him out of the memory.

Vance rubbed his hands over his face, feeling the dampness of sweat. The cop had had a newborn. *If I'd only been faster...* With an effort, Vance kept himself in the present.

His partner—Mama Kouros—watched him for a second and took up the story, drawing Sally's attention away. "After surgery, we ended up in the same hospital room. I'd caught a bullet in my leg." Galen gave a rueful glance at his knee. "After we were released, I stayed in his place until I could get around and until he could use his arm. Between us, we made one whole person."

And Galen had talked him into switching to the FBI. Turning away from everyone, Vance flipped a cheese sandwich and slid it onto a plate. Only a bit scorched. "Sally, can you dish up the soup?"

"Sure." Face pale, she stopped next to him at the stove and squeezed his waist. She stayed, pressing her warm body to his chilled one. Softhearted little sub. "Did you guys stay together?"

"Nah. But we stayed friends. When we were both assigned to New York, Galen dragged me into my first BDSM club. Taught me how to top."

"Really?" She set a bowl of soup in front of Galen and gave him a chiding look. "You corrupted an innocent youth?"

"Nah. I just bent him a bit," Galen said in a dry voice, as if he were a decade older instead of three years. "He had the last laugh, because I realized it was fun to partner up to torture little submissives." He fisted Sally's hair and gave her a light kiss that quickly turned long and deep.

Fuck. Vance was getting hard just watching.

Sally looked thoroughly aroused when Galen let her go.

Maybe they should skip the meal. Or on second thought, he'd almost forgotten this was Friday. "Eat up, imp. Galen and I are supposed to fill in as dungeon monitors tonight. And Z said he's missed seeing you." He grinned at her bounce of glee and told his partner, "How about you beat on her for a while tonight."

"I can do that."

An enticing anxiety appeared her wide brown eyes.

Galen added, "It'll be a good chance to break in that heavy flogger I bought last month."

The little subbie pulled in her lips as if to restrain a laugh, and her dimples appeared.

Galen was reaching for a sandwich and didn't notice.

Vance did. Might be an interesting evening ahead.

—✦—

Dressed in her favorite leather miniskirt and dark red bustier, Sally followed Galen into the Shadowlands with Vance behind her.

Ben, the security guard, stood behind his desk in the entry. His big-boned face split in a welcoming smile as he shook hands with Galen. "Little Sally. I thought you were back with us, but you disappeared again."

At the welcoming boom of his voice, she felt her eyes burn, and she leaned over the desk to kiss his cheek.

His face turned red. He might appear like an evil giant from some barbarian world, but he was one of the nicest men in the world.

"Good to see you, Ben." Vance slapped his shoulder.

The guys waited for her to stuff her shoes in a cubby before conducting her into the main club room.

Oh, it was good to be back. Music from Metallica mixed with the sounds of floggers and hands against bare flesh and moans. Yelps. Groans. The heady smell of leather. Even the air seemed to have a special weight and feel different from anywhere else in the world. She gave a loud sigh of happiness and noticed both Feds were smiling down at her.

"Come on, pet. Let's see what Z has in mind for us." Galen put his hand behind her to get her moving. Vance took her other side.

As they passed the dance floor, gazes turned toward them, and Sally felt rather like a sweet cocker spaniel between two massive guard dogs.

Uzuri was dancing, and her chocolate-brown eyes widened as she looked from the men to Sally. She gave Sally a thumbs-up.

Vance laughed.

"Glad we meet her approval," Galen said in a dry voice. But a quick peek upward showed he was smiling.

Sally grinned at him. Returning to the Shadowlands after

being with Frank, she'd felt as if she'd never reach a happy time, kind of like Sleeping Beauty's prince trying to chop through the forest of thorns to find his love.

This time she could almost see the Yellow Brick Road. She glanced up at the men. What would they do if she linked arms with them and started chanting, *Lions and tigers and bears. Oh my.*

Galen's razor-sharp gaze met hers. One eyebrow went up, and his hand moved from her back to her nape. "Whatever you're thinking," he said, "think again."

She scowled. "Only Master Z can read minds. How did you know I wanted to—"

His grin totally lifted her heart. God, he didn't do that enough. He bent and whispered in her ear, "It's a Dom secret."

"Oh fine." Maybe she'd decorate his canes and paddles too. Draw something girlie...pretty pink flowers.

Yeah.

At the bar, Vance lifted her onto a bar stool and stood at her right. Galen took her left.

She frowned. Did they always set themselves up that way? Were they protecting her or restraining her? Why did it make her feel so squishy inside?

Cullen spotted them and made his way down the bar, filling drink orders as he came. He paused to swat Andrea's butt and nuzzle her cheek on the way. Sally smiled, pleased at how Andrea's color heightened at his overt affection. Even though they'd been together for over a year, they still acted like new lovers.

"It's good to see you, love," Cullen said to Sally. He put his oversize hand under her chin, studying her face. "You look—"

She felt Vance put his arm around her waist.

Cullen's hand dropped, and he straightened. He looked at the Fed. "Sorry, gents. I forgot she wasn't still a trainee."

Sally froze. She really wasn't, was she? She remembered the thrill when the Masters had told her she'd be a trainee. How special it had been to belong somewhere and to have the Masters watching over her. The loss...hurt...like something had ripped away inside her.

Galen nodded; his face an unreadable mask. He set a hand on her shoulder, squeezed, and some warmth trickled back in.

"No problem," Vance said easily to Cullen. His arm stayed around her, holding her even tighter against his side as if to tell her where she belonged. "What time did Z want us on duty?"

Cullen checked a paper on the low counter behind the bar and pulled two gold-trimmed black leather vests from the shelves. "Looks like you're on now. Kouros gets the front of the room; you're in the back."

"Got it," Vance said.

Sally gave herself a mental shake and turned her mind to lighter—shallower—thoughts.

Like watching her Doms. How would they look in the dungeon monitor vests?

Vance dragged on the vest over his tight T-shirt. *Very nice.* Somehow his shoulders looked even broader, and the curve of his biceps stretching the shirtsleeves was more obvious.

Yeah, shallow thoughts weren't a problem at all—because she was having trouble not jumping his bones. With incredible control, she managed to keep her hands in her lap.

Galen turned to Sally. Somehow the vest over his dress shirt had a different effect, yet was equally amazing. His shirt was unbuttoned at the top, displaying just a hint of the steely, lean musculature. God, she just wanted to unbutton his shirt and lick her way down.

"We're only doing monitor duty for an hour," he said. "After that, we'll have time to play. Will you be all right by yourself?"

She sniffed. "Of course."

"Good." Galen touched his finger to the tip of her nose. "Remember you're no longer a free agent, pet. Stay here at the bar or sit with the other submissives."

As he strolled away, her mouth formed sarcastic words even though his statement made her feel all happy inside. *I'm not a free agent.*

Vance tilted her chin up and took a blatantly possessive kiss before smiling into her eyes. "Be a good girl now."

He headed off to the back before she finished sighing. As dungeon monitors, the two men would stroll through the room, checking each scene for safety, making sure the submissives were being treated well. Master Z was a great believer in the safe and sane practices, especially for the newer players. More experienced, hard-core players would practice RACK, and although "Risk Aware Consensual Kink" didn't exactly mean safe or sane, everyone agreed on the consensual part.

"Want a drink, Sally?" Master Cullen asked.

She looked up, up, up at the craggy-faced bartender. He and Ben sure made a girl feel height challenged. "How about a diet..." No, on second thought, any drink that sent her bladder into overtime was a bad idea. She still had trouble asking for stuff, and unlike Vance, Galen would probably make her wait until she ended up with her legs so tight together that she wouldn't be able to walk. "I'll grab some water from the munchie tables."

"You were told to stay—"

"Hey, Cullen, need a first-aid kit," a Domme called from the end of the bar.

"Coming," Cullen grabbed a white kit from under the bar and headed toward the Domme.

Galen had said to stay put. Sally sat for a second...considering. Doubtful that they'd notice if she visited the food tables.

The munchie table in the front corner was stocked with water, soft drinks, and finger foods. Master Z said having food available was not only healthy but also encouraged the community spirit of the dungeon, which was why the corner also had tables and chairs. The scenes were far enough away that people could talk without disturbing anyone.

Sally picked up a bottled water, cast her gaze over the table spread, and *yo baby*, there were quiche bites. God, she loved those. *Just a few though, girl.* Eat or drink too much and she'd totally regret it if the guys went for a heavy scene.

She was on her second bite when a couple of the younger Doms approached—although she probably shouldn't call them younger. They were her age, after all. But after being with the Feds, these two seemed...unfinished.

"Hey, Sally. Long time no see." Carter was tall and lanky. His glasses flashed in the light from the wall sconces.

"Hi, Carter."

Like Vance, Donald was football-player-sized. He moved a step too close, looked down at her, and the derisive twist of his lips made her uncomfortable. "Guess you wanted time off after your faking-it performances. Did you come back to give everyone another shot at getting you off?"

She straightened, anger flaming through her veins. Yes, she'd fooled him. Now she had to wonder why she'd ever agreed to play with him at all. "No, there won't be another shot."

His sneer was ugly, and he'd obviously taken her words as an insult.

Smart boy.

"Bet I can get Cullen to let me scene with you, *trainee.*"

"I'm not—"

"This submissive is not a trainee. She's mine." A hand curled around her arm, pulling her away from the two men, and Sally looked up to see Vance. His blue eyes had turned the color of gunmetal—hard and cold and deadly.

The startled look on Donald's face was—Sally bit the inside of her cheek to keep from snickering—wonderful. "Uh. Sorry. We didn't know."

"Now you do."

Sally's moment of pleasure lasted only a few seconds until Vance dragged her away from the quiche bites. "Wait. I wanted—"

"Disobedient submissives don't get their wants met." He stopped beside the bar and saw that Dan had replaced Master Cullen as the bartender.

Dan smiled at Sally, his eyebrows lifting at Vance's grip on her arm. "Got yourself in trouble, sweetheart?"

"I—"

"She did," Vance said, interrupting her with a stern look.

He hadn't given her permission to speak. *Got it.* Maybe she'd let him get away with the restriction, considering he'd just rescued her from asshole Donald.

Vance asked Dan, "Z still have collars in the spares basket."

"A collar? For Sally?" Master Dan's brows drew together as if he didn't approve. After a pause, he moved down the bar and pulled a laundry-sized basket from the bottom shelf. "Here you go." He set it on the bar.

Still holding Sally as if she'd run away, Vance poked through the items before pulling out a dark red collar. "This should work." He fastened it around her neck.

And as he fastened the buckle, as she felt the encompassing touch of the leather, her heart started to hammer. A few Doms had collared her as part of their idea of a scene, but she'd never felt like this. Like the collar was pulling her toward him, like his intense eyes were seeing past the leather and past her skin, like his hands were tying a leash on her soul. She could feel the tug of the attachment deep inside her. "Vance," she whispered, unable to look away from his hard face, his high, wide cheekbones, the jut of his strong chin.

He cupped her chin. "Look at you," he said softly, and the feeling of being possessed engulfed her.

As he straightened, he released her. "I like the way you look in a collar, sweetie. I think we'll put one on you every time we're here—and you can consider yourself collared by Galen and me until we take it off."

Words like that shouldn't make her heart feel as if it were break dancing inside her chest.

His lips turned up. "Silence from our little subbie? Do you understand, Sally?"

She swallowed. "I understand." Her voice came out so hoarse that he ran his finger around the inside of the collar again, checking to be sure it wasn't too tight. But it wasn't the collar that was choking her. It was the way her heart was pushing at her throat, as if it wanted out. Wanted to give itself away.

When had he become so...so important to her? So dear. God, she was such an idiot. He'd collared her for an evening; she wanted more.

"Sally, what's wrong?" He touched her cheek as his eyebrows pulled together.

No, don't be a fool. Players, the both of them. But they'd never stayed with a submissive this long. So...what did that mean? "I— Nothing." She forced her mouth to curve into a smile. "Thanks for keeping the other Doms away."

"My pleasure." He gave her another long look, making her want to drop to her knees and beg him to keep her. To love her.

Sally, you're a disgrace to your gender. "I should be fine now."

"Let's just make sure of that." He picked a leash—a damned leash!—out of the basket and clipped it to her collar.

Love him? She'd rather kick him right in his pride and joys.

He led her around the bar to the area where the subs liked to hang out. Sure enough, there were a few there now, including Gabi and one of the trainees—Maxie. If Gabi was in the subbie area, Master Marcus must be around somewhere. He didn't let her come to the Shadowlands without him. Maxie was probably taking a break and figuring out who she wanted to play with. The pretty blonde was totally sweet, although a bit on the insecure side, always trying to disguise what she called her fat ass.

"Ladies," Vance greeted them politely. "Sit, Sally."

She settled herself, and he picked up a chain from the floor beside the chair. One end of the chain was attached to an eyebolt in the floor; he secured the other to her collar. When in grade school, a 4-H friend had a pet goat that she'd tie up in the backyard. Yeah. Would Vance notice if she baaaed at him? She scowled at him instead.

"You have the prettiest face, even if you try to look upset." He tucked one finger under her collar to hold her as he kissed her. Softly, then completely aggressive. He tilted his head and took it deeper. Taking until her scowl melted, until her bones melted. Until her heart melted. Demon Dom.

Finished, he kissed the tip of her nose. "Stay put. Right here. If you unclip that chain, I'll paddle your ass—and not in a fun way."

She hadn't forgotten the sting of the wood or the unhappiness of disappointing him. "Yes, Sir."

"Oh yeah, that sounds nice," he murmured, running a finger over her wet lips before he strode away. Back to his DM duties, leaving her stuck in subbie-land. Well, at least the company was good.

"Stay put?" Gabi was giggling. "Miss Mouthy Sally gets an order like that and says, 'Yes, Sir'? Oh. My. God."

Maxie fanned her face. "I think it was totally hot."

"You're both right," Sally muttered, unable to keep from glancing over her shoulder at her Dom. She even liked the way he walked. Not graceful. Not aggressive, but...powerful. Darn football player with that linebacker's confidence of knowing he could flatten anyone in his path. People picked up on it and cleared out of his way. With a sigh, she turned back to the women.

"I wish I could find someone with that confidence. And authority. Some authority would definitely be nice." Maxie pouted. "In my last scene, the guy asked every two minutes if I liked what he was doing. 'Are you sure that's okay, Maxie? Not too tight?' He must have flunked out of Dom school. Seriously."

"Don't you hate that? When you give them the right to command, and they don't?" Sally shook her head. "Would you believe one man put nipple clamps on me...and the second I squawked, he took them right off. No Dom cookies for that wussy."

But her Feds...her majorly dominating Feds would earn an entire box of chocolate chip cookies.

"Oh man, I think I did a scene with that wimp. Totally forgettable." Maxie slouched back on the leather couch. "Last month, Master Sam put clamps on me. When I whimpered, his eyes lit up, and he tightened them until I was up on tiptoes." She gave a happy sigh. "There's no one like a Master."

"Well, even the Masters have weak moments." Gabi toyed with the blue streak in her shaggy red hair. "Marcus actually brought me breakfast in bed last weekend."

Sally considered. "I wouldn't mind that at all."

"I guess." Gabi shrugged. "But I was in a bitchy mood; I told him he was a failure as a Dom. A disgrace to the world of masterly men."

Maxie's eyes almost bugged out of her head. "No!"

Sally shook her head. Knowing Master Marcus, he'd probably laughed and—

"He spanked me so hard I had to eat breakfast standing up. I almost threw the eggs at him, but"—Gabi grinned—"even bratty submissives know there's a time to stop. And that's the wonderful part about it all."

Sally bit her lip, remembering the cabana. Her punishment. Or how Galen had pinned her facedown on the kitchen counter and taught her what ice felt like. And each time, how...settled...she'd felt afterward. She'd never felt like that before in her casual playtimes here. "Yeah. It is."

Gabi leaned back on the couch. "Since Marcus is helping out with a suspension scene, you have plenty of time to tell me what's going on with you and the Feds. Spill it, girl."

CHAPTER TWELVE

Waiting beside a freestanding St. Andrew's cross, Galen smiled as Vance brought Sally into the dungeon. She displayed the bravado that had initially attracted him, but now he could see the underlying vulnerability, which she'd concealed so well.

She'd done the homework he'd assigned. The essay. Even though she hadn't documented all her father had done, he could see the effect of the bastard's actions. And because she'd been writing—thinking rather than reacting—Sally realized how her thought processes had been twisted. She was an incredibly intelligent woman—but even under the light of her intellect, the problems weren't going to disappear overnight.

He'd been impressed at how doggedly she was trying. She had guts, all right.

And she also had a bubbly-as-champagne personality. Merely being on the receiving end of one of her smiles could lift his mood...and he found it disturbing how much she'd come to mean to him. Christ, where was he going with this?

He didn't want a permanent submissive. Or a lover. Or anyone who could be hurt by his job or actions...or anything. And yet the thought of losing her made him feel as if he'd run into a wall.

He and Vance needed to talk. Soon.

As the two approached, Galen crossed his arms over his chest. "Nice collar, pet." He ran his finger over the leather, brushing the satiny skin of her neck, listening to the hitch in her breathing.

Her lip trembled slightly, and he paused. The collar meant something to her, didn't it? Did she want to be claimed? By them? Possessiveness surged through him like a rising tide.

"She looks good in a collar, doesn't she?" Vance had his hand on her shoulder, displaying the same ownership Galen felt.

Odd how they'd never run into problems with territoriality. But Vance felt like the brother Galen never had—sharing with him felt...right. "She does." Galen lifted his eyebrows. "Was there a reason she needed one?"

Standing behind Sally, Vance winked and said gravely, "I'm afraid so. Tell him, Sally."

Her lip poked out. "I didn't do anything that awful. I just detoured to get some food before I went over to be with the other subs."

"I see." Testing her limits, was she? Was this just a normal response of someone independent to getting orders—or was there a need he and Vance weren't meeting and she was acting out to get their attention? The imp wasn't easy to read sometimes; she kept a lot buried deep. From the sulky set to her mouth, she wasn't going to share right now.

But maybe they could get her to a place where her reticence would be set aside. He started to speak before realizing something else. Vance wouldn't have collared her for just straying. "How did that work out for you?"

A flush crept up her face, and she dropped her gaze.

Vance said, "Some Doms weren't happy that she'd faked her orgasms. And the word that she isn't a trainee hasn't gotten around."

"Uncomfortable situation, eh, pet?"

Without looking up, she nodded, all defiance gone.

And his heart ached for her. She might have dug her own hole, but— "Sally, you took your punishment. As far as Vance and I— and other experienced Doms—are concerned, your slate is clean. A good Dom won't throw past mistakes in your face."

Her gaze lifted, her eyes a liquid brown. "Thank you, Sir."

"No thanks needed." He glanced at the cross. "We're planning to play with you a bit. I have a craving to dispense a flogging.

Vance will warm you up and decide on your restraints."

Vance smiled and turned her around. "Hold still now." He slipped her top off, his eyes lighting as her breasts were exposed.

Galen shook his head and leaned against the wall, facing her, and settled in to watch his partner play. He'd seen the clothespins case in the toy bag. Galen might like impact toys, but Vance definitely enjoyed teasing breasts.

After Vance had savored Sally's breasts for a while, he started placing the clothespins, taking a pinch of skin several inches from the nipple and putting the clothespin on, then moving down an inch to set another one. By the time he finished, Sally had a circle of clothespins on each breast.

Brave pet, she'd only whimpered once and suffered through the rest. She looked a little glassy-eyed now, but not in subspace. Galen planned to get her there...eventually.

Vance unzipped her short leather skirt and yanked it off her hips. Sally's eyes widened at the move, and Galen grinned. Apparently she expected that kind of aggression from him, not Vance. *Surprise.*

"Open your legs," Vance ordered her. He stepped behind and reached around her hips. His fingers opened her labia, exposing her to Galen's sight. "She feels wet and swollen. What do you think?"

He thought her flush now included embarrassment as well as arousal. Experienced submissives were used to being naked...it was fun to give them back that exposed feeling. And he loved keeping Sally off balance. As he studied her silently, her flush increased.

But he did enjoy the view. Her inner labia were puffy and gleaming slickly. Her clit was already swollen, a dark, glistening pink and poking out from the hood. *I think she'll get off quickly.* But that wasn't the plan. "I'd say she's ready for me."

An obvious tremor shook her short body. Yes, she was definitely ready for him. He tilted his head toward the St. Andrew's cross.

"Wait, sweetheart. I want access to your breasts." After eyeing Sally's height, Vance adjusted the footboards—pedal-like boards that could be screwed into the bottom of the X frame to position the submissive higher on the cross. In this case, so that her breasts wouldn't be pressed into the center of the X.

"Up you go," Vance said and helped her step onto the boards, facing the frame. She reached up and closed her hands around the eyebolts, putting her top half into a V position. With the higher position, her stomach rubbed on the center of the X, and her breasts pushed out between the wooden arms.

Vance walked around in front of her and smiled. "You know I like restraints. I consider them a visible symbol of the trust between a Dom and a sub. But tonight, I'm not going to use any. You'll stay in position—because we want you to. Can you do that?"

Her breathing had slowed as her body unconsciously prepared itself, as her mind slid her down the path to submission. "Yes, Sir."

"We're going to start light, baby girl," Galen said. After moving behind her, he ran his hand through her rich brown hair and used an elastic hair tie from his pocket to anchor it on top of her head and out of his way.

She looked over her shoulder at him. Her eyes held a touch of anxiety and—

His heart seemed to expand into a glowing ball of pleasure. "You trust me, don't you?" For that was what he saw in her eyes. Open, defenseless trust.

"Yes, Sir," she answered without thinking.

This was the wonder of being a Dom, that someone would let him have control over her, that she trusted him to care for her when she did. "Remember you have a safe word. This time I want you to use yellow if I get close to your limits. Is that clear?" He ran his hand up her neck, kissed her slowly. Soft, sweet lips.

"Yes, Sir. I will."

"All right then." Galen picked up his light deer-hide flogger and used it to warm up her skin, walking back and forth behind her, striking her upper back, occasionally going down on a knee to work over her pretty, round ass. Her golden skin colored beautifully to a rich red color and gradually showed a slight pebbling. Her breathing evened out, came slower as she sank into the sensations.

He loved watching the descent, the slide of tension out her body.

Sally's head was still up. Galen chose a heavier flogger and positioned himself where he could see the side of her face as he laid the leather on her back. Harder. Her expression would tighten, and she'd breathe out through the burst of sensation. Not real pain—not yet. But getting there. A pretty sight, watching her take what he gave her.

He moved behind her and increased the intensity.

CHRIST IN NEVER-NEVER land, that felt as if she were being slammed into by a million tiny hammers. He wasn't going to go easy on her, was he? She closed her eyes and inhaled through the edgy pain, through the edgy response that followed. The arousal simmering under her skin kept growing, even though the last strike had been powerful enough to knock her body forward against the cross and jostle the clothespins around her breasts, adding a whole new level to the sensations inside.

Whap. Whap.

No time to breathe between. Each blow just a little more forceful than the previous ones. She filled her lungs and opened her eyes. Galen was beside her. His dark gaze swept over her, studying her, before meeting her eyes. "You're doing good, pet. Give me a number for the last couple."

He wanted to see if their assessments added up. How hard had the blows been? "Maybe six?" God help her if he ever got to a ten.

"About what I thought. Can you take more?"

Oh, she wanted to; she'd do anything for him. And she wasn't close to her limit yet. "Yes, Sir."

The small smile of approval made her melt inside and resolve to take anything he could give her. Her mouth firmed.

Rather than looking pleased, he frowned. "I expect to hear yellow if we get to that point, Sally. Don't disappoint me."

"Okay. Yes, Sir." *Yes, Master. My Master.* When he looked at her like that, when she knew that he saw *her*...she could take so much, much more.

"Good." He unbuttoned his black shirt and tossed it to the side. He was pumped up by the flogging, and his olive skin stretched tightly over his exquisite musculature. Streamlined steel. A triangle of black hair on his chest pointed down toward his black jeans. Tight abs. God, he had a great body.

As he used a figure-eight technique, he moved behind her, hitting her on the left upper back and swirling the tails before striking the right upper. The left slightly lower. The right. He'd lightened his blows, and the flogger felt wonderful. She had a feeling her endorphins were kicking in, flooding her system with happy juice. Leaning her head against her arm, she waited for the next one.

A burning feeling detonated in her outer breast. "Ow!"

Vance stood in front of her, holding the clothespin he'd just removed.

The flogger hit her back, shoving her into the cross. Another clothespin came off, and she squeaked at the sharp pain. The flogger hit a second later.

"Breathe, pet." Galen's cheek rubbed against hers as he checked in with her. His voice was as dark as his eyes.

Tilting her head, she stared at him, seeing his enjoyment with the scene, with the flogging, with her submission. With her.

She sank into his pleasure, opening under it like a night-blooming flower. And she pulled in a breath.

"Good girl." As Galen stepped away, she managed to turn her face forward and meet Vance's dark blue gaze. The same pleasure showed there.

And the floor seemed to drop from under her feet. Everything in her wanted to continue, for them to push her to new places, take her higher.

As if she'd spoken the request, Vance nodded. With the next clothespin, he wiggled it slightly, teasing her, and just as the flogger struck her back, Vance removed the pin. Her back felt as if she were glowing, her breasts...the sensation was...was...not quite pain, but a thick burn, like a syrup of sensation. She was starting to feel as if she'd been breathing the dentist's gas. Wonderful, wonderful place.

The Doms worked together, clothespins coming off, flogger like punctuation. Heat increasing front and back. Over and over.

Galen moved to her other side, using his backhand, and damned if it wasn't harder yet. Vance had removed all the clothespins.

Her breasts were swollen, and each throb somehow coincided with the pulsing in her pussy. The flogger blows were sending her higher, making her giggle even as some tears spilled over.

"She's sliding into subspace." Vance moved into her field of vision, and he had the nicest smile.

"Adorable, isn't she?" Galen's voice was like the velvet dress her mommy had made her. "Time for something a little harsher."

With a contented sigh, she leaned her face against her arm, waiting for the next thumpety strike.

"What the hell?" Galen sounded so pissed off that Sally blinked and turned her head.

Oh shit. The pretty fog in her head receded.

Standing over his toy bag, Galen held up his heaviest flogger. The strands had been tied into pretty bows until the business end looked like a mass of ruffled leather flowers.

Don't laugh; don't laugh. Giggles rose so fast and violent that she choked, trying to hold them back until her ears were ringing. She couldn't...and then she was laughing so hard she had to hold her stomach. *Oh God, stop.* The stunned expression on Vance's face set her off again until her sides hurt worse than her back. A wave of laughter spread from one side of the dungeon to the other. Oh man, they were going to kill her. Tears streamed down her face as she gasped for breath.

Warm hands closed over her breasts. "You're in big trouble, sweetie," Vance murmured, playing with her breasts, rolling one nipple and the other, sending molten zings down to her clit in surges of pleasure. He ran his fingers over the tender areas where the clothespins had been, and her entire body turned as liquid as a snowman on a sunny day.

With a glint in his sharp eyes, Vance tugged at her nipples until she moaned for more. His scent wafted to her, crisp and bright, like a spring morning in Iowa. And when he kissed her, she wanted him so bad that if they'd been in private, she have tried to rip his clothes off.

His tongue invaded, played; his lips were firm. His hand cupped the back of her head, positioning her so he could take her deeper until her lips were swollen and her body hummed with need.

"All yours," he said eventually, and he wasn't speaking to her. To Galen? *Oh God.*

She felt Galen's warmth a second before his body leaned into her from the rear. Even through his heavy jeans, his erection was solid and thick against her buttocks. He closed one hand over her breast, using it to anchor her to him. His other hand cupped her face, turning her so he could take her mouth in a punishing kiss. Even though her breasts were aching and tender from Vance and the clothespins, when Galen pinched one nipple, she felt only want. Even her pussy felt swollen as she rubbed her bottom against his erection.

He released her, smiling at her whimper of need. "You need a spanking, little brat."

Naked over his knee. "Okay," she breathed.

And he laughed. "No. Instead you're going to take three more. About an eight. Can you do that?"

"Is that my punishment?"

His flash of a grin seemed to ignite whole new areas of need. "No, pet, that's just fun. Mostly for me. And you'll take it because I want you to—won't you?"

Oh, when he looked at her like that, she'd do anything. His eyes softened at the answer in her face, and he ran his finger down her heated cheek. "That's my girl."

Yes. Please, yes. She breathed out and tried to collect herself despite the happiness running through her.

He shook out the flogger he'd used before. Not the one with the pretty bows. Heh. At least he wouldn't be using that heavy sucker today. Her attempt not to smirk failed miserably.

He must have seen, because he shook his head. "Any flogger can reach a level eight, pet. It just means more work on my part." He looked her up and down. "Curve your shoulders in."

To make sure he didn't hit a shoulder blade. *Oh man.*

"Look at me, sweetie." Still in front of her, Vance wrapped his big hands over her wrists, pinning her to the cross. Restraining her physically for his partner. One holding, one hitting. God, she loved being right here, overpowered and taking it. Her insides turned molten. Vance bent slightly so she could look into his eyes. She pulled in a breath. Exhaled.

Wham!

The pain exploded in her upper back as her body slammed against the cross. Tears wavered, blurring her vision as she pulled in a breath, and then, like a slide into a tub, the pain turned to a sweet heat that filled her body. No one had ever hit her so hard.

And yet—she wanted another.

"Brace your forearms on the cross," Galen said.

Vance helped her adjust her position before securing her again.

"Breathe," Vance murmured.

In. Out.

Wham!

Ow ow ow. She shook her head as the burn turned liquid and wonderful.

"One more, baby girl." Galen's voice came through the surging in her blood, through the endorphins buzzing into her brain, as she slid right back into her happy place. *Happy, happy, happy.*

Vance's face wavered in her vision as he studied her. She could feel Galen's watchful gaze like a pressure on her side. "Green," she whispered. "I'm green."

The corners of Vance's eyes crinkled, and he tightened his grip on her wrists.

She pulled in a breath. Let it out.

Wham!

Her eyes went unfocused as the impact reverberated through her whole body. Past the surface, deeper, shaking into her bones. Blast, burn. The sweet rush like hot rain flowed over her skin. She was sliding in and out of subspace, happy and warm and yet...there.

Something pressed against her back, startlingly cool, ever so wonderful. It rolled over the burning skin on her shoulders, working up and down. It must be the long metal cartridge that she'd found in Galen's bag, the one for which she couldn't figure out the use. What a nice, nice use. With a sigh, she put her head back on her arm and let him care for her.

"Sally." When she slid back into the present, Vance kissed her lightly and opened his hands, releasing her wrists. Galen put an arm around her waist to steady her.

As Vance headed for the cleaning equipment, Galen helped her over to a couch against the stone wall. He sat down and pulled her, facedown, across his thighs.

He wants a blowjob now? She tried to reach for his zipper and had her hand caught.

"Lie still, Sally." The splash of liquid between her shoulder blades made her gasp. The feeling of him massaging the superbly cool gel into her burning skin made her eyes almost cross.

He hit a tender area.

"Ow!" She tried to push up, but his free hand was on her collar, holding her in place. God, she loved that feeling. "Easy, baby girl," he murmured. "This will help the swelling and keep you from bruising."

But she kind of wanted a few bruises to remember this by. Because she'd done it. Taken it.

Liked it.

He continued until her whole back felt as if an arctic mist had settled on a bad sunburn.

"I'm proud of you, Sally," he said, his voice grave and impossible to disbelieve. "I asked you to take something, and you did. For me. That makes me feel good." He massaged her scalp gently.

With a sigh of happiness, she laid her cheek on his muscled thigh and relaxed into his care. "But I didn't think you were a sadist," she whispered.

He caressed her cheek, and she could smell the leather on his skin as well as the hint of shaving lotion he'd used earlier. His beard growth was heavy enough that he often shaved twice a day.

Because of her.

His relaxed chuckle made her feel good, as if their scene had pushed him to the same happy place she was in. "I'm a Dom, and I like taking a submissive to her limit and an inch beyond. Pain is one of the easiest ways to get there."

She'd definitely gotten there. No one had ever pushed her as Galen did, demanded what he did. And somehow, Vance's hands-on restraint had felt like the same demand—and had let her go further. She'd submitted to the Masters before, but never…never like this. Never been taken so far. Been left so clear and sparkling inside.

As she rubbed her cheek against his thigh, she thought about the creek in the back pasture in Iowa. Frozen until the spring thaw. Then the little stream would flood, and the dirt and debris of the long winter would be scoured away, leaving the water so clear that even the tiny stones on the bottom could be seen.

The couch dipped as Vance sat down. He picked her up and set her in his lap. Her knees and calves rested on Galen's thighs. Despite the discomfort of having Vance's iron-hard arm behind her tender back, she loved being in his arms. With a happy sigh, she laid her cheek against his broad chest.

He pulled the elastic tie from her hair and tossed it to Galen. Her hair spilled down over her shoulders in a soft, cool wave.

After tucking the tie away, Galen picked up a blanket—Vance must have tossed it on the couch—and spread it over her legs and stomach. Snuggly, snuggly, snuggly. He smoothed the fabric, stroking her legs. "Should I ask what else you did in my toy bag?" he asked.

She started and bit her lip. Christ in pigtails, if she told him about the anal plugs, he'd probably hitch her to the cross for more flogging.

Vance's chest bounced with his laugh. "From her expression, I'd say you better check the rest of your equipment."

She tried not to grin. Vance liked to examine his bag's contents before a scene, but Galen usually cleaned and set up his stuff right after using it. He rarely messed with his bag before a scene. That's why she'd chosen to sabotage his stuff rather than Vance's.

Well…and because she'd been mad at him. At the time.

Galen gave a grunt of exasperation. "You are a sore trial to me, pet. So. Aside from my toy bag, have you done anything else of which we'd disapprove?"

"Sometimes you really sound like a Harvard grad." Her attempt at humor didn't help the tightening in her stomach. If they found out about her hacking, the two Feds would have her head—or worse, have her arrested. They'd be so pissed off. They must never, ever find out.

The silence of both of the men warned her that she'd woken their suspicions. But she…couldn't manage to lie. She didn't want to lie. "Nothing that concerns you."

Vance tightened his hand on her shoulder, his eyes shrewd. "Everything about you is of interest, sweetheart." His lips tipped up. "Especially if we wouldn't be pleased."

How could she feel so happy with their attention—and so worried? When she dragged her gaze from his, she realized Rainie stood nearby, waiting to be noticed.

Yay, saved by the girl. "Hey, you waiting for one of us?"

Quite properly, Rainie didn't talk to the submissive but waited for a Dom to speak.

"Go ahead, Rainie," Galen said.

"Sir, if you're done, Master Z hoped you'd join him and the others in the main room. They're near the center."

"All right. Please tell him we'll be there shortly."

Dismissed, Rainie moved away, shooting a worried glance back over her shoulder at Sally.

Galen leaned forward to tap Sally's chin. "We'll discuss your refusal to answer another time. For right now, how does your back feel?"

Thank you, God. She leaned forward and wiggled her shoulders. "I'm okay."

"Good. You may put on your skirt," Vance said. "Leave your breasts free for my enjoyment."

As she slid off his lap, she felt her face flush. Yet a thrill ran along her nerves. She'd always envied subs who had their own

Doms.

As a trainee, once a scene was over and aftercare done, she would have been sent back to work. But the Feds considered her "theirs," even if temporary, and instead of dismissing her, they were keeping her close. For more than just a scene. Had she ever been so happy?

"Drink this, imp." Galen handed her a bottle of water before putting his hand on her back—in a nonsore area—to keep her beside him. She looked up to see Vance on her other side, and the…rightness…of the arrangement settled into her heart.

The Masters and Mistresses—the ones with the official titles—were in a sitting area in a rough circle. Olivia and Anne bracketed Cullen on a couch. Most of the rest sat in chairs, with Sam, Nolan, and Jake standing. Even Jake was there.

"Galen, Vance." Master Z motioned toward an empty couch.

After putting Sally's water on an end table, Vance sat down in the middle of the couch with Galen to his right. The two Doms pulled her down and arranged her so she lay, faceup, her head and shoulders on Galen's thighs.

Her butt rubbed against Vance's jeans. *Ouch, ouch, ouch.*

"I don't see any other submissives, Z. Is it a problem if Sally is here?" Galen asked.

When Sally turned her head, trying to see, Galen laid his hand on her cheek, stalling her. "Close your eyes, pet," he said softly. "You're here for our pleasure, not your entertainment."

"You're welcome to have your toy," Master Z said, and she could hear amusement in his voice. "We released the others to spend time together and have something to eat."

Oh, that sounded like much more fun. Sally tried to sit up.

Galen put his hand between her breasts, pressing down strongly enough to push the air from her lungs. "Did I give you permission to move?"

But… She looked at Vance, who had a softer heart. Maybe…

He met her gaze, reading her question. "No."

Fine. Maybe she wasn't certain if she loved them—but she was positive she didn't like them right now.

OH, THEY WERE on a little subbie's shit list now. Vance smothered his laugh and saw his partner doing the same. The imp was in for a shock. They hadn't planned to get her off so publicly but, in all reality, he didn't mind the audience. The behavior of other Doms—especially other Masters—had gotten fucking annoying. Yes, she'd been a trainee for a long time, so the Masters considered her under their care. But that time was over.

He figured that both the collar around her neck and playing with her now would be an unspoken way of drawing a line in the sand.

"Before we start, tell me what happened to the man who attacked Sally?" Z asked Dan.

"Borup did some time in county and has to go through anger management and alcohol counseling." Dan frowned at Galen and Vance. "For some reason—which I don't want to know anything about—he sent Sally's landlord more than enough money to cover cleaning, repairs, and replacements for what he busted."

That "reason" had been Anne. The bounty hunter winked at Vance. Mistress Anne not only despised abusive Doms, but she considered it a treat to beat the shit out of them, and she'd persuaded Vance to let her take his place in giving Borup a lesson.

"Do I need to take steps?" Z asked.

"Don't think so, Z." Anne smiled sweetly. "Not only has his health suffered recently, but rumor says some annoyed Fed made him think he could get picked up for slavery."

Sally opened her eyes to stare at Anne and Galen in disbelief.

"Indeed." Z's lips quirked. "In that case—"

"No, I won't!"

Vance turned at the woman's shout and saw Uzuri.

Hand on her hip, the trainee shook her finger at one of the newer Doms.

A few shades darker than Uzuri, the Dom looked absolutely startled. Six-two, probably two-ten pounds—all muscle. Shaved head, dark brown eyes, classically handsome. Considering his looks and the way he was narrowing his eyes, the man wasn't accustomed to being turned down. "Why?"

She tossed her head defiantly, making the beads in her kinky hair clatter. "You only want me because I'm black."

"I have watched you do scenes with white Doms. Might you have a problem with black skin, young miss?" The man had a faint English accent. He took a step closer.

"No, dude. You do." She shoved him back, a baby bear cub taking on a grizzly. "You're all tied up in race issues. You don't see me—just the color of my skin." She spun on her heel and walked away from him, tossing back over her shoulder, "You come find me if you ever cut free of your bullshit and decide you like me—*me*—not what you see on the outside." She stomped across the room—and out the exit.

Vance glanced at Z, curious as to how the Shadowlands owner would handle the Dom-sub altercation.

"Well," Z said after a pause. "Normally, I'd bring her up short for her display of temper to a Dom, but *if* what she said is true, I can't disagree with her conclusions. Comments?"

"Huh, that's not a problem I'd have caught," Anne commented. "How well does Alastair know her?"

"He played with her once last winter in a scene I arranged. I figured they'd suit since he does prefer African-American submissives." Sam crossed his arms over his chest. "Didn't consider how a woman might not take to that. Want me to talk with him?"

Z steepled his fingers and considered. "No. Let's see how this plays out. She did present her objections quite eloquently."

Jake snorted. "No shit."

"If she's that pissed off, the poor bastard might need a guard." Anne grinned. "Her idea of revenge can be—"

"Fucking warped." Cullen finished for her. "Like supergluing all Nolan's ropes together? Or the miniature bag of Sam's? I about busted my gut with that one."

The other Masters roared with laughter, adding in other Uzuri tales.

"What's a miniature bag?" Vance asked Sally under his breath.

"She switched out all his toys and put in doll-sized ones. All his rope was replaced by yarn. She made him a mini single-tail. She even found clothespins that were only an inch long."

The light in the imp's eyes was a bit worrisome, and Vance decided to lock up his bag. Maybe his whole room.

"She made a pretty sight when you used that entire bag of tiny clothespins on her, Sam," Raoul said.

"The begging wasn't too bad either," Olivia added with a grin. "How much of a sense of humor does Alastair have?"

"I do believe Uzuri saves her pranks for the Doms she likes," Master Marcus said. "Hopefully, she doesn't like Alastair enough to attend to him."

"Doesn't matter. He was gone all spring, and he's returning to Europe for the rest of the summer," Cullen said.

"Good enough." Z looked around the circle of Masters. "I think the altercation serves as a good introduction to the matters I want to discuss."

Z began to talk about the future of the Shadowlands, how the membership had changed and now had a greater percentage of experienced Doms. However, the Masters group had also evolved. Originally, most had been single. Now, aside from Jake, Anne, and Olivia, they were all in relationships, and—Z included—were having difficulties juggling family and club obligations.

Vance shifted uncomfortably and met Galen's concerned eyes. Apparently, he'd also caught how they weren't considered "single" Masters anymore. A serious relationship wasn't in the plans...and yet, when Vance collared Sally, it had felt right. In fact, he couldn't see a future without her in it. He and Galen definitely needed to have a talk.

"Did you have a solution in mind, Z?" Olivia asked.

"I have some ideas to run past you." Z leaned forward. "We already plan to expand the Masters group with more single Doms. And we need at least one Master who prefers male subs."

Cullen nodded. "There are a few who might suit."

"Meantime, I want to phase out the trainee program."

Under Vance's hands, Sally stiffened. Considering how she worried, she probably thought she or someone had done something wrong.

Z looked at the little sub and gave Sally a smile she couldn't see. "Not because of problems with the current group, but with the lack of single Masters, the trainees don't get enough attention. I want to focus on finding them Doms. Once that is accomplished, I'll put the program on hiatus."

"Gonna hire barmaids?" Nolan asked.

"If needed." Z glanced toward a group of submissives who were chatting and eyeing the Doms at the bar. "How do you feel about taking volunteers? Serving is still an excellent way for quieter submissives to meet the members in a nonthreatening fashion."

Cullen scratched his cheek and nodded. "I like it. I can keep a sign-up sheet at the bar."

"Might could be we'd have some fun with it." Marcus unbuttoned his suit coat and stretched out his legs. "I'd like to be able to *draft* submissives who need a kick in the pants to meet more people."

As the discussion continued, Vance felt Sally's thigh muscles bunch under his palm, and he glanced at his partner.

Galen was running his fingers over her swollen breasts, teasing the lingering, red dimples left by the clothespins. Circling her nipples. Pinching. After a minute, he slid closer to the middle of the couch and Vance.

Without the support of his thigh, her head tilted back, further enforcing she had no say in what they'd do to her. A quiver ran through her.

Vance smiled. She liked being helpless. She might fight them, but she loved the feeling of being overpowered. Mastered.

With an ear tuned to the discussion, he watched as she reacted beautifully to Galen's teasing. Their earlier scene had left her aroused—now Galen increased that need.

Might as well lend a hand. Vance slid his fingers under her skirt to the soft, silky skin of her inner thigh. At the apex of her legs, he leisurely explored. Slick folds, puffy enough to flower outward, leaving her entrance open to his touch. With his free hand under her ass, he slid her farther down on his lap until her ass rested on his left thigh and he had a better angle to play. He pressed his finger inside her and watched her color heighten.

With a glance of amused annoyance, Galen shifted to using his left hand and continued playing with her breasts.

Leaving his finger barely inside her cunt, Vance spoke to the Masters. "We have to make a trip to New York next weekend—hopefully for not more than a few days. Unless she has other plans, Sally will stay at our house, but we'd appreciate if someone checked in with her every day. The Shadowkittens are welcome to visit her at the house."

"As long as they stay away from the toy bags," Galen muttered.

Raoul, who'd been in the dungeon when Galen found his abused flogger, laughed.

Vance glanced at Sally who had lifted her head to frown at him.

GOD, SHE WISHED they'd stop playing with her. Every touch made her needier, and sheesh, they'd hardly get her off here in front of the others. Sally couldn't quite believe they were being so...blatant.

And now, they were going to fly off and leave her alone in their house? Why the hell would she want to be there without them? Sally noticed Vance's frown—right, she was supposed to keep her eyes closed—but she had *concerns*.

Vance's brows pulled together. *Uh-oh.* Galen could intimidate without frowning, but Vance... When Vance actually got annoyed, he was downright scary.

With a huff of disgust, she laid her head back. But before she closed her eyes, she scowled back at him. Abandon her like a stray puppy, would he?

"Bad move, pet," she heard Galen say to her very quietly.

Like there was anything they could do, right here in front of—

Vance rammed two fingers into her, forceful and fast, and the slick burst of pleasure through her sensitized tissues was like a jolt of electricity. She gasped.

He didn't stop, thrusting firmly over and over until her need gathered inside her, tightening, heading for an orgasm.

No. No way. Not in front of all the Masters during a *meeting*.

She tried to move, to make him stop, and felt Galen's palm press down just below her throat. With his left hand, Galen continued to play with her breasts, rolling the nipples between his fingers, increasing the pressure to pain before easing back.

She opened her eyes and shook her head. *I won't get off.*

"Not your choice, is it?" Galen said, still so quietly.

Not here. I don't want to come here. She turned her head. Raoul and Marcus and the Mistresses were discussing something. Master Z looked...pleased. But Dan and Cullen were staring at the Feds in disapproval.

She stiffened. She'd known she shouldn't be here. Shouldn't be aroused—

Vance paused, his fingers still deep inside her. "Problem with the way we handle our submissive, *Masters?*"

At Vance's slight emphasis on the final word, Cullen stiffened, his mouth tight. Then he shook his head and pulled in a breath. "Hell. We try to ensure the trainees don't attach to us. Guess we should do the same for ourselves. We're all pretty possessive."

Sally felt tears sting her eyes. She hadn't realized that they actually...cared.

Dan narrowed his eyes at the two FBI agents but finally leaned back in his chair, the tension leaving his body. "I knew you'd be good for her. I wanted that. But I didn't realize how rough it would be to see her move on. She's been—was—a trainee a long time." He gave Vance a chin lift. "Sorry."

"Not a problem," Vance said.

"Back as a pup, I dated a young thing whose daddy was a cop. My balls'd shrivel up at his glare because I knew he'd geld me if I made his baby unhappy." Cullen gave the two Feds a very un-Cullenlike warning look. "I'm feeling a bit like that daddy just now."

"Understandable. Warning received," Galen said, drawing Sally's attention back to his very, very disapproving gaze.

Disapproving? She saw that Vance had the same expression. *Saw...oops.* She hastily closed her eyes. *Bad Sally.*

"Your lack of discipline means we will now play longer," Vance said, his voice low enough that the others wouldn't hear. "You may come—if you can. Otherwise, you must ask for our help."

Fine. She'd just go ahead and get off—quietly—and have this over. Why she felt embarrassed right now, she didn't know. She'd scened with tons of Doms here, getting off in front of everyone. Master Z and the others had used her for demonstrations.

But she hadn't been...hadn't been the only submissive in a group of Masters who were having a serious discussion.

And she'd never been emotionally involved with any Doms. Now, it felt as if her feelings were in a washing machine and set on spin. Whirling around and around and around.

Maybe once she got off, they'd let her join the other submissives.

As Vance slowly withdrew his very slick fingers, she trembled at the exquisite sensation. How could she be embarrassed and yet excited at the same time...and her obvious arousal made her feel even more humiliated.

His fingers pushed back in, ever so slowly. And he kept it up, over and over.

Galen tugged on her nipples, pinching them right to the edge of pain, until her breasts were so swollen that they ached with tightness.

Vance's thumb came down on her clit.

Every single nerve in her body flared into warp drive. She managed not to moan, but God, God, God, she needed to come. He wiggled his finger slightly, and the pressure grew, tightened, rolling toward her like a—

Vance lifted his hand; Galen stopped.

No. No nonononono. She didn't halt her glare in time. *Shit.*

"Add one more," Galen said to Vance—not to her—and slapped her breast lightly.

With the surprising burst of pain and the realization of exactly how they were punishing her, she felt her arousal sputter and die. Disbelieving, she stared at Galen.

With a slight smile, he widened his eyes at her.

Christ with a leather crop. Growling, she dropped her head back and closed her eyes. And could swear she heard Master Dan laugh.

Vance pushed his fingers inside her, and she felt them drag across the front of her vagina. Rubbing firmly, occasionally moving in and out. Her insides tightened around the intrusion, loved the intrusion.

Galen must have licked his finger before circling her nipples. The air on her wet skin made her nipples tighten to rigid peaks.

Slowly she realized they really *would* use her how they wanted, in front of anyone they chose, despite her objections, despite what was "proper." And the understanding dissolved the bones inside her body and turned her willpower to water.

And aroused the hell out of her.

Then Vance stroked his thumb over her clit. Just the side, but she was so sensitive, a touch was enough. Her muscles tightened as she neared orgasm. Her hips lifted.

The men stopped again.

A squeak of dismay escaped her. Everything in her lower half ached and burned with frustration. Her muscles quivered. How did they know she was close?

She realized her hands had fisted when Galen wrapped his calloused fingers around her hand and lifted it. He kissed her white knuckles, and his lips were soft. "I'm sorry this is hard on you, imp, but we won't let you get away with disobedience. You can test us as much as you want; you'll get the same response."

Testing them? She hadn't been...but, oh, she had. Every time they'd ordered her to do something, she'd disobeyed at least once or twice. Just to see... What? Why was she doing that?

In the same low voice, Vance said, "We care for you, Sally. You don't have to misbehave to get our attention. It's our pleasure to watch over you." His words were like a soothing caress.

And then they started moving again. Driving her back up. Slower, this time. And as the haze of arousal filled her body, she heard Vance say under his breath, "I did rather like the pretty bows on the flogger."

"It wasn't your flogger, asshole," Galen retorted. "Sally, sometime this week, I'm going to beat your ass with that flogger." He rolled her nipples until she arched at the delightful pain. "And then I'm going to get you off—using it—as a reward for making me laugh."

He did like to laugh; she knew it.

Her smile died as the two Doms used small caresses and pinches to drive her to the verge of orgasm. Her leg muscles were so tight they trembled as her arousal reached the edge of pain.

"Something you want to ask, sweetie?" Vance prompted.

Ask it. Dammit, ask it. "Please," she whispered.

"This time, you need to spell it out," Vance said. "Sally, hearing you ask will make me feel good."

Her words tried to stop up in her throat, but it helped to know that she'd please him—if only she could overcome her past. She stuttered out, "P-please, will you"—God, why did her body cringe?—"make me come?"

"Good, good girl," Galen murmured, and the sweetness of his deep voice washed over her like a blessing.

"Beautifully asked," Vance agreed. "I'm proud of you, Sally."

Galen caressed her breasts gently before his clever fingers closed on her tender nipples. Squeezing and releasing in burst after burst of exquisite pain.

Vance thrust, pulled out, pressed in. Each time, his thumb circled her clit, pushing her up, up. He rubbed his fingers just inside her entrance, reawakening the G-spot with a vengeance.

God. Her whole body went rigid as she shook, needing just another little bit. *Please.*

Vance's gaze met hers, holding hers as he deliberately set his thumb on her clit and pressed down. Wiggled.

The spark set off a conflagration. Her body lit, burst into flame, and exploded. Wave after wave of pleasure whipped through her. Her neck arched as she screamed and swore and screamed.

After a wonderfully long time, she felt the waves die back. God, that felt good.

Then she heard Vance mutter, "Let's try for seconds." His fingers pushed in—three fingers—stretching her as his finger rubbed right on her clit. And like a giant storm surge, another orgasm hit, flattening everything before it.

Her own wails seemed to echo in her ears as she panted and quivered with aftershocks.

"Pretty girl," Galen said. His hands were gentle on her breasts, circling and caressing her abused nipples. Vance was stroking her thighs.

After a minute, when she could actually breathe, Vance gathered her up into his arms. "You did well, sweetheart," he whispered. "I thought I'd have to tease you for another half hour before you asked for help."

The Dom had his own sadistic nature, cleverly concealed beneath a caring manner. She pinched him.

His answer was to silently slide his big hand between her legs again. To press against her oversensitive pussy. His smoldering gaze said he'd be perfectly happy starting the whole routine over again if that was what she wanted.

"Sorry," she whispered.

The sun lines beside his eyes deepened with his smile.

Oh God, she really did love him.

CHAPTER THIRTEEN

In his office, Assistant District Attorney Drew Somerfeld sat behind his desk as he discussed a case with his newest intern.

All was well in the great metropolis of Manhattan. Crime continued. Law enforcement put the criminals behind bars. The Harvest Association was on hiatus, but he had a few million in bank accounts overseas. Another few million and he'd be ready to retire. He'd take Ellis with him, buy an island, and live like a lord.

"Thank you, Kathleen," he said. "I think that covers it."

She was a bright young woman. Quite efficient. Somerfeld started to stand before noticing the intern was fidgeting rather than exiting his office. "Something else?"

"I remember how angry you were about Lieutenant Tillman's death."

"I still am," Somerfeld said in a tight voice. Mostly angry the bastard had gotten his claws into the Association. A shame the lesson hadn't taken hold with the other members of the investigation team.

"You'll be pleased to hear one of the so-called managers was arrested. He's singing like the proverbial canary."

Somerfeld froze for a second, then closed the folder on his desk as he forced a smile. "A manager? That's excellent work. How did it come about?" Yes, he needed to know. His managers were to have shut down all communications.

"It's that informant." Kathleen's smile was wide.

He wanted to slap her mouth hard enough to rip her lips away from her gopher-like teeth. "Go on."

"The informant sent the captain e-mail addresses and files for three managers. One was arrested. The tech department is working to get locations on the other two."

Son of a bitch. "Have we managed to identify the informant?"

"No. The computer experts say the man is bouncing his provider address through several places. Careful guy."

"Just as well," Somerfeld forced out. "The Association wouldn't take such a betrayal lightly." Wasn't that the truth? But before dealing with the informant, he'd have to shut that manager up. Yes, that caged canary was going to have his beak roasted right off.

Somerfeld smiled pleasantly at Kathleen. "I appreciate you sharing the good news."

Good to have a cure for Ellis's growing restlessness. Burning the manager—and the marshals and safe house—would calm him right down.

Pity his twin's slave would have to be sacrificed to get them into the house, because, right now, procuring a slut to replace her wouldn't be easy. But Ellis expected to be *reimbursed*, so to speak. Actually, the way things were going, maybe he'd order an extra. Be nice to have a spare.

Once the manager was ash, Drew could turn his attention to finding the informant. For that bastard, he'd push his brother aside and light the first match.

—✦—

Time does fly when you're having fun. In the second guest bathroom, Sally worked off her lousy Monday at the police station as she sponged grout from the blue-gray stone tile floor. A bucket of water sat beside her.

She grinned, realizing she was cleaning a floor on hands and knees. Sheesh, tales of Cinderella...

But Cinderella hadn't been the one to tile the floor, had she? Smiling, she swiped off another tile. Now she knew why the men liked doing their own construction. There was a simple pleasure in creating something both useful and beautiful.

Sally sat back and surveyed her work. Well centered. Around the walls, the partial tiles were all the same size. No tipped-up corners. Damn, she was good. Of course, she'd had a lot of practice over the weekend while the Feds were gone.

In between visits from her friends—and thank God for the Shadowkittens—the house had felt far too quiet, and she'd been lonely. And bored.

No Vance to cook with—or Galen to clean up. No discussions or arguments at meals.

Kari had come over one evening but had to return home early to put Zane to bed. She'd been her usual sweet, fun self—Sally frowned—except for the time Dan's name was mentioned and she'd looked...unhappy. But then she'd changed the subject.

But in the late evenings, Sally had been lonely, missing her guys.

Vance liked sports and movies, although he refused chick flicks or animations like *Mulan*. A typical guy, he preferred shoot-'em-ups like *Die Hard*. But after she forced him to watch *Alien*, he'd been converted to science-fiction films. *He can be taught.*

And how weird was it that Galen was a World of Warcraft addict? Even worse, his shaman was still kicking her ass online. But, as if to apologize, he'd taught her how to paddle his ancient wooden canoe.

She sighed. Kisses and canoeing on the lake in the moonlight.

But all that togetherness meant she really missed them. Although Glock had joined her in her giant bed, the sweet fur baby didn't compare to the men.

Thank God they were back...although they'd kept her up most of the night. Seemed like maybe they'd missed her too.

"Well, look at that. You got her doing manual labor." The rough voice made her jump, and she spun around.

Master Nolan stood in the doorway, arms crossed over his chest. He was so big he seemed to fill the doorway. With the scar down his darkly tanned face making him look cruel, he'd always made her a bit nervous, but his wife insisted he was actually sweet.

Beth must be delusional. Seriously.

"How are you, Sir?" Sally asked politely. She'd decided, in honor of her Doms' homecoming, she'd be super-supersweet and the best submissive in the world.

She could do it, right? At least for today?

"Before we left for New York, she helped me tile the laundry room," Galen said from behind Nolan. "She finished while we were gone and started this room by herself. She's even better at it than I am." The pride in Galen's face made her eyes burn.

"That's fine work, Sally," Nolan said. "If you don't find a computer job, you can work for me."

The contractor never bothered with politenesses, so if he said she'd done well, she had. She couldn't keep her smile back. "Thank you, Sir."

"If you're at a good place to stop, Beth is downstairs," Galen said. "I'm sure she'd like some company."

"Yes, Sir!" G and V had asked Nolan over to advise them on tearing out a wall in a downstairs bedroom. She hadn't realized Beth would come too. "I'll go right down."

Washing the gunk off her hands, Sally made a face at herself in the mirror. Company and just look at her. Her denim shorts were spattered with grout, her faded T-shirt had the sleeves ripped off, and she'd yanked her hair back into a ponytail to keep it out of her way.

Once downstairs, Sally set up a tray with a pitcher of iced tea, glasses, small plates, and a bowl of snack mix, and carried it with her as she searched for her guest.

In the game room, the cat sat on the fireplace mantel, imitating a statue of Bast, the feline God. Glock asserted that—no matter what humans believed—Bast was in charge of the universe. "Hey, Glock," Sally said. "How goes it?"

Glock gave her a tail flick indicating he found the world satisfactory at the moment.

When Galen had overheard her having a theological discussion with a house cat, he'd laughed himself stupid. *Frigging Fed.*

No one but Glock was in the game room, so Sally moved on. The office was empty. She finally found Vance and Beth in the great room.

Sally felt better, seeing that Beth was still in working clothes—cutoff overalls and a white tank top, red hair pulled back in a ponytail.

"There she is," Vance said as Sally entered the great room. "If you'll entertain the lady, sweetheart, I'll go talk with Nolan about manly subjects." He pulled Sally close enough to kiss the top of her head before making his escape.

"Hey, Beth." Sally set the tray down on the coffee table and winced at the clutter of combs and brushes, nail polish, and cotton balls. Early last night, while waiting for her men to get home, she'd needed to feel girlie and had played with new hairstyles and given herself a manicure and pedicure.

She should have a sign on her—hopeless at housekeeping. "Sorry about the mess."

"Like I care?" Beth gave her a quick hug and dropped down on the sectional. "But I'd love some of that iced tea. My project is in full sun."

"Where are you working?" Sally asked, pouring them both drinks and nudging the bowl within reach.

"Seminole Heights. A couple from Boston are having an old Victorian remodeled, and they want the grounds landscaped." After drinking half a glass of tea, Beth gave a pleased sigh. "How's job hunting?"

"Well." Sally frowned. "I've had offers and interest from a few places up north, but nothing down here. And I'd like to stay in Tampa." Because her friends were here. The Shadowlands was here.

The Feds were here. Odd how quickly she'd changed her mind about leaving town.

Beth patted her hand. "You'll find something that's perfect for you. Just be patient."

"Patient isn't exactly a word in my vocabulary," Sally grumbled.

"So very, very true."

Sally threw a pretzel at her for the insult. "At least only working part-time with no school lets me pretend to be a carpenter, and see you guys, and, even better, to play with Zane."

"Zane is such a darling." A shadow crossed Beth's face. "Kari is so lucky to have him."

What was that about? Beth and Nolan had been together about two years and had married last year. "Are you planning to follow Dan and Kari down the baby trail?"

When Beth flinched and averted her gaze, Sally wanted to hit herself on the forehead. *Bad question, stupid.* "Want to watch TV...or make some dinner?" *Or do anything to get that unhappy look off your face?*

"I—" Beth bit her lip. "It's okay, Sal. It's just that I can't have children. The damage from my previous marriage was too much."

Her husband had been a sick, abusive bastard, and Beth had scars all over her body. But she had internal damage too? "Christ in a swamp, it's not fair that the creep left you even more—" Unable to think of the right word, Sally sat and put her arm around the slender woman, needing to comfort at the same time she wanted to kill Beth's ex.

But Nolan had already taken care of that little task.

Beth leaned against Sally's shoulder. "I don't mind as much for me, but Nolan..." A tear slid down her sunburned cheek. "He said he'd like children, and I can't. I feel so *guilty.*"

"But..." Sally opened her mouth, searching for the right words, needing just the ones, but nothing came. "You shouldn't. It's not right—"

"What's not right is not telling me what the fuck has been bothering you." Nolan stalked into the room. His eyes were black ice, and his mouth twisted into a threatening line.

For a moment all Sally could do was cringe. But then she jumped up to stand in front of Beth. Maybe she could hold him off until her Feds got there. "Don't touch her."

Nolan stopped, way too close.

Sally felt her muscles tighten; the memory of being backhanded was awfully clear still.

A corner of Nolan's mouth tipped up. "The rabbit has a Chihuahua to protect her?" He grasped Sally's upper arms, lifted, and set her to one side.

"Hey!" Her lunge forward was stopped by a steely arm around her waist.

Vance chuckled. "Easy there. He's not going to hurt her."

"I should." Nolan went down on one knee, still tall enough that his eyes were even with Beth's. With a scarred hand under her chin, he lifted her face. "I had a nasty scene planned to pull answers out of you. To find out what's made you unhappy."

Her lips quivered. "I'm sorry, Master. I wouldn't have married you if I'd—"

"I would have."

His blunt statement made her blink. "But—"

"My family has kids to carry our bloodline." He released her chin and tucked a stray strand of hair behind her ear. "If you want children, we'll adopt them."

"Really?" she whispered. Her blue eyes filled with tears.

"Sugar, I love you. I'll do about anything to make you happy." He picked Beth up and sat down, cuddling her in his lap. She buried her face against his chest, her shoulders shaking as she cried.

With a sigh of happiness, Sally slumped back against Vance. Despite scaring the spit out of people, Nolan really was as sweet as Beth insisted.

Vance kissed the top of Sally's head before whispering, "See what happens if a submissive keeps secrets from her Dom. She's miserable although she doesn't have to be. Why don't you tell me what you're hiding, Sally?"

She stiffened. Would the FBI special agent cuddle her sweetly after hearing she'd hacked into the Harvest Association's e-mails? Oh yeah, and she could tell him she was acting as a modern-day Robin Hood. He'd definitely understand her reasoning.

Not.

Pulling out of his arms, she smiled politely. "Would you like some iced tea, Sir?"

His eyes narrowed. "Guess I should ask Nolan what he'd planned for that nasty scene."

Oh crap. Master Nolan liked using a flogger—and Galen

would be all over any scene like that. Time to escape. "Perhaps I should check on my other Dom."

"I'm here." Galen tugged her hair as he limped past to take a seat on the far end of the sectional. "I'd like some tea, please, pet."

"My pleasure, Sir." Her answer got a suspicious look. What? Didn't they think she could be a sweet submissive? *Jeez.*

First she served Vance a glass.

He nodded his thanks and took a chair beside Galen.

She handed a drink to Galen. When she knelt beside him without being ordered, he raised his eyebrows.

Master Nolan and Beth were talking quietly, not ready to be disturbed, so Sally asked her men, "Did Master Nolan have suggestions about tearing the wall down?"

"It's not load bearing, so we're good to go." Vance took a sip of his tea. "We'll need an electrician for some rewiring though."

"Might be good to put in an intercom while we're at it," Galen said.

An intercom? How old-fashioned. Be more fun to put in some voice-activated software and...

Voice activated. Oh my God. Totally jazzed, Sally rose and left the room, keeping her back to the guys so they wouldn't see her plotting. *Wire a light switch to turn on the receiver.*

In the bathroom, she grabbed a handful of tissues, breathed through her excitement, and headed back. Think of the havoc she could create if she rigged her laptop to mess with the house functions—lighting, maybe—upon command.

As Sally walked into the great room, Beth was sitting up and wiping her cheeks. Excellent timing. Sally handed her the tissues before taking her place between the men. Kneeling.

Ignoring the two sets of suspicious eyes, she looked at their guests.

Beth's hand was shaking as she cleaned off her face. She was too pale.

Nolan lifted his submissive to her feet. "Perhaps something to drink, sugar?"

Seriously? She bawls her head off, and he asks her to serve him? Sally scowled and started to rise to wait on the insensitive jerk.

Galen set a detaining hand on her shoulder and whispered, "She isn't like you, pet. Nolan knows serving him will calm her down."

At the coffee table, Beth slowly fussed over fixing a tiny plate of snack mix and pouring a glass of iced tea. By the time she handed the plate and glass to Nolan, her hands were steady.

Setting the drink on the end table, he spread his legs and nodded at the floor.

She gave him a pleased smile and knelt between his feet, facing outward.

When Master Nolan looked down at her, love had turned his eyes a soft sable. He stroked a hand down her bare arm and offered her a tiny pretzel. Feeding her.

Beth leaned her head against her Master's thigh with a look of peaceful contentment as he fed her tidbit after tidbit.

Feeling far too envious, Sally turned her attention to her glass, swirled her tea, and watched the ice cubes bob.

"Pretty rare," Nolan said.

Sally looked up to see the Master studying her and Galen and Vance. "Rare for two Doms to share a submissive for more than a scene," Nolan commented. "Especially since you're not gay."

"More like brothers," Vance said, shaking his head. "But you don't see it much."

Sally nodded. There were poly relationships in the Shadowlands, but most were one Master and female slaves. Or a Domme, like the one who had a nonlifestyle partner, a female submissive, and a male pup. Two male Doms weren't that common.

"Actually..." Beth glanced up at Nolan. "Sir?"

He ran his knuckles down her cheek. "I'm not enforcing high protocol, sugar. You're on your knees only because you needed to be there for a bit, but this is just a visit with friends."

Turning her head, she kissed his hand. Given permission to speak, she said, "I vacationed at a town in Colorado called Happiness or Joy or something, and the place had a lot of male-dominated ménages."

"Uh-huh," Galen said. "Jake told me about a place in Wyoming—King's something or other—where polyamorous relationships with multiple men are common."

Really? Sally straightened. She'd thought her time with the Feds would be only short-term, just for the month or so until she snagged a job. But now…her heart quivered as if it had caught a chill.

Would the guys ever consider something long-term? And would she want that? With two men? Was she totally insane?

She scowled at the floor and then realized Nolan and Beth were leaving. After scrambling to her feet, she hugged Beth and whispered, "Let me know how it goes with the adoption stuff."

Beth's smile was far brighter than when she'd arrived. "I will."

Nolan nodded at Sally, shook hands with Vance, and Galen walked them out.

After grabbing the bowl of snack mix off the table, Sally set it on the floor beside her and popped a cashew in her mouth. "Do you suppose they'll try for a newborn or adopt an older child?"

Vance sat down beside her and picked up the bowl, earning himself a frown. "I could see Nolan wanting to give an older kid a chance."

"Do you think it would bother him that the child wouldn't be his own?"

As Nolan had with Beth, Vance fed her a pretzel.

A fuzzy, contented feeling invaded her chest.

"Most parents don't think of their adopted children as anything but their own," Vance said. "My mother tends to forget she didn't carry me or my sisters in her belly."

"You—you're adopted?" Sally stared at him.

"Um-hmm. Chew before you choke, sweetheart."

Adopted? He tapped her lips, and she chewed obediently.

He picked out a couple of cashews and fed them to her. "Mom couldn't have children." His eyes darkened. "My birth mother was only thirteen when she was pregnant with me. She was a cousin of my father's."

Christ in the flowers, thirteen? "Have you ever met her?"

"Once I understood what adopted meant, I asked to meet her. Turned out that she'd died having me." He stared out the window, where an egret was wading, stork-like, in the shallows. "For years, I felt so damned guilty. Like her death was my fault—that I'd killed her."

"No." Sally wrapped her arms around Vance's legs and hugged them. "No, you didn't. You were a baby."

"Yeah. Once my parents realized how screwed up I was about it, they got through to me." Vance stroked her hair. "Kids can feel guilty for the stupidest things."

She looked up. His eyes were understanding but held the determination that she'd work past her own guilt.

Maybe, someday, she'd stop feeling so guilty for causing her mother's death.

Hearing a noise, she turned her head.

Galen had been watching from the doorway.

He walked in, pushed the clutter on the coffee table to one side, and took a seat facing her. "In my case, I decided my crappy behavior was the reason my father divorced my mother." Galen gave her a wry smile. "Soon after college, I ran into him in a restaurant, and we talked. He didn't remember any of what I'd always thought was so bad. He hadn't asked for visiting rights because he didn't want any contact—at all—with my mother."

"Oh God." She wiggled her way between his legs until she could put her arms around his waist. "Your father sounds like a complete douche bag."

"You're a vicious little sub." Galen laughed, and the darkness cleared from his voice. He hugged her back.

Happiness filled her. Staying between his legs, she settled herself with her back to him so she could lean forward and grab a handful of snack mix from the bowl beside Vance. And like a dutiful submissive, she twisted around and offered it up on her open palms to Galen.

Rather than taking it, he laughed at her and ran his finger down her cheek. "Don't try to warp yourself into something you're not, imp. Vance and I are happy with you as you are. We don't want a full-time submissive. If I decide to take control at an unusual time, you'll know it; you won't be confused."

Well, that was true enough. She remembered how on her first day with them, he'd tossed a cushion on the floor and pointed to it. "But—"

"You're adorable when you try to be a slave, but that's not who you are."

"But don't you like—"

"Makes me nervous to be waited on hand and foot," Vance said.

"Oh." She frowned. "But...I don't feel as if I'm giving enough."

"Works for me to share the chores. In the bedroom, I expect a submissive." Vance grinned. "You don't seem to have a problem with that."

She flushed, remembering the early morning fucking that he liked so well. Galen liked to get up before dawn, but she and Vance would sleep until the alarm went off. And Vance would definitely take charge. The headboard probably had her fingernail marks on it.

Behind her, Galen tugged the scrunchie from her ponytail, and to her shock, he picked up her hairbrush from the table and started to brush her hair.

Long, smooth strokes. He even worked the tangles out with his fingers if he hit a snarl.

With a moan, Sally fell into the pleasure. "God, Galen."

Galen laughed under his breath, his voice husky. "I used to do this for my mother."

"Seriously?" Vance asked. "I can't imagine your mother letting anyone touch her."

"She got worse with the divorce. Totally retreated into the arctic zone."

"Ah." From the lack of expression on Vance's face, Sally had to guess he didn't like the woman at all. Which made Sally figure she must be a royal bitch.

And Galen had thought he'd caused that divorce, and afterward his mother pulled away into a cold shell. How would that affect a kid?

Sally frowned. Galen seemed like a gaming computer. Sensitive and responsive and always functioning at high speed. Far too easy to break. She wrapped her arm around his calf, holding him close as if she could make up for all the affection he'd missed as a child.

"Are you sure you don't need more from me?" she asked, wanting just to...give.

"No, baby girl. What you bring us is more valuable than labor. The house is happier with you in it. More fun." Galen's hand stroked down her head after the pull of the brush, a double hit of tenderness. "Imp, wherever you go, the air practically sparkles."

Her eyes blurred with the rush of tears.

And for one second—one second only—she could see herself staying. Long-term.

CHAPTER FOURTEEN

*N*ice to be home. In the short hallway to their home office, Galen stretched. His shoulders and neck ached as if he'd taken Vance on in a weight-lifting competition rather than spending a day doing paperwork at the field office. Being an agent wasn't all car chases and gun battles as he'd dreamed as a child.

The older he got, the more grateful for that he was—no matter how many reports he had to fill out.

In the office, Glock was stretched out on the center table. Galen walked over to stroke him. The rumbling purr merged with the country-western crap that Vance loved. Least it was a female vocalist this time.

Vance looked up from his desk. "Hey."

"Where's Sally?"

"Just left. Her job hunting must not be going well, since she looked pretty miserable. Shut her laptop down and went out to swim."

Galen set his briefcase down on his desk. The thought of the imp moving away didn't sit well on his chest. Nonetheless... "She'll find something pretty soon, I'm sure."

"Right."

Galen frowned at the gruff answer. He knew damned well Vance didn't want her to leave. "You two have a fight?"

"Not with her. Figure I'll be having one with you." Vance sounded tired. Discouraged. "I got an e-mail."

"Go on."

"The safe house holding the Harvest Association manager burned last night. The manager didn't survive; the marshals are dead as well."

"*Fuck.*" Galen slammed his hand on the desk, welcoming the flare of pain.

Glock gave him an offended stare for his behavior and stalked out of the room.

"God fucking dammit to hell." Arson. What a fucked-up way to die. A coldness grew in his belly as he took the logical next step. How soon before the Harvest Association extended their targets to those in the FBI—or their loved ones? "We need to let her go."

Vance didn't even pretend to misunderstand. In fact, he looked almost resigned to the argument. "You think she'd do better without us? What about the next asshole who uses her for a punching bag?"

The memory of her bloody face made Galen scowl. "We can't keep her safe."

"Since the other quadrants shut down, the Association's hits have all been in New York." Vance shook his head. "Our residence isn't listed; phones are unlisted. No one knows she's here except the Shadowlands members."

"True." The tightness in his chest receded. Maybe he was being hasty. After all, Sally's desire to be needed could lead her into more danger than the remote chance the Association would notice her. He thrummed his fingertips on the desk as he thought. "No outings. Let's keep her out of the public eye until this is over."

Relief filled his partner's face. "You're going to be reasonable?"

"Sure wasn't your logic that swayed me." It was because he liked having her here as much as Vance did. It was because hearing about her job applications had sent his mood spiraling downward. It was because he *wanted* her.

Real soon he and Vance needed to think about the future. Before it was too late. But for now... "It's been over a month since we had our first scene with Sally. I've been thinking about taking things to the next level." He smiled suddenly. "It might be a way to coax out what she's been hiding."

—*—

Sally dived into the pool behind G and V's house, hammered out a lap, another, and another. Breathless, she stopped at one end and tossed her tangled hair back. Despite the late afternoon sun, the rising wind cooled her wet shoulders.

Redolent with the fragrance of the lush green vegetation around the lake, the breeze this far inland held only a trace of the ocean. The slight scent of chlorine came from the water.

Chlorine was supposed to make a person feel clean, but she had a feeling she'd never feel clean again.

Three men had died. The Association manager...she didn't know anything about him, but he'd chosen his destiny by dealing in human trafficking. His death was of his own making. But—God, those other men. Marshals, trying to protect the manager. Dead. A sob shook her chest, and she dived for the bottom of the pool.

Her fault.

And yet... *If I hadn't sent the New York cops information about the three managers, more women might have been enslaved. Might have died. I did the right thing.* She'd been telling herself that since she'd checked on the manager they'd caught and found out about the fire. How long before she stopped feeling guilty?

To make it worse, she knew Galen or Vance could have been in that house. They'd talked about flying up to question that manager. And they'd be dead. She kicked to the surface and treaded water.

How could she bear it if they died? To be without them, never touch them again. Never hear Galen's rare open laugh, feel him stroke her hair, reading her soul with his dark eyes. Never feel Vance's hands as he rolled her over in the early morning and pushed inside her, taking her so slow, murmuring what he expected her to do.

How could she live without them?

Dammit, you weren't supposed to fall in love with them, you stupid, stupid girl. Talk about a pitiful cliché. Silly submissive falls in love with the Dominant she's working with.

And in Sally's case? *Oh yeah, I fell for two of them.*

She turned over, lying in the water facedown in a dead man's float. On the bottom of the pool, the shadows of the nearby trees wavered and danced. The dying rays of the sun brushed over her back—although she didn't think she'd ever be warm again.

"Sally." Despite being muffled by water, the word still summoned her attention. Of course, it would. Hell, even laughing, Galen radiated authority.

She came upright, treading water. "Sir?"

"Take a shower and wait for us in the dungeon."

Her breathing almost stopped. A scene? Everything in her thrilled at the idea of being totally at their command and the focus of their intense attention.

But...her feelings were a mess. She didn't want them to know how she felt. Galen would pitch her out if he realized she was emotionally attached. God, what would—

"Did you happen to hear what I said?"

Shit. "Yes, Sir. Shower and wait. Right away, Sir. Please forgive me, Sir. It won't happen again, Sir."

A snort. "Don't make promises you can't keep, pet."

As he strolled back into the house, she was already scrambling out of the pool.

VANCE SAUNTERED DOWN the overgrown dirt path to the cabana.

Because of Sally, they'd abandoned working on the game room and had been fixing this one up instead. It was going to make a hell of a nice dungeon.

He—and his *apprentice*—had painted the walls and ceiling. A king-size bed had replaced the twin beds. Some of the equipment had already arrived and would be tested out tonight.

About fifteen minutes ago, the back door had slammed as Sally headed for the cabana. Hopefully she'd spent that time in anticipation of what would come. He grinned. With the little brown-eyed submissive, any assumption was liable to be wrong.

In fact, Galen had removed his toy bag from the cabana—just in case.

Vance opened the door. To his surprise, she was dutifully

kneeling naked in the center of the room. Her posture was perfect: hands open on thighs, back arched slightly to display her breasts, eyes down. From the way her hair fluffed over her shoulders and curled down her back, he knew she'd taken the time to wash and blow it dry.

She might drive him crazy sometimes, but she never neglected to prepare her body for his pleasure.

He flipped the switch to turn on the music, and the sound of Enigma filled the room. "You look beautiful, sweetheart."

A visible tremor shook her.

"Open your legs farther for me, please."

She shifted position, spreading her thighs apart as he went down on one knee in front of her. Her pussy already glistened in the bright lights. Yes, she'd been anticipating the scene.

As he cupped his hand over her crotch, he leaned forward to whisper, "Galen and I are going to take our pleasure tonight—and if you're very, very good, we'll see that you're rewarded for your patience. Very well rewarded."

He heard her gulp. "Yes, Sir. I'll be good."

"You won't get the chance not to be." He moved his fingers through her plump folds, teasing her clit with his thumb. Her inner thigh muscles flexed and tightened. From the silky smoothness of her skin, she'd applied lotion. The scent wafted up, making him think of sunlit honey. Smiling, he moved back, sucking on his fingers, enjoying the first taste of what the evening would hold.

She stayed impressively still, only her heightened breathing and pink cheeks showing her anticipation.

"I'm going to warm you up a bit before Galen arrives; then we'll start." He stroked her hair, silky and bouncy, like her personality. "First, all the lab tests came back clean. Apart from anal sex, we won't use protection." And he was looking forward to having no barrier between his cock and her tight, wet pussy.

He continued, "Tonight, anything you haven't marked as a hard limit might be used. You have your safe word. Use yellow if you're getting overwhelmed. Otherwise, we're going to do what we want."

Her eyes were no longer down. She stared up at him, practically begging him to continue. A submissive's wish was to be pushed until she knew to the depths of her soul that she'd given up all control. Tonight, that's what she'd know.

He lifted her to her feet, molding her against him, taking a slow, drugging kiss. Her lips were soft and sweet, her tongue teasing.

Curling his fingers under her round ass, he pulled her closer, and her long hair silkily drifted over his arms. Nice.

With a smile, he pulled the set of nipple clamps from his jeans pocket. "Let's see what these look like on you."

Her nipples were the smoothest, softest skin on her body and a dusky pink that reddened quickly as he tightened the first screw. He could see her decision not to complain. Her facial and throat muscles turned rigid as she fought the pain.

He quickly loosened the clamp. "Let's do this again." He lifted her chin, giving her a firm look. "I know some submissives think their Doms are God—but I'm not. I can't read your mind." Thank God, she had such expressive body language. "You need to tell me if something starts to hurt." He grinned. "Then I'll decide whether I want you to take it anyway. Is that clear?"

For a second, she pouted. "Yes, Sir."

"Good." He tightened the screw slowly. Waiting. Nothing came from her, so he cleared his throat. Fuck, but he wanted to kill her father when he saw her struggle to force herself to speak.

"That hurts," she whispered.

"Good. Very, very good." Vance hugged her, feeling how her heart pounded against his chest. But she'd done it. "Next one." He attached the right clamp, and this time, she managed to speak without prompting.

He stepped back to admire his work for a moment. The shiny metal clamps were beautiful against her reddening nipples. *Very nice.* Next time, he'd add a chain between them. "Now, take my shirt off, imp."

She made a pretty ritual of disrobing him, button after button, pressing velvet-lipped kisses to his chest. Her hand blazed a trail downward, her mouth following, until she pushed his jeans down.

He stepped out of them, and before he could move, she closed her lips around him. *Fuck.* The sweetheart had a mouth that was made for sin.

She released his cock and pushed his legs apart. Curious, he went along with her unspoken request. She cupped his balls, dipped her head, and kissed down his groin to his testicles. Licking and nuzzling. The sensation of wetness on his overheated skin was disconcerting, and he had to smother a groan when she sucked one ball, then the other into her mouth, tonguing them.

Almost too much.

Time to stop. With what he considered a superb amount of control, he tugged on her hair to get her to release him before pulling her to her feet. "Thank you, Sally." He shook his head. "Tomorrow morning, I expect more of that."

Her eyes lit with her delight—and the knowledge she'd pleased him.

"Now let's get you ready for some action."

She had the most beautiful brown eyes he'd ever seen, filled with a shimmering excitement and trust, and he struggled against his own urges. Fuck, but he wanted to bury himself in her as deep as possible. Instead he kissed her again, enjoying the feeling of her heated skin against his. There was an almost palpable vibration of need growing in them both.

When Galen walked in, Vance gave him a rueful smile. Yeah, he was behind their mapped-out schedule.

His partner grinned. But Galen had never resented making adjustments for unexpected twists in a scene.

Vance nudged Sally forward. "Help Galen out of his clothes too, sweetie."

"Yes, Sir."

Galen's clothes soon dropped to the floor. Color crept into his face as Sally treated him to her talented mouth.

With a guttural growl, Galen pulled her away from his dick and motioned to the red leather-covered spanking horse, which had been delivered the day before. It was the one she'd lusted after in the catalog. "Let's break this in, pet."

She actually bounced up and down with anticipation.

He'd never known a submissive who brought so much joy to a session. Grinning, Vance lifted her onto the sawhorse, positioning her stomach-down so her knees and forearms rested on the lower padded areas.

He took a moment to adjust her breasts on each side of the narrow top, flicking the nipple clamps to hear her suck a breath in. *Mmmhmm.* He strapped her down, watching her eyes dilate as she tested the growing restrictions to movement.

While Vance worked, Galen idly fondled her ass and pussy, smiling at her increasingly urgent squirming.

"Let's put a stop to that." Vance tightened a strap over her low back, ensuring that her sweet, round ass would be nicely immobile as well as poke out invitingly from the end of the bench. "Can you move, Sally?"

She managed to lift her head and tried to wiggle. "No, Sir."

"Good. Now listen, Sally; you aren't permitted to come." He grinned as her face scrunched adorably. "That's right. Don't disappoint me, sweetheart."

Vance's chest squeezed at her immediate answer: "I won't."

Fuck, how did she keep making him want her more? "Good girl. You sing out if you're getting close, and we'll back off. Clear?"

She actually looked relieved. "Yes, Sir. Thank you."

"All right then." As they'd discussed earlier, Vance took a place at her head.

Without warning her, Galen positioned his cock and thrust into her cunt, fast and hard.

She gasped, her back trying to arch.

Taking advantage of her open mouth, Vance slid his dick in. She sucked on it immediately, and the sensation of her hot, wet tongue swirling around the tip almost sent him over.

Galen was working her up, his left hand under her pelvis to tease her clit as his right hand prepped her anus with lube and fingers. By the time he finished, she'd be in a real state of need.

But on this rare occasion, they'd come before she would.

So Vance concentrated on his own pleasure.

Fuck, but he appreciated how Sally focused on him, trying to make it perfect for him.

"Heads-up," Galen warned, and Vance pulled out and stepped back.

Galen rolled on a condom and pressed his cock to her tiny asshole. As he slowly worked his way in, Sally gritted her teeth...and Vance was grateful for the warning.

"In," Galen said.

"All right." Vance smiled down at their little sub. Flushed, sweat at her temples, eyes a little wild. "Open up, sweetheart. If you can finish me off in the next three minutes, Galen won't feel the need to spank your ass."

She tried. She really did, but despite her sucking and licking, Vance managed to hold out long enough for her to collect a half-dozen swats on her ass.

However, if he'd had to last any longer, his heart might have given out. She was astonishingly good at using her mouth.

With a low groan, he gripped her hair and came so intensely that the floor seemed to shake. She swallowed fast, and each contraction of her throat muscles made his dick spasm again. "Thank you, Sally," he murmured. Her little tongue swirled around his cock as he gave a few more, purely indulgent thrusts. She was truly a sweetheart.

As Galen fucked her asshole, slowly increasing his pace, Vance moved to her side so he could tease her breasts. Her nipples were a dark red now, and when he flicked the clamps and ran his fingers around the edges, she kept trying to wiggle.

"Oh, I'm so close..." Her whine was absolutely beautiful.

Pulling his hand away from her clit, Galen stopped with his cock buried deep in her ass.

Vance stepped back as well...and grinned as she panted, fighting back her orgasm.

"That's a very good girl," Galen murmured, running his hands up and down her sides. After a minute, he started thrusting again, and Sally groaned as he sped up.

Vance pressed down on her back to increase her feeling of being restrained as his partner finished off with a low growl. Vance could see the contentment on Sally's face—not from having come, but from having pleased Galen.

Vance stroked her hair. She fit with the two of them. Like with a construction set, two upright pieces might be tied together, but they'd fall. A three-dimensional one formed a stable tripod.

He and Galen needed her...and she needed them. "You did very, very well, sweetheart," Vance said softly, meeting her gaze. "You were wonderful."

HAPPINESS FILLED SALLY at his words, even as she closed her eyes, trying not to pant. God, she was so turned on that she might die. When Galen had been thrusting into her ass, she'd gotten way too close to coming. And he must have known, since he'd never returned to playing with her clit...which still pulsed with seething tension.

Vance started unstrapping her.

Galen returned from the bathroom and went down on one knee beside her right shoulder. She turned her head to look at him, wary of the amusement in his eyes. "Time to get these off, pet."

These what? She stiffened when his fingers touched her breast. Loosened a clamp. Removed it.

Blood rushed back into the abused tissues with a long, flaring pain, which poured right down to her core, turning into hot, hot need. "Sadist," she whispered around a moan.

"A bit of a one, ayuh." Grinning, he rubbed her nipple gently.

Only, he really wasn't. Not compared to Master Sam. After giving her an unhurried, wonderful kiss, he walked around and removed the other clamp. The pulse of pain made her toes curl, yet somehow felt as if someone was rubbing her clit, upping her arousal almost unbearably. Dammit, weren't they ever going to let her come?

And yet, despite her painful need, it felt...right...to leave everything in their hands. She just had to do what they said. Take what they gave her.

God, she loved that yielding feeling.

"Here we go, sweetheart." Vance lifted her off the sawhorse, dropped her on the king-size bed, and rolled her onto her back.

He didn't do anything else. No kisses, no touching, no sex.

Want sex. She looked up at him, trying to beg silently.

"You know I'm a sucker for puppy-dog eyes," he murmured, lying down beside her, "but you still have to tell us what you want. If you want to continue, say it, imp."

Say it, say it, say it. She was so sick of hearing that. How could he be so mean to her? *I want...* Her eyes filled as she tried to say the words. Why was it harder when she was so...so needy?

He made a sound low in his throat and pulled her on top of him, hugging her closely. "Just ask, Sally. You know I want to give you what you need."

A tear splattered on his chest as she heard her father whispering, like the echoes in a cave. *"...always asking for things you don't need."*

As a tremor shook her, Galen sat down beside her shoulder and turned her to his intent gaze. "Who are you hearing, Sally?"

"Father."

"Ah. That's a good baby girl for telling me," he said. His thumb stroked her cheek.

Vance tightened his arms, and his heart was steady and sure under her ear. "He sure didn't like you asking for things. What exactly did he say, pet? You're hearing it—tell us now."

She whispered his words, "'Stupid, selfish girl. Always asking for stuff. Who will you kill this time, huh?'"

"He really is a son of a bitch," Vance muttered. The words rumbled through the solid wall of muscle under her cheek. "Accidents happen, sweetheart," Vance said, somehow shaking her without moving. "You aren't in charge of the universe. And if you start playing the 'if only' game, you'll never win. Listen: If only Sally hadn't asked for a dress. If only your father had been generous enough to give you nice clothes so you didn't need more. If only your mother had been paying more attention. If only the tires hadn't been bald."

She blinked. "How did you know about the tires?"

"Just guessed. He sounds like a tight-fisted bastard."

Something inside her relaxed. Not much, but a little. They

didn't blame her. And Vance was still holding her.

Galen's eyes were steady. Honest. "You are a beautiful, intelligent, sweet woman, Sally. If your father can't see that, it's his failing, because everyone else can. Wherever your mother is, I'm sure she's very, very proud of you."

Tears spilled over and ran down her face. "I-I..." The look on Galen's hard face was more than affection, and the warmth emanating from him surrounded her heart. She rose up enough to look down at Vance, and his eyes held the same...caring.

Not love. Mustn't love them.

I love them. She licked her lips, trying to find the words.

And Galen slid off the bed.

Moment lost. Her arms gave out, dropping her back down on Vance. With a sigh, she rubbed her cheek against the springy hair on his chest.

He didn't speak, simply stroked her back, his hands sure and strong and comforting. Whatever happened in the world, this man would be as steady as the cliffs over the ocean, shedding the fury of a storm as if it were nothing.

Galen reappeared with a glass of water. "Sit up for a minute, pet." He lifted her off Vance, helped her sit, and curled her fingers around the glass.

She sipped slowly, feeling more herself. Damn them for being so darned persistent with their emotion probing.

Behind her, Vance sat up, putting one hand behind her back. He reached around with his other hand to play with her breasts.

Her sore nipples peaked immediately, sending a buzz of hunger straight to her clit. She wiggled and pushed his hand away.

Galen gripped her chin. "What are you doing?"

Oh God. Her bones turned to pudding under his level, merciless gaze. "Sorry, Sir."

"Good answer," Vance said and took advantage of her immobility by using both hands, cupping her breasts, warming them for a moment, kneading gently before pinching her nipples, sending her remorselessly back into need.

Galen didn't release her, simply held her gaze, a slight smile on his face. And the intensity of his attention, the way he secured her with both physical and invisible bonds for his partner's pleasure was the most erotic sensation she'd ever felt.

When Vance ran his hand down her stomach, she knew she was even wetter than she had been before. Her back arched the second he touched her throbbing, swollen clit.

A tiny touch. Another. God, if—

He removed his hand.

She made a sound.

"That's right. You have to ask us to continue, remember? Otherwise, we'll go watch television," Galen said gently, but she heard the unrelenting tone. They'd hold her and comfort her...yet make her do what they wanted.

"C'mon, sweetie. Let's hear it." Vance's chest pressed against her from behind, his voice a grumble in her ear.

"I need—"*No, not like that.* "Will you—" Her father's voice echoed inside her.

"My voice. Vance's voice." Galen squeezed her chin, the bite of pain snapping the ties of the past. "That's all you hear. Clear?"

"Yes, Sir," came out automatically, but the past had gone. Maybe all that homework had helped because once she started, the words came readily enough. "Can we continue? Please?"

Galen actually smiled at her, his deep voice rich with approval. "Very, very good, Sally."

And Vance echoed his words in a sweet stereo effect.

ANGER SMOLDERED IN Galen's gut. Next time he met Sally's father, he'd give the bastard a few lessons in how to treat a daughter. And then he'd hand him over to Vance, who had just as much rage. But this wasn't the time.

Right now, Sally was trembling with anticipation, flushed and beautiful, and Galen wanted to take her that extra step further into submission. She was ready.

He glanced at Vance. "My requirements are that she lay on her back, ass on a pillow, legs out of my way. Otherwise she's all yours."

His partner grinned, studying the bed and Sally, obviously formulating his plan for restraints.

The imp's eyes were wide.

He ran his finger down her cheek. "This might be uncomfortable, but if it really hurts, I'll stop."

The questions—and worry—in her eyes added spice to the scene.

After clipping her wrist cuffs to ropes on the sturdy iron headboard, Vance took a minute to suck her nipples until they stood up, distended and dark red.

Her pleasingly round ass was already squirming. By God, she responded beautifully.

While Vance worked the restraints, Galen checked his fingernails—already clipped as short as possible—washed his hands, and donned a long surgical glove on his left hand.

Vance had put a wide leather belt around her waist and with rope, secured each knee to the belt at her sides. "Ready for you, pard."

Ass high, knees up and out, arms restrained. "Perfect." He looked at Sally. "Your safe word is red. But for this, I will be talking to you. *No* will be the same as yellow. I'll stop and check how you're doing. Clear?"

He was sadist enough to enjoy the way apprehension creased her forehead.

After propping a pump-action bottle of lube against her hip, Galen settled himself on one elbow perpendicular to her position.

Slowly he explored her entrance before inserting a finger. Her cunt clenched down on him, making him smile. He pulled out and teased her clit until she squirmed. Two fingers. Play for a bit. Three fingers.

Vance was caressing her breasts, kissing her mouth, her neck.

And within minutes, she was wiggling and close to begging.

Four fingers. He'd done four with her in the past, pressing in far enough to feel the stretch, to hear her worried squeak. This time, he worked her for a while. In, out, play with the clit. He stretched her with each set, adding more lube. The musky scent of her arousal was heady, and he was already growing erect again.

Raised on one elbow, stretched beside her, Vance teased his favorite bits between kissing her.

After covering the glove on his left hand and wrist with even more lube, Galen stroked her clit, taking her to the edge. And this time, when he worked his fingers into her cunt, he kept going, folding his thumb inside his fingers to make a duckbill shape.

"Galen!" Her head jerked up as she felt the press of his hand. She stared at him, panic starting to fill her face.

"Give her a pillow so she can watch," he told Vance. Once her head was propped up, he looked at her. "Do you trust me, Sally?"

"Yes." The instant answer warmed his heart.

"I'm going to fist you—put my hand inside you. Can you trust me to do that without hurting you—not more than you can take?"

Her gaze went right to his free hand and his face, showing her disbelief. And a shudder went through her. "I can stop you?"

"Ayuh, pet. You can call a stop at any time."

She blew out a breath and said dubiously, "I'll try."

"Brave baby girl." Galen smiled at her and met Vance's gaze.

Vance reached down, his hand settling over her engorged clit.

FISTING. OH GOD, why hadn't she put fisting on her list of hard limits? Sally wondered. Vance's touch on her overly sensitive clit made her clench around Galen's fingers, and she gasped.

"Breathe, pet," Galen murmured, pressing forward, stopping, pressing in again. "This is the toughest part—"

It hurt, didn't feel good at all. His knuckles were hard. Huge. "You won't fit."

His grin flashed white in his tanned face. "Women's bodies are designed to stretch. My hand will fit." He tilted his head at Vance. "His might not."

She moaned as the pain increased.

"Easy, baby girl. I'll go slow," Galen said as he pulled back slightly.

Vance took another kiss, teasing her lips, whispering how well she was doing. Between kisses, he'd run a finger around her clit, rubbing firmly on one side, on the other, then up and over the hood.

Within minutes, in spite of the pressure from Galen's advancing hand, she felt the tendrils of nerves gathering, working toward an orgasm.

"Sally," Galen said. "I want you to tighten your cunt and hold." He waited until she did. "Now take a big breath. Exhale and relax everything. Push out if you can."

When she clenched around him, his hand felt huge, huge. She hauled in a breath, held it, gave a powerful exhalation and let herself go limp, inside and out.

As his hand pushed inward, she gritted her teeth against the pain, yanking at her restraint, holding back the "no" that threatened to burst free.

"In," Galen murmured.

She was panting in little gasps. The pain was gone, but the feeling—oh God, the feeling. She was terrifyingly full.

Head up, not moving, Galen was studying her, his black gaze moving over her face, her shoulders, her hands.

As Vance moved his fingers, light and slow, over her clit, he was doing the same. His lips curved up. "Look at you, filled with his fist."

She'd never felt anything this overwhelmingly intimate. Never felt quite so vulnerable. Galen's hand filled her completely; he could hurt her badly. And yet, she knew he'd never do anything to really hurt her. The trust in him was bone-deep—went deeper than his hand.

He was smiling too. "I didn't know if you'd be able to do this, even though I'd been working toward it."

Her mouth fell open. He had, hadn't he? Sneaky bastard.

"Tell me what you feel, Sally," Galen said.

"I— Strange. A little scared. Full. Very full." Neither Dom moved. Just waited. She tried harder. How could she express the...intimacy? "It feels as if there's a...a tie between us, all of us," she said, looking at Vance. "Even more than I can say." She shook her head.

Galen nodded, understanding in his face. "I feel it too, baby girl."

Vance leaned up to kiss her, so very, very sweetly and she knew she could never have relaxed enough to permit this without his presence. "Yes."

She pulled in a breath. *Okay.*

Galen smiled. "I'm going to move, pet. You tell me if it's too much."

The hugeness that was his hand opened slightly, growing even bigger, moving ever so slowly up toward her cervix, and down.

And suddenly she felt each little caress of Vance's slick fingers on her clit. With every movement of Galen's hand and the stretching of her center, more and more sensations poured into her with sheer sparkling brilliance. Like a star being born inside her, everything began to whirl and coalesce, turning into a hot, hot core as her entire body tightened around Galen's fist, as her world inside her and around her utterly exploded. The nova of pleasure expanded outward, filling her universe, shaking her body until her bones dissolved. "Aaahhhh!"

On and on and on.

As she moaned, as her eyes started to focus, Galen opened his hand inside her, and she went over again in long, sweetly terrifying spasms of pleasure.

And again.

He'd wait long enough for her to settle—then move his fist, just an inch or two, and she'd come hard, devastatingly hard. Like nothing else. Sweat rolled off her forehead, between her breasts. Her breathing came in harsh gasps; her heart was slamming inside her rib cage like a rocket with no controls.

"The next time you come, I'm going to pull out, pet," Galen said, the crinkles around his eyes showing his enjoyment.

Vance was chuckling. He slid his hand back to her clit and licked her breast even as Galen turned his hand completely over inside her.

The rush of the orgasm was huge, screamingly huge. "*Ooooh, noooo.*" As her hips tried to buck, Vance ruthlessly pressed down on her mound, keeping her flat and in place. The roaring sun at her core shot flares of sensation streaming through her and filled the air around her with sparkling lights. *Oh God, oh God, oh God.*

As she went limp, Galen pulled out slowly. She felt a flash of pain as his knuckles passed through; then she was empty inside.

He rose off the bed, leaving her feeling like a deflated, exhausted balloon.

Vance moved up beside her, kissing her, slow and sweet, his arm over her keeping her from disappearing into the foggy air around her.

Hands cleaned, Galen removed the restraints on her wrists and helped her lower her aching arms so she could hold on to Vance. He released her legs and removed the belt. When he stretched out on her other side, she was pinned between the two Doms.

My Doms.

Vance ran his fingertips over her damp cheek. "Sweetheart?"

She looked up into his concerned blue eyes and whispered, "I love you."

His expression changed to a stunned pleasure.

Turning her head just a few inches, she stared into Galen's smoldering gaze. "I love you."

And his eyes softened in a way she'd never seen before.

The bond between all of them was as real and alive as the blood moving through her veins. As alive as her beating heart. As she snuggled down, fading away and into darkness, she'd never felt so accepted.

So loved.

Their hands stroked over her, petting her. *Loving* her, even if they hadn't said anything.

CHAPTER FIFTEEN

For an hour or so, Galen watched Sally as she slept, tucked in her favorite position between him and Vance. Vance had dropped off a while back, but Galen couldn't. Not after what she'd said.

Surely the imp had been only half-conscious to have blurted that out. And she probably didn't mean it. It was the aftereffect of being so close, of having such an intense scene.

And yet, the warmth he'd felt—still felt—from her words was disconcerting. Impossible. He didn't want to love a woman. Would prefer not to love anyone, for that matter. People were far too fragile.

Even men could die.

Hell, he'd always worried about any partner being hurt during any action. But now... With a pained sigh, he glanced at the man sleeping on the other side of Sally. *My brother.*

It was twice as hard to have two people for which to fear.

Needing to think of something else, he ran his hand over Sally's soft stomach. The rich fragrance of her lotion mingled with the scent of sex. Her lips were swollen from being kissed. Her nipples had softened but remained a dark red. He ran his finger around one, enjoying how the tender white skin of her breasts contrasted with the velvet smoothness.

And, hell, he'd woken her up. Heavy-lidded with sleep, she was just watching him, too limp to move.

He had to smile with that satisfaction, although she'd worried him when she talked about the ties between them...because he could feel them too.

The fisting might have been a mistake. The little imp had sucked him and Vance in from the moment they saw her, and with each revealed facet of her personality, she drew them in further.

And thinking of revealing things... Something had been bothering her, making her feel guilty. Now, he didn't think painting faces on anal plugs was a serious crime...if he didn't notice the resemblance to Disney dwarfs. *Christ, that is just wrong.*

Was that what was bothering her? Might be something else. But no matter what she'd done, a little subbie shouldn't keep secrets from her Doms.

He eyed her. She'd blurted out that she loved him. What else might she spill?

Lowering his voice, increasing the command, he said, "Now, pet, tell me what you've been hiding."

Waking with a yawn, Vance gave him an amused glance. The bastard had laughed his ass off at seeing the plugs. "Yeah, what did you do, sweetheart?"

What would be a deserving punishment for the serious crime of defacing anal plugs? Or had she done something else? Couldn't be too—

"Hacked into the Harvest e-mails...Association."

Every muscle in Galen's body petrified such that he couldn't even draw in a breath. *She did not say that. She did not.* "You—"

Vance interrupted, asking quietly, "You've been reading the Harvest Association e-mails?"

"Mmm." The sleepy murmur was an assent.

God fucking dammit, he wasn't going to—

Vance closed his hand on Galen's shoulder in a bone-bruising grip. "Sweetheart, what do you do with the information?"

"Send it to New York. Need to tell my Feds." A crease appeared between her brows, grew into a frown, before her beautiful soft brown eyes opened.

His wife's brown eyes had been lifeless, had unblinkingly stared at him in reproach from her broken body. Had shown terror and agony that even death couldn't erase.

He hadn't saved her. He'd caused her death.

And now this little imp was… He rolled to his knees. The fury expanding through him mixed with an icy fear that sliced apart every control he had. "You did *what*?"

At her gasp, he realized he'd shouted the question. *Fucking right.* "You hacked into the deadliest—" Kneeling on the bed, he gave her shoulders a shake.

Vance shoved him back. "Jesus, Galen, get ahold of yourself."

Sally struggled to sit upright, her back against the headboard. Her face paled—but hadn't reached the gray-white it would if she were fucking *dead*.

Galen glanced at Vance. "Did you hear what she said? Do you believe—" His throat closed up, and he choked on the words.

"I didn't…" Sally's eyes were wide. "I was careful."

"Careful!" He saw her flinch, couldn't stop. "You have no—"

Vance had rounded the bed and now dragged him back even as he said, "Sally, the Harvest Association isn't"—Vance's voice was gravel-rough and shaken—"isn't safe. You could be—"

Raped. Enslaved. Eviscerated. Burned alive. Galen yanked his arm out of Vance's grip and leaned over her. "By God, you are not—"

She shoved him away and scrambled out of the bed.

Galen shouldered Vance away and stalked after her.

Shaking visibly, Sally was yanking on her clothes.

Fuck, what was he doing? This wasn't the way to handle this. He forced himself to not loom over her, tried like hell to get his voice to even out. "We need to talk—"

"No." She had her face turned from him. "We don't."

"Not right now," Vance agreed, skirting Galen to put his arm around her. "Later we'll sit down and—"

"Only if you actually listen to me." She pushed Vance away.

"*Listen* to you!" Galen stared at her. No one had listened to Ursula. His wife's mouth had been open. Because she'd died screaming. He grabbed Sally's arm. "I'm fucking not going—"

"Shut it, Galen," Vance snapped. "Sally, let's go inside and talk about this."

"I'm leaving." She ripped her arm out of Galen's grip. Her expression was frozen, posture rigid.

He remembered the soft lushness of her body, how she'd accepted him inside her. She couldn't die. He wouldn't let her die. "You're not leaving. You're going to sit down and listen to me."

Thank Christ he'd parked behind her in the drive. She couldn't get out unless he moved his car.

As if the realization of her trapped car occurred to her, she scowled. "Fuck you, Galen Kouros." She spun toward the door.

Galen lunged after her.

A cannonball of a fist impacted his jaw, and pain burst like fireworks in his face. He slammed into the wall. Regaining his balance, he shook his head. His vision unblurred barely in time for him to block the next punch. His reflexes took over. *Block and punch.* He drove his fist into his partner's gut.

Vance grunted and laid out a set of one-twos to Galen's torso. "You. Fucking. Idiot." *Left-right.* "You. Control. Your. Temper."

Galen lost it. "She'll die!" He blocked, spun, and kicked Vance into the wall. "Are you fucking blind? They'll *target* her."

GOD, WHAT HAVE I done? Standing on her bedroom balcony, Sally heard the men yelling in the cabana. And fighting.

They loved each other. Were closer than brothers. Now they were hitting each other.

She'd caused that.

And Galen was so *mad.* She'd known he'd be upset, but he was far, far past that.

Blinking back tears, she stepped inside. On the bed, Glock sat erect, ears pricked forward. The fighting was affecting him too.

Damn them, she wasn't going to stay and have Galen yell at her some more. Hear them yell at each other. She'd done that, broken the two apart. Made them hate her.

The trembling inside Sally increased as she shoved her laptop and her clothes in her school backpack. Her hands shook as she secured pillows around the outside with a belt.

If only she could turn back time, keep the words from spilling out. Why had she told them?

But she had. She pulled in a breath and stared down at the backpack. Was she really going to leave? Run away?

She should stay. Talk to them. Maybe if they calmed down...?

The shouting grew even louder.

What had she done? *"Stupid, selfish girl. Always thinking of yourself."* Her father's words oozed into her mind.

She'd hurt them, the two men she loved. Because she was selfish and stupid.

No. No, I'm not, dammit. I was trying to do good. To save people. Why could they risk their lives and be heroes, and she couldn't?

A sob welled into her throat, choking her. *Just go. You've done enough damage.* She picked up Glock and kissed the pale streak on his soft gray head. "I love you too, you know," she whispered.

He rubbed his furry cheek on her chin, marking her with his scent. Establishing ownership.

If only her Doms had done the same.

After setting the cat outside her bedroom door, she turned the old-fashioned key, removed it, and jammed a bunch of twisted-up bobby pins into the large keyhole. "Unlock that, you j-jerks." *Beloved asshole jerks.*

On the tiny balcony outside her bedroom, she used another belt to dangle her pillow-padded backpack over the side before letting go. Carefully, she crawled over the railing and hung by her arms. *I'm a nerd. I'm not supposed to be dropping from balconies.*

With a small *eep*, she let go and fell the last few feet onto the grass below.

After tossing the pillows behind the bushes, she slung her backpack over her shoulder and ran down the drive to the road.

In the darkness, she frowned at her phone. Who lived close? Who wouldn't tell on her? Jessica or Gabi.

Gabi was closer, but she'd try to counsel her. Get her to talk to the men.

Sally's lips tightened. She'd had enough yelling to last her a lifetime.

"Jessica, are you busy right now?"

—✦—

Watching Galen rummage in the freezer, Vance rubbed his aching jaw. Caught a good one. More than one. His ribs would be purple tomorrow.

Galen tossed over a pack of frozen peas. "Need more than one?"

"Probably." Vance grinned ruefully. "I'd forgotten how much brawling hurts afterward."

"We're getting old." Galen applied a bag of frozen corn to his left cheekbone, which was already swelling. "And I'm an idiot."

He wasn't the only one. Vance frowned. Why the hell had he jumped into the altercation like that? He'd made it worse. Hell. "She hit all your triggers." And done it far too soon after she'd said she loved them. Nothing would have set Galen up so perfectly for a fall.

But Galen had overreacted in a fucking major way. "Bad timing all around, bro."

He caught the flicker of a dark glance and realized what he'd said. *Bro.*

One drunken evening, Galen admitted he felt Vance was the brother he'd never had. They'd never spoken of it again.

Well, tough. Tonight Vance wasn't in the mood to worry about Galen's hang-ups. "If I can't beat up on the guy I consider a brother, who can I use as a punching bag?"

Galen froze, then snorted. "I scored the most hits, you asshole."

"Maybe. But mine were more effective."

"Point." Galen touched his jaw gingerly. "You think she'll feel sorry enough for me to keep from killing me?"

"She has a soft heart." And considering the way she could ignite... "And a temper. I'd call it fifty-fifty you'll survive the next hour."

"Thanks." Galen pulled in a breath. "I can't believe I lost it like that. Some fucking Dom I am."

"Scene was over. Aftercare was done." Vance studied his partner. No matter the provocation, Galen wouldn't have reacted like that during a scene—he kept his control too tight. But after? Yeah, his defenses had been way down. "You didn't react as a Dom but as a lover."

That got a wince. "Makes it worse."

"Nah. Lovers are allowed to explode if a little female puts her pretty ass in danger." Vance's gut tightened as his own anger surged.

"That in the rule book somewhere?"

"Hell, yeah. If you hadn't yelled at her, I would have."

"Best it was only me." Galen glanced at the liquor cabinet but shook his head. Neither of them resorted to alcohol for liquid courage or solace. "Guess it's time to beg forgiveness."

Vance nodded and started to rise.

"No. Give me a minute to bear the brunt of her anger—I deserve it. If needed, you can play good cop."

"Got it." Vance held the frozen vegetables to his face as he listened to Galen's footsteps climbing the stairs.

A knock. "Sally?"

If she answered, her voice was too faint for Vance to hear.

"Sally, please answer the door."

Silence.

"I'll give you space if you want, but right now I need to know you're all right."

Silence.

"Open the door. *Now.*"

Nothing happened. Vance frowned. When Galen punched up the power in his voice, all submissives—and quite a few others—responded.

Silence.

With a grunt of pain, Vance rose. Where the hell had they put the extra key to that room?

Not long after, Vance managed to shove out the metal crap she'd pushed into the lock, insert the key, and unlock the door.

Galen walked over to the unrumpled bed. "She hasn't been in the bed."

"Shower and tub are dry." Vance glanced at her desk, worry increasing. "Her laptop is gone."

Galen limped down the stairs.

Following, Vance held his aching ribs.

The grassy area under her balcony showed she'd jumped. And walked toward the drive. Her old red Toyota was still parked, blocked by Galen's black sports sedan.

In the cold twilight, Galen's face looked stark with worry. "Where the hell did she go?"

———✴———

Early that morning at the airline terminal, Sally slid out of Jessica's car. *Well, this is it. Leaving.* Her whole body pulsed with pain. She wrapped her arms around herself, as if the aching could be relieved by physical comfort.

How could she have been so stupid? She should never have told them about her hacking.

Should never have fallen in love.

Jessica pulled the backpack from the trunk and set it on the curb. "I'm going to park the car so I can sit with you."

"You don't need to do that. It's not that long till my flight, and I still have to get through security." Sally frowned at her watch. Six in the morning? "I... God, Jessica, I dragged you out of bed, didn't I? You're going to get in trouble with Master Z. I'm really sorry." How self-centered she'd been. "I should have called a taxi."

Jessica scowled. "If you'd done that, I'd have given you a good bitch slap. Shadowkittens hang together against all comers, even Doms." She hugged Sally with a grin. "I just told Z a friend needed a ride. If the Feds figure it out, well, Z understands loyalty. He won't spank me too hard."

Tears rose to Sally's eyes, and she blinked them back. "Thank you. For the ride. For buying my ticket on your card."

"Pffft. You gave me a check; not like I'm out any money. But...for the trouble, you can pay me back by calling once you get...wherever you're going. Or else I'll worry."

Sally nodded. "I can do that. For my...for the Feds, if they ask, can you just not tell them anything?"

Jessica crossed her arms over her chest. Braless. Barefoot. She'd obviously run right out of the house to rescue Sally. "Did you tell me where you were going?"

"No. You said not to."

Jessica smirked. "Exactly. I won't lie to Z, but I can honestly inform him that you never told me."

Despite the sick feeling in the pit of her stomach, Sally found a smile. "You're a sneaky little brat."

"I am. But your Doms are FBI, girlfriend. They'll find you."

"They're not mine." Not anymore. "And they won't try very long." Not after she'd caused a fight. Ran away from them. "If they figure out you drove me here, can you tell them I said I'm sorry for causing them trouble. That I'm safe and thanks for the fun times."

"Pretty crappy times if they made you look like this, the assholes."

"It wasn't their fault. I did it all." Sally felt tears rising. "Gotta go." Blinking hard, she hugged Jessica, grabbed her backpack, and ran into the terminal.

—✦—

She loved him. Sitting at his desk in the home office, Galen scrubbed his hands over his face. He couldn't get the memory of her soft expression out of his head. Flushed and beautiful, she'd looked him straight in the eyes and said that. *"I love you."*

He hadn't said it back. But he did.

Didn't want to. *Shouldn't.* But he did.

Law enforcement and relationships weren't a good mix. Maybe some couples could deal with knowing that one partner could well die young, leaving the other to grieve. Not all—there was a reason the divorce rate for cops and agents was so high.

But most hadn't experienced the grief and guilt of losing a

loved one to criminals seeking revenge. Ursula hadn't volunteered to be murdered.

How could Galen ever risk putting another woman in such danger?

But did he have the right to step away from someone who loved him? Or to hurt two people besides himself.

Sally loved Vance—and Vance loved her back. Fuck, his partner deserved a sweetie like Sally. Vance had always wanted a wife and children; maybe not this soon, but a person couldn't dictate when love arrived.

What kind of a bastard would Galen be to let his fucking worries mess up his partner?

He should step away now. Let Sally go...and tell Vance to keep her. Perhaps it would hurt less if he knew they were together.

But Galen would lose them both. Pain stabbed into his chest so sharp and swift that he put his hand over his sternum. *Hell.* He'd known losing Vance would hurt, but the thought of being without the imp was just as bad.

After another breath, he nodded. He'd do what he had to do.

The door to the office opened, and Vance walked in—and stared. "Fuck, pard, mellow. We'll find her. She hasn't used a credit card, so she's probably still in the city."

"That's not the problem." Galen's voice came out sounding as weak as if he lived in a nursing home. *Christ, pull it together.* "After I help you find her, I'll back out."

"Back out...how?"

"You and Sally are good together." Galen forced his mouth into a smile. "You can name the first kid after me."

Vance's nostrils flared as he pulled in a breath. "You stubborn asshole."

"We never talked—"

"Didn't think we needed to." Vance crossed his arms over his chest. "But we will now. Lay our fucking cards on the table so I can kick your ass."

Galen felt the rise of anger like a slow burn. Couldn't Vance just say thanks and move on? "I don't want a wife."

"Bullshit. You don't want to risk losing someone you care about. Can't stand feeling guilty. You pussy." Vance stalked across the room and stared down at him. "Bet if you'd been in a car accident and your wife died, you'd never drive again."

"You don't know—"

"Jesus, bro, I lost a partner in a takedown. Been through the if-I'd-only-moved-faster remorse. Had a partner turn into an alcoholic. Been through the if-only-I'd-been-more-supportive remorse. We all feel guilty about shit we could've done better. The rest of the world gets past it."

Galen stood. Considered smashing his fist into that sarcastic mouth.

Vance's gaze met his. "It's time to move on, Galen. You've hung on your guilt too long."

Maybe. But the past didn't just disappear. Neither did worries over someone's safety. Galen closed his eyes and exhaled. But others made it through to the other side. *Time to man up.* "Anything else you want to get off your chest," he asked in a dry voice.

Vance grinned and leaned his hip against the desk. "Long as we're being all girlie here, yeah." He crossed his arms again. "We live together. Top together. Co-Dom when there's a sub in the house. Always figured we'd co-husband together if we found someone."

Fuck. "You get any more in touch with your feminine side, and you'll need tampons."

Vance's lips quirked. "Yeah, well..." His voice changed into the tone he used to coax information from suspects and submissives. "Can you trust me enough to share your idea of the future?" He waited.

Fucking Dom manipulative techniques were fucking effective.

Galen paced across the room and stared out the window. The glossy hibiscus shrub boasted a wealth of flashy red trumpet flowers...and they'd wilt away by late afternoon.

No lasting power.

He scowled at the bush. When he'd joined the FBI, no one

mentioned one of his enemies could be his own mind. But he'd never backed away from a fight before. Wouldn't start now. And he'd win this one.

So. Although he still wouldn't mind putting a fist in the pushy bastard's face, Vance deserved an answer.

Galen sighed. If he could conquer his worry and guilt, then...then, he could think of nothing better than living in the future with Sally. With Vance at his side.

Ayuh.

He turned and looked his partner in the eye. "Being the older husband, I expect to name our first kid."

—✦—

A few hours later, Galen followed his partner through the back gate into Z's private gardens. A distant rumbling made him look up. The air was muggy, and black clouds piled up like skyscrapers on the western horizon. Yeah, it was almost June. The afternoon thunderstorm season had started. Getting drenched would be a fitting end to a dismal day.

They still hadn't found Sally.

Since she didn't carry much cash, they figured she'd holed up with a friend, and so they'd called the trainees. No luck. Tried the Shadowlands submissives, one by one. Good thing that grad school had limited the imp's social time or they'd have been calling every female in her university.

They'd gone through the entire list of Shadowkittens without success.

Then Z had called after hearing from the other Masters. Although Jessica was home, she hadn't mentioned receiving their voice mail.

Yeah, she knew something.

"Think Jessica will tell us where Sally went?" Vance asked as they walked across the veranda.

"Not a chance." That little banty hen had a rep for defending the submissives. She was as protective in her way as Z was in his, so coaxing information out of her might be tricky.

Jessica lived with Z on the Shadowlands mansion's third floor, and by the time he reached the top, Galen's knee hurt like a son of a bitch.

Z opened the door to their knock. "Gentlemen." Dressed in black jeans and a loose black shirt, he led them through the kitchen, the dining room, and into the living room. The light from arched windows streamed over the creamy walls, the dark red carpet, and glinted off Jessica's long golden hair. Curled in a corner of the leather couch, she stared at them with wary eyes. The determined tilt of her chin was worrisome.

Vance lifted an eyebrow at Galen, showing he recognized they were dealing with a hostile subject.

As Vance leaned against the stone fireplace, Galen picked up a ladder-back chair from the dining area and set it next to the couch. Inside her comfort zone.

Wisely staying out of the kill zone, Z took a chair at the other end of the couch and leaned back with his fingers steepled on his stomach. From his reserved expression, he'd intervene if he felt they were overstepping their bounds. And during the phone call, he'd made those bounds quite clear.

Galen straddled the chair, resting his forearms on the back. After giving Jessica a smile that wasn't returned, he asked gently, "Did Sally tell you what happened?"

Her mouth opened. Her eyes narrowed as she recognized the trap. This wasn't a submissive who would lie to—or in front of—her Dom, so she couldn't say, *I haven't seen her.* But she would have no problem with evasions. "I'm sorry, but I believe conversations between friends are private."

"Jessica, we're worried about her," Vance said, forcing her to split her attention between them. "Our lakeshore drive isn't a safe area for a woman on foot at night. Can you, at least, tell us if you picked her up?"

"I don't want to talk with you." Her mouth turned mulish.

"I think that was a fair question, kitten," Z murmured.

"Dammit," she muttered and glared at Vance. "Yes, I picked her up. But she's not anywhere on Shadowlands' property. And she's safe."

Thank God. The tension in Galen's chest eased slightly. Jessica wouldn't say that unless she was sure. "Thank you, pet."

"That's all you're going to get from me, even if he lets you beat me. You made her cry."

The verbal hit sliced into Galen's heart like a knife. "I did. And I'd like to apologize to her and make amends. Won't you help us find her?"

"No. I won't." The glance she cast at Z was antagonistic. "No matter what *he* does."

Oh hell. Now he'd caused trouble between two people he liked very much. The exhaustion weighing Galen down was joined by frustration and a goodly amount of despair. Everything he'd done in the last twenty-four hours had gone wrong.

But he could start by fixing this. Maybe.

He glanced at Vance and saw his partner was willing to let him take a stab at it. "Jessica. I'm sorry. Sorry if we created trouble between you two. Z is our friend, and he was trying to help us, much as you helped Sally. I've never met a more loyal man."

Her gaze dropped.

"You can be angry at us, because we—I—hurt Sally, but Z is trapped like you, right in the middle. Please don't be upset with him."

When her lips trembled, Galen felt her unhappiness like another blow. He pushed to his feet. "We're leaving."

Vance walked over to crouch in front of Jessica. "You're a good friend, sweetie. Sally is lucky to have you."

She glanced at him and Galen. "You two are pretty effective, aren't you? No wonder she had trouble resisting you."

Galen's spirits lifted slightly. Hopefully she still would.

Vance patted Jessica's knee. "With such good friends, I'm surprised she's not staying with one of you."

"Well, she felt—" Jessica caught herself, and this time Vance received the you're-a-cockroach-that-needs-to-be-squashed glare.

But the good-guy trick had worked. If Sally was at a friend's, Jessica would probably have said, *But she*—rather than starting an explanation.

The imp might or might not be in town, but she wasn't with one of her buddies.

Galen's eyes narrowed. Just how far would Jessica go to help her buddy? He'd checked on Sally's credit card...but they hadn't checked anyone else's.

Gotcha, imp.

Vance held his hand out to Jessica, not moving until she gave him her fingers. "I'm sorry for the trick, sweetheart. But we really are worried. I don't know if she told you, but she did something that will get her targeted by the Harvest Association. That's what we fought about."

Jessica's mouth formed an O. "Sally didn't talk about why. Just said she'd caused problems, and it was time to leave."

"Time to leave?" They'd just see about that.

CHAPTER SIXTEEN

U nder a blue, blue sky, the green fields of Iowa rolled out as far as the eye could see. Sally took her time, smiling at the weathered farmhouses, the occasional dog barking and racing along a fence line, the peaceful cattle grazing in pastures.

Her plane had gotten into Des Moines yesterday. She'd planned to drive straight to the farm, but after fighting back her tears and anger, she'd known she couldn't deal with her father. Instead, she'd holed up in a hotel for a night of weeping and throwing things.

Plastic hotel glasses hurled across the room? No satisfaction in that whatsoever. And what inconsiderate jerk had replaced heavy—breakable—coffee cups with Styrofoam? To hell with them.

And to hell with the Feebs too.

They were wrong. And Galen had no right to tell her what to do.

She could hack the Harvest Association e-mails if she wanted to. And she'd started before she'd moved in with them, anyway. And she'd saved women from being kidnapped. She'd done good. She'd been a hero.

They're just totally shortsighted dipwads.

But why did it have to end so badly? She tightened her fingers on the steering wheel and blinked back the tears. *Don't visit Father with red eyes.*

Really, she was making too much of all this. She hadn't planned to stay with the Feds, right? She didn't want a long-term ménage. That would be insane. Sure it had been fun for a while, but obviously the *while* was over.

God, she just wanted to stand in the middle of one of those cornfields and scream at the top of her lungs, *I wasn't ready...*

With the way her luck was going, some farmer would probably shoot her.

Shaking her head, she turned in at her father's drive. As she pulled her rental car up to the two-story farmhouse, she saw little had changed.

How long had it been this time? After high school, she'd returned every few years to catch up with high school friends. Each time, she'd made a dutiful visit to her father...always hoping that one day he'd decide he wanted a daughter.

Not going to happen this lifetime, stupid.

She walked across the yard, breathing in the fragrance of growing crops yet missing the slight tang of the sea. Planting was done. The corn wasn't up to her knees. Soybeans were in. Tall trees marked the creek banks in the south pasture. Everywhere were gently rolling hills. Iowa didn't have take-your-breath-away mountain ranges or ocean vistas; it just felt...cozy. Pretty.

It should have been a wonderful place to grow up.

Well, here goes. The backseat was filled with flattened boxes she'd bought so she could pack whatever was still here. But where would she send her stuff? Back to Tampa?

It would be best not to return there. Christ in a cornfield, but she wanted to slap Galen—and Vance too. Yelling at her. Fighting with each other.

But seeing them meant she'd probably fall into their arms and cry. Descend into a wussy girl. No, she didn't want to be anywhere around them. *And damn them for turning me into an emotional puddle.*

She lifted her chin and picked up the boxes. Time to face her father. She pulled in a breath and released it out slowly, letting calm flow over her like a second skin. *Don't show emotions. Don't ask for things. Be obedient and quiet.*

A startling flare of anger almost tripped her on the steps. Most parents wanted obedient children, but to expect them to be quiet? All the time? *That is bullshit.*

Settle, Sally. Settle. She knocked.

Her father opened the door.

She looked into his bitter eyes and watched his lips pull back into his cheeks, like a dog suppressing a snarl. *Well, nothing has changed, has it?*

She could barely remember him being different—when her mother was alive. He'd never been affectionate to his children—especially Sally—but he'd loved his wife. Absolutely doted on her. And with his wife's death, everything inside him had twisted up.

"I'm here to remove my things from your house," she said politely. Looking at him with new eyes—thanks to Galen and his frigging homework assignment—she suddenly wondered if her father had been jealous of Sally, jealous of the time Sally's mother had spent with her. "I'll have everything packed and be gone by tonight."

"Fine."

—*—

The mailbox read *Hugh Hart.* According to the records, Sally's brother lived on the adjacent farm. When Vance spotted a rental car parked at the father's white farmhouse, relief loosened his shoulders.

As Galen had figured, Sally used Jessica's credit card to book her flight. But she'd had to show her own credit card to obtain a rental car. "Parked right out there in the front. She obviously doesn't think we would come after her."

"My fault," Galen said. He'd been unnaturally quiet, even for him.

"Shut up." At the dark glance, Vance elaborated. "You fucked up by yelling at her, yes. But she also knew we wouldn't react well or she wouldn't have hidden what she was doing. And she broke the law." He slid out of the car and glanced back. "So get your head out of your ass."

The flush of angry red on his partner's face was rather rewarding, and Vance barely managed to smother his laugh. Being a peacemaker might be costing him some fun—maybe he'd start poking at his friends instead.

As Galen knocked on the door, Vance glanced around. An equipment building. A barn just past the coop. Chickens in a pen. Cornfields. No barking dogs. Maybe Hart had decided they were too much work.

The door opened to show Sally's stocky father. Where Sally's brown eyes were filled with sweetness or alive with mischief, Hart's looked like frozen dirt in his weathered face. The farmer shifted to block the doorway. "What d'you want?"

Well, there was a welcome. "We're here to see Sally," Vance said, using his nice guy persona. "I see her car is here," he added, forestalling any lies that she wasn't home.

"She didn't tell me you were coming." Hart took a step back as Galen moved into his personal space.

Using his cane as a prop, Galen sidled past the old man and into the foyer.

"Stop, you—"

"Is she in her room?" Vance shrugged off his denim jacket before slinging it over his shoulder. Nothing like a pistol in a shoulder harness to silence bluster. Probably didn't hurt that he and Galen looked battered enough to have been in a bar brawl.

"Upstairs." At the ringing of an old-fashioned landline phone, the man abandoned the fight and stomped away to answer it.

As Vance followed Galen up the stairs, he heard the man saying, "She's here."

A pause. A protest, "Won't work. She has men visiting her."

Pause.

Perhaps the brother? Was he causing trouble? Vance stopped on the steps to listen.

"Bring them? Hell, boy, are you out of your mind? I don't want to—"

Pause.

"Fine. Six o'clock. Yeah, I'll come."

"There's a grudging acceptance," Galen said under his breath. His gaze was cold as he looked back down the stairs. A second later, he resumed the climb, using his cane. The hours in the cramped flight obviously hadn't done his knee any favors.

The hallway at the top led both directions, but thumping noises came from the end room on the right.

When his partner squared his shoulders, Vance wondered if the imp realized how much Galen cared. How easily she could damage him.

Not just Galen, either. Vance shook his head. The thought of losing her hurt deep enough to hit the marrow.

Galen tapped on the door.

It opened. "Yes, Fath—" Sally's eyes went round. "Galen?" Her voice came out a whisper. "Vance?" But the flash of joy she showed transformed into a frozen, distant expression that was more ominous than anger. Her hair was down, no makeup, old T-shirt and jeans. Red-rimmed eyes.

They'd made her cry. Vance felt that like a stab in his chest.

Her mouth firmed into her more-stubborn-than-a-mule expression. "Go home, guys. The fun is over."

She shoved the door shut so fast that only Galen's cane kept it from closing. *Good reflexes, pard.*

And without a second of thought, he and Galen applied their shoulders to the door.

The imp staggered back into a very stark bedroom. Three boxes sat on the bed, another on the floor. No pictures, no knickknacks. Walls with peeling paint. Splintering hardwood floor. No carpet. The drapes were filthy and fraying on the edges. The room was as welcoming as her asshole of a father.

"Dammit, get out," Sally spat. The ice was gone, and she was looking meaner than Glock on vaccination day.

Galen held up his hand. "May I have ten minutes? After that, you can kick us out, if you wish."

TEN MINUTES. COULD she keep from crying for that long? Sally wasn't sure. Letting Galen talk would be the quickest way to get rid of them. Undoubtedly he'd explain how hacking the Harvest Association was dangerous and threaten her with arrest if she didn't stop. She could handle that. She'd say okay, and they'd leave. Crossing her arms over her chest, she snapped,

"Fine. Go ahead."

Galen hesitated. He looked so tired. Despite her teasing, she never really thought of him as being older—all his energy and passion made him seem her age—but the lines around his mouth and the corners of his eyes had deepened. His cheekbone was bruised and swollen. His jaw had two days of beard growth. He hadn't shaved...since she left?

"I lost my temper with you," he said gravely. "You don't need to forgive me, but I want you to know why I reacted so badly."

She opened her mouth to say something flippant and stopped. Galen always apologized if he did something wrong, and she admired that. But he'd never looked so—exposed. All she could do was nod.

"A few years ago, I was married."

Yes, he'd mentioned he was a widower, and his expression had been so closed she hadn't asked any questions.

"I was on a violent crimes task force, concentrating on gangs. We'd just arrested several members of a gang." He pulled in a breath. "Threats to agents aren't uncommon, but I never thought..."

Vance stood apart, watching silently. He'd shaved, and beneath his dark tan, a purpling bruise ran along his right jaw, making her heart ache.

Galen leaned on his cane, something he rarely did when just standing. Tough Guy never wanted to show weakness. But she could see he was hurting, and her hand trembled with the need to hold his, to comfort him.

His voice was rough as he said, "My wife was home. Decorating for a birthday party for her sister the next night."

He stared at the wall, his eyes tormented. Filled with pain.

God, Galen. As if pulled by a chain, Sally took a step forward, hesitated, and hugged him. She heard the cane hit the floor, and his arms wrapped around her so tightly she couldn't breathe.

He held her there, a second, another.

"Go on," she whispered against his shoulder.

His voice was husky. "She planned to meet me at a

restaurant, since I had to work late. She didn't arrive. Didn't answer her phone." His cheek was against her hair. "I drove home. Too late. Far too fucking late. Some of the gang had busted down the back door. They...took their anger out on her, used her as a lesson to me. And killed her."

"Oh, Galen." Sally rubbed her cheek on his chest, wanting only to comfort. How could someone so protective live with that?

"She died...in terror. In pain. I wasn't there, Sally. I didn't keep her safe. Instead, she was murdered because of me."

And suddenly the reason he'd totally freaked out in the cabana blasted into her brain. She'd told him she loved him, and there she was, taunting the Harvest Association. If she died at their hands, what would it do to Galen?

A shudder ran through her. Turning her head, she looked at Vance. Jaw tight, eyes haunted. He was hurting too. She held her hand out to him, and he pushed off the wall.

Once he was close enough, she wrapped an arm around him. Now that she wasn't blinded by anger, she realized he'd been as upset with her hacking as Galen. He'd just handled it better.

If they thought the Harvest Association would murder her as they had Lieutenant Tillman, of course they'd be afraid.

Sure she knew how good she was, but her Doms didn't. Not that they'd given her a chance to explain, the jerks, but...

"I'll stop," she said. She pulled away and faced them, feeling a tug of loss for her work. She'd wanted to be hero. To do something special. Worthy. "I'll give you my files. And I won't do any more hacking."

At one time, Galen had been able to make his expression unreadable, but either he'd lost the ability or her gaze was keener. She saw how his relief cleared some of the pain lurking in the shadows of his eyes.

Now that she knew what haunted him, maybe she could help.

"Are you sure, sweetheart?" Vance asked.

She wanted to hug him for just being his wonderful reasonable self. His steadiness balanced Galen. Okay, he balanced her too. And right now, she very badly wanted to see him smile. See them both smile.

Wrinkling her nose, she gave them her cutest pout. "If quitting is what it takes to keep you two safe, I guess that's what I need to do."

Galen rubbed his hands over his face as if to move on. "Keep *us* safe?" he asked in disbelief. When he glanced at Vance, his eyes held the amusement she loved to see.

"I like being safe." Vance touched the tip of her nose. "I think we should take her up on her offer."

"Well. Thank you, pet." Galen nodded at the boxes on the bed. "Why don't we load those into your car? We have rooms at the hotel in town. The one hotel. We can go back there and talk."

"But—" She was done packing. No need to stay here. "Okay. But talk about what?"

Vance took her shoulders. "Don't you want to stay with us?"

Stay?

Vance was frowning, and the expression on Galen's face probably mirrored her own—indecision, worry. "I... Let's talk at the hotel."

She heard the heavy thud of her father's boots on the stairs and a rap on the door. "Sally, Tate's having us there for supper. The men are invited, as well. We leave in fifteen minutes."

Great. A horribly uncomfortable meal at her brother's. Could she refuse? No, it might—probably would—be the last time she'd ever see them. Why the realization should make her heart hurt, she didn't know. It wasn't as if there'd been any love there. Ever. She looked at the men. "Do you two mind?"

Vance's mouth was set in a line. "You're sure not going there without us."

Galen nodded. "Let's load up your car first so you don't need to return here."

God, she really did love them, and how scary was that?

—✳—

Leaving their vehicles—the Feds' rental, her rental, and her father's truck, Sally followed the three men up to her brother's house, escorted by an elderly yellow lab and an energetic

Australian shepherd.

Before reaching the porch, Sally looked around. Their grandparents had owned the place, but they'd died when she was little and, although her father planted the fields, he'd let the farmhouse and barn deteriorate.

Tate had put everything back into perfect condition, and the old two-story clapboard was a pristine white with navy-blue shutters and trim. The barn had been painted the traditional red-brown. The eight-foot spirea bushes that lined the gravel road to cut down the noise and dust were pruned. And to her surprise, pink petunias lined the concrete sidewalk.

Since when had Tate planted pretty flowers? Or owned dogs, for that matter?

Probably alerted by the barking Aussie, her brother came down the porch steps, sidestepping the dogs. He was clean shaven, brown hair cut short, wearing jeans and a Willie Nelson T-shirt. "Sally. It's good to see you."

The welcome in his voice and his smile made her stare. "Uh. And you." Flustered, she turned and pointed to each man in turn. "Vance Buchanan, Galen Kouros. Guys, this is my brother, Tate Hart."

Tate's eyes narrowed as he looked over her scruffy, bruised men...and he could probably see Galen's weapon under his open leather jacket.

Off to one side, her father watched with his usual frown.

As the men performed a guy handshaking ritual, Sally noticed more changes. A small bike with training wheels and a bright red trike were parked by the porch. A football lay near an overturned dollhouse, where dolls were scattered around like victims in a war.

Tate hadn't had children three years ago...had he?

"They're here!" The childish scream came from one of the two children tearing out the front door. A boy, perhaps around eight, was followed by a slightly younger girl. Both blond and blue-eyed. Maybe not Tate's then.

"C'mere, you two." Tate motioned. The boy stepped up to his right.

The girl pressed against his left side and studied Vance and Galen warily. Her attention turned to Sally. She beamed. "You're Daddy's sister."

Tate a daddy? Sally gave herself a mental shake, grinned, and held her hand out. "That's right. I'm Sally. Who are you guys?"

The boy took her hand. "I'm Dylan, and she's Emma. Do you really live in Florida?"

"I do. I'm—" She was interrupted by a woman's voice.

"Tate, don't keep them standing out there. Bring them in." With coloring that matched the children's, a woman in a V-necked silky red top and blue jeans stood on the porch. She gave Tate a frown and waved at the group. "We have beer and wine and pop. Come on in."

"Beer sounds good," Vance said, hooking an arm around Sally. "And something smells delicious."

"Leigh Anne is a great cook," Tate said. He waved them up the steps, dodged the stream of children and dogs, and followed with their father.

It was a welcoming house. The living room held comfortable-looking, worn couches and chairs in dark greens, a large-screen television, and toys spilling from a wooden trunk. The woman led the way through and into the dining room. "Since the food's all ready to go, why don't you go ahead and be seated. And what would you like to drink?" She rolled her eyes. "I forgot—I'm Leigh Anne."

Tate entered the room in time to hear her, and he laughed.

Laughed.

Sally barely managed to close her mouth. As he started another round of introductions, she watched. Since when had Tate been so...relaxed? Nice? She wanted to poke the guy and ask what he'd done with her real brother.

Drink orders were taken, and the men opted for beer, except for Galen, who requested wine.

Sally grinned at him and whispered, "Wussy."

"That's me." He tangled his hand in her hair—a Dom's ready-made leash—and tugged her closer. "I've missed your mouth," he murmured, bent closer, and whispered, "And I intend to use it later tonight."

The ruthless grip on her hair and the promise in his black eyes sent heat stampeding through her veins. She might tease him about being unmacho, but no one ever doubted he had far more testosterone than was good for a man. She swallowed hard and whispered the only answer possible, "Yes, *Sir*."

"Good enough." A faint smile played at the corners of his mouth as he released her.

The jerk. With just a few words, he had her body humming with arousal. As she considered kicking him, she caught a wink from Vance and a frown from her brother.

Right. She turned and followed Leigh Anne into the kitchen. Feminist or not, a woman always offered her assistance to another woman, especially if needing to escape from the men. "Hey, can I help?"

"Of course. How about you get the beer from the fridge while I open the wine." She gave Sally a half smile. "Your father doesn't believe in predinner conversation, so we're skipping that part."

Just as well. She couldn't think of anything to talk about anyway. Sally pulled out three beers for the men and one for herself. "Your children are adorable."

Leigh Anne's powder-blue eyes danced with good humor. She was probably about Tate's age, so several years older than Sally, and comfortable with herself. Her clothes fit her curvy body, and her makeup was muted. She wore a man's watch on her wrist and hadn't bothered to put on shoes. How could Sally not like her? "The munchkins might be adorable, but you can figure on being grilled tonight. They're very curious about you."

"Ah, right." *The feeling is mutual. Like where did Tate find such a nice woman?*

Setting glasses on two trays, Leigh Anne gave her a perceptive smile. "Tate hopes you'll stay for a bit after Hugh leaves. To talk and do some catching up."

"Ah..." Talk to Tate? That would be a first. As if he had ever wanted to talk with her... "I don't think—"

Out of her buried past, a memory bubbled to the surface. *"Faster, horsy, faster."* Sally'd been perched on Tate's shoulders, using his shaggy hair for reins. *Squealing with laughter as he bounced her and trotted in circles.*

Shaken, she pulled in a slow breath. How had she forgotten that, at one time, he'd been her adored big brother, right up until her mother died? Her refusal trailed off, and she nodded instead.

Leigh Anne's smile turned full wattage. "Good. That's good. Now we just have to survive a dinner with your crabby father." She winked at Sally, picked up her tray, and led the way to the dining room.

Her brother sat at one end of the table. Her father had the children beside him on one side; on the other, Vance and Galen had left a chair empty between them.

Sally circled the long oval table, handing out the drinks on her tray.

"Thank you." Vance took his beer and said quietly, "You make a gorgeous barmaid. Z taught you well."

"Why, thank you." She leaned down to whisper in his ear, "Trainees get to play after finishing their shift, right? Do I get a scene later?"

"Oh yeah, sweetheart." A crease appeared in his cheek, and his wicked gaze set her pulse to hammering. But when he added, "You have a lot to answer for, after all," she almost dropped her tray.

Seriously? They'd punish her, just because she disobeyed their order to stay in her room, left without permission, and forced them to track her down? Didn't they have any sense of humor at all?

Unfortunately, the threat had her libido sitting up like a well-trained poodle begging for treats. With an effort, she conjured an insulted scowl before escaping back into the kitchen.

Once she and Leigh Anne had brought out milk for the children, meatloaf, mashed potatoes, rolls, corn, and a large salad, they took their seats. Tate offered a quiet prayer, which startled Sally. When her mother died, so had religion in their house.

Conversation was general, a catching up on the years that had passed. Leigh Anne told how she'd met Tate on the Fourth of July. Emma had become hysterical at the loud fireworks, and Tate had come to the rescue. "He was so sweet," Leigh Anne said, giving him a loving smile.

Sweet? Tate? Sally frowned. Not in her experience. But, come to think of it, he'd been wildly popular in school and a good friend to his buddies. Just not to her. She hadn't even gotten a wedding invitation. "And then you married?"

Tate toasted his wife with his beer. "Yep. We were married by a justice of the peace with a couple of friends to witness. No party."

"Shoot, we either did it with no one or would have to invite the whole town." Leigh Anne gave her guests a wry smile. "My first wedding was huge and expensive and obviously didn't bestow any special magic."

Sally bit her lip, feeling unwelcome tears sting her eyes. Why would she feel relieved Tate hadn't left her off his invitation list? Shoot, they didn't even talk. Breathing slowly, she got her emotions tucked back down where they belonged before looking up.

He was watching her with a small, concerned smile.

So was Vance, who patted her knee.

After a keen glance, Galen turned the subject to the gangs moving into Des Moines.

During dessert, Sally asked for news about her classmates. Leigh Anne and Tate probably knew all the town gossip.

Several had married. A couple of the guys were serving overseas.

"Last winter, Clare—I think she was a year behind you—died in a car accident," Tate said. "She left two children and a husband behind."

Sally's father looked up from his plate and gave her a cold stare. "Clare probably had a selfish brat who demanded something, or she'd never have been on the road." His unexpected attack slapped the table into silence.

Guilt rolled over Sally like a winter fog.

Wide-eyed, Emma pulled her hand back from the basket of dinner rolls.

No, that wasn't right. Sally rose and handed the little girl a roll. "It's okay, baby. He didn't mean you."

Without a word, Vance slung his arm behind Sally, pulling her chair close enough she could feel the reassurance of his body along her side.

Galen leaned back, lazily swirling his wine in the glass as he asked in his blunt New England voice, "You obviously meant those words for your daughter. What exactly did Sally ask her mother for?"

"A new dress." Her father's mouth twisted. "Couldn't be happy with what she had. Wanted something special for a party. And even though I'd said no more money for clothes, her mother drove her to town."

"Well, no wonder you treat her like a criminal." The diamond edge of Galen's voice could cut through metal. "A little girl asked her mama for a party dress? Get out the handcuffs, Vance. Haul her to jail."

Her father jerked back as if he'd been punched. "Now listen—"

"We should draft a law," Galen said. "Make it a crime for a child to ask for clothes."

As Sally struggled against dark memories and self-reproach, his words took a while to sink in. She stared at him. "What?"

Vance huffed a laugh. "Won't work, pard. I have sisters, cousins, nieces, and nephews, and they've asked for new clothes about every other day from preschool through college. Although one nephew didn't—he wanted video games."

Galen's brows drew together. "That's even worse."

Sally closed her mouth as the Doms' cold logic broke through. The shadows around her lightened as she remembered the essay she'd written for Galen. As she saw her father's actions through the men's critical eyes.

Seriously? Treat a child like a criminal for wanting a dress? She thought of her friends' children, how they'd ask for things— and beg if they didn't get the answer they wanted. They were normal kids.

"Oh dear." Leigh Anne widened her eyes. "I'm afraid Emma and Dylan will be the first to be arrested."

Sally saw Tate struggling with laughter.

After a quick glance at his stepfather, Dylan snickered and played along. "Oh no, Mom. Not *jail*. I only wanted one pair of running shoes. Not like John—he wanted three."

"Can I have new doll clothes, Mommy?" Giggling, Emma bounced in her chair. "I have to go to jail too. Like Dylan?"

Turning a furious dark red, Sally's father slammed his fist down on the table, making the dishes rattle and the children jump. "That's enough! It's no joking matter that the brat got her mother killed."

Galen rose and leaned forward, his hands flat on the table. "A car accident is a tragedy. Blaming a child for behaving like a child is criminal. Personally, I'd call it abuse, and if anyone here deserves to go to jail, it is you."

"You can't say that to me!"

"He shouldn't." Sally stood, seeing her father clearly for the first time. Anger swelled inside her. If he'd treated Emma the way he had her, she'd have removed the child from his care.

When she put her hand on Galen's shoulder, he studied her for a second and conceded by taking his seat. Vance's hand warmed her lower back; he'd defend her if she faltered.

Her father blustered, "That's more like—"

"He shouldn't, because I should have, years ago." Her lips felt numb, her hands chilled. But...she was ready. "I let you verbally abuse me, shut me in an unlighted barn. You locked me in my room for three days just for crying over a cat that died."

And Tate had left food in the tree house for her that time. She'd forgotten that. "You made me feel as if I caused the car accident, like I was a monster." Guilt wavered in front of her like a black curtain, but she ripped it down. The air felt fresh as she pulled in a breath. "But I was just a normal child. Mom was a normal mother. The car skidded in a bad place. The only monstrous behavior...was yours. *Is* yours."

"I didn't—" He pointed to her, face twisted in hate.

He wouldn't change. The sorrow of that filled her chest, but she knew what she needed to do. Her voice was firm. "I won't speak to you again. I no longer consider you my father."

His mouth worked, but under her unwavering stare, his gaze

fell.

Sally took a stiff step back. Vance squeezed her side and took his hand away, leaving her free to chart her course.

Her knees wobbled as she turned, but she lifted her head and walked steadily out the back door into the quiet night. Her chest hurt—her whole body hurt—but there were stars in the sky. She'd forgotten how beautiful they looked in Iowa.

GALEN FELT PUMPED up with pride in Sally, at how she'd said exactly what she needed to say. And he hurt for her, because he knew just what it had cost her. Which was why he wanted to plant a fist right in the bastard's face.

He curled his fingers around his cane and knew if he spoke now, it would be too much.

"My turn," Vance said under his breath. He rose and put his foot on the chair, resting his forearms on his thigh. "Mr. Hart. After hearing all this, I'm sorely inclined to see if I can't talk Sally into a civil lawsuit. Although the statute of limitations would hinder the outcome, your reputation in this area would definitely suffer."

Direct hit. The man's color faded, leaving his tanned skin an ugly yellow. He rose and glared around the table as if expecting someone to leap to his defense. His stare came to rest on Tate. "You gonna let them talk to me like that?"

"Yes." Face pale, Tate straightened his shoulders. "I didn't hear anything that wasn't true."

With a growl, the old man stomped out. The front door slammed a minute later.

"Well." Leigh Anne puffed out a breath. "That was rather a mess, wasn't it?"

"He was really mean." Emma looked as if she wanted to cry, and Galen felt a pang of regret that she'd witnessed the altercation. "Is Sally okay?"

"I think she'll be fine." Leigh Anne pulled her daughter into her lap and looked down the table at her husband. "I think we all will now."

Galen followed her gaze.

Tate looked shell-shocked. After a second, he attempted a smile. "Emma, Dylan, if you two get ready for bed, maybe Sally will come up and say good night before she leaves."

Emma's face cleared. She slid off her mother's lap and trotted toward the stairs. "I'm going to show her my dolphin and my octopus. She'll like them."

Dylan followed only a step behind. "She'll like my books better. Bet she likes to read."

Thank God, children were resilient. Galen turned to look at Leigh Anne. "I'm sorry your children were subjected to that. We should have taken it elsewhere."

Leigh Anne shook her head. "Although he never treated them the way he treated Sally, they sure heard enough about what he thought. Tonight was ugly, yes, but I'm glad they saw him receive his comeuppance."

"Me too," Tate said under his breath.

When Leigh Anne rose, the men did also. She nodded at Galen and Vance. "I'm going to check on the children, and I know you want to be with Sally. Go on, now."

"Thank you," Vance said. "You've been a generous hostess."

As Galen moved toward the back door, he heard Leigh Anne say, "Honey, this is a good time."

"I hope so," Tate answered. "I'll clean up the dishes a mite and have that talk."

Galen paused in the door. What talk would that be? He considered going back inside, then saw Sally.

She was sitting on the wide back steps, head against a railing slat, watching the stars. She gave him and Vance a weak smile. "Sorry for leaving you. I kind of wanted to have the last word."

"Worked a treat," Vance said. He gave her a quick kiss.

Using the railing to assist, Galen sat down behind her and a step above. Legs apart, he pulled her closer so she could use his stomach as a backrest.

She was trembling.

"You're cold," he said. Probably also suffering from postfight adrenaline.

Before she could answer, Vance dropped onto the step below her. Leaning against the railing, he slid his legs along the step so her thighs would rest on his. After curling his hands over her knees, he smiled at her. "Just consider us portable heaters."

"You two." She sighed and pulled Vance's hand onto her lap.

In the distance, an owl hooted. The corn rustled in the breeze that was scented with freshly cut grass. Peaceful area. When Sally leaned her head back against him, Galen felt the evening's turmoil drain away, replaced by contentment. His partner, his woman. Both safe.

He wrapped his arms around her. Later, they'd discuss what had happened and do some digging into the parts their little submissive had revealed tonight, but right now, she needed a break.

And that she'd accept comfort from him, that she'd really forgiven him, was more than he'd expected...and exactly what he needed.

AS THE MEN'S concern wrapped around Sally, the awful shaking of her insides lessened. They stayed silent, letting her recover on her own. The quiet countryside had always soothed her, especially when she'd hidden herself up in the huge maple behind the house.

God, she'd loved that tiny platform. Looking back, it seemed amazing that a skinny twelve-year-old could have made it. How much skin had she lost trying to drag scrap lumber up into the branches? How many times had she climbed out the window of her bedroom prison, onto the porch roof, and down the trellis? *Wonder if the platform is still there?*

While building her little refuge, she hadn't considered the future...like how the leaves would disappears with a brisk autumn wind, leaving her tree "house" totally exposed. Her father had definitely noticed. But he'd been amused, thinking Tate had built it.

Her brother had never revealed her secret. Odd how Tate's later behavior had made her forget so many of his small kindnesses.

A few minutes later, the screen door opened. Tate stepped out and nodded at the two men. "Sorry to disturb you, but I wanted to talk to my sister before she left." *My sister.* When they were little, he'd said those words with such pride. But after the world changed, he hadn't claimed her any longer.

Resentment flared and died. "Have a seat."

Vance said, "Would you like us to give you some time alone?"

Tate sat down on a step the same level as Sally's and leaned against the railing. "Stay. After that dinner, I doubt we have many secrets left."

Sally twisted in Galen's embrace and rested her forearms on his bent knee so she could face her brother.

The starlight heightened the shadows and lines in Tate's face. He looked old, and she realized in disbelief that he was over thirty. His eyes, so like her father's—and hers—met hers. "Sally. I'm sorry."

For the evening? "Tate, I'm the one that blew up at Father, not—"

"Not that. Hell, he got what he deserved—and nothing I hadn't said to him before once I realized..."

Sally stared. He'd argued with their father?

He sighed. "The fact that you look at me like that means I was even worse than I remember." He pulled at his ear. "Shit. I didn't know back then how bad I was. It's like... All brothers tease their little sisters, right?"

"I guess..." she said cautiously.

"No!" He slapped the step, making her jump.

Vance squeezed her leg reassuringly.

"No," Tate said more quietly. "See, Leigh Anne moved in here with the kids." He smiled. "I love the rascals, but they're a handful. Dylan teases Emma, and yeah, it's normal. But it's normal because we keep it from going too far. He gets in trouble if he hurts her or makes her cry or breaks her toys. I realized, watching them, that kids lack a sense of proportion. Limits."

Sally couldn't find anything to say, so Galen, Dom that he was, stepped in. "You went too far with Sally?" he asked so quietly she wasn't sure Tate even realized someone else had spoken.

"Yeah. Dad didn't set limits. Hell, he egged me on. And I bought right into his story, putting all the blame on you for Mom's death. Cuz, I was angry. Grieving. She wasn't my real mom, but I loved her."

In the silence, a whine sounded, and the old Labrador shuffled up the steps to lean against Tate's side with a gusty sigh.

Tate put his arm over the dog and ruffled its ears. "Funny, huh. She's the one who taught me that love is more important than blood."

Sally nodded. Her mother had loved everyone and everything. And back then, her father had—okay, he'd never wanted a daughter, but he hadn't been cruel. After her mother died, the light had gone out of her father's life, and he'd grown...twisted. "You changed with her death."

"Yeah. Dad blamed you, so I did too. I took her loss out on you." He shook his head. "As a kid, I felt kinda guilty about being mean to you. But now, when I imagine Dylan treating Emma the way I treated you...I'm sickened. God, Sally, I'm really sorry."

She stared at his face, open to her scrutiny. Slowly, slowly, a knot in her chest started to loosen.

He *was* sorry. Yes, he'd been mean, but her father had been the one to make it a battle of them against her. Tate had been a teenager who'd lost a mother he loved, and her father had pointed the finger at her. Would she have been different if the roles were reversed? Hopefully so, but still... "I think I understand. And I forgive you."

"Well, hell, sweetheart, you're taking all the fun out of the evening. Your pa got to walk out, and now I don't get to pound the crap out of your brother?" Vance grumbled, his tone light, but she recognized the underlying frustration. He really had wanted to beat someone up for her. She laid her hand over his and squeezed.

"Speaking of which... Since I'm now restored to big brother status"—Tate gave first Vance, then Galen a resolute stare—"would you explain exactly which one of you is with my sister?"

Oh my God. Sally held her breath.

"Both of us," Galen said. "Do you have a problem with that?"

Tate blinked, obviously not anticipating a straight answer. Or to be put on the spot. He studied the men, and she remembered that about him. He never decided anything quickly. Finally, he spoke to Sally. "I liked the way they stood up for you, even after you left. But if they're pushing you into something—"

"They're not," Sally said firmly.

"I guess that's all right." He stood up slowly and hesitated. "I just want you to know, you've got a place to come if you get into trouble. Or just need a home. Okay?"

Hell, she was going to cry after all. As tears ran down her cheeks, she pushed at Galen's leg. With his hands around her waist, he helped her stand.

Sally took a step forward and hugged her brother. "Thank you," she whispered.

"Thank you for forgiving me, Sal." He kissed the top of her head and stepped back, eyes gleaming with moisture. "I'll just check on Leigh Anne. The kids are hoping you'll come upstairs and say good night to them when you're ready."

"Will do." As Tate disappeared into the house, Sally scrubbed the tears off her face. And a slow grin blossomed. Family. She had *family*. "I just realized—I'm an *aunt*."

CHAPTER SEVENTEEN

Lying on the king-size bed in his partner's hotel room, dressed in just a pair of jeans, Vance felt his muscles unwinding. As usual when he and Galen traveled, they'd booked two rooms, although he damned well expected to spend tonight in this one.

But since the small hotel had equally small showers, Vance had left Galen to help Sally and had cleaned up in his room across the hall.

From the noise coming from the bathroom now, they should have an interesting evening. Galen wouldn't let the imp reach climax...not yet.

Although Tate and Leigh Anne had offered their guest room, Sally had refused. *Thank you, Jesus.* She'd wanted to be with her Doms. And they wanted to be with her.

But he and Galen hadn't had a chance to plan out the evening...aside from enforcing their displeasure at her running away.

After that, they'd show their pleasure that they were together again. Definitely that. That was a good enough plan for a scene.

He grinned at the sound of her giggles and Galen's deep laugh. His partner hadn't been so happy in a long time. He'd needed someone like Sally to remind him that life held more than work.

Vance needed her too. It wasn't until she had asked him about his wife, that he'd realized how much he'd avoided any serious involvement with women. Yeah, he'd been as much of a coward as Galen had.

And he trusted Sally. Really did. Yes, she'd deceived them about the hacking and sometimes about her feelings, but she'd never cheat on him. She didn't have a disloyal bone in her body.

She had a sense of honor that he could respect. A rather interesting sense of honor, in fact, remembering her statement in the cabana. *"And if you ask me if your hips look fat in a dress, I'll tell you the truth."* Grinning, he looked up as the noise escalated in the bathroom.

"But I want a robe," Sally whined as the door opened.

"No point." Galen pushed her out into the hotel room and returned to the bathroom, closing the door behind him.

Her hair was clipped on top of her head; her eyes were bright. Her full breasts were waiting for Vance's hands. Nipples puckered and erect.

"Oh now, that's nice," Vance murmured.

She was already pink from the hot shower—and arousal—but at his look, her color deepened and she tried to cover herself with her hands. "Uh, you're already here."

He grinned. "Sweetheart, you've sucked our dicks, had us inside you just about every way possible, had our mouths everywhere—how can you possibly feel modest?"

"I don't know. Because I'm in Iowa?" With the prettiest laugh a woman ever had, she jumped on the bed and flopped on top of him. Moist skin, scented with lotion, soft woman.

He'd died, bounced off hell, and gone straight to paradise.

He ran his hands past her lush ass to open her legs, and yanked her up, straddling him. Her pussy rested on his cock, and he could feel the heat right through his jeans.

When he rubbed upward, her eyes drooped, half-lidded. "Are we going to play?" Her voice came out husky.

"Soon. Talk, punishment, talk, sex. I think that's how it'll go."

Her frown wrinkled her brow. "Why can't we jump straight to the sex? Isn't it better to finish making up?"

Where was Galen? The inconsiderate bastard was still in the bathroom—probably shaving—leaving Vance to answer questions. Maybe because Vance had been the moron who'd felt Sally shouldn't escape the consequences of her actions. Not if their relationship was to continue. And he wanted that more than he could say.

"It's like this, Sally." With Sally still on his lap, he worked his way up to a half-sitting position with his back against the headboard. "Galen lost his temper and yelled at you."

"He did."

At her pout, he grinned. He knew full well she put on that cute face just for effect. Even better, she knew that he knew, so she didn't do it to manipulate...but rather for fun. "Galen and I yelled at each other after that."

"More than shouting. You hit each other." She gently touched the purple bruises over his gut, his ribs. His jaw.

"True, but that's what"— *brothers do*—"we do, whether it's mature or not. Then we get on with life." Would he ever get tired of looking into eyes of such a rich brown? Or of running a finger over her plump lower lip...which was still sticking out slightly. "Unfortunately, it's difficult to get on with life if one of the people is halfway across the country."

Her gaze dropped. "You're angry because you had to follow me here?"

"No, sweetheart, we're unhappy because you scared us to death when you disappeared. You usually tackle problems head-on. Why not this time?" Ah, but she didn't deal well with emotional upsets. She'd run from them before. *"Red red red."* Safeworded out of a scene, quit the Shadowlands, all because they'd gotten too close and she'd felt too vulnerable. So this time—

"I saw you punch Galen," she admitted. "My fault. You've been friends forever, and you were fighting each other because of what I'd done."

A movement caught his eye. Clad in jeans, Galen leaned against the bathroom door frame. Yep, he'd shaved. He jerked his chin for Vance to continue.

All right. "You felt guilty because you'd upset us," he fed back. "Maybe Galen hurt your feelings by yelling at you?"

She shrugged as if that part was unimportant.

Bullshit. When she forgot to hide, her face was as expressive as her body was responsive. "You told us you loved us, and before the night was over, Galen was yelling at you."

Touchdown. Her eyes turned liquid, and she looked away. "I know why he yelled now. But it hurt."

"I'm sorry, Sally," Galen said, walking to stand beside the bed, pain obvious in his face.

"I know now. It's okay." Her irrepressible spirit resurfaced, and a dimple appeared. "Does that mean you won't yell at me again?"

"'Fraid not. If we're together, I'll probably yell at you again, just as I'll probably exchange punches with Vance." Galen rubbed his knuckles on her cheek. "But Vance and I can survive fighting, because we will be around later to make peace. You weren't."

She winced.

"You disobeyed us," Galen continued. "You risked your safety by crawling out a window and walking down a road at night. You didn't phone to let us know you were all right." He pulled in a breath. "You had a right to be mad, pet. Even to come to Iowa."

"But I should have let you know." Sally's voice dropped. "I acted like a little girl."

Vance sighed. She broke his heart. "You acted like a woman who grew up having to hide her feelings." He gripped her hands and squeezed even as Galen pulled her to lean against his body.

"And I need to work past that reaction. Is that what you're saying?"

"Very good." Galen kissed the top of her head, his face gentle. Sally wasn't the only person learning to let her feelings show.

Since Vance's ribs still hurt, he kept that thought to himself. Galen certainly had no trouble expressing his feelings with his fists.

"I'll try."

"Thank you, sweetheart," Vance said.

"So this was the talking part of the show." Sally hauled in a breath, gave herself a shake, and her breasts shimmied in a way that made Vance's mouth dry. Seemed really unfair that a woman got those fascinating bits, and a man didn't. A woman could simply pull her shirt down, show some extra cleavage, and mesmerize every guy in the room. If a man opened his jeans and let his cock poke out, every woman in the place would be calling for the cops. Or worse, screaming, *Ew. Gross.*

Well, if he didn't have breasts of his own, seemed only fair the woman should share hers. He put his hands on her breasts, stopped the wiggle, and circled his thumbs over the pretty pink areolae.

Galen snorted. "Talk about a lack of control."

Grinning, Vance secured his grip and pulled on her breasts, drawing her forward until she gave up and buried her face against his neck. "I'll just restrain her using these lovelies while she learns the consequences of not informing her lords and masters of her location."

"What?" She tried to sit up to protect the vulnerable little ass that stuck up in the air.

Vance didn't let her. Hell of a restraint system. It wouldn't work with small breasts, but Sally's were the size where a Dom could get a good grip. Oh yeah.

"Whatever works." Galen shook his head. "Sally, this won't be a long punishment. I'm going to give you three strikes of the switch, hard enough that for a few days, the welts will remind you of our expectations." He ran his hand down her back.

Vance felt her quiver.

"No relationship escapes battles, so these are the rules of combat," Galen said. "The combatants may withdraw at any time during a fight. If you need to retreat farther than the house, you let the others know where to find you. The time limit on making up is twenty-four hours, whereupon discussion must begin."

Silence. She turned to look at him and sighed. "That's fair."

"Good." Galen picked up a slender, peeled length of wood and slashed it through the air. The whipping noise showed it was green and very flexible.

Vance grinned. No wonder Galen had volunteered to drive Sally's rental back alone. He must have stopped to cut the branch from a tree on the way back and taken the time to smooth it out.

"Sally, it's going to hurt," Galen warned. "And we're in a hotel. If you yell, I'm going to gag you, and I don't want to. We've come too far in getting you to talk to want to silence you now. Can you be quiet?"

"Uh-huh." She buried her face back in Vance's neck. And he wrapped his arms over her shoulders and held her, his amusement fading. Fuck, he hated punishing anyone, especially Sally.

The first blow made the distinctive sound of a switch hitting flesh. Her body jerked. No one in the next room would hear, but he knew it was damned painful.

HOLY SHIT. SALLY pressed her face to Vance's corded neck, gritted her teeth, and breathed out through the icy-hot sting. She trembled with the need to cover her ass for the next—

Smack. Oh God. She felt her arms try to move, but Vance held her immobile. Restrained by one man for the other. She keened into his soap-scented flesh and—

Smack!

It felt as if Galen had laid lines of fire on her butt. She sucked in air through her teeth, waiting for the intense stinging to die down.

"All done, pet." She felt Galen run his hand down her back, over her bottom. Fiery pain erupted again when his fingers traced over the welts. "You'll definitely feel these for a couple of days."

Slowly, she pushed up.

Vance curled his hand over her nape, holding her still, forcing her to look into his piercing eyes. "You scared me, Sally," he said softly.

Oh God, she wouldn't have hurt him for the world. "I'm sorry." Her eyes began to burn, and she blinked back tears. "I really am."

"You've been punished enough, sweetie. But don't ever do that again."

She buried her face back into his neck, feeling his hand stroke over her back in the sweetest of forgiveness. "I won't," she whispered.

"Then give me a kiss and we'll move on."

After hitching herself up, she ran her fingers into his thick hair—because he liked that—and kissed him, trying to tell him without words how much she loved him. How much she liked feeling the guilt fade with his honest forgiveness.

Lifting her head, she had to bite back words of love.

She heard Galen say, "Sit up now, pet."

She pushed upright, keeping her weight off her bottom, and flinched when she saw him hand the switch to Vance. Vance was going to hit her now?

B-but, he said he forgave her.

Hands around her waist, Galen lifted her off the bed and onto her feet. He framed her face between his hands, looking into her eyes. "Are you sorry you ran instead of talking to me?" His expression was open, showing her how much her lack of trust had hurt him.

Tears welled in her eyes. She hadn't meant to hurt him. God, she hadn't thought he'd care.

"Yes," she whispered. "I won't do that again. I'm sorry."

A smile flickered over his lips. He kissed her, so, so gently, and it felt as if he was washing away the anger and hurt. And forgiving her.

He took the switch from Vance and handed it to her. "I'm at fault as much as you were. People do yell, but I overreacted and at a very bad time. I should have left and returned once I regained control. Give me three welts."

"No!"

"Yes." He touched her nose and gave her his half smile. "Don't look so upset. I'm not offering my ass. Put them on my shoulders."

No, please. "I don't want to."

"I didn't ask what you wanted, pet." He turned and went down on his good knee.

The sight of his beautiful back, the contoured muscles beneath the olive skin, could still take her breath away. "But..."

"Go on. Let's get past this," Vance said.

Is this horrible, ugly unhappiness what Galen felt when he hit her? How could he ever manage?

The men wouldn't back down, so she needed to get it over. She tried to summon some anger, find the feeling of desolation from that night or the sense of betrayal when Galen hadn't let her explain. He'd punched Vance; he should pay for that.

She couldn't.

"Sally," Galen said in a guttural command. "*Now.*"

Pulling in a shuddering breath, she struck. *One. Two. Three.*

Any last trace of anger died as she saw the red lines marring the perfection of his back. Tears blurred her vision, and she threw the stick across the room as hard as she could. "I hate you!"

"Oh, imp." Galen rose and tried to pull her into his arms.

How could he? "I don't *hurt* people." Weeping, she hit him, her fists bouncing off his jaw and the ridged muscles of his stomach.

He ignored the blows, scooped her up, and sat on the bed, pulling her against his chest.

"I *hate* you." He'd yelled at her. Made her cry. Punished her. Made her hurt *him*. Head against his shoulder, wrapped in his arms, she choked on sobs, unable to stop.

"Get it out, baby girl," he murmured.

She felt her legs tucked over Vance's, and his fingers enfolded hers. She tried to pull away and got nowhere, so she glared through tears at the fuzzy lines of his face, the intensity of his level gaze. "I hate you too."

"No, you don't, sweetheart." His thumbs rubbed the backs of her hands. "Being mad at someone doesn't mean you hate them." He gave Galen a smile. "Punching someone doesn't mean you hate them. Neither does punishing them."

Her sobbing gasps eased as she reached the end of her tears. "I know," she whispered.

"Your head knows, but deep down, you believe if you care for someone and they get angry with you, that they'll pull away like your father did," Vance said.

"We're not pulling away, baby." Galen tilted her chin up so he could look into her face. "I love you, Sally."

What? Her mouth dropped open, and her heart came to a complete halt right along with her breathing.

"No."

His lips curled into a wry smile. "Yes."

Galen loves me? Me? Her processing unit had just suffered a complete power failure, she thought, even as she tried to store everything away—with extra backups—so she'd never lose the memory of the soft look in his dark eyes. The feeling of his fingers under her chin, the slight roughness of his voice.

After Galen released her, Vance cupped his big hand against her cheek, turning her to face him. "Sweetheart, I love you. Very, very much."

"But…" Her breathing stopped again. There was a serious lack of air in the room; she should complain to management. She tried to shake her head—he held her still as he studied her face. "But you can't," she whispered.

"But I do." Vance's cheek creased.

They love me? Both of them? Love me? "But-but you guys could have anyone." Submissives were always trailing after them, flirting with them, even kneeling to catch their attention.

"Very true," Vance said agreeably, making her want to hit him. "But we want *you.* Aside from being gorgeous, you're compassionate—"

"Spirited and fun," Galen said.

"Intelligent and generous," Vance finished. "And, oddly enough, you love us. Both. So we'll just make sure you get all the love you could possibly desire—"

"And all the control you need," Galen added.

That's what she felt—that wonderful merging of being controlled and cherished. Galen's strong arms kept her in place; Vance's gentle hand on her face kept her centered. Their love poured over her like the warmth of the sun.

Yes, she wanted them. Both. So very much.

Vance's lips curved up. "Say it, sweetheart."

And Galen gave her a tiny jiggle as if to shake the words loose.

She elbowed him—just to show she wasn't a complete wimp—and as he grunted, she smiled sweetly at Vance. "I love you."

His blue eyes brightened like sunlit glass.

Christ in a carriage, how many times had she cried today? Eyes blurring with tears again, she looked up at Galen and saw his stern face could no longer conceal his deeper emotions. "I love you," she whispered.

"Thank you," he whispered back. With his hand behind her head, he gave her a kiss sweeter than she'd ever known. Then he set her on Vance's lap.

Ouch. The welts burned, and she got in only one breath before Vance squeezed the air right out again. He kissed her, gently at first, growing more demanding. Wetter. Deeper. He released her only long enough to lay her on the bed and follow her down.

He kept kissing her, caressing her breasts with a hard hand, and the sweeping arousal shook her.

She heard Galen moving around the room. Country-western music came on—*poor Galen must have lost the toss*—with a slow love song. He joined them on the bed. When he took her lips, Vance slid down to kiss her breasts, sucking and licking, sending streamers of pleasure to her core until she felt as if she could almost come without anything else.

Her lips were swollen when Galen raised his head. He studied her face with a faint smile. "You are so beautiful."

And under his scorching gaze, she felt beautiful.

After another leisurely kiss, he moved down and settled between her legs.

Oh God. "You don't have to do that," she said hastily. "I don't—"

He stared at her—Dom to impertinent submissive. "I know I don't. I do what I want—and I've missed the taste of you." He glanced at his partner. "Vance likes sucking on your breasts; I like playing with your cunt."

"Well, that's direct," she muttered, feeling her face flush as both men chuckled.

Galen lowered his head. The tip of his tongue brushed her clit lightly, as if to wiggle the hood and expose it farther. As if it weren't engorged and throbbing. Just that infinitesimal touch shook her body like an earthquake.

When she wiggled and reached for him, he said, "Uh-uh, pet. Hands over your head. No moving."

She barely managed to smother a whine. Instead, obediently,

she put her hands over her head, hearing the pleased sound Vance gave as the position pushed her breasts higher. Why couldn't the bed frame have something to grab? *Don't move.*

Galen glanced at Vance. "I don't want to wait long; I need to be inside our girl."

"Agreed." Vance pushed her breasts together, licking each nipple between light nips that sizzled straight to her clit...which Galen had fastened his lips around.

Galen's tongue teased the sensitized bundle of nerves up one side, down the other, rubbing in the same rhythm as Vance was using. After a second, she fought her way up long enough to know they were licking and sucking in time with the music. "I thought white guys didn't have rhythm," she said in a raspy voice.

"That's rude, sweetheart." Vance nipped her sharply.

"Ow." She brought her hands down to cover her stinging nipple.

Vance raised his head, and the warning in his eyes stopped her, sent her arms back over her head.

Galen just laughed and pushed two fingers inside her. The feeling of thickness, of being filled was outrageously good, bringing back memories of his hand inside her, and making her blood boil with the increasing inferno.

To her relief—and regret—he didn't increase the number of fingers. With his shoulders, he pushed her legs more widely apart and curved his fingers, probing until he hit a spot that dialed up the sensitivity of her clit into the thousands and the slightest touch of his tongue made her gasp. "That's definitely the spot," he murmured.

Before she could stop herself, she lifted her hips, trying to increase the friction.

He tsk-tsked in disapproval and slid his hand under her ass. His calloused palm rubbed over the fresh welts.

"Frigging hell!" The blast of pain shot straight into burning pleasure.

Even as Galen squeezed, increasing the blistering pain, Vance pinched her nipples, sending jolts of pleasure splashing into the liquid pool of need inside her.

Galen released her ass and pushed his fingers back into her vagina, pumping mercilessly, wakening nerves until her core coiled tight with need.

And as they both sucked—clit and nipples—everything inside her clamped down onto Galen's invading fingers, increasing the feeling of the wonderful slide and penetration. The pressure grew and grew, not stopping, not pausing. Her breathing turned to ragged gasps. Her back arched as everything...tightened...and suddenly released in a rush of sensation so intense that she cried out. Wave after wave pulsed outward with mind-blowing pleasure.

Shimmering inside and out, she gave a sigh of sheer happiness and opened her eyes to see Vance smiling down into her face. He winked at Galen before taking her lips, kissing her deep and wet, ravaging her with his tongue, even while he mercilessly rolled her nipples between his fingers.

Galen's mouth closed over her clit again, sucking in long, vigorous pulls. He forcefully pumped his fingers, over and over.

Before she could object—or even move—another orgasm slammed into her. She moaned into Vance's mouth, and his kiss gentled, as if he were drinking in her pleasure.

As she flattened onto the bed in a comfy postorgasm glow, he rubbed his nose along hers and murmured against her lips, "Breathe while you can, sweetheart."

"Why?"

Without answering, he rolled off the bed and stripped off his jeans. His cock was rigid, straining upward, and she rolled toward him...just wanting to touch.

Instead, he yanked her out of bed, backed her against the door.

"Vance, what are you doing?" Her head was spinning, and her knees started to buckle.

He caught her around the waist.

WASN'T SHE JUST the prettiest sight after she'd come a couple of times? Smiling, Galen removed his jeans, rolled a condom over his painfully distended shaft, and lubed it up.

And watched the show.

"Up you go, sweetie." With a grunt, Vance lifted Sally. As he pressed her shoulders against the door, she instinctively put her legs around his waist, making it easy for him to slide right into her cunt.

"Oh God." Her eyes closed, and her expression of pleasure was so lovely that Galen savored it, storing it in memory to enjoy later.

"Fuck, you feel good, Sally. Now hang on to me." As Vance pressed her harder into the door, she put her arms around his neck. After a few hungry thrusts, which Galen couldn't begrudge him, he secured his grip on the back of her thighs and turned, putting a sweet little asshole out and available. "Come and get it, bro."

Galen grinned at him, positioned himself behind her and kissed her neck.

Her head jerked up as his slick fingers traced the rim of her back hole. He slid in one finger, then another, stretching her. Preparing her.

Vance pulled out, holding her steady, and moved his hands on her butt cheeks so he could pull her open as well as holding her up. Her squeak at the contact of his palms on her welts made him chuckle.

Laughing at the tiny annoyed growl from their submissive, Galen set his shaft against her asshole. He slowly worked through the tight little ring of muscles. Easing in and out.

Her fingers clamped onto Vance's shoulders, her head was up, neck rigid. She still couldn't take a cock easily, and he could feel tremors of anxiety running under her skin.

With an unheard *pop*, the head of his cock made it past the rim. He surged in steadily, feeling her engulf him. Her ass provided less snugness than her cunt, but the squeezing as the constricting ring of muscle slid down his shaft was very, very good.

A second later, Vance worked his dick back in, and the pressure was almost overwhelming.

Not just to him. Sally gave a little mew and buried her head in the curve of Vance's neck.

Vance's gaze met Galen's, sharing the pleasure.

As Galen slowly pulled back, Vance slid deeper.

So their little submissive didn't get too accustomed to their habits, Galen listened to the music on the radio for a second and held up his hand. *Index finger, index finger, thumb.*

Vance's swift grin showed he realized the beat would give him twice as much fun. Gripping Sally's ass firmly, he pumped smoothly twice, and pulled out as Galen plunged in hard.

They continued, thrusting in time with the music. Da-da-*dum.* Da-da-*dum.*

The increasing volume of Sally's moans was a carnal joy, and she grew louder when Galen slid a hand around her so he could play with her breasts. Fuck, he loved the way she squirmed.

He managed to worm his other hand down to lay a finger against her clit, and her whole body stiffened. "Oh, oh, *oh.*"

Galen managed to hang on—barely—as her insides did a vise clamp on his cock. He saw Vance grit his teeth, fighting off his release as well.

But from the feel of Sally's engorged clit, from the increasing clenching of her little ass around his shaft, she was close to coming again.

Da-da-*dum.* Da-da-*dum.* Galen wiggled his finger over her clit with each thrust. Sweat dampened his brow as he fought for control, as his body demanded he simply pound into her and get off.

But fuck, she felt good.

And he wanted to feel her get off while he was inside. Nothing was more intimate or rewarding.

His balls drew up against his groin, demanding release. *Not. Yet.*

And there she went. Sally's body froze from her head to her toes, and she turned to a rigid statue in their arms. Even her breathing ceased.

She broke with a series of high mewling cries, and he felt the exhilarating pulse of her core around him.

As she slumped against his partner, Vance grinned, although the muscles in his face and neck were taut from holding back, and his face was moist with sweat.

Go, Galen mouthed. He could hold on another minute. Maybe.

Vance's fingers tightened on the imp's striped little ass, and he started pumping forcefully. Sally moaned, rubbing her head against his shoulder as, with a long, low groan, he shoved in and came. "Fuck, sweetheart, you're killing me," he whispered.

Galen couldn't keep his smile back. It all felt fucking good. He loved seeing them both sweaty and satisfied. By God, he loved *them*.

Vance hauled in a breath and gave Galen a chin lift. *Go*.

Hell, yes. Sucking air, Galen worked in and out of Sally's tight little asshole, then drove deep, deep inside, pressing in hard, enjoying the lingering clenching of her muscles as he went over the edge. A growl escaped him as his cock poured out heat in long, mind-bending blasts.

"Makeup sex." Vance sighed, nuzzling the imp's cheek. "Fuck."

"Yeah," Galen agreed as he pulled out. "Let's fall onto the bed and sleep for a week."

"Really?" Sally looked up and wrinkled her adorable nose. "Guess at your age it takes longer to rest than it does to get tired."

Biting back a grin, Galen swatted her tender butt for the insult, getting a satisfying *eep*.

Old, my ass.

The imp was asleep before Vance even laid her down on the bed.

CHAPTER EIGHTEEN

I n the back of the taxi, Sally snuggled closer to Vance, resting her head on his shoulder. Seated in the front, Galen turned to smile at her before resuming his conversation with the driver about some scandal in the legislature.

Too bad the drive to Galen's mom's house wasn't longer. A nap would really be nice. After all, the past couple of days had been pretty stressful. Breakup with two Doms, lose a father, gain a brother, get punished with a Jesus-help-me switch, and conclude with mind-boggling makeup sex.

She sighed. For a while after the breakup, she'd figured she could leave everyone behind and find a job in some remote corner of the world. A simple solution, if more than a bit lonely.

With the derailment of that plan, her yes-no questions were suddenly multiple choice. Like, okay, Galen and Vance said they loved her. What did that mean for the future?

And how could she handle a long-term relationship with *two* men? Hell, she hadn't even been able to keep one Dom happy.

And if she could, what about marriage and babies and stuff?

And finding a job?

She rubbed her cheek on Vance's shoulder, fortified by the slow sweep of his hand up and down her back. Eventually, she needed to sit down and figure out her future. So far, all they'd decided was that she'd return with them.

Jeez, but a girl sure had to be careful what she asked for. Two months ago, she'd been pining away for a Dom to love, and God had decided to gift her with two.

Maybe Glock was right, and God really was a cat, just toying with the human race.

But…her two Doms said they loved her.

If that wasn't a miracle, she didn't know what was. As her heart went all mushy, she leaned up to kiss the blunt angle of Vance's jaw, inhaling the fragrance of his crisply sexy aftershave.

He rubbed his knuckles over her cheek. "You okay, sweetheart?"

"Oh sure…"

When he narrowed his eyes at her nonanswer, she scowled. "You can sure be a pain in the ass, Mr. Buchanan, Sir."

"Yeah, and I can give you a definite pain in your ass, Miss Hart," he growled. "Tell me. Now."

"Fine." Skipping over her vast field of problems, she plucked something from the miniworry garden. "I'm kinda paranoid about visiting Galen's mom. She doesn't sound very nice."

"She won't be rude, Sally. She's just… Hmm. You know how cold Maine is in the winter?" His voice stayed low enough so Galen wouldn't hear.

"Probably like Iowa."

"Right. Well, Thea Kouros fits right in with the climate she lives in—chill enough to freeze your face off."

"Oh lovely. And *why* are we visiting this woman?"

Vance chuckled. "If Galen is in this section of the country and has time, he stops by. About once a year."

Once a year? Guess she couldn't tease Galen about being a mama's boy.

The taxi stopped in a neighborhood of elegant brick houses. The yards had been manicured with more fussiness than Gabi with her nails.

After climbing out of the cab, Sally looked around in disbelief. Who'd ever think that a man raised in a house like that could be so comfortable sitting on the back steps of a farmhouse?

Galen finished paying the driver and shut the cab door.

When he joined her, Sally gave him a nice squishy hug.

"What's that for?" he asked, his expression a little distant as he looked over her head at his mother's house.

"Because I like you. Maybe almost as much as I love you."

The way his eyes turned soft and his mouth curved affectionately would probably sustain her through a battalion of ice mothers. Pulling her close, he rubbed his chin on her head. "You are a gift I never expected," he said under his breath.

Oh hell. Once released, she had to turn away to swipe at her damp eyes.

With a wink of approval, Vance handed her a handkerchief and ruffled her hair...just so she'd have to laugh and hit him.

By the time they caught up to Galen, he had already rung the doorbell.

The door opened. Galen's mother was around sixty, almost obsessively thin, hair colored to a rich brownish black, with eyes as dark as her son's. "Galen, it was a surprise to hear from you."

Oh boy, Vance was right. Darth Vader at his worst had shown more warmth. Sally frowned. Mrs. Kouros didn't even appear to notice the bruising on his cheek and jaw. Jeez, most mothers would be busting with pride to have a son like Galen.

Of course, Sally's father sure wouldn't win parent of the year either.

Mrs. Kouros looked at Vance. "Vance, you're looking well."

Sure and he looks just fine. That knuckle-sized purple bruise on his face is from nicking himself shaving, right?

"Likewise, Thea," Vance said easily. Trust Vance to not let anything upset him.

Sally was surprised when Galen tucked his arm around her. "Mother, this is Sally Hart. Sally, my mother, Thea Kouros."

"How do you do," Sally said, since the standard *it's nice to meet you* simply wasn't true.

"Quite well, thank you." Thea's eyes narrowed as if assessing how closely Galen was holding Sally. Her lips thinned even farther. "How nice you could accompany my son. Please come in." She stepped back to let everyone enter.

Christ in a corset, if this was Galen's role model growing up, no wonder he had trouble showing affection. The woman hadn't even touched her son. As Sally walked past into a house that was as stiffly formal as its owner, she decided on a couple of things.

First. She was going to totally swamp Galen with loving—enough to make up for Popsicle Mama there.

Second. Visits to Maine were going to be very, very rare.

—✦—

Another day, another parent. Sally suppressed a sigh as Vance drove their rental car through Cleveland, Ohio, and out of the city into pretty tree-lined streets. His parents' turn today.

She was liable to have a neurosis by the time she returned to Tampa.

They'd spent last night in Mrs. Kouros's house in three separate bedrooms. And Galen had grown increasingly distant.

But this morning, she'd pounced on him in the shower. It would take a stronger man than Galen to stay uninvolved while having shower sex.

He'd been back to normal—even smiling—at breakfast, and the way Vance had looked at her had made her feel like a hero.

Hopefully, the Buchanans would be nicer. She just had to survive this afternoon, and then they'd be on their way to New York.

As they piled out of the rental car, Galen stopped Sally. "Bring your laptop in, pet. If we have a moment, I'd like you to turn over the Harvest Association files."

"I said I'd stop." Hurt made her take a step away. "Don't you trust me?"

"Oh, baby girl, it has nothing to do with trust." He put his palm under her chin, stroking her jaw with his thumb. "Since the crime is already committed, I thought I'd see if you picked up anything useful. Be a shame to waste all that illegal information."

She smacked his arm. "You are so bad."

"Ayuh." He waited for her to pull her laptop out of the backseat.

They followed Vance up the sidewalk.

Here goes. As they approached the house, Sally braced herself for another set of disapproving eyes.

The door opened, and a swarm of children emerged.

"Vance. Galen!"

"Uncle Vance!"

"Unca Vance, hold me!"

The children, ranging from three to ten years old, were treating Vance and Galen like portable jungle gyms to be climbed. Sally grinned as Galen's deep laugh joined Vance's easy one.

"Oh my goodness, you'll think we're raising barbarians." The woman in the doorway was probably the same age as Galen's mother, but there the similarity ended. Chin-length dark brown hair, probably colored to hide the gray, no makeup, no jewelry. In jeans and a blue plaid top the color of her eyes, she gave Sally an entirely comfortable and welcoming smile. "You must be Sally." She held her hand out. "I'm Bonnie, Vance's mother."

"Yes, ma'am." Sally took her hand, started to shake it.

"Ma'am? Oh heavens, what stories has that boy told you? I stopped beating him years ago. Really." Still holding Sally's hand, she pulled her into the house. "Come on in."

Sally blinked, sputtered out a laugh, and stopped long enough to pick up a three-year-old who'd been left behind in the climb-a-Fed game.

—✦—

Lunch had been a production with overwhelming amounts of food. As usual, Vance's sisters had each tried to outdo the others. After being the victim of too many oh-just-try-this-I-made-it maneuvers, Galen felt overfull and in dire need of a nap—which would undoubtedly set the imp off on a bout of old man jokes. Sally had listened wide-eyed as the gang went around the table, each taking a turn at reciting their recent activities. Vance and Galen had gotten grief about the bruising on their faces...and Sally hadn't smothered her giggles very successfully.

For a bit, everyone dispersed into different rooms and conversation. Galen had joined a couple of Vance's brothers-in-law to walk off some of the meal in the backyard.

But now work called. After retrieving Sally's laptop, Galen went searching for her.

In the Buchanan-filled family room, Galen located Sally and Vance. Cross-legged on the rug, she was playing patty-cake with a toddler and giving the child her complete attention as if no one else existed in the room.

Galen's chest tightened. She would be an incredible mother, wouldn't she? From across the room, Vance met his gaze. They shared the same vision.

After watching for a bit, Galen pulled Sally away, smiling at the complaints. She was a hit with Vance's family, both old and young alike. He tucked an arm around her as they left the crowd behind.

"What's up?" she asked as they crossed into the quiet of the formal living room.

Before he could answer, he heard footsteps behind them. He turned.

Bonnie was hurrying after them with Vance's father, William, right behind her. She stopped.

"Bonnie, is there a problem?" Galen asked.

"Galen, my dear, I do love you dearly," Bonnie said. She dropped her gaze to his arm, which was around Sally's waist. "But I thought Sally was with Vance."

He felt Sally stiffen. "She is," he said quietly.

Entering the room, Vance obviously heard the question. He stopped on Sally's other side and said, "She's also with Galen. And that's how it's going to stay."

"Hmm." William studied Galen and Vance before turning his attention to Sally. "I'm not surprised, but I know how pushy these two can be, especially if they gang up on a person. Are you all right with this, sweetheart?"

By God, he liked Vance's father, and even more when Sally's eyes filled with tears. *Yes, pet, this is what a father should be.*

She gave William a radiant smile that wavered slightly as she said, "Thank you for worrying about me." Before he could answer, she said with the courage and honesty that had won their hearts, "But I'm sure. I love them both."

"Oh my." Bonnie shook her head. "Well, you two have been stepping outside the box since you met; why stop now?" With an easy laugh, she and William returned to the rest of the family. And her voice drifted back in response to a question. "Yes, both of them. Brave girl, isn't she?"

Sally looked at Vance with wide eyes. "I love your family."

"Told you there wouldn't be a problem." Vance kissed her forehead. "Let's commandeer Dad's man cave."

Galen grinned as they entered the room. Each time he visited, the place looked cozier. A few summers ago, William kept complaining about his daughters' chick flicks, so Galen and Vance had converted a spare bedroom into a "den." Everyone had helped furnish it.

The wide-screen TV was a Father's Day present from him and Vance. The leather "guy" furniture came from William's daughters. His wife had added pillows and quilts and a wall of shelves for his books.

Taking a seat on the couch, Galen patted the cushion beside him. "Sit here, Sally. Let's see those files."

She sat with Vance on her other side. After booting up her computer, she set the laptop on the coffee table where they could all see the screen. "This is what I've got.

"I think of it as being a geeky Robin Hood," she said. "Taking information from rich criminals and giving to the poor cops." She clicked on a file.

A spreadsheet. Rows and columns. Names and URLs of the senders. Dates of the e-mails were linked to files with the contents. More e-mails were documented each time someone responded.

"Jesus," Vance muttered.

The imp's gaze dropped. "I just wanted to help. To save people."

She hadn't saved her mother. Her father didn't value her. *"I think of it as being a geeky Robin Hood."* Galen turned to look at her downcast face. Despite her aversion to violence and blood in the police station, she kept insisting on working in law enforcement of some kind.

Someone wanted to be a hero.

Galen put an arm around her and pulled her close. "You've done a magnificent job, pet. Illegal or not, I'm proud of you."

"Really?" Her face brightened.

Vance noticed. After giving Galen a nod, he smiled down at her. "Really. You've saved a lot of women."

Leaning against Galen, she opened another set of files. And another. A series of notes showed her efforts at...tracing locations and personal data.

He and Vance both frowned at her.

"Now that's going way too far," Vance said.

"Hey, I was one of the targets, remember?" She gave them an indignant look. "This is sheer self-defense. I'm protecting myself from being kidnapped."

Galen felt a laugh rising. "There's a unique justification."

"Even more effective than the Robin Hood one." Vance tugged a lock of her hair and grinned at Galen. "If she used that self-defense line and added in those puppy-dog eyes, no jury in the world would convict her."

"Hell, don't encourage her."

Too late. She was smirking as she pulled up the next set of files.

Not fair that any one woman should be both adorable and brilliant. "Let's see the actual e-mails, little brat."

"Yes, *Sir.*"

Galen skimmed through the documents and stopped at one. He pulled up the notes where she'd traced the sender back to the originating provider. Then checked a list containing the user's name and address obtained from the service provider. His mouth flattened. "Vance, take a look at this."

Vance leaned forward. "You have fucking got to be kidding me."

"What?" Sally asked.

"Well, pet, looks like you moved a rock, and an assistant district attorney crawled out." Galen scrubbed his hands over his face. They'd have to play the rest of this by the book, but just knowing where to start...

He pulled Sally onto his lap and kissed her, long and well. So wicked smart. She just might have broken the back of the Harvest Association. However, along with the elation came a more sobering thought.

She's going to be impossible to control after this.

CHAPTER NINETEEN

Wearing his most conservative gray suit, Drew stood at the black granite-topped island in his kitchen and drank his coffee. Since the maid had been in yesterday, the chrome and stainless steel appliances and fixtures gleamed. Black and white ruled his decor—he found it amusing since the law tended to hover around a dark gray.

He glanced at a metal sculpture that displayed the time. He needed to leave soon. Get in early.

Something was going on, and whatever it was, he wasn't privy to the information. Even worse—at the weekly general meeting yesterday, he'd felt a chill. The district attorney had looked past him as if he weren't at the table.

But why? He did good work, hadn't screwed up any cases that would put him on the shit list.

"Don't you look like a fancy attorney?" Yawning, Ellis wandered out of the guest bedroom, his raspy tenor more grating than normal. "What's for breakfast?"

"Up to you. I have to get to work." Drew poured another half cup of coffee. "Thanks for coming in."

"Yeah. But I'm going back this morning. The two sluts are chained to the wall in the cabin. The food and drink will run out soon." Ellis glanced out the window at the other brownstones on the narrow street. "I hate this place."

"I know." A week was about Ellis's limit for being off the mountain. After that, he'd lose control. Drew didn't mind a few slaughtered women, but cleaning up was a nightmare. Better to give him a slave and keep him isolated until his skills were needed.

"It was fun to play with your fancy computer. Sorry I couldn't figure out the informant."

"You got further than I did." Nice to have a brilliant, twisted brother, although he'd undoubtedly left behind snuff films on the drive, which Drew would have to delete. "Fuck. If he keeps outing my people, I'll have to start from scratch." And that had been fucking tricky.

He took his last sip, grabbed his briefcase, and slapped his brother on the arm. "Lock up when you leave."

"Yeah. Will do." Ellis took a cup out of the cupboard. "Come up for a fuck break if you get needy. I'll try to keep at least one of them alive for you."

Grinning, Drew left, taking the stairs rather than the elevator. He'd noticed Ellis was in better shape—uglier but leaner. Time to join the gym again. Maybe pick out a female personal trainer. Preferably a blonde with big tits.

Where the wooden steps curved around and opened onto a landing, Drew glanced out the tall window. Rain was over. Should be a nice day. He frowned at the unusually high number of cars parked on the narrow street.

One was a taxicab with two men in the front seat. Drew narrowed his eyes. Passengers didn't sit in the front seat...and yellow cabs were often police cars.

Two men emerged from a nondescript car. Fuck, even a schoolchild would make them as cops, if only from the looser hang of their suit coats to conceal a weapon. They walked into the building. More men followed.

Drew sucked in a breath as he went cold. He heard low-voiced orders drifting up the stairwell. They were posting men on the exits. *Fuck.*

Drew ran back up the stairs.

ELLIS LOOKED UP at the sound of the dead bolt turning. Had his twin returned?

Drew burst into the apartment, his face white. "I think I've been made. We've got to get out of here." He ran into the bedroom where the window overlooked the backyard.

Ellis joined him.

The back area held a small concrete patio with four heavy wooden Adirondack chairs and a narrow strip of lawn. A six-foot privacy fence divided it from the towering apartment building on the other side.

As they watched, two men emerged from the back of the building and stationed themselves where they could guard the rear door.

"Fuck." Drew ran back to the kitchen and opened a thick metal safe built into the island. He pulled out cash and two revolvers, and handed one weapon to Ellis.

Ellis checked the cylinder. Already loaded.

"Once the cops are down, you jump first," Drew ordered, closing the safe. "I'll take your back. After you get to the top of the fence, guard me while I cross the yard. Split up once we're in the apartment complex, and we'll meet at the cabin."

"Got it." Ellis gave his brother a grin, knowing his scars would twist his mouth into something hideous. "Been a while since we went hunting together."

"Yeah. We'll start with the two-legged ones." Drew kicked the screen out of the window.

Ellis aimed, shot one dead center. The cop's arms went up, his pistol went flying, and he fell back. No blood? Fuck, the bastards wore body armor.

Ellis's next shot took off the top of the second cop's head. His third blew a hole in the first man's leg. He wouldn't be getting up anytime soon. And the screaming wasn't bad either.

Fuck, but he loved that sound. *Oh yeah, indeedy yeah.*

Stuffing his revolver into the back of his jeans, Ellis dropped out of the window, hit hard, staggered a few steps, and scrambled toward the fence.

AT THE SOUND of gunfire—three shots—from the back of the old brownstone, Vance pulled his weapon and ran toward the side of the building, quickly outdistancing his slower partner.

Welcome to New York City. NYPD was already inside the brownstone, heading for Drew Somerfeld's condo on the second floor. They were taking point. Their city. Their territory.

He rounded the back corner into the yard. *Jesus.*

A man dashed across the yard jumping over the body of a uniformed cop to get to the six-foot wooden fence. Another police officer lay nearby groaning.

The running man leaped, caught the top of the fence, and tried to pull himself up, feet scrambling on the wood slats. A pistol stuck in the back of his jeans fell, hitting the ground.

"Halt. FBI," Vance shouted as he aimed and— Something hit his back like the kick of a mule, followed by a blast of pain. *Fuck.* He retained his weapon as he fell forward. His head smashed against the concrete patio as he rolled off the edge, ending half on his side.

His lungs couldn't pull in a breath through the agony that was his torso. Above him was an open upstairs window. A man's face. *Somerfeld.* And the bore of a pistol pointed toward him.

Jesus. He tried to bring his pistol around. Couldn't move.

A barrage of shots split the air. A bullet struck the concrete patio in an explosion of fragments. *Missed, thank you, God.*

No one remained in the window. Vance managed to pull in a breath. Under the bulletproof vest, he was going to have a hell of a bruise for a while.

He turned his head and saw Galen lower his GLOCK. Eyes dark with fury, he looked toward Vance.

Vance gave him a painful nod—*thanks, bro*—and saw the tightness ease from his face.

With a low groan—it felt as if one shoulder blade had been pushed a foot forward—Vance rolled over.

The man who'd been climbing the fence was gone.

Goddamn it.

"Hey." Two officers appeared in the window, both holding their weapons. A ruddy-faced one yelled to Galen, "Somerfeld's dead. Where—"

From the other side of the fence came a man's scream, shrill with rage and anguish. "Noooo. You bastards. *No!*"

As orders and shouting filled the air, Vance lurched to his feet. Tried to breathe through the pain. Felt warm blood trickle down his scalp to his neck. Remembered hitting his head.

He staggered toward the downed officers.

One stared up at the sky with blind eyes. The other—he knelt beside him to put pressure on the leg wound. There was too fucking much blood. "Get an ambulance here. *Now.*"

———✦———

Goddamn fucking knee. As the hospital elevator dinged out the different floors, guilt was like lead in Galen's blood and bones, weighing him down. If he'd only been a few seconds faster, Vance wouldn't have been shot.

Thank God for body armor, but *fuck.* His partner could have died, could've ended up with his head blown off like one of those two cops.

The elevator doors slid open.

Sally tried to push past him, but Galen snagged her with an arm around her waist. "Walk, pet. Or they'll toss us out." He knew just how she felt—he wanted to run as well.

"I need to see him." She shoved at his restraining arm.

"You will. He's going to be fine." *Vance is alive.* Galen had to keep repeating the reassurance as they hurried down the hospital hall.

Against his side, Sally glowed like sunlight, a comfort against the coldness inside him. "I'm so...so angry," she growled. "I want them all to pay."

"Somerfeld is dead," he reminded her. Galen's bullet had taken him in the skull, and the two officers who'd broken into the flat had put two rounds in his back.

"There are others. One got away," Sally muttered. As they dodged an orderly pushing past with a food cart, Galen saw her face. Mouth pressed into a determined line, eyes glittering with resolve. A vengeful female—one who knew computers. Not good.

Galen frowned down at her. "I did have a promise from you about no more hacking, correct?"

She glared before reluctantly nodding. "Yes, Sir."

"Good." He relaxed. She might evade questions, but she had a personal honesty that was damned refreshing. She wouldn't break her promise.

In the hospital room by the window, Vance was in a bed. The back had been raised so he was half sitting. Pale, but awake. *Alive.*

With a relieved breath, Galen released Sally.

She darted over and halted, obviously afraid to touch him.

Vance smiled. "C'mere, sweetheart. You look like you feel worse than I do." He painfully held an arm out to her and smiled as Sally snuggled closer. He asked Galen, "How's the cop?"

"Still in surgery, but he has a chance." Galen stopped to clear his throat. The X-rays reported Vance hadn't even suffered any broken bones from the bullet's impact, although he wouldn't be moving quickly for a while. He'd hit his head. And he was *alive.* The knot in Galen's gut loosened with visual confirmation. "The shooter got away."

"Fuck," Vance said under his breath. "If I'd only—"

"No," Sally said. She shook her head. "You told me that. 'If onlys' will drive you mad."

Galen met his partner's rueful gaze. They'd managed to get the lesson through to Sally; now they needed to take their own advice. "At least we got the head of the Association. In case no one told you, Somerfeld is dead. The cyber team resurrected enough deleted files on his computer to know he ran the organization. And we've got addresses for the rest of the managers. They should be picked up later today."

"Maybe one of them will be the shooter."

God, he hoped so. Galen had an itch in the back of his skull. That scream the man had let out...hadn't sounded normal. Hadn't sounded sane. "Yeah."

Despite the lines of pain in his face, Vance actually smiled. "We're done, partner. Somerfeld and his managers were the last of the bastards."

"Yeah, you're right." Galen's spirits started to rise. "Thanks to the imp, who won't ever get any of the credit."

"No problem," Sally said. "I like my handcuffs for fun, not for real." With a hand on Vance's cheek, Sally gently turned his head. "You're a mess, Sir." She frowned at the blood in his hair and touched a spot near the back of his head.

"Fuck!" He jerked his head away and gave her a dark look. "You keep poking at me, subbie, and I'll wallop your behind."

Despite her obvious relief at the threat, she smirked. "This time—for a change—that might hurt you more than me."

He moved slightly and winced. "Good point." He glanced up at Galen. "Would you mind beating on her for me?"

"I'd be delighted to help out, bro."

—⊹—

Ellis was going to make them pay, the bastards who'd murdered his twin. His only family. He shuddered, seeing again the hole appearing in Drew's forehead, how his whole face changed, blanked, how he'd jerked as the other bullets hit. He fell.

Should have been me. I should have let him go first. Safe back at his mountain cabin, Ellis raged, kicking the walls, kicking the furniture, kicking the sluts—the two that Drew had delivered just a few days before.

Ellis had shackled their collars to bolts in the rough wooden floor. Purple splotches ranged up and down their bodies. One had ragged breathing. Maybe had busted ribs.

Like he gave a fuck.

Drew had saved his life. Ellis had been easy meat there on the fence, and that fucking cop would have shot him if his twin hadn't shot first.

"Somerfeld's dead." The bastard cops.

Ellis's head buzzed as angrily as if the bullets had hit him instead and were raging inside him like angry wasps. He felt like he did when he stayed around the chaos of people and noise too long. Worse. This was worse.

How could he live without Drew? His family. His brother.

Ellis raised his hands to his head, realizing exactly how ruined he was. He had no money, no credit cards, no job.

But Drew had cash. Kept spare credit cards in his safe.

Fuck. What should he do? He needed someone to tell him what to do. Who to kill. What to burn.

But Drew was gone. Ellis's rage flamed higher, burning through his insides like the fire that had scarred his face. The one he had set with his twin's help. Standing in the bedroom, watching the fire, they'd listened to their father screaming. Begging.

Indeedy yeah, begging. He chuckled, the memory so vivid he could almost taste the fat-laden ash. His father had needed to die.

Drew's murderers needed to die. All of them. There'd been one in the backyard, and the two smug-faced cops in the window—he remembered all their faces.

A stillness settled inside him as he realized he knew what to do. What to burn.

Them. All three of them.

His gaze fell on the two sluts on the floor, one gasping with pink froth on her lips. He only needed one for what he had planned.

CHAPTER TWENTY

"There we go, Glock. Ready for action." Chatting with the cat in the quiet, empty house, Sally screwed back on the four-switch outlet plate located in the game room.

The first two switches hadn't changed and would still turn on the overhead and track lighting. But now the third switch regulated the well-hidden audio receivers for her customized, voice-activated software.

Perched on the mantel over the fireplace, Glock observed, occasionally taking a break to groom down an obstinate section of fur. He'd expressed his displeasure with the paw-clogging sawdust in the still-being-remodeled room.

But Sally was enjoying being part of the progress. The hardwood floor was in. Walls were a textured sand color. They still had to put a ceiling fan in over where the pool table would go. Eventually a bar would curve out from one corner, but the building had gotten no further than the framework of two-by-fours.

"So, let's see if R2D3 is awake and listening for commands." All orders would have to be preceded by *her* voice saying, *Please, please, please.* She turned toward the receiver and said, "Please, please, please. Are you awake?"

"I'm awake, darling," came her own voice from the wall speaker of the in-house intercom.

And she scores! Sally whooped, doing a gangnam-style dance. Unfortunately, she had only two command responses set up so far—just this one and the recording she'd done with Gabi the day after she'd come up with the idea. Now that had been a wonderful drunken time.

But once she got this going, it would really liven the place up.

Something sure needed to. A depressed Dominant was not a pretty sight, and both of her guys were majorly grumpy.

They had good reason though. In the hospital, they'd been so pleased that the Harvest Association was finished.

The very next day, Drew Somerfeld's condo had burned. In the ashes, they'd found a metal safe—opened. The creepy arsonist was still on the loose, and no one had been able to figure out who he was.

So they'd left the search to the New Yorkers and brought Vance back home to Tampa to recuperate. After nearly two weeks, he was pretty much back to normal.

Thank God. Sally rolled her eyes. Every time Vance had trouble moving, Galen had gotten all quiet. Because of his bum knee, he hadn't been there before Vance was shot, and he blamed himself. As if he could have prevented Vance's getting hurt. She snorted. He'd just have gotten his own ass shot off. Christ in a computer, but her beloved stubborn Doms sure had I-am-God complexes when it came to protecting other people—probably caused by the overload of testosterone in their gorgeous bodies.

As she picked up her small tool case, she sighed. She'd been trying to help out. Doing the household chores so they could concentrate on work. Making sure they ate regularly. Comforting them. Nothing had worked.

She couldn't even coax Galen into taking her on in World of Warcraft, even though he usually won. Vance hadn't watched a game on television since he'd been back. She'd made a kick-ass three-layer chocolate cake last night—Vance's favorite—and he hadn't eaten a bite. Galen hadn't taken the canoe out at all.

Something *had* to be done.

After flipping the switch off, she scooped up the cat and headed for her room to tuck the tools away. "So, Master Glock, do you have any brilliant ideas on how to use the system to screw with Fed heads," she asked him on the way up the stairs.

He gave her an ear flick indicating he didn't think it could be very difficult. They were only humans, after all.

"This is true. I'll figure something good out." And she wouldn't use the software until then.

In the meantime, she'd resort to a less ingenious prank. She nuzzled the Glock's furry head. "This is your warning, fuzz face. You might want to stay somewhere out of the way tonight."

Cuz she was going to do her best to break her Doms out of their downward spiral. Ready or not, Master Grumpy Pants and Master Frowny Face were going to get it.

—❖—

Vance stripped and tossed his clothes toward the corner of his bedroom where yesterday's clothes were scattered on the dark blue carpet. Pretty sloppy. His ex would have had fits. He frowned.

Only one day's worth? He hadn't done his laundry since they'd returned from New York...which meant Sally must have taken it on.

Jesus, they hadn't brought her here to be a maid.

He rubbed his neck wearily, wanting to curse his brains out. Couldn't he fucking do anything right? Got himself shot. Even worse, he'd allowed a criminal to escape. Sure he'd done the best he could, but he still felt responsible.

Even worse, Galen was fucking morose. Probably blaming himself for not being Super Fed.

And neither of them was seeing to their submissive. Hell, they'd taken her on to help her, not ignore her. Certainly not to have that beautiful, brilliant woman turn into their slave.

She wasn't happy either.

He sighed. He and Galen had been spending days and nights working, surfacing only to watch an hour of late-night news. Hardly speaking.

An hour ago, Sally had said she was tired and wanted the night to herself. Not good. Usually either he and/or Galen joined her in her bedroom. Even when she had her menses and didn't want to fuck, she liked having someone to cuddle with and to put a warm hand on her cramping belly.

She'd never wanted to sleep alone before. Yes, something was up with her. And he didn't have the time or the energy to stop and figure it out.

Fuck. His back was almost back to normal. No longer ached as if he'd been run over by a train. Just let him get a good night's sleep—one without nightmares of the dead cop and gunfire and previous shootouts and blood and... Yeah, if he could sleep, he'd be able to pick up the reins of the D/s relationship.

After brushing his teeth, he lifted the toilet lid to take a piss. "What the *fuck*."

Words were printed on toilet paper draped over the bowl. *Dear Master Frowny Face, keep on swimming. Life will get better.* The water, tinted light blue, contained two toy fish, swimming in happy circles around the bowl.

Jesus. He started to laugh, knowing exactly who'd sabotaged his bathroom—one little impertinent brat.

GALEN STRIPPED AND gathered up his clothes. Exhaustion weighed down his shoulders. Seemed like his life had been playing the same tune for the past year. "Two steps forward, and one step back."

Every break they caught was followed by some disaster. To have the damned arsonist be the one who escaped... God, he couldn't live like this.

He hadn't been able to sleep since his partner'd been hurt. Vance could have been killed. Could still be killed.

Galen opened the closet door and— "What the hell!"

Just inside the closet sat a miniature potted tree. A stuffed orange kitten was hanging by its little paws from one branch. *A toy cat?* He looked up and read the banner that hung from the closet ceiling. *Hang in there, Master Grumpy Pants. Life will get better.*

God. Damn. His blood still churned through his veins at the surprise. He took a step back and started to laugh.

—✦—

Still grinning, Vance left his room and saw his partner, his face flushed and the remnants of laughter.

Galen gave him the same look back. "She got you too?"

"Master Frowny Face." Vance's lips quirked. "And you?"

"Master Grumpy Pants," Galen said ruefully.

Grumpy Pants? Laughter ripped through Vance so hard he felt as if he'd herniate a gut. "Fuck, she's out of control."

"I love that little brat," Galen said under his breath.

Vance felt the warmth in his heart. "Oh yeah."

"Not sure whether to spank her or fuck her."

"I think—" A blast of icy water hit Vance in the chest, shocking the breath right out of him. "Fuck!"

Water splashed off Galen. His gasp turned into a low growl. "Spank, for sure."

"I'm on it." Vance charged down the hall, sucked in air as he got struck again, and put his head down and bulled through. Freezing water hit his stomach and soaked his jeans. His balls shrank, probably to the size of marbles.

"She's got a water gun," Vance snapped. And she'd loaded the fucking thing with ice water. *Jesus.* He checked over his shoulder for backup.

Galen had grabbed his cane and was a few steps behind.

A stream of water went past Vance to hit Galen...and drizzled to a stop.

With an unhappy *eep*, their assailant fled down the stairs. Her skin—including a curvy, jiggling ass—shone white in the dim stairwell lighting.

Despite the freezing jeans, Vance's cock hardened.

"Naked war games?" Galen huffed a laugh. "I'm in."

Sally disappeared into the darkness of the ground floor.

After reaching the foot of the stairs, Vance waited until Galen caught up. "Plan?"

"Hold on." Galen flipped on the game room light, studied the floor, and pointed to drops of water heading into the dining room. "The perp's rifle is leaking."

Vance led the way, following the wet trail into the kitchen. When he stepped out the back door, the humid night air wrapped around him. He listened and heard nothing except the frogs and crickets on the shore and the hoot of a barred owl.

In the light of the full moon, he saw glittering drops of water in a line toward the pool.

Something moved to the right. Vance spun—and saw two furry gray ears. Yellow eyes.

Glock was watching the insanity from a patio chair near the pool. Good thing Vance hadn't had a squirt gun or that would be one offended feline.

Just past Glock's chair, Sally knelt on the edge of the pool, filling her gun.

"Now there's a target," Galen said under his breath. "Can you pull off a tackle without hurting your back?"

Vance grinned. "Just watch me." He charged across the deck and, rather than a tackle, grabbed her as he dived past into the water.

She gave a startled squeak before they went under.

Oh yeah. She was slick and squirmy, and finding one of her breasts under his hand, he closed his fingers. Fuck, he loved the feel of her.

As they surfaced, the underwater lights came on, and then Galen cannonballed into the pool, causing an explosion of water.

Holding his prisoner tightly with her back against his chest, Vance swam toward the shallower end and stopped at a depth where he and Galen would have footing. Wasn't it a shame that Sally was short and her feet wouldn't reach the bottom there?

Vance wrapped one hand around her upper arm—to keep her safe—and the other stayed on her beautifully plump breast where the nipple was so distended it poked into his palm.

Her ass wiggled against his cock. *Jesus.*

"Having trouble subduing the criminal?" Galen grinned at him. "I'll help." When he slid a hand between her legs, she jolted.

Galen fisted her hair and pulled her head back so they could both see her face. "You got our attention, pet. Was there something you wanted to say?"

"I-I-no..." Her voice shook so hard Vance froze. Was she crying? Fuck, had he hurt her?

Or...she was *giggling*. Giggling so violently she was choking with it.

Vance shook his head and grinned.

Galen started to laugh.

DESPITE A MOMENTARY worry they might be furious with her, Sally couldn't stop giggling. She had too many moments to savor, like the shock on Vance's face as the ice water hit him. And Galen's face when he saw her with the water gun.

When they'd left their rooms, she'd heard their laughter—Galen's deep and rich, Vance's rougher and infectious. They could still see the fun side of life and were no longer on their way to zombie-land.

However, there *was* someone who was mad. A gray form showed in the dim lights. Fur matted down with water, a very indignant cat jumped off a poolside chair and stalked toward the house. Well, heck, she'd warned him—his fault if he didn't listen.

"Sorry, Glock," Galen called and received a slit-eyed glare in return. "Guess I caused some collateral damage. But we got the perp, eh, Vance?" Galen's hand tightened in her hair. "What should we do with this little miscreant?" His voice had gone lower, the deep timbre vibrating across her skin, wakening every nerve in her body.

Vance's big hands on her upper arm and breast burned into her skin. "I could suggest a few things," he whispered into her ear.

Galen's gaze was on her face as he palmed her mound and stroked his fingers over her clit and labia.

Oh, oh, oh. She couldn't keep from rocking into his hand. He knew just where to touch her to drive her straight into need.

"Someone is getting very wet," he murmured.

"Duh. Someone is in the water." Her attempt at flippancy was spoiled by her breathlessness. Annoyed, she tried to push away, but her feet didn't reach the bottom, and they had her well restrained.

Intimately restrained.

Vance's chest warmed her back, and his thick erection pressed against her bottom. God, she wanted him inside her.

Releasing his grip on her arm, he claimed her other breast to scissor his fingers around the nipples. "I love it when they're all tiny and hard."

Galen snorted. "Have you ever seen Sally's breasts in a state you didn't love?"

"That would be a no." Vance nibbled her shoulders, sending quivers through her. "Now how should we pay her back for name-calling and ice water?"

"Well..." Galen considered, never releasing her hair. He slid a finger inside her, in and out, slowly. Wonderfully. She trembled as her need kicked up a notch. His lips curved. "I was ready for bed before this little subbie interrupted me. I'm still pretty tired. How about you, bro?"

He was calling Vance *bro* a lot now. That was so cool.

Vance derailed that thought by saying, "Exhausted. If she has this much energy, she should have to do some work."

"Ayuh." When Galen's eyes darkened to pure black lava, Sally knew she'd do anything he wanted. "Run to the cabana and fetch a condom and lube for me, pet. Pick out a waterproof bullet vibe as well."

She gaped at him. They hadn't used a vibrator on her before. "I... Yes, Sir."

They released her, and she shivered as the cool water slid where their warm hands had been. Vance lifted her out of the water and onto the side.

When she returned, Vance still stood in the water.

In the corner of the pool, Galen reclined on the concrete stairs with a chair cushion behind his back. The water bobbed around the base of his very erect shaft.

"A cock sticking up out of the water? It looks so perverted." She handed him the lube and condom and vibe.

He grinned. "Guess you'd better hide it." He twirled his finger in a circle for her to turn.

"Excuse me?" He didn't want her to straddle him?

Galen rolled on a condom and thickly lubed it. "No questions. Sit on me, Sally."

But. That meant he'd take her ass...now? From that angle? Her feet didn't move.

With firm hands on her shoulders, Vance turned her around and guided her up a step so she stood between Galen's legs. "Bend your knees, sweetheart."

Why did this feel so much less...controlled? As she complied, Vance pulled her butt cheeks apart, and she felt Galen's cock press on her asshole.

Ouch! She tried to stand, but Vance was bent over her, a barrier to escape.

Galen guided himself in, working past the ring of muscle. Slowly. They were always careful, but... *Oh. My. God.*

The position was different, and she hadn't come a couple of times first. "What are you doing? I don't like this."

"Ah, but we do," Vance said. His mouth tipped up slightly, but his gaze was that of a Dom, reminding her that sometimes a submissive was pampered and sometimes she was...not.

The world shifted around her, and she stopped struggling.

Galen's cock slid in all the way. Stretching. Burning. Yet, the knowledge of being controlled, taken, *impaled*, was so decadently wicked that it almost sent her over.

"Imp, you feel very, very good." He gripped her shoulders, pulling her until her back met his chest. He rubbed his cheek against hers, and his beard stubble was scratchy. Sexy.

The water in the pool splashed over the very bottom of her butt cheeks, leaving the rest of her out of the water.

She jumped when Vance spread her legs open before stepping between them. He put an arm under each knee. Lifting. Forcing her down on Galen even farther, sending a quaking sensation through her. So full...

Galen wrapped an arm around the outside of her left elbow and across her waist, immobilizing her. His other arm went on the outside of her other elbow, and his hand settled on her breast.

"She's all pinned down—ready for you, bro."

He pinched her nipple.

The sensation was almost too much, and she whined.

"God, I like when she clenches," Galen muttered. "You planning to stand there all night?"

"I want a taste first. See if I can make her squirm on your dick," Vance said. He put her legs over his shoulders and lowered his head.

At the slide of his hot tongue over her engorged clit, everything inside her contracted...around Galen's thick shaft. "Aaaaah." And she couldn't keep from wiggling as Vance's tongue teased her with little flicks.

"Didn't take you long," Galen said. He groaned, holding her tightly enough that only her hips could move. Slowly he rolled her nipple between his thumb and fingers, and another layer of sensation built on top of the others. She started to shake.

With his thumbs, Vance pulled her labia apart. He settled his mouth over her clit. Hot, hot, and so wet. Pausing, he gripped her hips and lifted her, pulling her almost off Galen's erection.

The slide of the thick shaft leaving her ass was an exquisite torment, and then Vance ruthlessly rubbed his tongue over her clit. Like cotton candy being formed, sensation whipped around inside her, catching and building. She was close to coming, shockingly close.

With a low laugh, Vance pushed her down firmly on Galen's cock, and she gasped with the stretch and slide. The wave of sensation sent her—

Vance lifted his head.

"Noooo."

A cruel pinch on her nipple made her struggle. The iron-like arm around her waist tightened. Galen's breath touched her ear. "You get only what we give you, pet. And you take everything we give you."

Her clit was throbbing. Needing. And yet, she had a moment to worry about that ominous-sounding *everything*.

Vance grabbed her ankles and lifted her legs up almost to her head. Afraid she might hurt his healing back, she didn't struggle at all.

His hands were big enough that he needed only one to restrain her ankles and hold her legs high, making her bottom fully accessible. With his other hand, he guided himself to her entrance and pressed in. Slow. Powerful. Putting pressure against...everything, especially where Galen filled her already. Nerve after nerve seared straight into flame as Vance continued, absolutely unstoppable until both cocks filled her completely.

God, with her legs pushed up over her head, she was past full. She could only moan at the overwhelming, uncomfortable—amazing—sensation.

From behind, Galen still had her arms pinned to her sides. Her legs were pushed up, leaving her ass completely at their mercy. She couldn't do *anything*.

By tilting his hips, Galen started sliding in and out in small, fast thrusts. Not even trying to coordinate with him, Vance pulled out very slowly and thrust in deep and hard. Very hard. Over and over.

The erratic combination of cocks was splitting her mind in two, leaving her nothing to focus on as the sensations bombarded her.

She felt Galen's hand ease downward, past where Vance was pushing her thighs against her stomach, between them, over her lower pelvis, and onto her mound. It took a second to realize his fingers were vibrating.

He had the vibe between his fingers.

Too much. If he put that on her clit, she'd die. She bucked violently. "I can't. Don't."

They stopped. But not to help her. Vance tightened his hand on her hip—forcing her bottom to be still.

Keeping the vibe above her clit, Galen put his other hand over her throat. Gently. Carefully. *Firmly.* "Lie back and don't move," he said, and the slight pressure on her throat served as his warning.

He wouldn't cut off her air. She knew that—and yet, with his hand there, with the primitive fear, her body...succumbed. Submitted completely. Her head fell back against his shoulder;

her hands lay flaccid in the water.

"Very nice," he murmured. "Stay just like that." And he slid the vibrator the last two inches to her clit. The whirring vibrations did nothing for a second, and then the ball of nerves sprang toward an excruciating peak. Her insides clenched.

"I like that." With a rumbled laugh, Vance pulled out and thrust in hard, hard, hard. Stretching and hammering, even as Galen's shaft pistoned into her asshole.

Everything inside her clamped down. Like two hands, her muscles fisted around the two penetrating cocks. The vibrator drove her higher; each thrust sent her closer, and even without Galen's hand on her throat, her breathing stopped. Her muscles froze. Every nerve halted.

She hung there on the pinnacle, almost...just almost. And then Vance rotated his hips, his cock slamming in short, rapid movements against a different area.

Galen drove in powerfully. Yanked back. Thrust in again.

And she came in massive waves of sensation.

She came. Screaming and bucking and flailing.

She came, as the men laughed and took her and took her and took her.

CHAPTER TWENTY-ONE

The Shadowlands was just starting to rev to life. With a sigh of exhaustion, Sally settled into a chair in a quiet part of the room. God, after the long, long night before, she was tired—and her body still hummed with satisfaction. Demon Doms.

Amazing Doms.

Okay, focus. She tipped her chair slightly, so she could watch the happenings and hopefully not be noticed.

She spotted Rainie. The trainee was at the bar, donning a starchy bib apron. Since she hadn't worn anything on top, her heavy breasts swayed in and out of concealment of the ruffles running up the sides to the straps.

In a tight dark red latex skirt and bandanna-style top, Uzuri was arranging a munchie table that didn't need any arranging. Her head kept turning so she could monitor the door between the main entrance and Master Z's office. It was the door to the Masters'—and Mistresses'—area where they kept lockers with their clothing...and their gear.

Master Z didn't keep the door locked, although that might change one of these days. Unfortunately, he might decide to solve the problem by simply handing over wayward trainees to a couple of the sadists.

Sally grimaced. She wasn't a trainee any longer, so Master Z wouldn't punish her without the Feds' permission. G and V might well frown on her...assisting...her friends.

But jeez, she and Rainie and Uzuri had been planning this forever.

A few minutes ago, their target, Mistress Anne, had entered the Masters' locker room. Sally tilted her head, trying to follow in her mind what would be happening.

Since the slender brunette had looked rather scruffy, she was probably showering over on the female side of the room. Master Z kept robes and towels in there, so she'd have donned a robe. She'd open her locker and...

No noise.

Huh. Well, maybe the rubber spider hadn't scared her, although it had probably pissed her off. But there were a few other treats tucked away, and one that—

"Shit!" The voice was Anne's, and even with that, she hadn't screamed. "Goddamn son-of-a-bitching brats!"

Gotcha.

Giggles rose in Sally's belly like champagne bubbles, impossible to suppress. At the munchie area, Uzuri had her hands over her mouth. Rainie—being smart—had turned her back to the door, but her shoulders were visibly shaking.

Oh God, we're all going to die.

Feeling a twinge of worry, Sally scooted her chair around and curled into a smaller, less visible ball, before peeking around the edge.

Mistress Anne stalked into the club room. A couple of scenes had already started. Anne glanced at them, and her mouth tightened. She was too experienced to start shouting and disturb the session.

Instead, she went to the bar and spoke to Master Cullen.

Both Master Cullen and Mistress Anne turned to stare at Rainie.

The big, beautiful woman visibly shrank.

Hell, that was way too fast. Sally scowled. Next time, they'd better stick to the newer Doms who couldn't read body language so easily—and who might be embarrassed to mention a prank to other Doms.

Mistress Anne didn't embarrass. *Shit.*

Look innocent, Uzuri. Facing the room, Mistress Anne slowly looked around the room. Her gaze came to rest on Uzuri.

The short trainee had turned her back and was unloading a tray. The red beads decorating her kinky black hair swung from side to side on her back as she swayed to the music. Yeah, obviously, she didn't have a care in the world.

Way to go, Uzuri. Who would have thought Rainie would have no acting abilities?

Mistress Anne strolled across the room toward the munchie table, looking just like Glock stalking a cricket in the grass. The Mistress set her hand on Uzuri's shoulder.

The trainee jumped. Spoke. Smiled. Everything looked good, as far as Sally could see.

Then Mistress Anne took Uzuri's chin in her palm, closed her fingers tight enough to make the trainee flinch, and said something.

Uzuri caved. Totally caved, going as spineless as an amoeba.

Sheesh, where'd the trainees' courage go? This was only Mistress Anne...the most *sadistic* of the Doms.

As Uzuri joined Rainie at the bar, Sally slunk lower in the chair. The girls wouldn't give her up. Not ever. But—with a sinking sensation, she saw Master Cullen point right at her.

Didn't it just figure he'd noticed her arrive? And he knew she'd been an accomplice to every prank committed in, like, forever.

Oookay. Look at the bright side—at least I don't have testicles to torture.

Like Darth Vader, Mistress Anne appeared and stood over her, looking down. A small cane swung from her braided leather belt.

Great. I hate canes. Sally endeavored a smile. "Good evening, Mistress."

Hands clasped behind her back, Mistress Anne stared at the ceiling. Silently.

More silence.

More silence.

Sally felt sweat bloom on her upper lip, on her low back.

Mistress Anne looked down. "I don't like bugs."

"Yes, Mistress," Sally said ever so politely. "We thought it was our duty as trainees to help you conquer that problem." *Don't laugh; don't laugh; don't laugh.*

"Did you," Anne said in a flat voice.

Sally's urge to giggle died as worry flooded in.

Master Cullen wouldn't let her be whipped to death...right?

Master Z would be upset to have dead trainees. All that paperwork.

Housekeeping might quit.

Anne's voice was level. Quiet. "I have had a bad day. My permanent submissive, Joey, moved out last week. My secretary is on vacation, and papers are piling up. I caught a fist to the face from a cheating husband who didn't appreciate the pictures I gave to his wife of him and his twenty-year-old fling." Anne gingerly touched a darkening bruise along her jaw.

And continued slightly louder. "But when I got here, I thought life was looking up. I had a nice shower and was starting to relax, and then I find that my locker. And clothing. And shoes. And *toy bag*"—her voice rose—"are filled with rubber *bugs!*"

Sally stared. Mistress Anne had lost Joey? But they'd been so good together, and although Anne usually had more than one submissive under command, Joey had been with her ever so long. "I...I'm sorry, Mistress."

More silence.

Why did the demon Dominants like to use stillness as a weapon? Sally's teeth ground together as she started to shake.

"You aren't a trainee, Sally," Mistress Anne said finally. "You aren't mine to punish...which means you shouldn't pick me as a target."

Ouch. Explaining that they'd planned the joke pre-Feds ownership of Sally probably wouldn't help, would it? "Yes, Ma'am."

"So my only recourse is to inform your Masters of your misbehavior. And how I feel about it." Mistress Anne fixed cold eyes on Sally. "I'm sure they'll think of something to do with you."

Oh shit. Oh man, this was bad. "Yes, Ma'am." As the Mistress walked away, Sally had to force herself not to run after her.

Please, don't tell Galen and Vance. Pleaaase!

When Mistress Anne reached the bar where Rainie and Uzuri waited, Master Cullen made a gesture, handing the two over to her. But she shook her head and said something.

Master Cullen glanced at his watch and nodded.

Right. She wouldn't punish a submissive if she was angry. Sally winced. Somehow she doubted a cold Mistress Anne would be any gentler than a pissed-off one.

Sally took out her phone. Maybe—if she could think of what to say—she could sneak in an explanation to her Doms before Anne talked to them.

"Hey, Sally. I've been looking for you." Kari walked over. "Are your guys here yet?"

"No. I'm going to call and see what's keeping them." *Should I sound sweet or cute or...*

"Cool. Dan's running late too." Kari shifted. "Too much diet soda—I'm going to visit the restroom. After you call, we can run upstairs and see Jessica."

"Sounds good." Sally stared at her cell phone, not quite ready to dial. *Maybe penitent? Remorseful? Or flirty...flirty might work well, especially after last night.*

—✦—

The door to Vance's office opened, letting in the noise from the main room. Early Friday evening, the FBI downtown field office was chaotic with the last rush of activity before the weekend.

He knew the feeling. If he could just get this report written, he and Galen could get to the Shadowlands and meet Sally.

As Vance looked up from his writing, Galen entered, looking sucker punched.

"What's wrong?" Vance pushed aside the court case.

"The arsonist." Galen's voice was harsh. Tight. He set a memo onto the desk. "Two houses burned down last night. Police detectives—and their families."

"Why would he kill cops now?" Vance glanced at the names of the deceased, and a cold chill ran through him. Those were the

two cops who—along with Galen—had killed Somerfeld. *Fuck.*
"Any other law-enforcement officers killed?"

"Just them."

Vance's jaw went tight as he remembered the scream of rage they'd heard at Somerfeld's death.

"Leads?"

"Yeah, actually." Galen looked even grimmer. "Research finally dug down to the untold story of the Somerfelds—although someone had done a pretty good job of burying the information."

"Yeah?"

"Drew had a twin named Ellis who burned down the family home with Daddy alive inside. Got caught in the fire himself but survived. Judged criminally insane. Committed. Mom suicided."

"Fuck, there's a mess."

"Ayuh. Drew went on to become a lawyer, assistant district attorney, and head of the Harvest Association."

"The brother is loose?" A proven arsonist and crazy.

"Discharged from the mental institute a few years ago. Cutbacks, you know, especially since Drew pulled strings," Galen said in a dry voice. "Once out, Ellis went off the grid. New York is searching Drew's records to find him."

"Goddamn it." The sick feeling in the pit of Vance's stomach increased. An insane bastard out for revenge. If Drew had kept him in check, that control was gone.

"Got a hit." Annabel hurried in, holding a folder away from her body as if it was contaminated. After swallowing a few times, she said, "Drew owned a cabin in the Adirondacks. We did an inquiry..." Her voice trailed off.

"Talk, Annabel," Galen said, taking the paperwork from her.

Vance's cell rang, and he answered automatically. "Buchanan."

"Aren't you official?" Sally's vibrant voice was clean and bright and beautiful, a complete contrast to the atmosphere in the office. "Where are you anyway? Kari and I are waiting for our law-enforcement boys."

As Galen opened the folder, several photographs spilled onto the desk. A woman's body. Her legs and torso were charred black, her face so battered that she was unrecognizable. A begrimed metal collar was around her neck.

Jesus. Fuck. Vance's mouth went dry.

Annabel was telling Galen, "...arrived too late to save her. She was already dead. If only..."

"Vance, what's wrong. Who's dead?" asked Sally.

He couldn't look away from the pictures. His stomach clenched as he moved the top photograph and saw another. Whip marks striped the back of the body.

A hand appeared in Vance's field of vision, setting down a folder over the photos. Covering them. Freeing him. He looked up.

Galen's gaze met his. "Where is Sally?" His voice was strained but controlled.

"The club. With Kari."

"Tell her to stay there. Dan can take her to his house."

"Vance, I can hear him," Sally said on the cell. "What's wrong? Did I do something—"

"You heard Galen," Vance said. His skin felt cold. Two cops were dead. Somerfeld was out for revenge, and Galen would be next on the list.

What the bastard had done to that woman... Sally needed to stay far, far away from them. Vance's voice was harsh as he said, "Stay with Kari. We'll send your things to you there."

WAS VANCE TALKING to her? Seriously? After staring at her cell phone, Sally put it back to her ear. "Send my things? But why? Who's dead?"

"Two police officers are dead—because of us." Vance took an audible breath. "And a woman."

"Because of us." Because they didn't get there in time. *Because of me.* "Was she..." *Did I cause that?*

"Go and stay with Kari. I don't want you to return to the house, is that clear?"

She froze, her mouth dropping open. "But you...you—"*love me. You said.* The words welled higher in a child's helpless cry. "Let me—"*be with you. Please.* Her request dried up like corn in a drought, leaving her mouth tasting like dust.

Because she'd caused those deaths. If she hadn't kept Galen and Vance up all night, hadn't begged for attention, hadn't made them late for work, maybe they'd have been in time to save the officers and the woman.

My fault. Because she was stupid and selfish and always asking for more. She stared at the empty St. Andrew's cross, and guilt crept into her blood like a transfusion of darkness. Because Sally had wanted her men to lighten up, a woman had died.

And Vance was disgusted with her; she could hear it in the lifelessness of his voice, the coldness. Vance wasn't cold. Not to her.

On the phone, she heard, "Buchanan, you need to—"

"Just a minute," Vance snapped. "Sally, did you hear me?" Someone in Vance's office was trying to get his attention. And she was interfering with his work again.

"I heard," she whispered. "Take care of..." She didn't have the right to say that to him. Didn't have any rights at all. "Bye."

She set the cell down beside her. Carefully. As if the phone would break if she handled it roughly.

Staring at the blank display, she curled into a ball in the leather chair. The leather skirt rucked up on her thighs. Making her look like a slut. And that leopard-printed top she'd put on earlier was stupid, not alluring at all.

She slowly pulled the cat ears' headband from her hair. She'd wanted to talk the men into playing hunters against the wild cat woman. Her eyes closed as humiliation made her stomach sink.

Always playing games. No wonder the Feds wanted her gone. Her childish whining for attention had meant they hadn't been there to prevent someone's death. Self-loathing lapped at the edges of her confidence, and pieces of her crumbled off, falling into the blackness. Disappearing forever.

She looked up to see Kari returning from the bathroom, her phone to her ear. As she reached Sally, she said, "Okay. Love you," and stuffed the cell into her pocket. "Dan says you're our new roommate."

"I heard."

Kari sat down beside her. "Are you all right?"

"Oh sure." *No. And probably never again.* "Just tired."

"Hardly. Tell me what's wrong."

She forced a smile. "Nothing. Really. But I could use a drink." Sally started to rise, glanced at the bar, and stopped.

Master Cullen was behind the bar. His submissive, Andrea, had her hands on her hips, and Cullen threw his head back, obviously roaring with laughter.

I don't want to see him. He'd been Master of the trainees the night she'd come to the Shadowlands. The thought of disappointing him, first with her practical joke, and next because Vance and Galen didn't want her anymore... She just couldn't.

"Kari?" Sally bit her lip. "Could you, maybe, get me a drink? Anything is fine. I just want to...sit...for a minute."

With a frown, Kari patted her arm. "Of course, I can. Stay put, and I'll be right back." She headed for the bar, pulling her phone out of her skirt pocket.

A check a little later showed Kari at the bar—and waiting in a line. *Good.* Sally rose and headed for the exit. Going to Kari and Dan's house was out. She didn't want to be around anyone and especially not a Shadowlands Master. Especially not Dan. He must think she was pathetic. She'd faked orgasms, chosen herself such an abusive Dom that Dan had to rescue her. Then once she hooked up with nice Doms, she was such a whiny bitch that she interfered with their jobs.

Got someone killed.

The Feds didn't want her anymore. Galen hadn't even talked to her to say good-bye.

Before she submerged herself in a complete mire of depression, she firmed her lips. She was a good person. Really. She had good friends. Was an honest, hardworking sort. Just couldn't function in a relationship. Wanted too much. *Selfish, self-centered. Stupid.*

Near the door, as she halted to let three submissives in full pony attire trot past, she saw Rainie approaching with an empty tray in one hand.

"Hey, Sally. Mistress Anne is seriously furious." Rainie patted her heavy breasts, looking worried. "She won't be able to adapt her cock crushers to fit on my tits, will she?"

"Ah. Don't think so." Sally took another step toward the door. "Listen, I need—"

"Thank you, God." Rainie grinned before frowning. "She's gonna talk with your Doms and let them deal with you. Are you going to be in trouble?"

The unexpected question stabbed into Sally like a pitchfork, leaving bleeding holes in her heart. Galen and Vance wouldn't be around to *deal* with her. "I-I... No. Vance and G-Galen don't like me anymore, so I guess it's not a problem." She blinked against the welling tears.

After a blank stare, Rainie snarled, "Those sons of fucking bitches!" She slammed her drink tray down on the closest table, startling the two Doms sitting there. Putting an arm around Sally, she pulled her close. "What did they do, baby? What happened?"

Baby. Galen liked to call her baby girl. Sally pulled in a shuddering breath. "I'm not really sure." *I was selfish. Needy.*

Like magic, Jessica and Gabi appeared in front of her.

Jessica was wearing the heavy black leather collar that Master Z required of her in the club, and the sight made Sally's heart ache. Vance had put a collar on her. "*...you can consider yourself collared by Galen and me until we take it off."* He'd liked her then.

"Sally," Gabi said, her voice gentle. "You look miserable. Let's sit for a bit."

"I don't think I want—" Before the sentence was finished, Sally was sitting on a couch with Gabi beside her.

"What's made you so unhappy?" Gabi asked, brushing Sally's hair back.

"It's those fucking FBI agents," Rainie said.

"The Feds? What did they do?" Jessica asked. Standing in front of the couch like a guard dog, she crossed her arms over her lacy bustier. "If they hurt you, I'm going to—"

Gabi clucked her tongue against her teeth. "Let's get the facts before you string them up by their pride 'n' joys, okay?"

"I'd rather hang 'em and get the facts later," Rainie said, taking the same aggressive posture as Jessica.

Sally stared up at them. Two subbie defenders in one club? Master Z would have a fit. And yet, knowing they'd take on the Feds for her...that she wasn't alone... Her chin quivered, and she bit her lip.

"Can you tell me what happened?" Gabi wrapped a warm hand around Sally's.

"It's not their fault. It's mine." She stared down at their joined hands. "I just wasn't—"*Ready. Prepared to break up.* "Vance told me to go home with Dan and that they'd send my stuff. Not to go back to their house." Not to go where she'd been so happy.

"That limp-dicked, slimeballed, fucking feckless FBI fart," Rainie growled. "Get the noose."

Gabi's frown silenced the trainee. "Why, Sally?"

"I don't know. I don't *know*!" Realizing she'd shouted, Sally covered her mouth with a shaking hand. "I do know," she whispered, grief filling her chest. "I wanted to— I made them late for work. People died." Remorseful tears spilled over, turning the room to a wavering darkness. "But Gabi, they said they loved me. They *did*."

Her breath hitched, and all she wanted was to crawl into a corner and cry and cry and cry. *I tried to be good. I tried so hard.*

"Huh. Sally, I know them—and can't imagine them using the 'love' word if they didn't mean it. Can you?"

Sally shook her head.

With a low humph, Rainie dropped into a leather chair on the other side of the coffee table. Jessica moved back beside her, resting a hip on the chair arm.

"Good, you're here," Kari said to Gabi as she walked into the area, holding a tray.

Sally pulled in a slow breath—*get it together*—and realized what Kari had said. "You called them?"

"Of course. They were just upstairs having a chat."

No schoolteacher should be that sneaky.

Kari gave her a concerned smile and set the tray on the table. "I brought drinks for everyone, but no drinking if you're planning to play later, okay?" She picked up a heavy mug and handed it to Sally. "Even from the bar, I could see you shaking. You get hot chocolate."

Something warm would be good. Icy slush seemed to have replaced her blood. But she'd almost rather have a serious drink. Or a bottle. "Thank you." Sally gulped down some of the hot chocolate and gasped as the liquid hit her stomach with far more potency than just milk. "What did you put *in* that?"

"Andrea wanted to come help, but Cullen said he needed her at the bar, so she mixed the cocoa with Baileys and Frangelico instead of water and said to consider that your hug."

"She's so sweet." Almost tearing up again, Sally determinedly sipped. All alcohol, the drink heated her insides quickly.

Friends and alcohol and chocolate—FAC—the ultimate postdisaster support system for women.

Kari handed out the rest of the glasses and took one for herself.

Time to change the subject. Sally said, "You never told me if you got spanked for drinking at my graduation reception. Did you?"

The others giggled...until Kari's mouth turned down. "No. I didn't. He hasn't—" She sighed. "Sex is okay, but I miss the D/s stuff. It's like... I guess he doesn't want me that way anymore." She shrugged. "But it is what it is."

As everyone stared at her, Kari took a hefty swallow of her drink. "Zane is staying with my mother tonight, so I can get drunk if I want to."

"That sucks," Gabi muttered. "If I get drunk and mouthy, Marcus knows I'm craving a fake fight and punishment. I get spanked."

Sally knew Gabi would never deliberately disappoint her Dom. But Master Marcus enjoyed that she provided him with reasons to tan her ass. Of course, being a Dom, he didn't need any excuse other than he wanted to, but punishment role-playing was just plain fun.

Sally managed to smile, even as grief threatened again. She and Vance and Galen had barely begun to develop those unspoken agreements. She shook her head to dislodge the thought and studied Kari. She'd been sick and exhausted for months after having Zane, but not anymore. And Zane must be around eight months old.

It would be nice to have a baby someday. Sally had wondered once or twice if Galen and Vance wanted children.

Guess I don't have to worry about that.

She'd worry about Kari instead. Starting now. Sally turned to Gabi. "Can I stay with you tonight? I think Kari needs to smack Dan upside the head while Zane's not around to watch."

"What?" Kari's drink stopped halfway to her lips.

Gabi simply smiled. "I totally agree. A good smacking is indicated, and yes, you'll come home with me tonight."

At Gabi's instant agreement, Sally felt the wetness on her cheeks. Jeez. "Thanks." She tried to furtively wipe her eyes and froze at the sight of a giant in leathers stalking toward their sitting area. *Oh shit.*

Silently, his submissive, Andrea, followed him into the group.

Master Cullen stared down at Sally. "Did you think you could hide in a corner and cry?" he asked without a hint of his usual good humor.

Unable to speak, she shook her head and stared at her feet.

He dropped to a knee in front of her. "Look at me, love," he said, a hand on her cheek turning her face back to his. As his perceptive green eyes studied her, anger harshened his features. "Are those Feds the reason you're crying?"

God, she didn't want to set one Master against another. "No. I'm just having a bad day. I'm not at all—"

"You're not at all a good liar." Cullen shook his head. "Were they annoyed at what you did to Mistress Anne?"

"No. They don't know." *Don't need to know now.* "Master Cullen, please. This isn't necessary."

"But she *is* crying because of the Feds," Rainie volunteered. "They dumped her. Fuck, the assholes just told her they'd send her stuff and not to come back. Over the phone no less."

Sally scowled at her way-too-helpful friend.

Cullen's face darkened with rage.

No no no. Holding up a hand, Sally stammered out, "It's my fault, all my fault. I screwed up. Don't—"

Andrea stepped up beside Cullen, her eyes sparkling with wrath. "*Cabrónes. Hijos de puta.*" She touched Cullen's hand, which had formed a fist, and actually nodded approval. "Sí, Señor, wipe the pavement with them."

A grin broke over his face. "You're definitely the woman I love." He gave Andrea a quick kiss. "Find Jake and give him the bar, and if I'm not back before you're ready to leave, text me."

When he headed for the door with a determined stride, Sally stared after him. "He wouldn't—"

"But yes. He will leave their bones scattered in the street for the dogs to chew."

Sally's mouth dropped open. Andrea really was a match for Master Cullen.

Andrea gave her a hug. "It will get better. Now I must do as Señor said."

As her friend headed back to the bar, Sally realized everyone was looking at her again.

"So, I want to go over this a bit more," Gabi said.

Jessica nodded. "I'm missing the logic too. They threw you out of the house because you made them late for work?"

"I wanted…" She wanted to hide under the couch rather than admit to her selfishness. With a sigh, she pushed her hair out of her face. She should own up to what she'd done. "They'd been so depressed, and I wanted to make them feel better." Her eyes filled again. "I didn't mean to make it all about me." But she had.

"Go on." Rainie prompted, "You jumped them in bed? Or forced them to endure blowjobs? Or cooked them an extra-big breakfast?"

"Last night, I attacked them with a water gun and started a fight." Her lips curved for a second before quivering again.

"They were angry?" Gabi asked softly.

"I've never heard Galen laugh so hard." Sally looked at her hands. "And yeah, there was sex."

"So this morning, you pulled them back in bed and started to cry because you wanted more sex?" Jessica asked.

"No!" Sally shook her head. "I'd never do that. We just slept too late, and, well, Galen decided he needed...and Vance agreed."

Rainie snickered. "I can guess how that ended. But sounds like they made themselves late. You didn't."

"But I did. It's my fault. I asked..." Sally stopped, playing the morning back in her memory. "No. No, I didn't. I didn't whine. Or beg. Or even ask them not to go." Relief was like an upwelling of clear water, so clear she could almost see to the bottom of her idiocy. "But still, they were late to work. They weren't there, and people died."

Kari was frowning. "Are you blaming yourself for those cops who died? Jeez, Sally, they died in New York. Yesterday evening. Galen and Vance couldn't have prevented that."

"New York?" Sally slumped back. "I...don't get it. And the woman?"

"A forest in New York state. A couple of days ago. Someone saw a cabin burning, but the fire department was too late."

The fire department? She closed her mouth. None of it was her fault.

"What else do you know?" Jessica asked Kari.

"Just that Sally was staying with us because Dan isn't officially on the Association case."

"So why did they kick Sally out?" Rainie asked.

Sally pulled in a breath as understanding lightened the darkness inside her.

"The Harvest Association?" Jessica asked. "But I thought they'd caught the head of the organization. That he was dead."

"The arsonist is still running loose," Sally said.

"Dan said the cops were shackled to something, so they couldn't escape," Kari said.

Gabi had turned the color of her white peasant blouse. "Shackles and death by fire. The Harvest Association signature."

"That's just sick." Rainie's lip twisted as if she wanted to spit.

"But if the deaths happened in New York, what does it have to do with me?" Sally asked. "I don't get it."

"Well." Kari bit her lip. "This stays with us, right?"

Heads nodded.

"The two cops who died were the ones who'd shot that Somer guy. Galen shot him too."

Sally's eyes widened. "They think the arsonist is after revenge?" *Oh fuck.* "That the guy might come here?" A knife of worry slid between her ribs almost soundlessly. Galen was in far more danger than she was.

Gabi pursed her lips. "Galen is definitely the type who imagines worst-case scenarios."

A chill crept up Sally's spine. Because he'd lived through them. "I didn't do anything wrong. And they do love me. But they don't want to see me hurt."

Kari nodded. "That sounds right."

She leaned back, relaxing for the first time in hours. Nothing had changed—she was still ousted from the house, separated from the idiots she loved—and yet everything was different. "So Vance sent me away—and Galen let him—because there's a chance some a-hole will decide to visit sunny Florida?"

She didn't need an answer. Oh yes, that's exactly what had happened. Because Galen wouldn't take any chance that she might get killed as his wife had. She growled. "Those fucking dickless—okay, maybe not that—lily-livered, spineless, impotent—okay, not that either—chickenhearted, dim-witted, gutless Doms."

Gabi snorted. "No Dom cookies for them?"

"There's the Sally we know and love." Jessica grinned. "What are you going to do?"

"Be nice if I could kick them to the curb." She considered that glorious scenario and sighed. "Only that would hurt me as well."

Gabi patted her hand. "I've seen shortsighted idiots do that though. I'm glad you're smarter."

Pulling out her cell phone, Sally powered it off. "I need to think and think hard before I talk to them." And she started thinking about what she wanted to accomplish.

"These are the rules of combat," Galen had said. *"The time limit on making up is twenty-four hours, whereupon discussion must begin."* Yes, G and V figured they were acting for her own good, but…discussion? *Hello?*

"Don't talk. Just use Mistress Anne's cock-and-ball torture devices on them," Rainie suggested.

"Clever idea." A laugh bubbled up in Sally, half relief, half amusement. "Assuming I want to have my arms and legs ripped off."

Jessica grinned. "And you might yet have a use for those manly bits. It's just not good makeup sex without them."

The Feds really had a knack for great makeup sex. Sally hugged herself. With luck, she'd soon have all those fully functional, manly bits back in her bed. "Somehow, I have to get the guys to see reason."

"Did you just use *reason* in the same sentence as *men?* You need a reality check." Grinning, Rainie shook her head—and froze, her gaze fixed on something beyond Sally.

"What?" Sally asked.

"Time to get to work." With a grunt of exertion, Rainie pushed herself up, grabbed the tray from the coffee table, and hustled away.

"What's with Rai—" Gabi glanced over her shoulder and flinched. "Oh hell, he said he was working late tonight."

Sally turned.

Master Z and Marcus stood inside the club room, looking directly at the group.

With a groan, Jessica slid down into the chair Rainie had vacated. "How does he always know if I sneak down here? Who ratted us out? It wasn't Cullen this time—he didn't notice anyone but Sally."

Feeling remorseful, Sally glanced around the room. Maybe she could sic the trainees on the informant. Around the bar, mostly newer Doms and Dommes had congregated. A few submissives were chatting with Andrea. Behind the bar was…the new Master.

Jake.

His gaze went past Sally, undoubtedly to Master Z, and he touched his fingers to his forehead in a make-believe salute.

"It was Jake," Sally told the others.

"That jerk." Jessica fumed. "I don't believe it. He's even coming to dinner tomorrow. I swear, I'm going to serve him a chocolate cake with a chocolate-flavored laxative for the filling."

Kari choked on her drink. "You wouldn't."

"Well no." Jessica glared at Jake, and his smile widened. She glanced in the other direction and shrank down in her chair.

Gabi picked up her glass. "They're coming this way, aren't they?" she asked Jessica.

"Oh yeah."

Gabi chugged the rest of her drink.

"Maybe I don't want the munch-ass Feds back," Sally said. "Not if they'd go all Dom on my ass just for coming here."

"It's worth it, sweetie." Gabi turned.

Shoulder to shoulder, the two Masters stood right behind the couch. Marcus folded his arms over his chest, looking down at his submissive.

Gabi gave him a brilliant smile. "Sir, how nice to see you here already. Did you know the Feds had—"

Sally noticed Master Marcus's steel-colored suit brought out the blue of his eyes, which were just a shade or two lighter than Vance's. And Vance's eyes acquired that same intensity when he slid into that dangerous Dom mode.

"Darlin' Gabi, I do believe we need to have a bit of a chat." Master Marcus's southern accent somehow had taken on an ominous edge. The way he loosened his tie was even more threatening.

Sally twisted around fully. "Master Marcus, it's all my—"

Laughing, Gabi rose, put a hand over Sally's face, and pushed her over backward on the couch.

Sally stared up in disbelief.

Turning slightly so Marcus wouldn't see, Gabi winked before smiling cheerily at her Dom. "Sir, would you really punish me for rushing downstairs to help my friend? Wouldn't that show you don't value loyalty?"

The smile that flashed across his face revealed why the man could positively mesmerize a panel of jurors. "That's a fine defense, sweetheart. Come along now and we'll discuss it."

With immense dignity, Gabi walked around the couch to her Dom. They hadn't gotten far when Gabi shouted, "Spank me! That's still a punishment. You bloated dickhead, you really *are* proof that evolution can go in reverse."

He turned her around, and Sally saw the twitch of his lips before he looked at his submissive sternly, raising his voice slightly. "Master Cullen would enjoy having a bar ornament if your cheeks aren't up to being reddened."

"I didn't do anything wrong. *Sir.*" Gabi crossed her arms over her chest. Her voice was syrupy sweet as she asked, "Did you ever wonder what life would be like if you'd had enough oxygen at birth?"

He was still laughing as he dropped into a chair, yanked her over his lap, and administered the first resounding whack on her bottom.

"Jessica." Master Z walked into the sitting area.

Jessica straightened in response.

Eeks. Sally scrambled to a sitting position so fast she almost fell off the couch. Her head spun for a moment. For God's said, how much alcohol had Andrea put in her drink. She shook her head and frowned. How could she help? Jessica was in trouble because of her.

Dressed in his usual black silk shirt and black tailored slacks, Master Z stopped in front of Jessica's chair and looked down at her. The deep timbre of his voice was even smoother than the expensive Scotch whisky he preferred to drink. "I realize you wanted to help Sally, but would a phone call to me not have been appropriate?"

Jessica sighed. "Yes, Master. I just...forgot."

"You've forgotten quite a few things recently," he said gravely. "Is there something—a need—I'm not meeting? Or some reason you might feel insecure?"

When Jessica didn't answer, he crouched in front of her, taking her face between his hands. "I love you, kitten. Whatever is bothering you, we'll work it out. But you have to let me in before that can happen."

"I don't think that there's anything." Jessica's whisper was almost inaudible. "Just that..."

"That you want a baby. I know, pet." He studied her for a minute. "Is that all?"

Jessica nodded.

"Then we will continue to work on the problem." Master Z gave her a flashing smile. "Perhaps some different positions will help. So while you are being punished, you may offer suggestions until I feel we have an adequate variety...or my arm gets tired."

When Jessica's mouth dropped open, he traced a finger around her lips. "I like that idea, but I'm afraid it won't help you get pregnant."

As she sputtered out a laugh, he pulled her to her feet. "Get my toy bag, please, and wait by the cross at the end of the room."

"Yes, Master." She rose on tiptoes to kiss his cheek and gave him a quick grin. "I hope you're flexible, Master."

He was chuckling as he turned.

And Sally realized—too late—that she should have fled the minute she had the chance. *Idiot.* She could have been safely in the parking lot by now. Hoping to level the playing field, she rose to her feet. Useless. She still had to look up at him.

He met her gaze, and his smile faded. "You've been crying."

"Yes, Sir."

As his attention focused completely on her, she felt as if she were being blasted with a fire hose, destroying her balance and pushing her backward. His darkly tanned face turned stern. "I thought Vance and Galen would be good for you, Sally. I'm sorry to discover I was mistaken."

"They were good—I mean, I think they're trying to protect me."

His eyebrows rose. "Indeed. Does that mean you are still with them?"

"Um, kind of?"

"Explain, please," he said softly, an underlying anger threading his voice.

But she couldn't let him be mad at her Feds. She chewed on her lower lip for a moment. "Because they told me to stay away, I thought I'd done something wrong, so I didn't"—she felt the prickling of tears again—"I didn't say anything. Didn't argue. And they were at work, so…maybe that's why they didn't explain, and I'm not sure, but I think they're sending me away to keep me safe."

"I see." His eyes filled with disapproval, and he was looking at *her*. "You didn't tell them how you felt. Again."

"N-no." She pulled in a breath and fessed up. "I was going to just…just leave." Without making them explain. Without fighting. "I'm an idiot."

"Good relationships don't have exit signs, pet," Master Z murmured, confirming her statement. He put his arms around her and drew her close, wiping out her sense of failure. "Little one, now that you understand, will you be able to talk to them?"

"Yeah," she whispered into his shirt. The strong arms around her were safety, reassurance, everything she'd never had from her father. Falling down in life was inevitable, and sure, a tough girl kept going anyway. But after collecting bruises and scraped knees, who wouldn't cherish a helping hand or two? "Yeah, I definitely am."

"Excellent. However, if they're worried about your safety, you shouldn't go there. I'll arrange for them to come here tomorrow so you can talk." He gave her a squeeze. "Good girl."

His approval filled her sails, and she felt as if she were skimming over the water. With a contented sigh, she dared to hug him back.

———✳———

Galen knew the photos of the cops, blackened and curled into fetal postures, and even worse, of the young brutalized woman, were going to haunt his dreams. Or nightmares.

Maybe he'd not bother to even attempt to sleep.

In the darkness, he walked the lakeshore path, checking their property for intrusions. A gray shadow in the night, Glock padded behind him, in case an evil rodent escaped the human's scrutiny.

Galen shook his head. Glock had wandered the house earlier in search of the female who pampered him, carried him, and, even worse, included him in conversations.

When caught trying to explain Sally's absence...to a cat...Galen had shrugged and given his partner a rueful grin. Did the imp know how much a part of their life she'd become? How she was changing them?

He sighed, fighting the longing to see her.

She was far safer away from him and Vance, but every instinct in his body urged him to keep her close where *he* could protect her.

His jaw tightened. Once he and Vance had reached home, they'd talked about her. And realized she hadn't argued. That wasn't like her.

And yet, he was relieved that she'd agreed so easily. Sally could raise stubborn to a whole new level. If she was so angry with them that she wasn't talking to them, at least she wasn't here in the kill zone, trying to change their minds.

The sound of a vehicle on the road made him turn. From the rumble of the engine, he'd guess it was a truck.

"Let's go see who's visiting, Glock."

THE HOUSE WAS too quiet. Trying to work, Vance kept listening for Sally's quick footsteps. The little submissive rarely walked slowly—sometimes he swore she actually vibrated with all that energy.

Fuck, he missed her already.

At a knock on the front door, he strode out to the foyer. This wouldn't be Sally. She still had a key. But his hopes drove him into haste, and he swung the door open without looking.

A fist slammed into his jaw.

The force of the blow—and the flare of pain—knocked him back several steps. "What the hell?" Shaking his head to throw off the effects, he saw a man completely filling the doorway. "Cullen?"

"I warned you not to fuck with her." Cullen took a step into the room.

"Hit me too." From outside, Galen pushed past the furious Dom to stand beside Vance. "We both agreed to send her away."

"You fucking *assholes*." Cullen's hands were still in fists. He took a step forward. "She's beautiful, spirited, intelligent. And you hurt her badly."

"Hurt?" The word was like a blow in Vance's chest. "Maybe she's angry that we told her to stay away, but—"

"Stay away?" Cullen growled. "You dumped her, and she blames herself. Thinks she did something wrong."

Goddamn it all. "We didn't—" He turned to Galen and saw matching alarm in his expression. "She thinks we dumped her?"

"Christ, no wonder she didn't argue," Galen muttered. He pulled out his cell.

Vance could hear the sound of ringing…and ringing…and the tinny voice mail response. His hands clenched. She'd turned her phone off.

Galen spoke into his phone. "Sally, we are not—I repeat—not breaking up. Try it and I'll paddle your ass. Call me. Now."

Cullen snorted, but a grin pulled at his wide mouth. "That was diplomatic."

Fuck. Vance stared at his partner. "Next time, I do the talking, you asshole." In fact, he'd call her himself and leave his own message.

"So why the hell did you pull that stunt to begin with?" Cullen asked. He leaned back on the door frame and crossed his arms, one immovable object not about to leave until he got answers. He looked at Galen. "Seriously, buddy, she's really hurt."

"Better she be hurt than dead," Galen snapped.

"*Dead*." Cullen straightened. "Explain."

Despite the ache in his chest, Vance huffed a laugh. *Mistake, friend. Never give Galen an opening like that.* Another special agent once said Vance might charm his way into heaven, but given time and opportunity, Galen would talk his way out of hell.

Shaking his head, Vance headed for the kitchen to fetch beer.

If he and Galen hadn't been ordered to remain at home, he'd haul ass to Dan's house so he could talk to Sally in person. Reassure her; comfort her.

Hold her. Jesus, fuck, he needed to hold her. He took out his phone and dialed Dan's number.

CHAPTER TWENTY-TWO

D an Sawyer walked through the quiet night, the sound of his footsteps and the clicking scratch of Prince's claws louder than the tree frogs and the distant hum of traffic. The German shepherd took the lead, anointing lampposts, terrifying cats, and inspecting the dark yards. A canine version of a uniformed cop walking a neighborhood beat.

Dan and Kari lived in a cul-de-sac of older homes, and she knew every single person. Hell, she'd probably baked cookies for each of them, one time or another. He smiled. His wife had the most generous nature of anyone he knew.

At the corner, he gave a whistle for the dog and headed back. Near the end of the block, their two-story house showed only a light on the porch and in the living room. Upstairs was dark. She'd already gone to bed.

Disappointment slowed his gait. With Zane gone for the night, Dan had wanted to talk a bit about their relationship. About what was missing.

But no, that wouldn't be fair. She'd been very clear she wanted a vanilla lifestyle. No more D/s.

And he'd do whatever she wanted. Hell, he'd screwed up her life more than enough as it was. His carelessness had made her a mother years before she'd wanted to be one.

Of course—he smiled slightly—she seemed to have forgiven him for that. Zane was irresistible, after all.

But the way Zane had arrived... Fuck, he'd heard people talk about labor. They'd never talked about a small woman trying to birth a big baby. Jesus, the labor had been so fast and brutal her body had actually ripped from the birth. And he could do nothing—*nothing*—to help.

She'd been miserable afterward. Stitches—actual stitches in her pussy. Hurting. Couldn't even sit comfortably. Exhausted. Depressed. She'd cried the first few times they'd made love—and not with happy tears. But, brave woman, she was the one to insist they keep going.

At least they'd gotten past that, but he missed the extra element the D/s dynamic had brought into their lives.

He was a selfish bastard, wanting it all. But, if vanilla was what she needed, he loved her enough to accept her wishes.

After holding the door for the dog, Dan closed and locked it, turned, and stopped.

Kari stood in the living room. She had a determined tilt to her pretty round chin and her mouth set in a straight line.

"What's wrong?" he asked. "I thought you'd be in bed."

Her lip wobbled, and she bit it—damn, he wanted to be the one biting it. "I'd rather be here."

"You're not sleepy yet? Would you like some wine or—"

"No!" The sharpness of her voice was a slap in the face. He'd heard that tone from her only once—at the Shadowlands the night she'd given up on him. She'd thrown her wrist cuffs at him and told him she deserved better than him. *"I'm going to find someone who will appreciate me."*

Worry tightened his gut. "Something has been bothering you. About us. Am I right?" *Please, God, let her say no.* True, he felt like an asshole for getting her pregnant, but he'd never been so happy. Never been loved so sweetly. His life was filled with the sound of Zane's joyful gurgle, of Kari's sweet laughter. "Let's—" He forced himself to say the words. "Let's hear it, sweetheart."

Her gaze dropped. She was wringing her hands. "When we met—remember how we met?"

After talking her into a beginning BDSM class, her asshole boyfriend had been so obnoxious she'd broken up with him on the spot. Dan had been more than happy to take his place and teach her the joys of submission. The little newbie had been appallingly, excitingly innocent.

He'd asked her what kind of submissive she was, and she'd answered, *"Submissives come in different types? I'm afraid I don't know what you're talking about. Can we try multiple choice?"* She'd been the most adorable little teacher he'd ever met. Still was.

"I'm not liable to forget." Just the memory of her wide blue eyes when he'd first restrained her made him smile. Made him erect.

"You liked me then. I... What do I have to do to have you like me again?"

The hurt in her voice sliced through his reminiscing like a fillet knife. *"Like* you? Kari, I love you. How can you—"

"I know you love me." Tears filled her eyes. "But do you *like...*" She gestured at her body. *"Like* me. Do I need to lose weight or—"

"Fuck." He yanked her into his arms. "Why the hell would you want to lose weight? Stay the way you are, dammit. Round and soft and— You're beautiful. Why the hell would you say that?"

"But you don't want me anymore."

And the wood in his jeans was because she didn't turn him on? "Kari, every time I get within two feet of you, I'm hard." He rubbed his erection against her. "We made love just last night."

"Yeah." The unhappiness hadn't left her voice. "I guess. Never mind." She wasn't going to share what was wrong.

Oh yes, she is. As if a switch had been turned, he slid into the Dom mode he'd avoided since she had Zane. "Don't bullshit me, sweetling. Tell me what the problem is. *Now."* Her chin still fit in the palm of his hand. When he tightened his fingers to keep her face raised, he could feel her yield. Submissive to the core.

"I want this." At his confused frown, she clarified. "I want to serve you. To have you order... Why don't you ever make me...?" She pulled in a breath and said clearly, "We go to the Shadowlands but only so you can be a monitor. Never to play."

He stared at her in disbelief. "You want to play." *No, more than that.* "You want the D/s side of our relationship back?"

KARI REALIZED SHE'D probably turned the color of a strawberry. But she mustered her courage and shoved down the embarrassment. "Yes. Yes to both."

"Well, damn." His calloused hand was hard and unyielding and turned her on so much she almost shook with it. Not just his touch but also the firmness. The authority.

She managed to get the words out. "Why did you stop wanting me as your submissive?"

"Kari—did you forget? You didn't want to be my sub. And I don't blame you." His jaw tightened. "I packed your bag for a bondage weekend *I* wanted—and forgot your birth control pills. Got you pregnant before you were ready. And that labor stuff— you went through hell during and after. Sheer hell. What kind of a Dom fucks up so badly?"

"You feel guilty? Because I got pregnant?" She saw his answer in his face. "Dan, I'm old enough to know to check my overnight bag. I don't regret having Zane in the least. So he was a few years early. He's perfect."

He started to speak, and she held her hand up. "Give me a second."

She paced across the room, her head reeling as if she'd chugged one of Sally's crazy drinks. *Guilt? Dan?*

Stop and think logically.

One, Dan always felt responsible for everything. Maybe it was a side effect of needing to be in control. If anything went wrong, he blamed himself. So, yeah, she could see that.

And in Dom mode, he was incredible. But as a normal guy, he could be a total idiot if his emotions got him going in a circle.

And then... *"You didn't want to be my sub."* That was just wrong. She stopped her pacing. "Why in the world would you think I didn't want to be your submissive?"

"You said so."

"I did not."

He looked at her as if she were losing it. "Kari, you said, 'No, I don't think I ever want to play again. Ever.' That sounds pretty clear to me. You said it more than once."

She frowned, having a vague memory of saying that. Back

when...

Oh, honestly.

"After I had Zane, my hormones were all over the chart." She put her hands on her hips and glared. *How could a man be such an idiot?* "I also said I never wanted to talk to my mother again. That I was going to stay in the bedroom and never come out. That you should take Zane and go live in the backyard for a month...with the dog. Did you take me seriously those times too?"

"Ah. No." The small dent in his cheek showed the beginnings of a smile. "Son of a bitch." He shook his head, his mouth tightening in annoyance. "I've been an idiot."

Saying yes was totally not a tactful response...and she couldn't stop herself. "Yes. You have."

"So, you want more than a vanilla love life," he said softly. His gaze changed, transforming into an intense focus that sent windmills spinning in her chest. "But you didn't say anything because...because you thought I didn't want you. Kari, why wouldn't I want you?"

The room seemed awfully small all of a sudden. She took a step back.

As if she were one of his criminals, he gripped the front of her shirt and pulled her forward until her face was only inches from his. "Explain this to me."

Half of her was dancing with excitement. The other half wailed, Oh no. Don't answer that. "Because."

"*Because* is not an answer." His grip on her shirt tightened, lifted, until she stood on tiptoes. "Do better, little teacher."

"I don't know. Because I'm a mother and boring? Not sexy or pretty." Her eyes closed as she whispered her worst fear. "I'm fat."

"Fat." He spat the word out as if tasting something incredibly foul. He'd never let her ever say that word. He'd spanked her with a ruler once for whining about gaining weight with Zane.

A second later, he released her shirt and stepped back, and she knew—*knew* he was so disappointed he'd just walk away.

He took his cell phone out of his jeans and shut it down. Picked up her cell from the coffee table and did the same. His dark, dark brown eyes held hers as he stalked back to her.

And then he ripped her shirt open.

Buttons pinged against the coffee table. The floor. "Dan!"

"Try again, little sub." His voice went lower and so deeply masculine that she dampened. He dragged her shirt off her shoulders, and in some arcane Dom technique, used the long sleeves to tie her wrists behind her back.

Everything inside her turned hot. "Sir. Sir, I—"

"I'll let you know if I want you to speak." He opened the front catch on her bra, letting her breasts spill out. Huge breasts still, even though she was weaning Zane.

But the heat in his eyes grew as he cupped them. "God, you have gorgeous breasts, Kari."

No longer gentle, he caressed her breasts with his calloused hands, rolling the sensitive nipples between his fingers until she was sucking in long breaths. His gaze stayed on her face, the crease in his cheek deepening.

He unzipped her jeans and yanked them and her panties down until they hobbled her ankles.

His powerful hands kneaded her bare bottom before he touched her between her legs. His quick grin showed his pleasure at finding her completely soaked. "We've been miscommunicating, sweetling," he murmured. "That stops now."

Mouth too dry to speak, she nodded.

After nudging the end table aside with his foot, he pushed her to the end of the sofa. With a firm hand, he bent her forward over the padded arm until her chest hit the seat cushions. Her toes barely scraped the floor, leaving her no leverage. Her hands were still bound behind her, and a merciless grip on her nape kept her in place.

The way he effortlessly conquered her attempts to move sent a lovely squishy sensation through her, right down to her toes.

Then he smacked her bottom, hard enough to make the skin sting.

Oh spit. Ow! She jerked and gritted her teeth. He wasn't going to be nice.

The spanking continued—deliberate and intense—as he punctuated each swat with a growling voice. "You. Are. Not. Fat."

The painful smarting widened, covering her buttocks. *Ow!* Her fists clenched.

"You're beautiful. Lush and womanly. And you're mine." Another and another, until each blow sent reverberations through her pelvis, lighting up every single nerve in her female parts.

His hand slid between her legs again, and he gave a hum of satisfaction, using his fingers in a way he hadn't since before Zane was born. He explored her pussy as if he had the right, and no matter how she wiggled, he would take that right. He stroked her clit until her toes curled, slid a finger around her entrance and pressed in.

Added another finger.

She moaned, wanting more. Wanting him.

Instead of taking her, he opened the drawer of the end table where he kept his supplies.

She craned her neck to see and...he was lubing an anal plug. *Oh jeez.* It was a small one, at least; *thank you, God.*

With a hand on one buttock, pulling her open, he pressed the nasty thing inside. And turned it on so it vibrated right there in her backside.

"Wait. Dan—" That earned her a swift smack on her stinging bottom.

"Did you have permission to speak?"

"No, Sir."

"Safe word is red. Are you saying your safe word?"

God, her behind stung and burned, and that plug was vibrating each nerve into a state of intense arousal that she hadn't felt in months. "Oh God," she moaned.

His chuckle was gruff. Pleased. "I've missed torturing your sweet body into orgasms."

She heard the sound of his jean's zipper, and his cock pressed against her entrance. He slid in deeply, ruthlessly, filling her.

Her bound wrists jerked—couldn't move—and she sank down, completely down, into acceptance. Couldn't do anything. Could only take and take.

And oh, he gave. Slow and steady, so very controlled, using his legs to pin her thighs against the sofa. He reached around and ran a finger over her slick clit.

"Oh, oh, oh." She was so ready. *Right there.*

"Give it to me, little sub," he murmured, and he rubbed ruthlessly. One side, the other, and she broke, exploding into a magnificent orgasm, the sensations lashing through her in a maelstrom of intensity, until she trembled under his hands.

His laugh was deep and satisfied. "Oh yeah, your body liked that. You haven't changed, pet." Gripping her hips hard, he drove into her, forceful and fast and rough, until she heard only the *slap, slap, slap* of their bodies. He drove her back up until she was squirming under him.

With a low groan, he pressed inside her and came, emptying himself in her.

Despite the hum of arousal he'd reawakened in her, she sank into the couch, happier than she'd been for ever so long. The tie—that elusive tie between them—was back. His masculine scent surrounded her; his arms were anchoring bands.

"You are beautiful. My wonderful little sub," he whispered in her ear. "Stand up, sweetling." He pulled her upright and helped her step out of her jeans and panties. He turned off the anal plug.

He didn't remove it.

Didn't remove the shirt around her wrists.

"Sir?"

His lips curved as he turned her around. "Time for a shower. I'll get my bag from the closet, and we'll start over." He thumbed her nipple back to a jutting point. "We have all night, you know."

The tremor that shook her body felt like heaven. *Oh yes. Sally, I owe you a big hug.*

As he tucked an arm around her and guided her up the stairs, she wondered if she'd be able to walk in the morning.

CHAPTER TWENTY-THREE

Settled at the table in Gabi's kitchen, Sally tapped her fingers on her laptop. Side by side on another chair, Gabi's two black cats watched her. Hamlet and Horatio. One sleek; one fluffy. The house was quiet since Master Marcus and Gabi had left to attend a karate tournament to cheer for some teenagers.

Sally had wanted to stay and do some thinking. Late last night, she'd had a long talk with Gabi and Marcus. They'd been wonderfully understanding.

And she'd reached a few decisions.

She'd been wrong to blame herself for what happened with her and the Feds. If she hadn't been so ready to believe she was a selfish person—*thanks, Father*—she'd have demanded an explanation from them.

So, once this was all settled, she'd take Gabi's advice and see about some counseling. The men had brought her a long way, but taking the next step—getting herself some help—was up to her.

And, dammit, she'd been wrong to blame the overprotective— *gutless*—men she loved. They were trying to keep her safe, and who knew, maybe she'd make the same decision if she were in their shoes.

Really, there was only one person to blame for messing up her relationship with her Doms. That arsonist.

He'd killed Tillman, the police, and that poor woman. His brother had shot *Vance*. The anger from that fed into her determination. She'd been content to promise to give up hacking since it seemed as if she'd done what she could. That the

Association would be destroyed quickly enough.

She'd been almost right. But there was one left, and he was the reason she hadn't woken up this morning snuggled between two muscular male bodies.

Since the bastard had ripped apart her relationship with the Feds, she thought it was perfectly logical that he'd also severed any promises she'd made to the Feds.

Logic is an excellent weapon when employed correctly.

She opened her laptop. Ever since she'd handed over her files to Galen and Vance, her hacking software had been calling her— *Sally, Sally, Sally.*

And now...she answered the summons. Mouth set in a straight line, she logged on.

In New York, Galen, being careful—*might even call him a bit paranoid*—had monitored as she deleted her computer worm program and Association files. And he'd even demanded she turn over the flash drives. She smirked as her fingers ran over the keyboard.

Wasn't it a shame that he'd missed seeing the tiny tray icon denoting a continuous online backup? And that he hadn't realized the e-mails came from an online mail program and weren't deleted?

"I never cheated. Never checked the software or e-mails," she told the cats virtuously. "I was a good girl."

She looked around the room. Even checked under the table. "Well, hell, guys. I don't see any good girls here today. Do you?"

Hamlet offered a tail flick of agreement.

"Yeah. That's what I thought." She clicked onto the Internet and smiled as her files opened up like a cannon barrage. *Target my Galen, will you?*

Fuck that. If war was what the arsonist wanted, war was what he'd get.

———+———

Seated in front of his computer, Vance was drinking coffee, typing up a report, and trying to ignore how empty the house felt without

Sally. The morning had passed with the speed of cold molasses.

Too antsy to sit, Galen had spent the last few hours working on the dungeon in the cabana before returning to the office and covering the center table with his weapons.

A timer went off with a quiet *beep-beep-beep*.

Vance glanced over his shoulder. "What's that for?"

Galen frowned. His rifle and three automatic handguns were dismantled and scattered over the table on opened newspapers, ready for cleaning. It was his ritual as he prepared for action.

On the far side of the table, Glock supervised from a safe distance.

Everyone reacted to impending danger in different ways. Galen liked to clean his weapons; Vance lifted weights.

"The timer is for the backsplash in the cabana. The grout is set; it's ready to be buffed and caulked." Galen wiped his hands on a paper towel. "I'll get that done and be back to finish up." His brief smile didn't get to his eyes. "Don't let anyone burn the place down until I get my weapons reassembled."

"Do my best." Vance took a drink of his coffee. "Though I'd rather be in New York, taking that bastard down."

Late last night, Drew Somerfeld's credit card had popped onto the FBI radar. Apparently Ellis had booked himself onto a flight to Florida this afternoon. He'd probably lifted his brother's ID and cards from the safe. Since he and Drew were twins, he'd pass well enough as his brother.

But the asshole would never make that flight. NYPD planned to nail his ass the minute he tried to check in. Only another half hour to wait.

If he wasn't just playing them.

Didn't matter. With two cops dead and Galen a target, the brass in Tampa wanted him and Galen to stay put. To keep them safe, sure, but also to serve as bait if needed. The only two ways to reach their property—the lakeshore drive and the lake itself— were being guarded.

Actually Vance had absolutely no problem with their caution.

"Not long to wait," Galen said, glancing at the clock. "If he doesn't get on that flight, then...hell."

"The bastard's definitely crazy as bug shit. It'd suck if he's also smart."

"True." Galen scowled, moving his shoulders. "Maybe that's why it feels wrong to be unarmed. Think I'll finish up here first and—"

"Leave that shit on the tiles too long, and you'll never get it off."

"Fine. Be a good guard dog till I get back." With a grunt of annoyance, Galen strode out of the office.

A couple of minutes later, Vance's cell rang. "You got a beat-up red Toyota Camry coming in." The call came from a special agent stationed half a mile away, watching the turnoff to the lakeshore drive. Pretty convenient that he and Galen lived on an isolated lake with only one access road. "Got a pretty brunette at the wheel. Looks like the one whose picture's on your desk."

"Got it. Thanks." Sally was coming.

Damn, but he wanted to see her. *Only, please God, don't let her cry.* Hell, he'd handled everything so poorly; she'd misinterpreted everything he'd said.

He'd *hurt* her.

Fuck. The knowledge ate at his gut. He'd tried to call her last night. Galen had as well. And texted her. No response. They'd left voice mails.

For God's sake, Dan was supposed to have explained everything before he took her home with him. When they'd finally reached him this morning, they'd found that Sally had gone home with Marcus.

So she didn't know...

But he knew the imp. Knew her strength. And intelligence. Even without Dan or Galen or Vance's explanations, Sally would figure out what was going on. She'd either hack out the info or weasel it out of someone. By now, she'd know why they'd sent her away.

He'd thought she would call.

He should have known better. Being Sally, she'd want to yell at them in person. Fuck, he loved her.

His smile grew. Even though he'd still have to send her away for her own safety, anticipation hummed through his body. After he apologized his ass off—and maybe swatted her ass for risking her neck by coming here—he could have her sweet body in his arms for a few minutes. Listen to her bright voice, her laughter...or, more likely, her shouting.

Just don't let her cry, please.

He walked out the front door and glanced around. Impenetrable growth lay on each side of their property—Florida's version of a chain-link fence—which would take a machete and flamethrower to get through.

Her car pulled into the drive. And just in case Somerfeld had gotten to her, was hiding in her car, Vance had drawn his weapon.

But she slid out, slammed the door, and scowled at him with an expression that was easy to read. Her chin was up, her shoulders squared. She certainly wasn't a terrified kidnapped victim.

She was prepared for battle. Damn, she made him proud. She'd argue, undoubtedly, that the chances of her being targeted were slim to none. That all the deaths had happened in New York. That she belonged with them.

But no. He holstered his weapon and stood where he was. Waiting.

As she walked toward him, her control slipped, and he grinned when she broke into a run.

She slammed into him and hugged him, holding him so tightly she shook with the effort.

Unable to help himself, he pulled her closer. Breathing in her clean, sweet scent was like unexpectedly finding almond cookies. So fucking sweet. "Shhh, sweetheart," he murmured. "We'll work this out somehow."

"You told me to move out." Her words were muffled by being said into his chest. "I'm really mad at you." Her arms didn't loosen in the least.

Don't laugh. "I know."

"I figured out why, but did you have to be so mean about it?"

Hell, exactly what they'd realized, far too late. "I should have explained." He rubbed his chin on her silky hair. "Trouble is, we'd just seen the pictures of the other cops who were killed. And you called, and while you were on the phone, I saw photos of the woman he murdered. It was an ugly death, Sally."

"Kari told me."

"After seeing those, all we could think about was keeping you safe. If the bastard comes after Galen for revenge, we want you far, far away."

The last bit of tension slid out of her body, and she leaned against him fully, all soft curves. "I don't think sending me away is the right answer."

And because of her spiteful father, sending her away would affect her more than most women. He frowned. What if the asshole didn't get caught in the next hour? If this dragged on and on. "Maybe we can find a way to compromise." Maybe all of them at a safe house? Maybe they could move. Or work from home. Or never leave Sally alone so she always had one guard. Teach her to shoot. Get a big dog—Raoul had found an excellent shepherd for his Kim, one from a company that specialized in protecting women. Move to Mexico. He huffed a laugh. Yes, he was losing his mind. She needed to leave. "Let me talk to Galen about it."

"Not going to happen."

"Sally, he won't let you stay long enough to argue."

She snorted. "Because he knows I'll win an argument. If he's in danger, this is where I want to be. I can help you stand guard. Three's better than two, after all."

Galen versus Sally. *I should sell tickets.* But he wouldn't let her stay either. "We'll figure something out. I'll talk with—"

"Vance, I-I need to see him. If nothing else, to know he's okay." She tipped her head back to smile up at him. Her brown eyes had light golden flecks that sparkled in the sunlight. Stubborn and mischievous, a terrifying combination. "But I'm glad I saw you first. I needed to know you were all right too."

That nurturing streak of hers was even stronger than he'd thought. Couldn't say he didn't prize that trait. In fact, he wanted, more and more, to give her a little one to mother.

He bent his head, taking himself another kiss. Her lips were sweet, soft, generous. Given the choice, he'd have hauled her straight up to his bed. "You sure you don't want me to pave the way?"

"No." When she straightened her shoulders, her full breasts strained against the bright red halter top she wore.

His mouth went dry. "Brought all your weapons to war, did you?"

"I'm a firm believer in outgunning a man—and kicking him once he's down." She fluffed her hair.

Although she grinned at him, he could still see lingering hurt in her big brown eyes, and he squeezed her shoulder. "I love you, Sally."

She leaned against him for a moment. "Love you too—even if you are an idiot."

He wanted to defend her, to at least accompany her back and take the brunt of Galen's anger. But sometimes two people had to battle it out, and stepping between them would only get the peacemaker slaughtered by both. "He's working in the cabana."

VANCE STILL LOVES me. Sally followed Vance through the house, out the back, and across the patio. There he stopped, looking out toward the lake. In a boat just offshore, two men in a motorboat were fishing. He lifted his hand to them in a short wave before turning back to Sally. "Good luck, sweetie."

After a final kiss, he gave her a slight push and remained where he was. Probably going to make sure she made it to the cabana before retreating out of hearing distance of the battle to come.

Smart guy. And actually, she was glad. When she and Galen argued, Vance tended to intervene, which wasn't good if tempers got hot. She'd never forget the men's fistfight...and all the bruises.

At least, no matter how angry Galen got, he'd never physically fight with a woman. And he'd said once that he never administered punishments when he was angry. Her ass was safe for the moment—because she intended to piss him the heck off.

Veering to the right, she headed down the overgrown path to the hidden cabana.

As she stepped inside, she spotted Galen in the kitchen area, buffing newly placed tiles.

He saw her. For an instant, his eyes lightened with pleasure, and everything in her surged up with joy.

A second later, his carved face turned deadly cold. "What the *hell* are you doing here?"

Feeling as if she'd walked into an ice storm, she looked away as she regathered her courage. A new bondage table sat across the room. Pretty, all dark wood and leather padding. It was the one she'd seen in the catalog. Her jaw set at the thought of them using *her* equipment with other women. *Never.*

And Mr. Grumpy Pants wasn't going to intimidate her. She set her hands on her hips. "Hiding out?" she asked, her tone frigid enough to match her insides.

He didn't even blink. "You were told not to come here. I want you gone. Now."

Don't you just wish, buddy. "I came to talk with you."

"No." He moved toward her, and she had no doubt he'd grab her by the hair to haul her off to her car.

"Damn you," she said, not exactly under her breath, and edged behind the bench. "If you won't talk, you can listen." *You beloved asshole.* "This is my home now. You and Vance insisted. Brought all my stuff here. Moved me in. And now, just because there's danger, you kick me out."

His fingers tightened on the buffing cloth as he stalked around the bench. "Because you could be killed."

"You didn't even have the courtesy to talk with me about it. Just—*get out, Sally.*" Her voice wavered as she remembered the hurt.

Under the thin white T-shirt, Galen's powerful shoulders were rigid. His angular jaw was tight. "Vance wasn't gentle with you, Sally, and I'm sorry for that."

She had a moment of hope. "That's all right, but—"

"Now that I've apologized, get your ass back to Gabi's house."

"No." Hey, if he could use one-word sentences, so could she. Just to drive home the point, she added, "I live here. I'm going to my room."

Even as she turned, his brows drew together into a straight black line.

She got two steps out the door before being yanked back into the cabana. "You will go back to Gabi's." His hands tightened on her shoulders, and he gave her a shake. "It's not safe for you here."

"It's not safe for you either, Mr. Hotshot FBI Agent." She realized her voice had risen. "I'm not going anywhere unless you do too."

"This is my job."

"No, dumb-ass, this is where you live!" From the startled look on his face, she must have shouted that. She waved her hand at the room. "Does this look like a downtown office? No, it does not."

A muscle danced in his cheek, and his grip on her shoulders turned painful. "Sally, Somerfeld's brother wants revenge. He's killed two cops—and their families with them. He—"

"I *know* that, Galen. Six people total if you count the woman from the cabin." She pursed her lips. "Actually, I think he did all the arson jobs. Even though the Association was countrywide, all the arson deaths were concentrated in the northeast area. If you look at the map I made, you'll—"

"What map?"

"Oh, please, do you really think I can't access any information I want?"

"Hell, I forgot who I was talking to." His hands eased slightly. "Then you know—"

"I know he's never left the northeast. He's brilliant but crazier than a hoot owl. I know it's still not one hundred percent safe." She curled her fingers around his wrist. "I also know I love you. This is where I belong."

"Fuck!" He stalked away from her and punched the wall.

Seriously? She thought that only happened in movies. He'd actually put a hole in the wall she'd spent so much time painting.

He punched another hole and turned. "I will not have another woman die because of *me*. Because of what I do."

His anger threatened to flatten her like dry cornstalks in a gale wind. Her back hit the door.

"You will get your ass out of here, and you will stay away."

"Forever?" she whispered. When grief darkened his eyes, she realized this mess had awakened his nightmares...and the idiot planned to push her all the way out of his life. "But you love me."

"That. Is. Irrelevant."

"That is *not* irrelevant." She stomped forward, kicked his toolbox out of her way, and punched him in the chest with all her might. Took satisfaction in the grunt—though *ow!* Had she broken her thumb? "You're just scared."

He bit back an automatic denial—such a guy—and nodded. "I am. I couldn't stand to see you hurt."

"Instead you'll rip my heart right out of my chest?" She punched him again and sucked in air against the flash of pain.

He grabbed her wrist and hauled her closer. "At least you'll be alive."

"If I'm alive, I want to live. I can't live inside a cocoon, Galen." She glared up into his eyes. "Do you think you're the only person who worries about a lover dying? Who had someone they love die? Because of something they did?"

Shock spread over his face as he realized she was talking about her mother. "Sally..."

"You can stay inside your cocoon, all wrapped up tight until you shrivel down to nothing." She opened her palm. "But I want to spread my wings—and love. You worked with me to be sure guilt didn't rule my life. You need to help yourself now."

His jaw stayed tight.

"I love you so much, you dumb-ass." She took the last step—and, thanks to him, the words came easily. Yes, she could ask. "Let me stay. *Please.*"

"God fucking dammit," he said under his breath and pulled her into his arms.

And it felt as if she'd come home.

After a minute, he said, "But would you just—"

"No."

"Maybe for only—"

"No."

"Vance and I spank submissives who say no to us," he muttered.

"Okay." Because in order to spank her, she had to be right there, within reach. And that was exactly where she intended to stay.

He pulled her up and kissed her neck before shaking his head. "I love you, but not even you can plant yourself in the middle of an FBI case. You'll get us fired, pet."

Oh. She hadn't thought of that one. "Maybe getting you fired would be a good thing." Jeez, maybe it was.

"I'd rather it be my decision, thanks," he said in a dry voice. "So, we'll talk for a bit. But if NYPD hasn't picked up Somerfeld in the next hour, you're going back to safety."

She eyed him. No, he wouldn't give way on this, but the unreasonableness was gone. He wasn't operating out of old fears, but logic. And she could live with that. "It's a deal."

FROM THE BACK door, Vance listened. He and Galen had installed excellent soundproofing in the cabana—he'd barely been able to hear the yelling.

And now nothing.

Hopefully, they were fucking up a storm. Makeup sex. He grinned as he started to harden. With luck they'd get a call in a minute or two that New York had Somerfeld in custody. If so, a victory fuck would be in order.

If NYPD didn't call, the imp's time would be up. He'd have to drag Sally out and stuff her in her car.

Meantime—he snorted—he was guard dog.

His cell chimed, reminding him to make the scheduled check-in call. Vance hit the number for the office. "Still alive. How are the guys doing out by the turnoff?"

"They're just fine, Vance." Hazel was around seventy and undoubtedly had won Mother of the Year when her children were young. "How is your back?"

"All healed. I'm going stir-crazy, being shut in."

She sniffed, unimpressed, as if he'd whined about a snow day. "You just settle down. And tell that boy to be careful as well."

Choking on a laugh, he assured her that he'd tell the *boy*. If Galen heard that... Then again, his partner adored the old woman. Fuck knew, she acted more like a mother than Galen's real one.

A few minutes later, his cell rang. The stakeout team reported an elderly woman had taken the lakeshore drive. One of the neighbors.

To stave off the urge to go to Galen and Sally, he went out the front. They hadn't checked the mail earlier. After pulling on a coat to cover his shoulder holster, he walked onto the front porch. Nothing. Couldn't even see the neighbor's houses through the dense surrounding growth. No cars. No people. All quiet.

He glanced at his watch. *Somerfeld, do your airport check-in. I want this over.*

His skin felt as if the air was filled with sand. Nerves.

It was a nice day; he should make an effort to enjoy it. As he ambled to the mailbox at the end of their U-shaped drive, he watched the brilliantly white puffy clouds float across the sky. No thunderclouds...yet. Chances were good they'd appear later in the day. The summer rainstorms had started up.

As he unlocked the metal mailbox, he grinned at the memory of Sally's insults about paranoid Feds. He pulled out a nice haul of letters and flyers.

A car appeared, slowly moving down the road. The gray-haired driver gave him a wide smile. It was his nearest neighbor, Mrs. Childress.

He stepped over to the car and glanced in the backseat—just in case. "Ma'am, how are you today?"

"I'm fine, dear. I was going to call you later. How nice to see you in person. We're having a small barbecue next week on Saturday. I hope you and Galen and Sally will come." The elderly couple had met Sally when she was on the lake, fishing with Galen. Like everyone else, they'd fallen for the imp.

"We'd be delighted." Somerfeld had damn well better be safely behind bars by then.

"Wonderful. Around four." With a sweet smile, the old lady put her car in gear and continued down the road.

Vance strolled back to the house. Before he'd opened the front door more than a crack, Glock darted out onto the porch.

"Have a good day, buddy." Must be pretty urgent feline business. Flipping through the junk mail, Vance stepped inside...and the world fell in on him.

—✴—

Why was he lying on his side on the floor? Vance wondered. Hangover? Hell, his head felt like an overinflated balloon, ready to pop.

His jaw clenched as memories trickled back in a slow returning tide. Mailbox. Cat. Letter. Nothing. Something was really wrong.

His heart sped up, increasing the throbbing inside his skull. Swallowing, he fought nausea silently. Blocked his urge to call for help. Didn't move, didn't groan, didn't touch his head. With his eyes opened only a slit, he tried to assess, even while cursing the slowness of his brain. His thoughts moved hopelessly slow, like bubbles fighting to rise through a thick swamp.

He recognized the game room flooring. God knew, he'd spent enough time putting it in.

He listened, hearing nothing except the painful roaring in his head.

Fingers felt numb. Ah, fuck, his wrists were cuffed behind him.

Dread burst inside him at the sight of the heavy iron shackles on his ankles. *Shackles.* The chain connecting the shackles was looped around a two-by-four—part of the built-out bar Galen was constructing in a corner of the room.

The ugly realization worked through the murk in Vance's head. Jesus fuck, he'd screwed up.

Somerfeld wasn't in New York; he was here. But how the fuck had he gotten past the stakeout teams?

Please, don't fucking let Sally or Galen walk in unknowingly.

Footsteps. In his narrow field of vision, he spotted the legs entering the room. A five-gallon container of gasoline was set down. The bastard was consistent, wasn't he?

Vance felt his stomach clench. Burning was dead last on his list of ways to die.

The man made another trip out and back into the room. After Somerfeld ran upstairs, Vance kicked the two-by-four holding him. And again. And again. The fucking chain kept him from exerting much force.

And Jesus, his head might split before the post did. Half-blind from the pain, he halted when he heard footsteps coming downstairs.

Somerfeld dropped bedding in a corner of the room and went back upstairs.

Kick. Kick. Kick.

This time, Somerfeld came down with a full laundry hamper. After tossing the clothing into another corner, he walked into the hall leading to the office.

Once Somerfeld disappeared, Vance slammed his foot into the post again. This time he felt a slight give in the screws holding the post in place. Or maybe it was his knee fracturing.

Footsteps. Humming to himself, Somerfeld set a can of paint thinner on the floor and tossed crumpled paper against the walls. He was rigging enough flammables to ensure the building would burn completely. Wonderful.

The legs approached. Vance closed his eyes.

Pain burst in his low back; the bastard had kicked him.

"Wake up, asshole, or I'll put a bullet in your leg." The voice was raspy with a New York accent.

Not worth pretending. Vance groaned and blinked—and got backhanded across the face.

His head exploded with pain again, and lights danced in front of his eyes. Bad treatment if he had a concussion.

Hell, he probably wouldn't live long enough to be diagnosed.

Meeting Somerfeld's eyes set off the crazy bastard like Vance had lit a firecracker. "Fucking Fed. I should just—" A pistol barrel jammed against Vance's cheekbone. "No. No, I want to hear you scream. And burn. Drew would want me to burn everything. Leave nothing behind."

Somerfeld stepped back, and Vance released the breath he'd been holding. Looked like he'd live another minute or two. As his vision cleared, Vance stared at the arsonist. *What the hell?*

A long blonde wig curled over the man's shoulders and down his back. He had on a frilly, long-sleeved top—something Sally might wear over her swimming suit. Nothing else was feminine.

His facial structure was like his twin's, but thick white scarring ribboned down his face like a waterfall. One eyelid was shriveled, the lower part drooping.

"How'd you get in here?" Vance slowly sat up.

"Sailboat."

But they'd had two agents fishing not far from the dock.

The scars twisted the bastard's smile. "Your watchdogs let us come right up to their boat. All they saw was a pretty brunette in a bikini sailing with her pregnant blonde friend." After patting his ruffle-covered gut, he pulled the wig off, revealing a shaved skull.

"Too slow to catch on." Somerfeld mimicked shooting with his finger—one, two—and blew the smoke from the imaginary barrel.

Two women? One had been Somerfeld. "You have someone else here?"

Somerfeld jerked his thumb toward the corner behind Vance.

Gagged and hog-tied, a young woman lay on her side almost on a flammable pile. Her blank gaze showed she'd gone past terror into resignation. She knew she'd die today.

"Kouros is at work?" Somerfeld asked.

The bastard had been all over the house...but he probably hadn't seen the isolated cabana. "Yeah."

"Give me his phone number."

Vance hesitated. Should he? *Think, Buchanan.* But his thoughts turned helpless circles as if lost in a forest.

Somerfeld turned the pistol toward the girl. "Wanna see her kneecapped?" A sickening hunger showed in his face.

"No." God, no. But someone was going to die. *Let it be me, not*

Galen. Not Sally. Could he manage to shout a warning or— "It's 555-8023."

"Good. When he answers, you tell him I'm here." Somerfeld tossed the phone in the air and caught it. "Oh yeah, indeedy yeah."

—✦—

Sitting on the edge of the bed, Galen cursed as his cell phone rang. Sally was in his lap. Her halter top was down around her waist, and he'd cupped a plump breast in his hand. All was right with his world and about to get better. Poor Vance, having to stay on guard.

Sally nipped his chin. "You better answer that."

"Ayuh." Shifting her over to sit beside him, he pulled his phone from his pocket and checked the display. The house phone? Maybe Vance had heard from the office. "You do realize I'm busy here," he said into the phone as he ran his knuckles over the prettiest nipples in the world.

Sally made a hungry sound.

"Galen, I can't join you at the field office. I'm still at home. I got jumped by Somerfeld. " It was Vance's voice. Thin and tight with pain and warning. "He has me shackled to the game-room bar, pistol to my head—when he isn't pouring gasoline around the walls. Got his slave here too. Hog-tied."

Christ. "Vance—"

He heard his partner give a low, painful grunt.

"God fucking dammit." Galen stood, anchoring the phone to his ear. "*Vance.*"

"You killed my twin, asshole." The grating whine of the unfamiliar voice sounded like a tile saw. "So I'm gonna kill your partner. I'm going to *burn* him."

Galen took two steps toward the door and stopped. *Don't charge your ass into the kill zone. Need more information.* "You're at my house?"

Somerfeld's voice had been controlled...barely. Now his laugh went over the edge into insanity.

Close enough to hear, Sally turned white.

"Buchanan's got oh, about five more minutes before I leave and toss a match behind me. Yeah, by the time you get here, your good buddy will be black and crisp. And dead."

The phone went silent.

Galen's mind went blank as fear rushed through him, permeating every cell. *God, Vance. No.* And then his brain kicked in.

Sally had pulled her own phone out and tapped 91. Holding it up, she waited for his nod before punching in the final 1. A second later, she was talking fast. "I need the fire department and the police. An FBI agent is being held hostage by an arsonist."

She had a good head in a crisis, Galen noted as he carefully cracked the door of the cabana. He heard her give Vance's name and the house address as he checked outside. He saw only the thick growth of lakeshore plants.

Vance had provided the essential facts. One crazy man. Armed. In the game room. Two hostages. Vance wouldn't be of any help. Gasoline. And less than five minutes? He punched in the number for the ones on the lake.

No answer. His jaw tightened over the grief. He'd known those men.

The lakeshore road took time to drive. The agents on the road stakeout wouldn't make it in five minutes.

Think, Kouros.

Somerfeld thought Galen was at the field office in Tampa.

"No, sorry, but I can't remain on the phone," Sally said to the emergency dispatcher and swiped the display to hang up her cell. "What now?"

"My weapons are in the office. Can't get to them—can't cross the dining room without being spotted. Windows are locked. Vance can't help." Galen rubbed his face, thinking bitterly of the handcuffs in his pocket. Wishing for anything else. Pepper spray even. "Give Somerfeld time to react, and he'll light the place up. I need a diversion."

"Well, that's me." Her fingers fumbled as she retied her halter top.

"No."

"We don't have a choice." She ran to the cupboard, pulled out her collar, and buckled it around her neck. "He's obviously into slaves. He won't shoot me."

"Then he'll have three hostages."

"It'll buy us a minute or two—and, um"—she gave him a half-guilty look—"I messed with the wiring. If I can flip on the switch in the game room, I can make it sound as if someone is trapped upstairs. Another woman."

He stared. A software prankster. Yes, she could do that. And he couldn't let her. "No."

"Galen, yes," she whispered.

She made sense. By God, she made sense, and Galen wanted to shake her for it. He wanted to shove her in a safe room somewhere, lock the door, and let her out once it was all over.

But look at her. Facing him. Arms folded over her chest. Willing to die. He loved her more than life, and the thought of seeing her die... "I can't." Memories of Ursula. Beaten to death. With each beat of his heart, more ice spread into his bloodstream. "I can't risk you."

Her stubborn little chin lowered as sympathy filled her eyes. "I'm not your wife." She hugged him, intending comfort, but he could feel her shivering. "If I go in, there's a chance. If I don't, Vance and that woman will die."

"*You* might die." He lifted her chin and saw both terror and resolve combined. She knew. She was willing to take the chance.

"God didn't promise us safety. Just a chance to live. To love." She put her palm on his cheek and whispered in his ear, "You know better than to bind someone too tightly. Loosen the restraints, Sir."

His mouth tasted of bitterness and sorrow, of ash and doom. To lose both Sally and Vance was his own version of hell. But she had the right to decide. He forced out the words. "All right."

She pulled in a breath and gave him a firm nod, despite the way her fingers trembled against his face.

For himself, he took a quick kiss, her lips as sweet as anything he'd ever tasted. "If you die on me, I swear—" He couldn't think of anything nasty enough.

"I won't." She kissed the side of his jaw. "And if you get hurt, Sir, I'm going to kick your ass." As she slid out the door, Sally mouthed, *I love you*, one second before she ran up the dirt path toward the house.

He closed his eyes for a moment, praying he'd see her again so he could give the words back. Praying the brother of his heart would survive.

Then he called the stakeout on the road. "Somerfeld is here. Hostage situation. Place is set to burn." Without waiting for an answer, he set his phone to silent, leaving the connection open. If they arrived in time, they'd have an idea of what was going down.

After grabbing a hammer from the toolbox, Galen followed Sally up the path.

———✳———

Don't look scared. Look lover-like. Happy.

As Sally stepped through the back door, she tried to call out.

Voice didn't work. *Slow breath.*

She saw Galen run across the patio and step to one side of the door. Out of sight. Didn't it just figure that he wouldn't have his weapon? What kind of an FBI agent did his carpentry unarmed?

Slow breath. She cleared her throat and reminded herself to smile. *I'm a happy, horny girl.* "Oh Vaaance. Are you home, sweetheart?" She walked across the kitchen, unable to hear anything but the pounding of her heart. It took an eternity to get to the dining room.

Would Somerfeld just shoot her? Her insides cringed as if trying to flee the impact of a bullet. *No. We're going to save Vance.* "Hoooney, I want to do a scene. You promised to spank me for being bad, Master."

She walked into the game room and saw Vance.

Arms restrained behind his back, he sat, one shoulder propping him up against the wall. His ankles were fastened to a post with heavy iron cuffs. Blood ran down the side of his face, and his eyes were glassy.

"Vance." Where was Somerfeld?

At a sound, she spun. He was right *behind* her.

The man slapped her across the face, knocking her backward. Pain exploded in her cheek. Tears filled her eyes and blurred her vision as she stared at him. *Dear God.*

His skull was shaved. One eye was bigger than the other because of the scars running past it and down that side of his face to distort his mouth. The girlie swimsuit cover-up he wore was bizarrely wrong.

As the pistol pointed at her, he smiled. His muddy hazel eyes lingered on her breasts, making her skin crawl. "I didn't hear a car. Where'd you come from, slut?"

Her face still burned with pain. She swallowed. "The lake. In a canoe."

He grunted his acceptance of her answer. "Sit over there." And motioned with his pistol toward Vance.

She ran across the room toward her Dom...and toward the light switch. *Can't kneel—need to stay on my feet. Need to be mobile. Get to the door.* "Oh, look at you, Master." As she spun and glared at Somerfeld, she edged two steps toward the door to the foyer. "What did you do to him? Who are you anyway?"

The scarring—and insanity—twisted his smile to something horrible. "I'm the man who's going to listen to you burn, slut. To your flesh crisping and your screams."

The ghastly rush of fear turned her body cold. No. Move. She backed up farther toward the door. "But why? I don't even know you!" Another step. Almost there.

He motioned with the black barrel of his pistol, and her mouth went dry. He'd shoot her. "Get over there," he said.

"No. I don't *want* to." All her years of defiance served her well, and the words came out without her forcing them.

Even as he aimed the pistol at her, she backed into the wall. The light switches poked her shoulder, and she nudged the far one up. "Okay, okay, I'm moving." She hurried back toward Vance.

"Too late." He turned the pistol and shot Vance.

—✦—

Moving through the kitchen, Galen heard the gunshot followed by Sally's high scream, "Noooooo!"

Vance. He'd shot Vance. Galen's throat tightened as he stopped just inside the dining room door. He'd have to cross that area to reach the game room. *Do the diversion, Sally. Do it.*

All he could hear was sobbing...and the splashing sound of gasoline.

Fuck.

He'd give her one minute and charge, no matter what.

A second later, he realized the cursing he heard was from Vance. The son of a bitch was alive.

His vision blurred for a second.

—+—

"Jesus, fuck." Vance gritted the words out over the searing pain in his thigh. Nice hole in the outside muscle. Bleeding like a river but not spurting. Hadn't hit an artery or even the bone. Hurt like hell.

Beside him, Sally dropped like a rag doll, her knees impacting the hardwood floor with a nasty thump.

Vance twisted to try to help. Couldn't.

Somerfeld's laughter sounded like the rough whine of a chainsaw. Out of control and revoltingly gleeful as he watched Vance bleed. He grinned at Sally. "See what you made me do, slut?"

"Wake up, Mommy." The imp's whisper held no reason, no knowledge as she rocked back and forth on her knees, arms limp at her sides. Her gaze had fixed on the blood creeping across the floor, dark red against the light wood. "Mommy. Wake up. Wake up."

"Crazier'n' me now. Oh yeah, indeedy yeah." Somerfeld licked his lips. "Nice tits. Could use a new slut."

Unable to help himself, Vance growled.

"Like her, huh?" Somerfeld nudged him with a foot. "Tell you what, I'll play the recording of your screaming when I fuck her." He rubbed his groin, cock half-erect. "Be sure you're not forgotten."

Vance's gut twisted with his revulsion. *No. It wouldn't happen.* He couldn't let that happen.

Humming again, Somerfeld picked up the half-full can of gasoline. Pistol in one hand, he carelessly splashed the liquid against the walls, splattering everything in the area.

"Sally," Vance said quietly. His partner must have sent her in here for a reason. If she needed to do something, she'd better be about it, or Galen would end up with a bullet in his gut.

She didn't even look at him.

Vance lowered his voice to that of command. "*Sally.*"

BLOOD EVERYWHERE. "WAKE up, Mommy." Dripping down the windshield, on her face, her clothes. On *Mommy.* "No no no." She tried to turn, to get to her mother, but her arm wouldn't move. She pulled and yanked. Pain tore through her. Nothing moved except the pouring blood. Red, so very red against the snow outside the car. "Mommy."

"Sally. Look at me." The steel in the dark male voice sliced through her nightmare and pulled at her. Her body obeyed, not under her control at all. Turned her away from the red, turned her toward the sound.

"That's a girl. Eyes on me. *Now.*"

Her head lifted, her gaze met blue fire, and the anger—and love—in Vance's eyes burned away the past. *My Vance.* Her skin felt clammy, and cold sweat ran down her face. What...happened?

As the stench of gasoline hit her, she was suddenly, completely in the present. *Somerfeld. Burning.* Vance had been *shot.*

He was *bleeding.* Shocked, she pressed her hands to the horrible wound. He groaned. How long had she been...elsewhere?

God, she was supposed to create the diversion.

"Ready to go. Indeedy yeah." Somerfeld tossed the container aside.

Get it together, Sally. The receiver for the voice-activated program was very sensitive. She didn't have to talk loudly. Sally tried to speak. A horrible sound emerged. *Get the tone right, girl.* A long breath. She turned to Ellis, holding up her hands in a pleading position. "Please, please, please, don't hurt me. I'm sorry I brought her here."

The dickwad stared at her. "You talking to me, slut?"

Vance stared at her. "Brought who?" he whispered. His face was pale, jaw tight from pain.

I love you, my Vance. Her hand closed over his. *Please, please, please, let this work.*

A high scream came from upstairs. "Master, help me. Master." Another long wail.

"Fuck!" Somerfeld ran up three steps, turned to glare at her, and pointed the pistol at Vance. "You leave, slut, and I'll shoot his balls off. You'll hear him scream no matter how far you run." He dashed up the stairs toward the sound of the woman sobbing.

"Run," Vance gritted out. "Whoever that is up there, Sally, I want you to run."

He didn't recognize the voice? Of course, Gabi had been pretty drunk the night they'd made the recording. "Not leaving without you, dummy."

"Goddamn it." He lifted his uninjured leg and kicked the post, grunting at the impact. On his other leg, the jeans were drenched with blood.

She pushed her hands down on the wound, holding it as he slammed his boot into the post, over and over. *Hurry, Galen.*

Yelling came from upstairs as Somerfeld searched for the illusive woman. *Screw you, bastard.* She spotted a mallet in the pile of construction tools.

Yes! She grabbed it and hit the post holding Vance as hard as she could. But it made so much—too much—noise.

Hit again.

The post moved.

Before she could swing again, Vance kicked. With a crack, the screws tore loose.

—✦—

Galen slid into the room with a quick check of Vance and Sally. Alive and alive. Although the amount of blood wasn't good. A hog-tied woman lay in the corner. Gagged. Alive.

A woman's crying and screaming sounded on the second floor—*was that Gabi?*—along with the thud of heavy boots.

Galen moved behind and under the stairs. Crappy hiding place, but the room held no conveniently concealing furniture.

Upstairs, Somerfeld yelled, "You fucking slut. Think you'd trick me? Huh?" From the worry on Sally's face, the bastard had discovered he'd been searching for a recording.

Boots pounded down the stairs. Once Somerfeld reached the bottom, Galen could jump him from behind.

The man halted most of the way down. "You fucking cunt!"

A trigger clicked. "Hell!" Galen stepped out from the stairs and threw his hammer. The tool struck Somerfeld's shoulder and knocked him a step sideways. The pistol fired.

Galen grabbed the railing and swung himself up and over, and hit Somerfeld in a half-assed tackle. The bastard lost his balance; Galen never found his.

Tangled together, they rolled down the stairs.

Galen's back, leg, head banged against the steps with bursts of pain. He landed badly but rolled to hands and knees, Somerfeld beside him, groaning.

Galen tried to stand. His leg gave out. His hip and shoulder hit the floor, knocking the air out of him.

Growling, Somerfeld made a grab for the pistol he'd dropped.

Twisting, Galen kicked the weapon toward Vance and rammed his knee into Somerfeld's chin. Pain knifed through his leg with the impact.

The bastard spat blood and managed to stand.

GALEN WAS DOWN. Somerfeld up. Vance had yanked the chain free from under the splintered wood post and tried again—and again—to get to his feet. Succeeded.

He tried to run and tripped on the two-foot chain between his shackled ankles. "Jesus, fuck!" Handicapped, he half hopped, half lunged across the room toward the fight.

From the corner of his eye, he saw Sally darting the other way, going for the pistol, which had skidded into a pile of bedding.

"Somerfeld," Vance yelled.

The bastard didn't hear him.

Galen was on hands and knees, trying to stand. Somerfeld kicked him in the gut so violently that Galen was flipped sideways, retching and gasping for air.

"You asshole!" Sally pointed the pistol at Somerfeld, the weapon shaking so hard she'd probably shoot Galen.

Somerfeld involuntarily retreated, and into that moment of silence came the wailing of sirens. Approaching the house.

The bastard's eyes went wide, fearful, then furious. Insane. "Burn it. Burn it *all*." He pulled a match from his pocket, flicked it with his thumbnail, and it lit.

Jesus fuck, Vance thought, if Sally shoots him... Gasoline everywhere.

Galen yelled, "Sally, hold!"

But Somerfeld was crazy enough to burn the place with himself in it. No way to win.

Fuck that. Vance dived at the bastard, rammed into him—chest to chest—knocking him back. Glass shattered as they slammed into the bay window—and out.

Somerfeld hit the ground with a grunt of pain.

Vance landed beside him, the impact yanking at his cuffed arms. The pain that ripped through his wounded leg took his breath away. Sent his brain spinning.

He groaned, opened his eyes, and saw *fire*. His shirt. On fire.

"Fuck!" Unable to use his hands, Vance rolled frantically, smothering the flame in the damp grass.

Panting, hurting everywhere, he rolled back over, trying to sit up. And froze.

Somerfeld's gasoline-splattered clothing had also ignited. And burst into a conflagration. He shrieked, slapping at the fire before he ran, straight down the drive. Flaming.

"Drop and roll, roll!" Vance shouted, trying to get to his feet. The chain clanked, reminding him he was hobbled. Could never catch the poor bastard in time.

The sirens on the approaching emergency vehicles didn't drown out the screaming. Somerfeld fell, finally fell, directly in front of the police car, the first vehicle down the lane.

From the following fire engine, firefighters jumped out. They surrounded Somerfeld, spraying him down.

More vehicles. Cops and FBI agents raced toward the house.

A knife of pain ripped through Vance's leg. *Shit!* He jerked around. "What the—"

Galen was tying a makeshift bandage around his thigh. "Nice tackle, bro. Still got some skill there."

As Vance hauled in a breath, he started to shake. Too fucking close. "Nice battle plan given the short notice, bro," he returned.

Galen switched his attention to unlocking the handcuffs around Vance's wrists, swearing under his breath at the torn skin.

As Vance pulled his arms around to the front, his shoulder joints hurt almost as much as the returning circulation in his hands. "I'm too fucking old for this," he muttered, wanting to scream like a little girl. Jesus, he hurt.

"Tell me about it." Galen turned.

Vance followed his gaze. The paramedics were loading Somerfeld into the ambulance with an IV. He must still be alive.

"Halt!" a cop shouted from the driveway.

What now?

Sally, halfway around the house, skidded to a sudden stop. She lifted her hands and obviously realized she still held the pistol. "Shit! Hey, I'm the good guy. Girl. What*ever*," she yelled. She carefully set the weapon on the sidewalk.

As the cop approached her, one of the FBI agents trotted toward the front door.

"There's another woman inside," Vance called. "And be careful. It's set up to burn." He nodded approval when a fireman yanked the FBI special agents back and went in first.

Glancing at Galen, Vance asked, "How'd you get here before

Sally?"

"Came through the window."

Vance saw the streaks of blood where shattered glass had ripped clothing and the flesh beneath. If Somerfeld hadn't gone out the window first, Vance would probably be as ripped up. "You must've missed the hole we left."

"Forgot to aim."

"Vance!"

He looked up in time to be attacked by a hysterical whirlwind who plastered his face with kisses and "I love you; I love you; I love you" before she spun away to smother Galen with the same.

When she slowed, Galen grabbed her and kissed her hard enough to silence her. Whatever he murmured in her ear made her tear up. Then he handed her back to Vance.

Vance pulled her into his arms. Warm woman filled with love. Risked her life to save him. Kept her head. He ignored the pain in his leg as the paramedics tried to cut away his jeans. He held her, kissed her hair, cupped her chin, and knew exactly what his partner had said.

"I love you, Sally."

CHAPTER TWENTY-FOUR

*W*e're all alive. Sally stood in an emergency-room cubicle beside the stretcher cart where Galen lay. *Galen is alive.* She kept repeating the reassurances to herself. *Vance is alive.* Didn't help. She still couldn't stop shaking. She was so dreadfully cold.

His shirt already off, Galen was talking to the skinny doctor setting out a suture kit. Beside Sally, a nurse in pink flowered scrubs pulled on sterile gloves.

Vance was in another curtained-off room, but his ER doctor hadn't let Sally stay with him.

This doctor was nicer.

With a gauze pad, the nurse started to wipe the blood away from the horrible rents in Galen's skin. All over his beautiful chest. The white gauze turned red. The nurse picked up another. So many long, gaping slashes.

Black shimmered around the edges of Sally's vision. Blood kept trickling down his side. Her mouth tasted like tin and—

"Christ!" Galen's voice danced through the mist. Someone cursed. Metal clanged as it hit the floor.

Hard hands caught her as her legs went soft and black clouds filled her head.

"Down you go, baby girl." Somehow on his feet, Galen backed her up, sat her in a chair, and relentlessly pressed her head down until her forehead rested on her knees.

She actually felt blood surge back into her brain. After a minute, she muttered, "Enough." He released her and set a hand on her shoulder, helping her sit up. "I'm okay." Aside from being really embarrassed.

His dark eyes held amusement. "You're far, far better than just okay, imp," he said softly. "But I want you out of here. I'll find you after I'm stitched up." He turned to the nurse, and even shirtless with blood streaking his chest, he was a force to be reckoned with. "Please get her something to drink, miss. And help her to the waiting room."

"Of course."

A few minutes later, she was tucked into the corner of the ugly sitting area. Plastic chairs ringed the room. A television on the wall displayed a sitcom. A woman held a towel to a cut on her face. Children were coughing. Crying.

Trying to not think about the past hours, Sally stewed about something less...traumatic. Like her future. Just look how she'd frozen up when Vance got shot. Because of the blood. She'd almost passed out seeing Galen bleed.

And I want to work in law enforcement?

Sally shook her head. Even if she concentrated on computers, she'd still come face-to-face with blood and death, whether in the hallways or picking up equipment.

Did she really want a job like that? *No.* With a sigh of both regret and relief, she mentally crossed off law enforcement from her list of potential employers. She'd find job where she wouldn't see dead people. Or blood.

But...

But what if Galen or Vance came home looking like they did today? Coldness took root in her belly, spreading outward. This was what they did. Day after day. How could she let them leave the house, knowing what they might face?

More chills ran over her body as she saw again the splattering blood, the pained grunt Vance had made at the bullet's impact. He'd been hurt, and she hadn't been able to help him. What if she wasn't even there next time? With a moan, she buried her head in her hands.

"Sally."

Master Z's smooth, deep voice pulled her from the dark places.

Shaking herself back to reality, Sally inhaled the scent of cleaners overlying the foulness of excrement and infection. She rubbed her fingers together, feeling the tackiness of old blood on her hands. The television was blaring. But she was back in the present. She looked up.

Master Z stood in the door of the waiting room, holding a brown paper grocery sack.

She frowned. "What are you doing here?"

"Dan called." After putting his sack on a chair, he lifted Sally to her feet, holding her steady as her legs wobbled. "Galen has hospital paperwork to fill out before he can leave. But Vance has been admitted for the night. Shall we go see him?"

"Please." And as if she had the right, she burrowed into his arms. He tucked her in closer, holding her firmly—anchoring her—and she knew that no matter what would go wrong, she had a refuge. A place of safety her father had never given her.

When she finally stepped back, her legs felt as if they belonged to her body again. "Thank you," she whispered.

His gray eyes softened. "You're one of mine, little one. Don't forget it again."

As tears pooled in her eyes, he touched her cheek gently, picked up his sack, and led her from the room.

Endless corridors later, he opened a hospital door and guided her inside.

Vance lay in the bed. Under his dark tan, his color was almost gray.

Her feet froze in place on the ugly linoleum floor. But after an eternity, his chest rose and fell. He was sleeping. She clenched her hands as she fought the need to wake him, to know—*know*—that he was alive.

"Sit there," Master Z murmured and gently pushed her down in a chair by the bed. "Galen should be up in a minute."

"He's coming." Dan and Kari walked into the room. "He wouldn't let them admit him," Dan grumbled. "Wouldn't even accept the loan of a wheelchair. Stubborn bastard."

Finally Galen came in, leaning heavily on an ugly metal cane, and Sally rushed to his side. She started to grab him, remembered the stitches, and—ever so carefully—put her arms around him.

He snorted. "I'm not as fragile as all that, pet." After leaning his cane against the foot of the bed, he pulled her into him. His arms were the same iron bars she remembered, his chest muscular, his body ever so solid. Z might be a refuge, but here was her home. "Sally?"

She was unable to release him, unable to talk. Every word thickened in her throat and clogged it. Her shaking returned, starting in her belly and moving outward. He could have *died*.

"Shhh." His cheek rested on the top of her head.

"Want to sit?" Dan asked him.

Galen's arms tightened. "No. I just need to hold her. Came too close to losing her. To losing them both."

Oh, she knew. She knew. He smelled of antiseptic, of sweat and blood, of danger and death and life, and she fully intended to relax her grip—in a year or two.

"If you're going to have a party in my room, I expect alcohol." Vance's voice sounded as if he'd dragged it over the gravel road to their house.

"I believe I have that covered," Z said. Everyone in the room looked at him. "Dan mentioned your aversion to pain meds, so I brought a different kind of a sedative. Although, I have to say, the pills are more effective."

Galen shrugged. "I'm not hurt that bad, and I have reports to fill out and imps to hold."

"Better be only one imp you're hugging, Sir," Sally muttered into his chest and heard his huff of a laugh.

"I don't like being blurry after action," Vance said to Master Z, sounding so irritable that he might win the Master Grumpy Pants title from Galen. "They always give me too much."

Galen kissed her head. "Someone else needs a hug, pet," he said under his breath.

Just what she'd longed to do...if she could find an uninjured place on his body. "Only if you'll sit down," Sally answered and got a nod in return.

She moved to the bed, put down the railing, and slid her hip next to Vance's. Then she waited for permission.

"God, yes," he muttered and reached for her.

His big hands closed on her shoulders, and he pulled her down onto his chest. When his arm wrapped around her as if he'd never let her go, she nestled her head in the hollow of his shoulder and sighed in contentment.

She could hear the almost inaudible sound of his matching sigh.

Galen limped over to the chair, shoved it closer to the bed, and sank into it. "You all right, bro?" he asked Vance.

"Hurts like a son of a bitch, but any gunfight you walk away from is a good one."

"Ayuh."

Sally wanted to smack them both. Her voice came out tight as she said, "How about you stay out of gunfights in the future, okay?"

There was silence, not the instant agreement she was hoping for. Instead, Vance asked, "The woman Somerfeld had with him— she going to be all right?"

"Eventually."

Sally lifted her head and saw Galen's jaw tighten as he continued, "A long eventually. But her husband and parents are on their way here."

Sally remembered the woman's blank stare and sent off a prayer. *Please, help her heal.*

"Hand me that, please?" Master Z said to someone. A second later came the distinctive sound of a champagne cork. "Galen. Vance. Since your doctors said you both refused pain meds, you can substitute this...if we can keep the nurses from finding out. Kitten, can you locate the glasses?"

Jessica was here? Sally lifted her head and saw more Shadowlands people had entered. Dressed in pale green slacks and top that brought color to the ugly room, Jessica was handing Z something from a sack. Master Cullen occupied one wall, and Andrea leaned against him. Marcus and Gabi must have come from the tournament. Nolan had an arm slung around Beth, who pressed into his side. Kari stood in front of Dan with his arm crossing her chest, keeping her back against his chest.

And they were all smiling and accepting drinks.

When Z handed a glass to Vance, Sally sat up and accepted one from Jessica. "What's the celebration?" she asked.

Master Z held up his plastic stemmed glass. "To the end of the Harvest Association. Well done, gentlemen."

As the hearty chorus of agreement echoed around the room, Vance stared at them.

Galen's face held the same stunned look. "Yes." His lips tilted up. "You're right. That really was the last one." He lifted his glass in the toast and took a sip. Blinked. "Now that's champagne." He took another sip and took the bottle from Z's hand to examine the label. "Blanc des Millenaires? You do us proud."

"You've earned it." Z took the bottle and refilled Galen's glass. "Enjoy. You're staying with Dan and Kari tonight—and Dan is driving."

"Got it all planned out, eh?" Galen gave Z a narrow look. "Thank you, Mama."

Into the stunned silence of the submissives, Z smiled and answered, "You're welcome, my boy."

The room broke up with laughter, but Sally didn't join in. "I want to go home," she whispered. She wanted her own room, her bed, her...stuff.

Vance had heard her. "Aside from being a crime scene, there's blood and glass all over. And it needs to air out. You and Galen need to stay somewhere else tonight."

To lose the hope of going home felt like having a Band-Aid ripped off. With an unhappy sigh, she took a sip of her drink. *Okay, it really was good champagne.*

Galen frowned. "We need to get the place cleaned up before—"

"I sent a crew," Nolan interrupted in his usual no-bullshit manner. "They'll fix the window."

Galen said, "But—"

"Andrea recommended a trauma and crime scene cleaning service," Cullen cut in, hugging his sub who ran a *normal* cleaning business. "They'll be out there as soon as the police give them clearance."

Vance stared. "You—"

Seeing the Feds' surprise, Sally hid her grin against Vance's shoulder. Her poor Doms had no idea what happened when a Shadowlands Master—or submissive—needed help.

"Gabi and I swung by and managed to coax Glock into a carrier," Marcus said.

"Boy, I use insults...but nothing like a cat in a foul mood." Gabi rolled her eyes. "It's a good thing Marcus doesn't speak feline, since your cat started with, 'Rat-turd human, if I throw a stick, will you leave?' and descended to, 'Chicken-butt human, you're so ugly, Hello Kitty said good-bye to you.'"

Sally could just see Glock with his tail twitching and hissing out insults. As she giggled, laughter swept around the room.

Galen's deep laugh turned into a groan, and he pressed his hand over his ribs where that bastard Somerfeld had kicked him. Horribly hard.

Sally glared at Gabi.

"Sorry, Galen," Gabi said, grinning unrepentantly.

"We took Glock to the pet boarding place we use during vacations." Marcus handed Galen a card. He glanced at Vance and tapped the hospital bed rail. "Happens I like having you on that side of the bed railing rather than me."

Vance grinned. "I'll be out tomorrow. And thank you for finding Glock." He held his hand out to shake and winced.

"Don't move," Sally snapped at him before turning a frown on Marcus.

The lawyer chuckled. "Easy, li'l spitfire. I know how much bullet holes hurt. At least, I was smart enough to take pain meds."

Yeah, he'd been shot last year—and Gabi had been crazed. As Sally put her head back down on Vance's shoulder, she remembered how Raoul had been shot as well. How upset Kim had been. But at least her friends' Doms weren't in law enforcement.

Hers were. So this might not be a one-time deal, not for them. Her Feds might have gotten rid of the Harvest Association, but there were always more criminals.

Criminals had guns. And knives. And gasoline.

—✦—

Sally's unnatural stillness on the drive to Dan's house had given Galen an uneasy feeling. And when she'd disappeared into the nursery with Kari, with barely a smile for him, he was downright worried.

"Problem?" Carrying a couple of beers, Dan motioned him out the back door.

"Not sure." Ignoring the patio swing, Galen settled into a dark wicker chair with a grunt of relief. In the future, he'd avoid kneeing a perp in the jaw. After leaning his cane against the chair, he stretched his leg out. "She's upset about something."

Dan sat down across from him and handed over a beer. "All three of you almost died. The house could have blown up. She watched a man almost burn to death. You seriously expect her to be cheerful?"

"No. But there are different kinds of upset. This one feels different." Galen took a long pull of icy-cold liquid.

From the window above came Kari's soft laughter. But Sally's infectious giggle was absent, and Galen felt the loss deep inside.

"You're a good enough Dom to know if something is off." Dan's eyes narrowed. "Thinking back, seems like she changed after she switched positions, from your arms to curling up against Vance. But I didn't get the feeling she has a problem with having two men. And you've been sharing her all along."

"No, this isn't related to threesome problems. I think it might be when Marcus reminded her that he'd been shot." Galen frowned. If she'd remembered that, she'd also remember Raoul's time in the hospital. And Vance had been shot twice now. *And my chest looks like I went headfirst through a paper shredder.* Far too much violence for a young woman who'd grown up on a farm rather than in a city. "She might have realized how dangerous our work can be."

"She knows. Hell, she works in my station."

"And she's not doing well with it. The sight of blood bothers her, even more than violence. I'm going to try to talk her out of taking a position in a law-enforcement area."

"You fucking asshole. I just got the brass talked into offering her a job."

"Now there's a pity." Galen grinned briefly, then sobered. "Did Kari have trouble with your job?"

"Oh yeah, for a few months. Now she's okay. But from what you said, Sally has suffered more loss than Kari. And has less family." He rose and looked down at Galen. "If she takes you on, she'll have *two* lovers at risk every day. You going to ask that of her?"

"Fuck."

"Yeah. You think about it. Better yet, talk about it. Fuck, I've learned recently that sometimes—Dom or not—there's no understanding what's in a woman's head." Dan tipped his bottle in a salute. "I'm going to see what Kari has planned for tomorrow. It's Father's Day—my first."

As Dan walked into the house, Galen repositioned his injured leg and tamped down his feeling of envy for the lucky bastard. Yeah, time to start looking toward the future.

In the west, the sunset slowly faded, leaving behind pink streamers like the sad remnants of a party.

—✦—

Sally held Zane in her arms, swaying back and forth, nuzzling his neck. He smelled like soap and baby powder—and love. Something about holding him settled her. With an adorable grin, he hit her nose with the rattle he held.

"Sheesh. I guess guys are just born violent," she muttered.

Kari finished putting away the stack of baby clothes and laughed. "Nah. My cousin's daughter pulled her hair so often that she started wearing it on top of her head." She pointed to the rocking chair in the corner. "Sit. He gets heavier with every minute you hold him."

Sally grinned and bounced Zane, making him squeal with laughter. "Yep, he's definitely getting heavier." After settling into the chair, she looked over at her friend. "Kari?"

"Mmmhmm." Another stack of clothing got tucked away.

"Doesn't Dan's job ever bother you? That he could get hurt?"

Kari turned, saw Sally's expression, and sank down onto the ottoman. "Oh, you got the cop's wife syndrome. No wonder, after today."

"Yeah." She kissed Zane's soft cheek, trying to keep the memories at bay.

"Yes, it bothered me. A lot. Still kinda does." She gave Sally a wry smile. "Although we talked about it, he could only promise that he'd be careful. The thing is, being a cop is who he is. Right down to the bone. And I can't love him and ask him to be someone different."

"I guess." Sally rocked a little faster, thrilling Zane, who decided to stand on her lap and bounce along. Didn't sound as if there was a good answer. But she was sure she now knew how Galen had felt when he was worried about her safety. God, how did he stand it? She gave Kari a bright smile. "You and Dan look...happier."

"Last night was..." Kari sighed with a happy smile. "Like we were before Zane." She rubbed a finger over her lips. "Maybe even lovelier."

"How's that?"

"We know each other better. I trust him even more because I've seen him with Zane. Dan really is as protective and caring and strong as I thought in the beginning. And when he cuddles our son, I just melt"—she gave Sally a mischievous look—"in a whole different way than seeing him in black leathers."

"You are too much." Sally lifted Zane and blew a raspberry on his belly.

"Sally, I owe you thanks for pushing me into talking with Dan," Kari said softly. "And so I'm going to do you the same favor. Talk with your guys. It's truly easy to decide someone is thinking about one thing, when really, you've got a whole different problem."

Hmm. And what had that discussion between Dan and Kari been about? Sally wondered. But she'd probably never know. Some women shared all. Others didn't. Sally nodded. "I will. In fact, can I sit up here and sing lullabies to Zane while I think?"

"Of course."

—✦—

Galen rubbed his face. Exhaustion, aching bones, lacerations—God, he felt old. And frustrated. He'd worried and worked to keep Sally safe, and instead she'd ended up front and center in a bloodbath. Insisted on being there. God, she was brave.

The door to the house creaked; Sally stepped out on the patio. With just the sight of her, his muscles and bones and soul seemed to inhale contentment. She was alive. No longer in danger.

She gave him an uncertain look, something he never wanted to see from her. "Can I join you or—"

"I can't think of anything I'd like better." He reached out.

She took his hand with cold fingers. Resisting his attempt to pull her onto his lap, she edged his legs apart and knelt between them.

Seeing her unhappy expression, he wasn't tempted by her provocative position. Instead he ran his hand down her silky hair. "Tell me."

She lowered her gaze...and he permitted it...for the moment. "Um," she said and paused briefly. "I knew your job was dangerous, but I didn't know—imagine—*how* dangerous. But you told me how you and Vance got shot up. I watched Tillman's funeral. Saw his children."

Look at her, launching herself right at the heart of the matter. Before he'd known her—back when he'd just watched her in the club, she'd been a bossy little sub. Finding out that she'd hidden her emotions had come as a surprise. But now she was still a bossy little sub, and even better, she was hiding no longer. He was wicked proud of her. "Go on."

"I...I just wanted you to know that I'm struggling with it. I know I can't ask you to give up your careers for safer ones, but..."

He chuckled. "Seems we've been having the same arguments with ourselves. You see, Vance and I planned to ask you to not take a job in a police station because they stress you out."

"You'd choose my job for me?" A sparkle of anger lit in her eyes.

Galen shook her head. No, she wouldn't want to give up her dream of working in law enforcement. She wanted to be a hero.

"Not because of the danger." At the slight lift of her chin, he admitted, "Not entirely. But face it, pet, you don't sleep well if you have to visit crime scenes."

"I haven't noticed you sleeping all that well either, Mr. Big Shot Special Agent."

"I don't have a pro—" He stopped his automatic...idiotic...response, because she was right. How many years had it been since he slept without worrying about problems? Or having nightmares?

Each new case dragged him further toward—he stroked her hair and smiled—toward what the imp would call the dark side. If he continued, would he be able to fight his way free?

Earlier, Z had stated the Association was finished, and Galen had been happy, feeling as if he'd stepped into the sunlight.

Slowly but surely, his life had grown...narrower. Less balanced. Even with Sally to love, he didn't see that changing.

So, what was he planning to bring to a relationship? To Sally?

As he looked down at the submissive at his feet, at his sweet imp, he knew he didn't want to spend his life in darkness. Didn't want to drag her down either, because, being Sally, she'd dive in to help.

And she'd worry when he got pulled back into another case. She'd be right. He wasn't able to distance himself from the cases he took. He never had been.

Apparently, she wasn't the only person who wanted to be a hero.

CHAPTER TWENTY-FIVE

S everal days later, Vance followed Galen onto their dock. Although his partner was using his cane more, his limp had returned to "normal."

In contrast, Vance could feel pain stab into his leg with each step. Fuck, he was getting old.

But it was fucking nice to get out of the house. To be outside. And alive. Under his bare feet, the wood was damp and rough. A thunderstorm had passed through earlier, leaving the night air cool, almost crisp. Reflections of the house lights danced on the dark water.

Turning to face Vance, Galen set one hip against a post, shook his head, and pointed at a chair. "Sit before you fall on your ass."

Ignoring the urge to remain standing to prove him wrong, Vance gingerly settled into a chair. "You wanted me out here—away from Sally. What's up?"

"I'm quitting the FBI."

Disbelief kept Vance silent as Galen talked. He'd break up their partnership? After everything they'd been through? The years together?

When Galen fell silent, Vance realized he hadn't heard a word. "Go through it again; I missed some." All, actually.

After a frown, Galen simply nodded and started over.

This time, Vance managed to listen. To process. Mostly.

Galen was talking about Sally's worries for their safety. About his need to protect her—and not see her upset in her job. That fair was fair. That he was tired. That he got too involved with cases—although Vance figured *obsessed* would be more accurate. That it was time for a change.

Galen stopped, looked at Vance for a minute, and turned to watch the water. Giving him space and time.

Vance realized he was rubbing the itching wound on his leg and forced himself to stop. Another scar for Sally to play with, to add to the others he'd collected. Some agents retired without their bodies looking like a battleground. Sally had good reason to fear for her Doms.

And if they died, she'd mourn them. She loved fiercely. Completely. She wouldn't recover from their loss easily. The thought of hurting her in that way was difficult.

Even worse was the thought of losing either her or Galen to violence. And, this was where Galen's logic had obviously taken him. They couldn't tolerate seeing Sally in danger; she felt the same about them.

So Galen wanted to quit.

Vance cleared his throat, unsettled at the rough sound. His partner turned, face dark, eyes remote, but Vance could read him. Always could, even from the start. Yeah, he loved the asshole, probably more than he'd have loved a real brother. "I'm not ready to quit the FBI."

As Galen's mouth tightened, Vance knew his response had hit his partner like a knife stroke.

Galen pulled in a breath. "I understand. I thought you might feel—"

"You talked," Vance interrupted. "Let me finish, you pushy bastard."

Galen blinked. His lips curved slightly as he stood straighter and crossed his arms over his chest in an intimidating alpha-male stance.

Vance stretched his legs out, settling down into the chair in a body-language response of: *I'm comfortable even if you are standing.*

Galen laughed.

Yeah, how many people would understand the unspoken

maneuverings and find them funny?

Vance couldn't see a life without Galen. And he didn't want his loved ones' terrified every day he went to work. There was a compromise, though. "I'm not ready to leave, but we've both turned down advancement into supervisory positions. Let me see if I can't move into one of those. As long as they can station me here."

"Seriously?"

"You're right, bro. It's time to get off the firing line. I might be three years younger, but I'm tired of waking up in a hospital."

Galen sank into a chair. "Didn't think you'd take this so well."

"I'm the flexible one, remember?" Vance tipped his head back. The moon was rising, a waning ball of light glowing over the treetops. The lake was quiet. Peaceful. Yeah, he was tired of cold winters. Snow. Could see sitting out here with a beer after the kids went to bed. "What will you do? Can't see you retiring." Couldn't see him giving up the thrill of the chase, either.

"I'm looking at starting an investigative company, specializing in locating whatever is missing—money, information, people. I have enough contacts to get it up and running."

Would probably work, Vance thought. The clever bastard had a Master's in business as well as criminology. He'd even started off in the white-collar crime division.

"I'll manage. We'll hire people for the fieldwork. To travel. Sally can do her computer magic from here."

Vance's mouth curved into a smile. "Clever. Very clever. You're going to lure her away from corpses and blood-streaked apartments."

Galen opened his hand. "Want in?"

Vance considered. He'd enjoy the work, and it was appealing to keep the partnership together. But no. "I want a few more years with the Feds. But after that, yes." He shook his head. "Might be good to have a bit more space anyway...if we're going to make this a formal sort of relationship."

"I'm not sure how to do that," Galen admitted. "Sally deserves a fancy wedding as well as legal protection."

"Well, now, I've been thinking about that."

———❖———

Inside, Sally ended the call on her cell with mixed emotions.

Tate had been calling each week...just to get to know her again. This evening, after regaling her with Emma and Dylan stories, he'd mentioned their father. Apparently the children had told their friends about the fiasco of a dinner party...and what Sally had said. Sally was still remembered fondly by the townspeople. Her father was now being avoided.

She sighed, trying to pull up either anger or satisfaction or pity, but found an absence of any deep emotion. Her father truly wasn't part of her life anymore.

And she had a new family.

Detouring to the kitchen, she glanced out the back door. Two men sitting at the end of the dock. No change there, dammit.

Growling to herself, Sally went into the great room. At least Glock would be some company. She dropped down on the couch and pulled Glock into her lap. After an indignant look, the cat stood and arranged himself more comfortably—in the same position.

"Jeez, you and Galen are real control freaks, aren't you?" She scratched his chin.

His rumbling purr was both agreement and enjoyment.

At least someone was content. Well, apparently everyone except her. Her two men had finished their beers long ago and now just sat outside. Talking and laughing—easy laughter, which she hadn't heard in far too long.

Fine.

Although three days had passed, Galen hadn't mentioned their talk at Kari's house and her concerns. That sure didn't seem fair. He was always after her to express her emotions, and now he was ignoring her?

Of course they'd been swamped in paperwork. And healing.

Still, she needed to decide what to do. She'd wanted to give Galen a little extra time to think, but now she should speak with Vance and at least let him know her worries. Then again, Galen might well have told him.

Would she stay, even knowing how dangerous their jobs were? She sighed. *Yes.* Kari was right. If the job was what they needed to feel complete, she had no right to change them. She loved their dedication and the way their protectiveness extended to the whole world.

But it'd sure be horrid to watch them go to work each day. Sure, anyone could die, but the odds of being injured or killed were a lot higher for law-enforcement types. Hopefully she wouldn't turn into as much of a worrywart as Galen.

But, whatever happened, she loved them. *This is where I'll be. In their home. In their bed. In their arms.*

If she didn't kill them herself before the week was out. What *were* they talking about? She stroked Glock's long gray body. "So, fur ball, I'm not real happy about being left in here with just a cat for company. If you were their submissive, what would you do?"

An indifferent tail flick was her answer.

"No, leaving them alone to enjoy their evening isn't the answer. I'm not nice."

The kitty smirk showed Glock's opinion of niceness. Felines didn't do nice. Felines did sneaky.

"Sneaky. I can be sneaky." She considered. "Maybe I should be a sweet service sub and take my men some fresh drinks. Excellent suggestion, Glock."

When she dumped him on the couch, she could swear the annoyed cat called her one of the names Gabi had mentioned.

After grabbing beers from the fridge, Sally headed outside...quietly. *Eavesdropping? Me? Surely not.*

Their voices were low murmurs that blended far too well with the soughing of the breeze in the tree canopy and the gentle lapping of water against the pilings.

Demon Doms.

A rough patch of wood on the dock caught her foot, and the beer bottles clanked together. As the men turned toward her, she smiled. "I thought you might be ready for refills."

"Did you now, pet?" Galen's smile was too darned knowing. "That was thoughtful of you."

Fine. She turned her back on him.

As Vance took his beer, he subjected her to a slow perusal. "Did you feel left out, sweetheart?"

Well, honestly, maybe she had felt left out, but that didn't mean she wanted to be interrogated. Stupid Feds. She gave him a smile that was 90 percent sugar. "Don't give yourself airs. I just brought you some beer."

She set Galen's beer on his chair arm and got three steps toward the house before one of them caught her shorts waistband and dragged her backward.

"Dammit, let me go!" She tried to twist around. Vance had her.

"Don't think so. Here, bro. Catch." Vance yanked sideways, flinging her toward Galen.

Galen leaned forward, grabbed her waist, and pulled her into his lap.

"Demon fucking Dom, I didn't come out here to—" She shoved at his hands until he trapped her wrists in front of her. "Let go, you asshole!"

"The little ones are fun when they wiggle," Galen said in a conversational voice.

"Got to agree with that." Vance set his beer on the dock and pulled his chair closer as Sally glared at him. "Can't say I care for that language—or attitude." He regarded her. "Been a while since we spanked our little imp."

Sally froze.

Both men burst out laughing, and it would only be justice if her glower could turn them into stone. Or at least boil their beer. But nooo.

Galen tightened his grip around her wrists before sliding his free hand under her shirt.

"No bra. Very nice." A calloused finger circled one nipple before his palm cupped her whole breast. He kissed the curve between her neck and shoulder, sending goose bumps down her arms. "She smells like vanilla."

Because she'd started to make the ungrateful bastards a cake.

"Yeah? Let's see." Vance pulled his chair next to Galen's, and his hand went under her shirt, possessing her other breast before he kissed the other side of her neck. Two men touching her, kissing her. Her insides began to boil, melting her resistance, her anger, her hurt feelings.

Vance took her mouth in a long, deep, wet kiss. "Have I mentioned how much I love you, sweetheart?"

"I—"

"I love you, imp," Galen whispered in her ear and nipped her earlobe, sending dark desire pooling in her belly.

"Mmm." A hum had started under her skin. In the moonlight, their faces were shadowed, but her hands knew their shapes. She flattened a palm on each cheek. Galen's hard beard stubble, Vance's softer.

Galen set his hand over hers, turning his face enough to press a kiss to her palm. "Want to know what we were talking about, Ms. Curiosity?"

"I certainly would, Master Grumpy Pants."

Galen's grin flashed before he ran his fingers over the breast he'd captured and used his fingernails to pinch the very tip.

A tiny zing shot straight to her pussy. He tugged on the entire areola, and the boiling anticipation coursing through her made her squirm.

Vance curved his hand over her upper thigh, his weight stopping her wiggles, his fingers rubbing lightly against her pussy. "We were talking about you, of course."

"Oh." Right. Her curiosity rose, vying with her arousal. "Anything you want me to know?"

"Aren't you just the well-behaved submissive?" Galen commented. His tone turned grave. "Yes, you need to know what we decided."

Her heart seemed to stop, and she chilled despite the heat inside. Were they going to send her away? She swallowed back her fears and lifted her chin. They loved her, and if they'd *decided* on anything short of living together, they'd have a fight on their hands. "Spit it out."

"I like when she gets all pissy." Vance grinned at Galen before his gaze met hers. "Galen told me about your talk. Your concern about our jobs."

Oh, no no no. They were going to call it quits. Ice invaded her bloodstream, and she had to clasp her hands together to keep them from shaking. "But I—I didn't give Galen an ultimatum. I just said I was concerned."

"Ah, but we're giving you an ultimatum, pet," Galen said softly.

Vance turned her face to his. "We'll change to less risky jobs…"

Less risky? They'd be safe? The surge of relief was a massive roaring in her ears. *Safe.*

Galen finished, "But in return, you will marry us. Both of us."

The roaring ceased as the word registered. The big *M* one. *Marry?* Her heart stopped. The world stopped.

She stared at Vance, at the certainty in his grin. At Galen with the calmness, the happiness in his smile. "Oh yes."

Lunging out of the chair, she wrapped her arms around Vance's neck and kissed him. "Yes. Yes, I will." The kiss was possessive. Hot. "I love you so much."

When Vance pulled back, he turned her around.

She put her hands on each side of Galen's face and kissed him, trying to tell him without words how much she loved him.

They'd demanded she free herself from her past—and cared enough to change for her. She lifted her head, looked into Galen's intense black eyes, and repeated, "Yes. Yes, I will."

As she turned and wrapped an arm around each man, she frowned. "You'd better not go and get all depressed again, or next time I'm aiming for your balls."

"Fuck, she's a mean subbie," Vance muttered before he recaptured her breast as if he had the right.

"Ayuh." Galen slipped his hand between her legs. "But she's *our* mean subbie."

EPILOGUE

Two months later

Afterter hanging a sign on the front door directing people toward the side gate, Galen made his way through the house and out the back.

The sound of easy conversation and laughter washed over him as he crossed the patio. Splashing came from the pool where Jessica and Beth were swimming token laps, stopping at each end to gossip and giggle.

The sizzle of steaks came from the grill where Raoul and Kim had joined Vance.

As Galen stopped here and there to talk with various clusters of guests, he noticed Sally watching him with concern. *The little mother.* The surgery on his knee was long over, the incision healed. Despite Sally's annoyance, he'd abandoned his cane a few days ago.

Odd how irritating—and amazing—it was to be so loved.

But he didn't want her fretting at her engagement party— although she had no idea that was what the celebration was for— so he picked up a beer and sat down with Z and Nolan.

"Has the new business started?" Z asked, idly stroking Glock. After rejecting several guests, the cat had apparently decided that Z's lap was up to feline standards.

"On the record no, although I negotiated an early contract for Sally where someone had embezzled a fortune from a credit union. She's been going stir-crazy since she quit the police station." And she was thrilled to be working. Completely, thoroughly happy with hunting through lines of software code. The imp was insane.

"But the company officially opens in a month," Galen continued with a smile. "It will be a pleasure to turn in a report and *not* have to arrest anyone." Even more of a relief that his work wouldn't follow him home with knives or firearms.

"I bet." Nolan leaned back, stretched out his long legs, and rested his beer on his stomach. "Any problems with the Harvest Association?"

"Paperwork is done. Court cases will continue"—he sighed—"probably forever. Ellis Somerfeld died last month."

Nolan grunted. "I'd call that a mercy."

Considering the percentage of burns, his prognosis had been poor. And he'd been quite insane. All Galen felt was relief mingling with pity. "Ayuh."

Jake dropped down in a chair next to Nolan, having scored a bowl of nacho chips.

With a sigh of exhaustion, Dan pulled over another chair.

"You okay?" Galen asked him.

"Been babyproofing the house. Did you know how many cupboards and shelves are in reach of a crawling rug rat?"

"I do know. Wait until he's a teenager and sneaking out windows," Z said.

"Shit," Dan muttered. "And Kari wants another one."

Sam obviously heard as he grabbed a chair and joined them. He gave a raspy laugh. "Enjoy life while you can. Once they're in college, they stay up late—and you'll find out how difficult it is to fuck quietly."

"Hell." Dan frowned before turning to Galen. "You mentioned your dungeon's available. You okay if I drag Kari down there? So we can enjoy life a little before we have two kids?"

The detective was fast on the uptake, wasn't he? Galen grinned. "Wait until Vance and I make an announcement, then escape during the confusion. Use the cabana for as long as you want."

"Thanks." Dan turned. His wife was by the pool, chatting with

Jessica. As if she felt his gaze, she glanced over her shoulder…and the look they exchanged scorched the air.

Nice. With that as a spur, Galen rose to gather his own family.

Over with Marcus and Raoul, Vance saw him move. He excused himself and headed toward Galen.

Near the dock, surrounded by the trainees, Sally was flushed with laughter. By God, she was lovely. And with one of the most beautiful habits of a submissive, she was always visually checking on her Doms to see if they needed anything.

When her eyes met Galen's, the love he saw made his heart glow.

Pull it together, Kouros. Crooking a finger, he beckoned for her to join him.

With instant obedience—not a given with Sally—she hurried over. He grasped her hand.

On her other side, Vance did the same and grinned at Galen over her head.

VANCE TOOK OVER as he usually did if a situation required a voice loud enough to be heard over shouting or gunfire. This was a hell of a lot more fun. He sucked in a breath and called, "People, may I have your attention?"

Conversations stuttered to a halt.

Looking down, Vance caught Sally's puzzled expression, and unable to resist, he ran his fingers along her jawline. Fine bones under the smooth skin. Stubborn little chin.

Stay on task, Buchanan. "I'd like to announce the engagement of Sally Hart to Galen Kouros. *And* Vance Buchanan." He added with a grin, "That would be me."

Sally's gasp was drowned out in the laughter and cheering and congratulations. The enthusiasm filled his heart. He liked having friends outside the small FBI community, ones he'd have around after he quit. Ones who'd be there for their marriage, children, maybe even old age.

"You didn't *tell* me. Just announced it." Eyes sparkling with outrage, Sally punched him in the stomach.

Fuck. Then again, he might not reach old age. That tiny fist had a concentrated impact. When his partner laughed, Vance tossed him to the wolves. "This was Galen's idea."

She spun around.

Warned, Galen caught her fist in one hand. "You want a public spanking to go with your engagement, pet?"

"You should have told me!"

"Seemed like we owed you something for the lights going off during our last scene," Vance said. Next time he heard *please, please, please,* he'd gag her before she got the third one out.

Galen huffed a laugh. "Vance voted for mercy; I wanted you naked and gagged for the announcement."

Vance could almost see her blood starting to boil.

Galen put an arm around her waist, pried her fist open, and held her hand out to Vance.

He pulled out the ring he and Galen had chosen and slid it on her finger. "You're ours, sweetheart," he said softly.

Stunned to silence, she stared down at her hand, and with the quicksilver changes of mood he loved, she burst into her enchanting giggles. She threw herself at Galen, bestowing kisses and hugs and love-you's before doing the same for Vance.

He lifted her over his head and treated himself to a long kiss.

Once back on her feet, she announced to the crowd, "Just wait. I am *so* going to make them pay for their sneaky ways."

Under the wave of laughter, Z walked over and hugged her. "Felicitations, little one. I'm happy for you."

She had tears in her eyes and a quivering chin when he released her. Z turned to shake hands with Galen and Vance. "Congratulations, gentlemen. She'll keep your home lively—and filled with love."

"Thank you." Vance smiled. "We know."

The stream of people continued.

Cullen slapped Vance's shoulder. "Glad it worked out."

"So am I." Vance rubbed his jaw with painful recollection. The bastard had a wicked right hook.

Cullen gave a bark of laughter. "Heard you're doing supervision rather than fieldwork. How's that going?"

Vance stroked his hand down Sally's mink-brown, mink-soft hair. "Safer. But it's harder to send people into danger than to handle the trouble myself."

Cullen nodded. "Know that feeling." He put his arm around his Andrea. "Having someone to talk with helps."

"So I'm finding. And I have two someones. Galen understands; Sally comforts."

Hearing her name, Sally stood on tiptoe to kiss his chin, her brown eyes warm with love.

As planned, the next one up was Marcus, with Gabi a step behind. Marcus was already grinning.

Vance swept his arm in a welcoming motion, giving Marcus the stage. "Your turn."

"I do look forward to the sound of an outraged pup." Marcus gripped Gabi's shoulder, pulling her closer, and raised a voice trained to reach the farthest corner of a courtroom. "Ladies and gentlemen, to add to yo'ah pleasure, I'd like to announce the engagement of Gabrielle Renard to Marcus Atherton." He shot Vance a smile. "That would be me."

The welling of laughter and outpouring of renewed congratulations didn't come close to smothering Gabi's shriek.

Marcus's little redhead whipped around so quickly she almost fell. "You...you douche bag. We were going to wait until winter. You said."

"I lied, darlin'."

Galen muttered to Vance, "Better warn him to keep Sally away from his computer."

"No shit." Last Friday night, when he'd logged on to finish some work, the screen had frozen while the speakers blasted out Alan Jackson's "Good Time"—an unsubtle hint his workweek was over. At least the tune had been country western, unlike what she'd done to his partner.

Postsurgery, Galen had given her trouble over taking his pills, and she'd booby-trapped the poor bastard's laptop with "A Spoonful of Sugar" from the Disney *Mary Poppins* movie. She'd set it off every time he refused his meds...which had been often.

Unable to resist, Vance hummed a bit of the song.

Sally snickered.

Galen's look was deadly.

As everyone clustered near, the noise levels continued to increase, but the mere clearing of Z's throat silenced the group. He pulled Jessica in front of him and wrapped his arms around her from the back. "Since announcements are the order of the day, I'd like to announce that Jessica Randall Grayson is expecting her first child. The father is delighted." He gave Vance an amused glance. "That would be me."

Jessica's shriek of outrage was higher pitched than Gabi's had been. "You, you, *you*. I just did the test this morning—I haven't even told you yet!"

Z captured the hands beating on his chest, smiled down at his submissive, and asked gently, "Did you think I wouldn't know?"

"I—" She sputtered for a moment before shaking her head. "Are you really delighted?"

"Absolutely. Incredibly. Completely."

The answer set her to glowing with a beauty that showed Vance why Z was so in love. "Well, okay." She snuggled closer to her husband with a low grumble, "But still..."

Peeking around Z's side, Jessica whispered to Gabi and Sally. "We are *so* going to make them pay."

LIKE AN INEBRIATED bumblebee, Sally's body buzzed with joy. Tucked between Galen and Vance, she bounced on her toes, wanting to dance. To sing. Her friends and her family surrounded her. She had a home. A cat. And *two* Doms.

When she sighed, Galen tightened the arm around her waist and studied her face. "You're happy."

"Oh yes."

To her joy, he stole a quick kiss. He'd changed over the past months. Not only was he more relaxed and happier, but also more open with his affection.

"I love you," she whispered.

Vance grinned at her, looking far too pleased with her surprise.

So she told him begrudgingly, "I suppose...maybe...I might eventually tell you I love you. Since you saved me from that palmetto bug and everything."

"Eventually?" The muscles in Vance's square jaw tightened, reminding her he still worked in law enforcement. "If I—or Galen—don't hear 'I love you' often enough, one little subbie will be punished." He glanced at Galen. "Right, bro?"

"Ayuh." Galen's lips quirked. "Either way, I win."

Fun punishment or bad punishment? Sally eyed her men warily. "I think we'd better talk about—"

"I like that rule." Master Sam's gravelly voice interrupted. Arm wrapped around Linda, he looked down at his redhead with icy blue eyes. "If you don't tell me at least once a day, I get to beat your ass."

"Really? Oh my goodness." Linda smiled slightly. "I don't think I told you today. Or yesterday. You'd better beat on me extra hard."

Galen snorted. "Got yourself an S.A.M., Sam?"

Sally snickered. No matter how motherly she was to the Shadowkittens, Linda was definitely one smart-ass masochist with her sadistic Dom.

"If you prefer not to delay the punishment"—Vance pointed to the nearby dirt path—"we made the cabana into a dungeon. The cupboard has a supply of toys for guests."

Sam's hand closed around Linda's nape.

Her eyes widened, and she protested, "Wait. This is a party. You can't just—"

"Yes." Sam's voice was flat. Uncompromising. "I can." Behind her back, he winked at Galen and Vance and steered Linda across the patio.

Nearby, Dan grinned. "*Seize the day*—before more babies arrive." With a swift move, he swept Kari up. She gave a loud scream as he tossed her over his shoulder and headed down the cabana path.

After a second, Sally managed to close her mouth. Kari had

said things were going well at home, but *dayum*.

Sometime later, Sally walked out onto the dock.

Jessica, Beth, Kim, and Andrea had been swimming and, near the end, they'd stretched out on beach towels to dry off.

Midway, Gabi lounged in one of the old chairs with her feet up on the railing.

"Gabi." Sally took the other chair. "Marcus is *fetching* you a drink and food."

"God, I love that man." Gabi glanced back at the patio, then smiled at Sally. "Great party, Sally."

As the rest chimed in with agreement, Sally flushed with pleasure. "I've never planned something this big. It was fun—although I'd have had better decorations if I'd known it would be an engagement-announcement celebration."

"Can I see your ring?" Jessica asked, sitting up on her towel.

Sally leaned forward and held her hand out. In the bright Florida sunshine, the jewels were almost blinding.

Jessica considered. "The big blue is a sapphire. After the huge diamond, what is the big yellowish one?"

"Citrine." Sally smiled, remembering how she'd started to walk into the office, heard them discussing her rings, and had managed to tiptoe away after only listening a…little…bit. "Birthstones. Vance's is sapphire, I'm diamond, and Galen's is citrine."

"Got you tucked between them, don't they," Kim said with a grin.

Andrea frowned at the gold band, so thickly encrusted with diamonds the metal had almost disappeared. "Please tell me that all the little diamonds aren't supposed to be babies?"

"No. Galen said they thought my ring should sparkle almost as much as I do," she whispered. Tears stung her eyes. They really felt that way.

Andrea's eyes filled. "Oh, don't start or we'll all be crying."

Kim blinked quickly. Jessica sniffled.

"It's perfect, Sally." Gabi leaned over, kissed Sally's cheek, and pulled in a long breath. "Okay, moving on, or the guys will stomp out here, wondering why we're all bawling. I'm snoopy enough to want to know how you're going to marry two men. Aren't there laws?"

"Oh yeah. Can't you imagine the headlines? *FBI agents arrested for polyandry.*" Sally laughed, remembering the night they'd proposed. "First, they offered to have me 'officially' marry one of them—and Vance said it should be Galen, because he's older."

Jessica frowned. "Well, that sounds—"

"Actually"—Sally snickered—"Vance called him an *old man.*" Which was just wrong since she should be the only one telling *old* jokes.

"Galen let him?"

"He shoved Vance off the dock." Sally shook her head. "We had to haul him out, before the gator got him."

"You've definitely improved Galen's sense of humor," Gabi observed. "Which one will you marry?"

"Neither. Oh, being they're crazy overprotective, they'll set up trusts and legal stuff for me and any children that come along." *Children.* Sally felt as if her heart actually swelled as she imagined Galen's face when he saw his baby for the first time. And Vance teaching a little boy to play football—or, being Vance, he'd teach the girls too.

"Yeah, that sounds like men." Jessica scowled. "And that's it? Just legal stuff?"

"No." Sally smiled. "They think we should have a ceremony." She glanced back at the crowd on the patio and whispered, "Actually, I think they want one more than I do."

Kim nodded. "Honestly, men are more romantic than women are."

"But, how?" Andrea asked.

"The guys talked to the other Masters about the local laws. They said Master Z has married people—and done ceremonies—before, and he volunteered." And wouldn't that totally appeal to Matchmaker Z. She beamed. *I'll be married by Master Z.* It seemed only right.

Jessica blinked. "I hadn't thought of that. He's mentioned

conducting marriages."

"Ohhh." Kim smiled. "That's actually pretty clever."

"I thought so," Vance said, coming up behind Sally. He bent over and kissed her cheek and handed her a cold soda.

Her other cheek received a kiss from Galen, and he set a plate of snacks in her lap.

She turned and smiled at them, her big Doms standing shoulder to shoulder.

"What's wrong?" Kim frowned at Gabi. "You're thinking so hard I can see steam coming out your ears."

"I had an idea." Eyes alight, Gabi grabbed Sally's hand. "Now if you don't like it, just say no, okay?"

Gabi always had good ideas, so Sally grinned. "Shoot."

"Okay, it's like this. Although Marcus's family is wonderful, mine is completely stuffy. And they'll try to score points with *my* wedding, going all fancy and inviting their clients. I'm not good at standing up to them."

"Oh God, seriously? That sucks." Sally shook her head in sympathy, remembering one sorority sister having hysterics because her mother-in-law-to-be messed up all her plans.

"Yeah."

Families. Sally stiffened. "Oh my God, Galen and Vance have families. I hadn't even thought about them. Oh no!" She turned to face her Doms. "We're flying to Vegas. I'm sure Elvis will marry us."

"Sweetie," Vance said, obviously on the edge of laughing. "I've heard rumors that Elvis has left the building."

Before Sally could answer, Gabi said, "See? You get it. You totally understand. Why do you think I kept putting Marcus off?"

Behind Gabi, Master Marcus had started to reach for her. His hand stilled, and he took a step back, eyes narrowing.

Yep, he'd heard. Sally started to warn her friend. "Gabi, you have—"

"No, pet," Galen forestalled her from finishing with a merciless grip on her shoulder. "Not your place."

Oblivious, Gabi continued, "Sounds like you have some

relatives like mine. Whose?"

Where was Gabi going with this? "My brother is nice, and he already said he'd come to the ceremony, and Vance has a fantastic family. But, oh God, Galen's mother could outfreeze icicles."

Behind her, Vance chuckled, and Galen gave an amused snort.

"Yeah, see?" Gabi bounced in her chair. "Daughters and potential daughters-in-law are obliged to be polite. But Galen's mom isn't related to me, so I wouldn't have to be nice to her. And you...you could totally flatten my parents." Gabi's smile grew. "So, do you want to?"

"Gabi—want to *what*?"

"Boy, those stuffy Feebies are slowing your wits, girlfriend." Gabi shoved the blue-dyed lock of hair out of her eyes and grinned. "Want to have a double wedding?"

"Oh. My. *God*." Sally sat up straight. "Oh, Christ in a paddy wagon, that would be past fun and into sublime!"

"Exactly. Think of the havoc we could create."

Master Marcus took a step forward and gripped her shoulders. "Gabi..."

Gabi stiffened, and her excitement faded away. She gave a resigned sigh. "Right. It was just a thought. I'd love to take on Galen's mama. And Sally's so tricky—she'd be great up against my dad. But...never mind."

His keen eyes softened. "Take yourself a breath, darlin'," he murmured, tracing his finger over the blue temp tatt on her shoulder. "I got a mind to wallop you for not sharing with me— and not thinking I can protect you."

"You can't guard me, big boy. Not for wedding stuff. That's girl country."

His surprise was almost laughable. But even a lawyer couldn't argue that one, Sally knew. He looked over at Galen and Vance and shook his head before looking down at Gabi. "As long as I get my ring on your finger in a timely manner, y'all have my blessing to create whatever havoc you want."

Under the sound of Gabi's elated scream, Sally heard Vance mutter, "Fuck, just shoot me now."

She turned to look at her Doms. "Um. Guys?"

"Sweetheart," Vance said. "Have you ever *met* Gabi's parents?"

Unbelievably enough, Galen was the one who laughed. "Up against our imp? They won't know what hit them." He bent down to kiss her cheek. "Go for it, pet. I know you can do anything you set your mind to."

Her eyes filled with tears at the utter confidence in his voice.

"Yeah, that's what I'm afraid of, bro. She'll make mincemeat out of them." After a second, Vance grinned. "At least the ceremony won't be dull."

God, could they be any more perfect? Blinking away tears, she remembered back in the spring, she'd given up on love. On finding a Dom. On hope.

Now she had love in abundance, hope for the future...and *two* Doms.

Even as she smiled down at the twinkling stones on her ring, she heard Vance mutter to Galen, "But she's not bringing that laptop and *voice* stuff to the wedding."

ᶴTHE ENDᶴ

CHERISE SINCLAIR

Now everyone thinks summer romances never go anywhere, right? Well...that's not always true.

I met my dearheart when vacationing in the Caribbean. Now I won't say it was love at first sight. Actually, since he was standing over me, enjoying the view down my swimsuit top, I might even have been a tad peeved—as well as attracted. But although our time together there was less than two days, and although we lived in opposite sides of the country, love can't be corralled by time or space.

We've now been married for many, many years. (And he still looks down my swimsuit tops.)

Nowadays, I live in the west with my beloved husband, two children, and various animals, including three cats who rule the household. I'm a gardener, and I love nurturing small plants until they're big and healthy and productive...and ripping defenseless weeds out by the roots when I'm angry. I enjoy thunderstorms, playing Scrabble and Risk, and being a soccer mom. My favorite way to spend an evening is curled up on a couch next to the master of my heart, watching the fire, reading, and...well...if you're reading this book, you obviously know what else happens in front of fires. :)

—*Cherise*

Visit http://www.cherisesinclair.com to find out more about Cherise and her books.

Loose Id® Titles by Cherise Sinclair

Available in digital format and print at your favorite retailer

Master of the Abyss
Master of the Mountain
The Dom's Dungeon
The Starlight Rite

——✦——

The MASTERS OF THE SHADOWLANDS Series
Lean on Me
Make Me, Sir
To Command and Collar
This Is Who I Am
If Only

——✦——

"Simon Says: Mine"
Part of the anthology *Doms of Dark Haven*
With Sierra Cartwright and Belinda McBride

——✦——

"Welcome to the Dark Side"
Part of the anthology *Doms of Dark Haven 2:*
Western Night
With Sierra Cartwright and Belinda McBride

CPSIA information can be obtained at www.ICGtesting.com
Printed in the USA
LVOW06s1219101213

364691LV00001B/169/P